A LOCKET FULL OF HOPE

Lily Fielding

PENGUIN BOOKS

TRANSWORLD PUBLISHERS
Penguin Random House, One Embassy Gardens,
8 Viaduct Gardens, London SW11 7BW
www.penguin.co.uk

Transworld is part of the Penguin Random House group of companies
whose addresses can be found at global.penguinrandomhouse.com

Penguin
Random House
UK

First published in Great Britain in 2025 by Penguin
an imprint of Transworld Publishers

A CIP catalogue record for this book
is available from the British Library.

ISBN 9781804993941

Typeset in 11.25/14.25 pt Baskerville by Falcon Oast Graphic Art Ltd
Printed and bound by Clays Ltd, Elcograf S.p.A.

The authorized representative in the EEA is Penguin Random House Ireland,
Morrison Chambers, 32 Nassau Street, Dublin D02 YH68.

For Liam, Ben, Johnny, Jaxon and Lilly.
With love x

CHAPTER ONE

1876

'You're not going out tonight, Ivan, surely?' Lydia Wheeler pleaded with her husband, her pretty face creased with fear.

'We'll be all right,' Ivan said, reaching for his heavy oilskin coat. 'Won't we, lads?' He turned to his two sons.

Thirteen-year-old Robert looked up from pulling on his boots. 'Course we will, Dad. The storm's only due to hit at first light. We'll be back long before that.' Like his father, he was stockily built with a shock of unruly dark-brown hair, a wide, strong jaw, and brown eyes.

'But you know how unpredictable the storms can be on this part of the coast,' Lydia said, wringing her hands. 'What if you don't get back in time?'

'*Elizabeth May* can outrun any storm,' bragged fifteen-year-old Simeon, playfully tugging his little sister's cornfield-blonde plait.

'Ow!' she yelped, batting at him with her hands.

Simeon laughed, easily dodging her. Like his father and brother, he was tall, dark and square-shouldered but, like ten-year-old Rebecca, he had inherited his mother's blue eyes.

'Stop teasing your sister, Simeon,' Lydia said automatically. 'You put too much faith in that boat,' she told Ivan, her gaze going to the small, lead-paned window that overlooked the bay. In the growing twilight the water appeared as calm as a millpond under the darkening winter sky.

'Look, love.' Ivan placed his big, calloused hands on her slender shoulders. Lydia looked into his warm dark eyes. Their love had sustained them through many a hard time over the sixteen years they'd been together. 'We haven't had a decent catch all winter. We're weeks behind on the rent. We've no choice.'

'I don't like it, Ivan,' Lydia said softly. 'I've a bad feeling.' He pulled her close, caressing her back.

Rebecca looked up at Simeon. 'Promise me you'll be all right, Sim,' she whispered.

'Course we will, Becky,' her eldest brother said, crouching so they were face to face. 'Look at it,' he said, motioning towards the window. 'It's as calm as anything. By the time the storm hits, we'll be home and snug in our beds, you'll see.'

Rebecca nodded, unconvinced. Her mother wasn't one to let her anxieties get the better of her. If she felt there was cause to worry, Rebecca worried too.

'We'll be home before dawn,' Ivan promised, releasing Lydia from his embrace as his eyes rested on his daughter. 'I've a feeling we'll make a good catch tonight, so we'll go into town tomorrow and buy material for a new frock, and a ribbon for your hair, Becky. What do you say to that?'

'Can I wear it to church on Sunday?' Rebecca asked, eyes shining at the prospect of a new hair ribbon.

Her father laughed. 'Course you can, my little one. Now, come and give your old dad a hug goodbye.'

Rebecca threw herself into her father's open arms, burrowing her face into his broad chest, the rough fibres of his woollen jumper scratching her cheek.

'You be good for your mum, Becky,' Ivan said, as he squeezed her tight.

'I will, Dad,' she promised.

'Now, we really must go,' Ivan said, releasing her with a pat on the head. 'We don't want to miss the tide. Lads?'

'Ready, Dad,' Robert said, grabbing his hat from the peg on the wall.

The fire sputtered in the cold draught that rushed in as Ivan opened the door. The horizon was the colour of ripe damsons. Water lapped musically against the wharf and *Elizabeth May* rocked on the gentle swell of the incoming tide.

Simeon gave Rebecca's pigtail an affectionate tweak and followed his father and younger brother onto the harbour wall. Rebecca and her mother watched from the cottage doorway. Lydia clutched the shawl at her throat. She shivered, but the chill that came over her had nothing to do with the cold wind blowing off the bay. She couldn't shake the dark foreboding that had taken hold of her. With her free hand, she pulled Rebecca to her, watching her husband and sons preparing to leave. Simeon hoisted the sails, which snapped in the breeze as Ivan expertly steered the fishing boat out of the relative safety of the harbour into the open waters of the English Channel.

Mother and daughter stood in the doorway until the little craft was no more than a speck in the distance. With night fast approaching, Lydia ushered Rebecca inside and lit the lamp. In relative silence, they washed up the supper things and settled in front of the fire. Rebecca picked up her schoolbook, but she couldn't concentrate on the words. She glanced at her mother. Lydia was sitting on the threadbare sofa, her fingers playing with the silver locket she always wore around her neck.

'Tell me the story of your locket again, Mother,' Rebecca asked, closing her book and snuggling up to her mother.

'You've heard it a hundred times,' Lydia said, managing a small smile.

'I want to hear it again,' Rebecca insisted.

'All right,' her mother said. 'As you know, my father gave it to my mother when they married.'

'It's very pretty,' Rebecca said, stroking the intricately engraved pattern on the oval-shaped pendant. It depicted vine leaves entwined with the initials HD. 'Hermione Durnford,' Rebecca murmured.

'That's right,' her mother replied. 'Though everyone called my mother Min. Even my father. I was only four when she passed away. I remember being very sad and frightened. The house never felt the same after that. My father was heartbroken and spent a lot of his time away on business, leaving me in the care of the housekeeper and my governess, Miss Robinson. They were kind, but I was a very lonely child.

'My father gave me the locket on my sixteenth birthday. I was so disappointed when I opened it. You see, I had a vague memory of my mother showing me inside her locket and I had expected to see portraits of my mother and father, but my father had removed them, just as he had every other portrait of my mother after her death.' Lydia's expression clouded. 'I could hardly remember what she looked like.' She gave herself a small shake and the smile returned. 'So now, as you know, it contains miniatures of your father and me.'

'Tell me again how you met Father,' Rebecca begged,

cuddling closer to her mother. She knew the story so well, but she never tired of it.

Lydia smiled. 'I had been quite poorly, and the doctor recommended I spend some time on the coast to rebuild my strength. So, my father arranged for Miss Robinson and me to take a house in Stoke Fleming. It was a lovely house set in small but pleasant grounds and afforded us lovely views of the sea. But,' she chuckled, 'it was set high on a hill and Miss Robinson was not a great walker so I spent much of my time exploring by myself. I liked to walk along the coastal path and one morning, as it was such a pleasant day, I wandered further than usual and ended up here, in Leonard's Bay. Your father was working on his boat. I thought he was the handsomest man I had ever seen.'

Rebecca grinned. Lydia knew she liked this part of the story. How her mother had been intrigued by the simple fisherman with the sun-browned skin and wild dark hair. And how she had given Miss Robertson the slip most afternoons to meet Ivan at the harbour. He'd taken her out on his boat several times over that long, hot summer.

'It was agony to part from him when I had to return to London. Sadly, your grandfather forbade me to have anything more to do with Ivan so we ran away together. We didn't have much money, but we were happy in our little cottage by the sea. Then, one day, a young man turned up on the doorstep. He was an artist, down on his luck and needing a place to stay for a few days. Well, the days turned into weeks and, to repay your father and me for our hospitality, he painted our likenesses in miniature.' Lydia pressed the clasp and the locket sprang open to reveal the two tiny paintings.

Clearly Rebecca loved examining them, seeing how her mother and father had looked in their youth. Her mother had been only a few years older than Simeon was now when she'd sat for the painting.

'Dad looks different,' Rebecca said, studying the pictures in the flickering lamplight. 'But you're the same.'

Lydia laughed. 'That's very sweet of you, Becky, but I doubt it.' She closed the locket, slipping it back beneath her clothes. 'Now, it's time for bed. Up you go. I'll soon be behind you.'

Reluctantly, Rebecca unfurled herself from the sofa. Her mother grabbed her hand. 'Be sure to say an extra prayer for your father and brothers tonight, love,' she said, giving her daughter's fingers an affectionate squeeze.

'Course I will, Mum.'

It was cold upstairs, her breath billowing in clouds before her face as she climbed the rickety staircase. Upstairs the single room was divided by a curtain. Rebecca shared one half with her brothers, and her parents slept in the other. She changed quickly into her nightdress and slipped under the covers. She was halfway through her prayers when she heard the creak of her mother's footsteps on the bare floorboards and saw the flicker of candlelight through the thin curtain.

'Mum,' she called. 'Can I sleep with you tonight?' She often shared her mother's bed when her father and brothers were away fishing.

'Of course, you can,' replied her mother.

Rebecca flung back the covers and, pushing aside the curtain, scampered over to where Lydia stood at the window. 'There they are, see?' she said, blowing out the candle.

Rebecca's eyes took a moment to adjust to the darkness but then she spotted it, a tiny pinprick of light far out in the inky black. The white flash from the lighthouse above the harbour

6

briefly lit up the sky, picking out swathes of calm, flat sea. Its sturdy presence, perched high above the small fishing village gave them a measure of comfort.

'Come,' Lydia said. 'Into bed now. The sooner you go to sleep, the sooner morning will come, and our boys will be home.'

Rebecca slipped under the covers. Her mother tucked the blankets under her chin and smoothed a strand of hair from Rebecca's forehead. 'Sleep well, my love.'

CHAPTER TWO

Rebecca woke with a fright. The house was shaking. A gust of wind slammed into the wall, making her cry out in alarm as she sat bolt upright.

'It's all right, Becky,' her mother's voice said in the darkness. 'It's just the storm. It's hit sooner than we expected.' The room was suddenly illuminated by the flash of the lighthouse, and she glimpsed her mother, silhouetted against the window, her back to the bed as she stared out into the night. The lighthouse lamp continued its circuitous route, plunging the room back into darkness.

Swallowing her fear, Rebecca crawled from beneath the covers. The air was bitterly cold, and she shivered in her nightdress as she joined her mother at the window. Lydia was still wearing her clothes, Rebecca realized. Had she been to bed at all?

'I didn't think there was any point in going to bed,' her mother said, as if Rebecca had spoken her thoughts aloud. 'I knew I wouldn't be able to sleep. Here, put this round you.' She tugged the blanket from the bed and draped it over Rebecca's shoulders. As she did so, the lighthouse lit up a swathe of foaming sea.

In that moment, Rebecca saw the waves pounding the harbour wall. The light faded and she strained her eyes, searching the vast blackness for the tiny pinprick of light.

'Please God, your father found somewhere to anchor until the storm passes,' her mother whispered.

Rebecca felt sick in the pit of her stomach and her chest hurt with the effort not to cry.

She must have fallen asleep again, for she awoke to pale thin daylight streaming in through the window. 'Mum?' Rebecca sat up with a start. 'Mum?' Scrambling from the bed, she ran to the window. The storm had blown itself out and the rising sun cast a golden hue over the gently undulating sea. The air was filled with the clamour of seabirds nesting on the cliffs behind the cottage. The tide was going out and already the water in the tiny stone harbour was receding, revealing large patches of black mud, seaweed and broken crab pots.

Her mother stood on the low wall, her back to the cottage as she stared out towards the horizon. Two of their neighbours, men Rebecca's father had known all his life, stood nearby. With a horrible sinking sensation inside her, Rebecca dressed quickly and, almost tumbling down the stairs in her haste, flew out of the door, and across the lane.

'Mum,' she shouted, the cold breeze snatching away her words as she sprinted up the stone steps onto the harbour wall.

Her mother looked strained, her face pale. The men's expressions were grave. 'Run up to the lighthouse, Becky,' she said, her voice faltering. 'Perhaps Mr Fisher has seen something.'

Rebecca nodded.

'Be careful,' one of the men warned her. 'It's blowing a hooley up there. Stay well away from the edge.'

'I will, Mr Ford,' Rebecca called, over her shoulder, as she jumped down the steps and raced to the foot of the winding pathway that led up to the lighthouse. She'd barely gone a few yards when she was almost bowled over by a gust of wind. The path hugged the hill but on the other side there was no protection from the elements. A low dry-stone wall was all that separated a person from certain death on the rocks below.

Rebecca pressed herself against the rough bracken that clung to the side of the hill. The wind snatched at her clothes and hair, like icy fingers trying to draw her towards the edge of the path. Swallowing her fear, she inched her way round the bend. There the wind lessened, and she could walk quicker, until she rounded the next bend, where it hit her full in the face, making her gasp. By the time she reached the lighthouse, she was panting and shaking.

She leaned against the cold white stone, fighting to stay upright as she caught her breath, looking down at the three fishermen's cottages nestled at the foot of the rugged cliffs below her. She could see her mother standing on the harbour wall. Their neighbour, Mary Ford, stood beside her.

Clinging tightly to the wooden handrail, Rebecca turned her gaze to the sun-dappled sea. White horses had begun to appear on the waters beyond the bay.

'I've been looking ever since first light,' said William Fisher, the lighthouse keeper, coming up behind her. He was stocky, with weathered skin and wiry grey hair that curled from below the thick woollen hat pulled low over his ears. His grey beard reached almost to his stomach. He was a solitary man, preferring his own company, but he'd always been kind to Rebecca, giving her a toffee or a pretty shell on the odd occasions when their paths crossed.

'There's nothing out there,' he said now. He smiled, treating Rebecca to a glimpse of crooked brown teeth. 'No sign of wreckage, which could mean they managed to hole up somewhere until the storm passed.'

'Do you think so, Mr Fisher?' Rebecca asked, her blue eyes scanning the empty sea hopefully.

The old man shrugged. 'Ivan's a seasoned sailor. He knows every sheltered cove and gully along this coast.' He gestured at the small group gathering on the harbour wall. 'Tell your ma I'll sound the bell the minute I see anything. Now, off you go, and mind yourself.'

'Thank you, Mr Fisher.' As Rebecca turned to leave, the old man pressed a toffee into her hand. 'For later.'

Thanking him again, Rebecca slipped it into her pocket and set off, careful to keep close to the hillside.

She reached the bottom to find her mother wasn't among the knot of people staring out to sea.

'Your ma's nipped home,' Mary Ford said, with a worried frown. Puzzled, Rebecca thanked her and hurried back to the cottage where she found Lydia stirring a large pot in the fireplace. 'Your father and the boys will be wanting their porridge when they get in,' she said, straightening as Rebecca entered the cottage. 'I think you should stay at home today, love. I don't want to be on my own.'

Rebecca ate her breakfast in silence. Her mother stood at the window, staring out to sea. The harbour wall was deserted now, apart from a flock of seagulls squabbling over the carcass of a dead fish.

As soon as she'd scraped up the last spoonful of porridge, Rebecca deposited her bowl in the sink and joined her mother at the window. Voices sounded outside. A door banged and the

Ford children spilled out into the lane. They were joined almost immediately by the Willis girls. Rebecca knew them all as well as she knew her own brothers. They were a subdued group as they walked past her window, with none of the usual banter and teasing. In such a small, tight-knit community, the news that Rebecca's father and brothers were missing would affect them all. Kitty Willis, Rebecca's particular friend, glanced towards her as they passed, her expression pale and anxious. Rebecca gave her a small wave. She wished with all her heart that she was going with them. It was a two-mile walk to the school in the next village and usually she relished a day off but now she would have given anything to be setting off for school while her father and brothers caught up on some much-needed sleep.

The day passed in agonizing slowness. Lydia spent most of her time staring out of the window or walking along the harbour wall. Amos Ford, Edward Willis and their older sons took their boats out, scouring the little coves and beaches along the coast in search of their missing friends. They returned early in the afternoon, shaking their heads, grim-faced. Mary Ford and Catherine Willis came during the afternoon to sit with Lydia. Rebecca was kept busy making tea and peeling potatoes for the evening meal. She found the toffee in her pocket and sucked it slowly, savouring the sugary taste of caramel melting on her tongue.

When their visitors left, the silence was deafening. Quietly Rebecca went about finishing off the meal. She hesitated as she set the table, unsure as to whether to lay five places or two. In the end she decided on five. She refused to give up hope that her father, Simeon and Robert would walk through the door at any minute. She'd been praying for a miracle all day and Miss Jones, her Sunday-school teacher, said that if you prayed hard enough, and believed without a shadow of doubt, Jesus would be sure to answer your prayers.

'This looks delicious, love,' her mother said, a few minutes later as she took her place at the table. She stared at the empty places, her eyes brimming with tears. 'You've been busy,' she said, forcing a smile as Rebecca set the bowl of fish stew before her, then took her own seat opposite. She tried not to notice the empty chairs, or that her mother only managed a mouthful before she pushed back her chair to resume her vigil at the window.

'Trim the lamp and place it in the upstairs window,' Lydia said, pulling her shawl tight around her. 'Just in case.'

Rebecca nodded. In the bedroom she trimmed the lamp and stood it in the window. The sea was being swallowed into the coming night. She hoped that, wherever they were, her father and brothers were safe.

She woke the next morning to a shout. Sitting bolt upright in bed, she heard the slam of the front door. Rebecca jumped out of bed, and flew to the window, her heart in her mouth. A small group was gathered on the shingle beach. Her mother was running along the lane, her hands to her mouth. Even with the window shut, Rebecca could hear her anguished cry and her blood turned cold. She ran down the stairs. Stopping only to pull on her coat and boots, Rebecca yanked open the door and sprinted towards the beach.

'Mum!' she screamed. The small crowd parted, and she could see Lydia. She was on her knees on the damp shingle, crouched over something lying just below the tide line, rocking gently in the shallow water. Not something, her brain amended. Someone. Her chest tightened. 'Mum!' she screamed again. Her boots crunched as she ran onto the damp shingle, the wind whipping at her hair. Then she felt arms tight around her waist, and she was almost lifted off her feet.

Squirming against the vice-like grip, she twisted her head round to find herself staring into the face of Mary and Amos's oldest boy, Paul. 'Don't go on the beach, Becky,' he said.

'Let me go,' Rebecca squealed. 'Mum! Mum!' she shouted, fighting against Paul's grip. 'Get off me!'

'Becky! Stop, please,' Paul pleaded.

'Becky, love, come with me.' It was Catherine Willis. She was a short, stout woman with flaming auburn hair and startling green eyes. On her broad hip, she jiggled her seventh child, a small red-haired boy of about two.

'Becky.' He beamed, stretching his arms out towards her.

'Not now, Sammy,' his mother chided him, turning slightly. 'Becky doesn't want to play.'

The fight went out of her and Rebecca's knees buckled. She would have fallen had Paul not been holding her up. 'Is it my dad?' she asked, tears running down her face.

Catherine and Paul exchanged glances and Catherine sighed. 'It's Simeon, love.'

At the thought of her beloved brother lying dead on the beach, Rebecca let out a shrill cry.

'Come on, love. Let's get you indoors.' Catherine nodded at Paul, and he swept Rebecca up and carried her away from the beach.

Catherine's dingy cottage smelt of fish and damp. Laundry was draped in front of the fire and Paul had to duck to avoid the lines of fish where they'd been strung across the ceiling to dry before he could lower Rebecca into the nearest chair. He ran a hand through his hair, as if at a loss as to what to do next.

'You get off,' Catherine said, filling the doorway. 'You'll

need to be scouring the beach for ...' She glanced uneasily at Rebecca curled up on the armchair, sobbing piteously. 'Well, you know ...'

Paul nodded grimly.

'Becky?' Sammy chirped, as Paul ducked out of the door. 'Becky sad?'

'Yes, pet, Becky's sad,' replied Catherine soberly, shutting the door. With Sammy on her hip, she went to stand by the window. Soon, she felt a small hand in hers and looked down at Rebecca's tear-stained face.

'Mrs Willis, is my dad dead, too?' she asked, in a small voice. 'And Robert?'

Catherine bit her lip. 'I think it's likely, love, yes.'

Rebecca nodded, wiping her eyes. Catherine fished in her pocket for a bit of rag and handed it to her to blow her nose.

From the window, they watched as Lydia staggered up from the beach, supported on either side by Mary and Paul Ford. They were almost at the lane when Lydia stumbled.

'Mum!' Rebecca shrieked. She flung open the door and raced out of the cottage. She reached her mother just as Mary and Paul were helping to lift her upright.

At the sight of her daughter, Lydia sank to her knees in the damp shingle. 'Oh, Becky,' she wailed, opening her arms. Rebecca fell into them, tears streaming down her pale cheeks.

'He's gone,' her mother gasped, sobbing unashamedly. 'Our dear Sim. Oh, our poor, darling boy.'

CHAPTER THREE

Rebecca clung tightly to her mother's hand. A cold wind swept across the cliff top, scouring her wet cheeks. Gulls and cormorants wheeled overhead in the dark-grey sky, the heavy clouds pregnant with the threat of rain. Far below, the sea was flecked with white horses. Waves crashed against the reef, throwing spray high into the sky.

Unable to bring herself to gaze upon the open graves of her father and brother, she kept her eyes fixed on the ground at her feet, straining to hear what the vicar was saying. She tried to swallow. Her throat ached from crying and her stomach felt hollow.

Only three days earlier they had buried Simeon among the generations of Wheelers who rested beneath the rough scrubland grass, and now they were here again to bury her father and Robert. Their bodies had washed up on the beach on the day of Simeon's funeral.

She heard her mother's sharp intake of breath. Raising her gaze, Rebecca immediately recognized the stout middle-aged man standing on the other side of the open graves as Gilbert Carter, the rent collector. She glanced up at her mother. Lydia's mouth was a thin, angry line in her white face, and she looked tense as the vicar brought the short service to a close.

'My condolences again, Mrs Wheeler,' the vicar said, taking Lydia's gloved hands in his. 'May you know God's comfort during this difficult time.'

'Thank you, Vicar,' Lydia whispered, watching Gilbert Carter from the corner of her eye. He was clean-shaven with dark hair, greying at the temples, and dark eyes under thick brows. Catching Rebecca's eye, he gave her and Lydia a curt nod. Replacing his hat, he strode casually to the stone memorial that had been erected fifty years ago in memory of the crew who had lost their lives when their ship had sunk on the reef off Leonard's Bay.

'Come on, Becky. Let's go.' Her mother took hold of Rebecca's arm, gently leading her away as Amos, Paul and his brother Arthur picked up their shovels. She heard the dull thud of soil hitting the wooden coffins, sending a shiver up her spine.

Buffeted by the cold wind, Lydia and Rebecca led the way down the steep, winding path. Mary and Catherine followed with their children and the handful of other mourners who had made the journey from the surrounding villages to pay their respects. Back at the cottage, Mary and Catherine busied themselves making pots of tea while the Willis girls offered plates of sandwiches. The vicar and Gilbert Carter stood by the fire, drinking their tea. The vicar had his head inclined towards the rent man, who was talking animatedly, pausing only to swallow another bite of his sandwich. Rebecca noticed her mother watching them nervously and felt a growing sense of unease.

The door swung open, letting in a cold draught, as Amos

Ford entered, followed by Paul, and Edward Willis, stamping their feet and blowing on their cold hands.

'Lizzie,' Catherine Willis called to her eldest daughter. 'Fetch your dad and Mr Ford a cup of tea. Kitty, where's that plate of sandwiches?'

Kitty fetched it from the kitchen and gave it to her mother, then joined Rebecca on the low window seat. They sat in silence, listening to the ebb and flow of conversation.

The night was drawing in and people were starting to leave. 'I'm sorry for your loss, Mrs Wheeler,' Gilbert Carter said, approaching Lydia, hat in hand. He stood in front of her, feet apart.

At once the air in the cottage felt charged. Across the room, Rebecca saw Amos and Edward exchange glances.

'I'm sorry to be the bearer of bad tidings, Mrs Wheeler,' Gilbert began, 'especially at such a time as this, but it is my duty to remind you that you are several weeks in arrears with your rent and—'

'Have a heart, Mr Carter,' Amos spoke up. 'The woman has just buried her husband and two sons.'

'I'm aware of that, Mr Ford,' Gilbert replied testily, looking not the least bit ashamed. 'And Mr Elliot has instructed me to pass on his most heartfelt condolences to you, Mrs Wheeler. However, the fact remains that you are behind on your rent and, unfortunately, if all arrears are not paid up to date by the end of this week, Mr Elliot will have no choice but to evict you.'

'Evict us!' Lydia rose to her feet, clutching her throat. 'He can't!'

'I'm afraid he can, Mrs Wheeler,' Gilbert responded brusquely.

'I can't afford to pay,' Lydia said, wide-eyed in panic. 'The fishing. It hasn't been good and now . . . Please, I need more time.'

'Mr Elliot has been more than patient,' Gilbert said. 'And as you now have no obvious source of income . . .' He cleared his throat, his cheeks reddening.

'I hope he chokes to death,' Kitty hissed under her breath, making Rebecca smile for the first time in days. 'End of the week, Mrs Wheeler. Good day to you.' He set his hat on his head and strode towards the door, which Paul held open, regarding the older man with barely concealed contempt. Uttering no word of thanks, Gilbert ducked out into the cold November evening. Paul let the door swing shut behind him as Lydia sank onto her chair. She was shaking. Catherine and Mary, who were washing up, left the dishes and hurried to her side.

'What will you do?' whispered Kitty, as Rebecca watched her mother, her lip quivering as she fought back tears. 'Where will you go?'

'I don't know,' Rebecca said, barely audibly. They had no family, no one they could turn to should Mr Elliott evict them. What would become of them?

'Have you no family you can go to?' Mary Ford asked. She had sent her husband and the children home, and Catherine Willis had left with her family, but Mary had insisted on staying, despite Lydia's protestations that she'd be all right with Rebecca.

Lydia shook her head.

'You could write to Grandpa?' Rebecca piped up. She had been pondering their predicament and, to her, the solution was obvious. They did have family. She had a grandfather. She'd never met him but perhaps he would help them.

'Your father is alive?' Mary asked Lydia. 'I assumed your parents were gone, as you've never mentioned them.'

'I haven't spoken to my father for sixteen years,' Lydia replied, with a sigh, 'He didn't approve of Ivan. The last time I saw him, he told me I was never to darken his door again.' She smiled sadly at Rebecca. 'I'm sorry, love, but I doubt he'd be willing to help.'

'Time is a great healer,' Mary said firmly. 'He may have come to regret his behaviour towards you. It's worth a try, surely.' Her expression softened. 'If I had the room . . . but with my brood we're bursting at the seams as it is. And Catherine, well, they've even less space than us.'

'Oh, Mary.' Lydia squeezed her friend's hand. 'I wouldn't dream of imposing. No, you're right. I shall write to my father immediately and attempt to build bridges.'

Curled up at her mother's feet, Rebecca couldn't help feeling a fizz of excitement. Her mother had often spoken about the grand house she had grown up in. How wonderful it would be to live in such a beautiful place. She hoped her grandfather would write back soon. She closed her eyes, imagining the large house from her mother's stories, with butter-yellow walls and a fountain in the garden . . .

'Becky . . . Becky.' Her mother's voice seemed to come from far away. Rebecca sat up, rubbing her eyes. Mary had gone and the fire had died down, leaving a chill hanging over the room.

'You fell asleep, love,' Lydia said, stroking her hair. 'It's been a long day. Off you go to bed. I shan't be far behind you.'

Rebecca made her way wearily up the stairs. She set the candle on the small nightstand, its flame flickering in the draught from the ill-fitting windows. Stifling a yawn, she got into her nightdress, shivering in the dank night air. Without her brothers' noisy presence, the room seemed unwelcoming. She slipped under the covers and squeezed her eyes shut, listening to the howl of the wind under the eaves. She could hear the waves pounding the shingle beach and her throat thickened. Turning on to her side, she buried her face in her pillow and cried herself to sleep.

'I wish I was as clever as you, Becky,' Kitty said, as they negotiated the narrow cliff path down to Leonard's Bay. 'I can never remember all my times tables.' She pulled a face, the humiliation of being made to stand in front of the entire class and recite the nine-times still smarting.

'I just find it easy,' Rebecca said, with a shrug. She was only half listening to her friend's chatter. She'd felt sympathy for her friend, red-faced and stammering as she'd tried to remember nine sevens, eights and nines, but Kitty had been moaning about it for the past fifteen minutes, and Rebecca had more important things on her mind. Mr Carter was due to collect the rent this afternoon, and when she'd left for school that morning, there had been no reply from her grandfather.

'My dad says it's a waste of time girls knowing their numbers,' Bertie Ford informed Kitty, with a sneer. 'You'll only end up in service.'

'Who says I will?' Kitty flashed back.

Bertie shrugged. 'What other jobs are there around here?'

'I'm going to apply at Maisie's Hotel when I leave school this summer,' Maddy Willis said. 'Rosie Clarke's sister's a chambermaid there and she says it's lovely. The wages are fair, and the staff are treated like family.'

'I heard it's very hard to get a place there,' one of the younger Ford girls said, shoving past Rebecca and Kitty. 'You've got to know someone. Oh, drat,' she said, as she snagged her skirt on a bramble.

'Rosie's going to ask her sister to put a word in for me,' retorted Maddy, as she twisted round to help the younger girl unhook her skirt from the prickly bush. Rebecca moved up the bank to squeeze past her and froze, causing Kitty and Bertie to crash into her.

'Becky!' grumbled Bertie. 'Watch what . . .' His words died on his lips as he followed Rebecca's shocked gaze.

'What's happening?' Kitty whispered, peering over Rebecca's shoulder.

'Oh, my word!' Maddy screeched, making them all jump. 'Becky,' she said, in a horrified whisper, 'he's gone and done it! You're being evicted.'

Her heart in her throat, Rebecca scrambled down the path as fast as she could, her gaze fixed on the scene unfolding below. Her mother was standing outside the cottage, her face ashen, as she clung to Mary. Catherine stood nearby, holding Sammy's hand. As Rebecca slithered over a small rocky outcrop, she saw her mother's work basket fly out of the cottage to join the small assortment of belongings that littered the road.

'Mum?' She ran along the quay, her breath catching in her throat. She could hear her friends following, but she didn't look back. 'Mum, what's happening?'

'Becky, wait.' Catherine put out a hand and grabbed her arm, bringing her to an abrupt halt. 'You're being evicted, love,' she said quietly.

Rebecca shook her head. 'They can't evict us,' she panted, struggling against Catherine's grip. 'We haven't heard from Grandpa yet.'

'Becky.' Lydia stretched out her hand. Catherine let her go and she flung herself at her mother. A frying pan flew out of the door, followed by Lydia's treasured china bowl, which shattered on the road.

Rebecca pressed herself against her mother, unable to bear the sight of the two big, bald men moving systematically through the cottage, throwing out everything that didn't belong to the landlord, but equally unable to look away.

A figure filled the doorway, and she flinched as Gilbert Carter strode towards them, his expression grim. 'All your things have been cleared from the cottage,' he said, his eyes hard as he handed Lydia a piece of paper. 'And you are no longer legally entitled to enter the property or you will be arrested for trespassing.'

Lydia scanned the notice, her hands trembling. Surrounded by her friends and neighbours, her meagre possessions scattered across the road, Rebecca was overwhelmed with shame. She couldn't bring herself to meet Kitty's eyes when her friend asked if she was all right. She simply nodded, keeping her eyes focused on her scuffed shoes.

'Where will you go, Lydia?' Mary asked, as the two bald men emerged from the cottage. One shut the door with a resounding bang, and stationed himself in front of it, arms folded across his broad chest.

Lydia took a shaky breath. With a determined tilt of her chin, she looked at Gilbert Carter with defiance in her eyes. 'We shall go to Dartmouth,' she said, a note of forced cheer in her voice as she smiled down at her daughter. 'It will be an adventure. Help me gather up all our things, Becky. There's plenty we can sell.' She turned her smile on Mary. 'We'll be all right for a day or two until I can find work.'

'Are you sure, Lydia?' protested Mary, her eyes brimming with tears.

'Of course.' Her confident tone belied the terror squeezing her insides. She took Mary's hands in hers. 'I'll send you my address. If a letter should come for me . . .'

'I'll send it on to you,' Mary assured her but, as their eyes met, it was clear that neither woman expected one.

Lydia turned away, her heart aching because she was leaving Ivan and her boys alone on the cliff top. But she couldn't stay in Leonard's Bay where fishing was the only way to earn a living. In Dartmouth she'd have more chance of finding work, even if it was mending nets. Lord knows she'd done that often enough. Even Becky knew how to mend nets. They'd be all right. She would make sure of it.

CHAPTER FOUR

It took the two of them an hour to navigate the two and a half miles of rugged coastline, and darkness was falling by the time Rebecca and her mother trudged wearily along the quay, dragging the small cart that held their possessions.

Water lapped against the harbour wall, the lights from the nearby hotel shimmering across its ruffled surface. The door swung open, affording Rebecca a glimpse of plush carpets and embossed wallpaper. She caught the tinkle of a piano before the door swung shut, cutting the music off mid-note.

Despite the bitter winter weather, the town was bustling with merchants unloading carts and wagons, horses whinnying loudly. Voices shouted in the darkness and the steady splash of oars drifted across the water.

'Excuse me,' Lydia said, as a well-dressed couple hurried past. The man looked down his nose at her and kept walking. 'Sir, can you help me?' she tried again, taking a step towards an elderly gentleman standing at the harbour wall, gazing contemplatively over the water.

'I don't encourage begging,' the man answered haughtily.

Lydia flushed beetroot red. 'I am no beggar, sir,' she said, in what Rebecca's father had always laughingly called her 'posh' voice. 'I was hoping you might direct me to a certain address.'

The man raised a quizzical eyebrow, clearly surprised that someone dressed as shabbily as Lydia should be so well-spoken. 'What address are you looking for?' he asked, in a slightly warmer tone.

'Mead's Emporium,' Lydia said, fishing a scrap of paper from her pocket on which Catherine Willis had scribbled the name of a pawnbroker her sister had used some years back when the family had fallen on desperate times.

'Mead's?' The man's eyes narrowed suspiciously, his hooded gaze alighting on the loaded barrow.

'Please,' Lydia said, with a defiant tilt of her chin as she pulled Rebecca closer.

The man shrugged. 'It's along the Butterwalk,' he said, indicating a covered walkway to Lydia's left. 'Big sign over the door. You can't miss it.'

'Thank you, sir.' Lydia gripped Rebecca's arm, ushering her towards the opening of the wide street, the rattle of the cart's wheels echoing off the buildings. The broad, decorative ceiling covering the pavement offered welcome respite from the wind. A nearby streetlamp sputtered, and a mangy cat slunk out of the shadows, startling them both.

'Goodness,' Lydia breathed, laughing nervously as she clutched Rebecca's hand. Their footsteps echoed on the frozen ground. They passed a narrow doorway where two women dressed in low-cut gowns were sheltering, their shoulders bare despite the freezing conditions. They eyed Lydia and Rebecca sullenly, their made-up faces macabre in the sickly yellow light of the streetlamp. Rebecca stared at them. One women flashed her a smile, displaying rotting teeth.

'Come along, Becky,' Lydia said sharply. Rebecca bowed her

26

head and quickened her pace to keep up with her mother, her heart pounding. The noise and smells of the town were intimidating after the quiet tranquillity of Leonard's Bay. She heard her mother's sigh of relief at the same time as she spotted the emporium up ahead, its name illuminated by a lamp swinging on a hook above the door.

Through the steamed-up window, Rebecca could see the blurred shapes of an assortment of household items. On the door hung a crudely painted sign which read: 'Mead's Emporium – Fair Prices Paid for Quality Goods'.

Taking a deep breath, Lydia pushed open the door. A bell jangled above their heads, summoning a large, overweight woman from behind a curtain. She had a round face and florid complexion, with tendrils of greying greasy hair escaping from beneath a grubby white-lace cap. She propped her ample bosom on the wooden counter, wheezing as she eyed Lydia and Rebecca with disinterest against a backdrop of shelves laden with every conceivable household item.

'Yes?' she said, in a bored voice.

'Good evening.' Lydia approached the counter, carefully manoeuvring the cart between piles of precariously stacked furniture. She cleared her throat and steadied herself, forcing a smile. It wouldn't do to let the woman see how desperate she was. 'I have a few items I no longer need, and I wondered if you might be interested in buying them.'

Rebecca clutched the edge of the counter, staring up at the woman nervously.

The woman eyed the loaded cart with indifference. 'I'll give you a shilling.'

Lydia blanched. 'Is that all?' Her voice quivered. 'The linen alone is worth more than that.'

The woman waved her hand. 'You can see how much stuff I've got in here. It could be sitting on the shelves for months. Take it or leave it,' she said, with a shrug. 'Unless you got anything else?'

Lydia's hand moved to her neck. She could feel the locket nestled against her skin. It was solid silver. They would be able to live comfortably on the proceeds for several weeks. But could she bear to part with her one link to her mother? She glanced down at her daughter's pinched, frightened face, and was about to unfasten the clasp when the shop bell jangled, and a small, thin man entered, bringing with him a draught of cold evening air. He removed his hat and peeled off his black gloves as he approached the counter, his oiled black hair gleaming in the lamplight.

'Ladies.' He nodded. 'Everything all right, Mrs Mead?' he asked the woman, resting one pale hand on the counter. The woman nodded, and told him how much she'd offered Lydia for her goods.

The man smiled up at Lydia, displaying yellow teeth. His eyes widened, as his smile brightened. 'Perhaps we can be a little more generous, dear wife,' he said, stroking his moustache thoughtfully. 'Erastus Mead.' He turned to Lydia. 'Owner of this establishment.'

Suppressing a shudder of revulsion, Lydia smiled back.

'May I?' Without waiting for Lydia's reply, he peered into the cart. 'Fallen on hard times, have we?' he remarked sympathetically.

To her horror, Lydia felt tears welling in her eyes.

'Mrs Mead, put the kettle on,' Erastus said, affably. 'This poor lady is clearly in distress. My dear madam,' he said, motioning towards the curtain, 'please come through to the parlour.'

As his wife bustled off to make the tea, Erastus settled Lydia and Rebecca in the warm, stuffy parlour. The room, decorated in greens, oranges and browns, had clearly been furnished with little regard to taste. A stag's head hung above the fireplace. Rebecca sat in an armchair, her feet an inch off the floor, while Erastus Mead attempted to prise Lydia's story from her.

'So, you and your little girl are alone in the world?' he prompted, with a sympathetic tilt of his head.

'Yes, sir.' Before Lydia could say any more, the door opened and Erastus's wife entered with the tea tray.

'Ah, thank you, my dear.' Erastus half rose from his seat. 'Has Mr Fox been in this evening?' he asked her, in a low voice, as she set the tray before him.

'Not yet.'

'Thank you, my dear.' He accepted his cup with a smile. 'Perhaps you might nip over to the Nautical Arms and see if he's in. I believe he may be able to help this lady.'

'Might Mr Fox be able to offer me employment?' said Lydia, feeling a surge of hope for the first time in days.

'It is a possibility,' Erastus replied, studiously ignoring his wife's scowl as she pulled on her wraps. Clearly she was not relishing the inconvenience of going out on such a cold night. She banged the door behind her, making Rebecca jump. Erastus winced.

'So, you were about to tell me how you came to be in this . . . unfortunate situation,' he prompted, leaning towards Lydia, having quickly recovered his equilibrium.

To her surprise, Lydia found herself telling him everything that had happened over the past ten days. Was it only ten days? she thought, as she paused to catch her breath. Less than two weeks ago, she had been a happily married woman, and mother of three. Now she was a homeless widow trying to provide for her only surviving child. Tears rolled down her cheeks as she recounted the bailiffs' visit.

'You poor lady,' Erastus said, pulling a clean handkerchief from his trouser pocket and handing it to her.

'Thank you.' Lydia sniffed, wiping her eyes. 'So here we are,' she said, with a shaky smile. 'All we have in the world is in that little cart. I was hoping for enough to tide us over until I can find work. The amount your wife suggested would barely cover one night's accommodation in a decent hotel.'

'I'm afraid you've caught me at a difficult time,' said Erastus, his hair gleaming in the lamplight. 'Most of my money is tied up in stock. However . . .' he continued, sucking his teeth. He clasped his hands under his chin and leaned forward, resting his elbows on his knees. 'If my assumption is correct, my esteemed acquaintance Mr Fox may be able to provide you with a solution. He's often on the lookout for new employees. Accommodation is provided.'

Lydia's eyes lit up. 'Do you really think he may be able to offer me a position?' she asked. 'I'm used to hard work.'

'I'm sure you're just the sort of person he'll be looking for.' Erastus smiled. Lydia's calloused, workworn hands, so at odds with her genteel manner, hadn't gone unnoticed. Fox would work her hard, he mused, with a glint in his eye. But not in the way she expected. 'More tea?'

Rebecca sipped her tea, trying not to make any slurping noises or spill on the furniture, watching Mr Mead. He must have felt her gaze for he turned to her and winked. She looked away quickly, feeling the heat rising in her neck and colouring her cheeks. Something about the man made her uncomfortable, but she had no time to ponder why for at that moment they were interrupted by the muted jangle of the shop bell, followed by the sound of voices. The parlour door opened, and a heavily built man came in. His ginger hair was shaved close, and he sported a neatly trimmed, red goatee beard.

'Ah, Mr Fox,' exclaimed Erastus, jovially, getting to his feet. The man gave his outstretched hand a cursory shake, his gaze going past Erastus to settle on the woman seated by the fire. 'Thank you for popping in,' Erastus continued, as his wife relieved the man of his hat, coat and scarf. 'Allow me to introduce you.'

Lydia rose quickly to her feet, indicating to Rebecca to do the same. She slid off her chair, clutching her teacup in trembling hands.

'Mr Fox, may I present Mrs Lydia Wheeler and her daughter, Rebecca? Mrs Wheeler, Mr Michael Fox.'

'Good evening, Mr Fox,' Lydia said, with a prim nod.

'Good evening, Mr Fox,' Rebecca echoed, staring shyly at the floor.

Mickey Fox's initial interest quickened. The woman was a bit long in the tooth. He'd hazard a guess at early thirties, but her upper-class accent, coupled with her striking looks, would be a big draw. Punters would pay over the odds for a woman like her. 'I believe you're in need of employment,' he said, stroking his beard contemplatively.

'I'm not afraid of hard work,' she said, a note of desperation in her voice. 'I'll happily turn my hand to anything.'

'I thought Mrs Wheeler would be just right for your establishment the moment I saw her.' Erastus smiled ingratiatingly at the younger man.

'Here's your brandy, Mr Fox,' Mrs Mead said, appearing at Mickey's side. He accepted the glass without a word of thanks and downed the amber liquid in one long swallow.

'How old is the girl?' he asked.

'She's ten, sir. Almost eleven . . . but if you cannot allow me to bring her with me I shall have to turn down any offer you may make. I cannot be parted from my child.'

Rebecca flinched as he cupped her chin in his fingers, tilting her head towards the light. He gave an approving grunt and let her go. Rebecca scuttled closer to Lydia, who wrapped a protective arm around her shoulders.

Mickey played with the glass in his hand, mesmerized by the way the cut crystal reflected the light. Rebecca inched even closer to her mother, pressing into her.

'Very well,' he said at length. 'I shall take you on. Here.' He reached into his waistcoat pocket and drew out a handful of notes. 'This is an advance on your wages. Mrs Mead, see to it that all of Mrs Wheeler's outstanding debts are paid. If you need any more, let me know.'

Rebecca stared at her mother clearly astonished. She'd never have seen so much money.

'Why, Mr Fox,' Lydia stammered, 'that's so generous.'

'I'm a generous man,' he said, with a semblance of a smile.

He glanced at the clock. 'It's time we were on our way.' He laid his hand on Rebecca's shoulder. Her cup fell to the carpet, tea seeping into it.

'Clumsy girl!' snorted Mrs Mead, and slapped Rebecca's face.

'Mrs Mead!' Lydia cried, outraged, as her daughter clutched her cheek.

'Mrs Mead,' Mickey repeated mildly, 'accidents happen.

Here.' He passed her a banknote. 'This should alleviate the inconvenience.'

Mrs Mead snatched the money. She glared at Rebecca and waddled towards the kitchen to fetch a cloth.

CHAPTER FIVE

Mortified, her cheek red and stinging from Mrs Mead's slap, Rebecca followed her mother and Mr Fox out into the cold night. Her breath clouded in the frosty air. The door shut behind them and she heard Mr Mead slamming home the bolts. They had left the little cart behind. Mr Fox had promised to send someone to collect it the following day.

'Come along, Mrs Wheeler,' Mickey said, offering Lydia his arm. After a moment's hesitation, she took it. Their footsteps echoed as they were buffeted by the salty wind blowing in off the River Dart.

Suddenly one of the women Rebecca had noticed earlier emerged from a doorway. Her lips were tinged blue, and she was shivering violently. There was a livid purple bruise on her cheek that hadn't been there before, and one eye appeared to be swollen shut. She smiled at Mickey, her remaining teeth gleaming yellow in the halo of light from the streetlamp. 'Here, Mickey,' she said, batting her eyelids suggestively. 'How about I warm your bed tonight?' She lurched forward, making as if to grab his arm but he stepped neatly out of her reach, pulling Lydia with him. Rebecca stared up at the woman nervously. She could smell gin on her breath.

'Oh, come on, Mickey,' the woman cajoled him. 'I'm a good girl. I'll make you good money.'

'Ignore her,' Mickey said, ushering Lydia and Rebecca along. 'She's drunk and no doubt her mind has been addled by the pox.'

'Mickey,' the woman called after them. 'Have a care, please. It's perishing cold tonight.'

'She looks very young,' Lydia said, with a note of sympathy as she quickened her pace to match Mickey's long strides. 'Is there nowhere she can go?'

'There's a doss house down near the quay,' he replied, walking briskly on.

They had gone almost the length of the covered walkway before it occurred to Lydia to ask, 'What line of work are you in, Mr Fox?'

'Hospitality,' he replied, shortly. 'This way.'

They turned a corner. A sign halfway up the blackened brickwork proclaimed the steep, narrow street to be Angel Terrace. It was lined by tall, narrow houses on either side. Wrinkling her nose at the damp, briny air that carried the stench of rotting fish, sewage and smoke, Rebecca followed close to her mother. Out of the corner of her eye, she saw a rat the size of a small cat: it sprang from the gutter and ran across her path. She screamed, clutching her mother's coat.

Mickey laughed. 'Rats are the least of your worries,' he said. 'Cutthroats and thieves are what you need to watch out for. Right, here we are.' They'd stopped in front of a narrow door. The black paint gleamed in the moonlight. The brass knocker was in the shape of a galleon, below the number fourteen, also in brass. A small plaque to the left of the door said, in small, discreet letters, 'Gentlemen's Club'.

Mickey pulled a key from his coat pocket and unlocked the door. It swung open slowly to reveal a small, dimly lit hallway. Directly opposite the door was a flight of stairs. By the light of the sconces on the wall, Rebecca could tell that the carpet was worn and threadbare. The black and white checked linoleum was scuffed and cracked.

Lydia regarded her surroundings with evident unease. Her grip tightened on Rebecca's hand.

'Mother,' Mickey called, shutting the door behind him. A door to their left opened, flooding the hall with light, and a tiny woman came out. She was barely taller than Rebecca and her facial features were strangely owl-like. Her greying fair hair was pulled back into a bun, and she wore a floor-length black woollen dress. The high collar was edged with lace, as were the cuffs, and she wore no wedding ring.

'What do you mean, bringing a child here?' she snapped, her blue-eyed gaze darting between Rebecca and her mother.

'Mrs Wheeler,' Mickey said, ignoring the question. 'May I introduce my stepmother?' His lip curled. 'Miss Tina.'

'Good evening, Miss Tina,' Lydia said pleasantly.

'I asked you what you mean by bringing the child here?' Tina narrowed her eyes in annoyance.

'I heard you the first time, Mother,' Mickey said. 'I need you to look after her for a bit.'

'Oh, no,' Tina said. 'I'm not playing nursemaid.' She jerked her head towards the parlour door. 'Nora can do it. She's between customers.' She raised her voice. 'Nora, get out here.'

A tall, slender woman with auburn hair and a pale, milky complexion appeared in the doorway. She wore a floor-length blue silk gown, open at the throat to reveal the curve of her breasts. Behind her, Rebecca heard her mother gasp. The hand resting on her shoulder trembled slightly.

'I need you to look after the kid while her mother and I talk business,' Mickey said, his tone brooking no argument.

Nora bent down to Rebecca. 'Come on, sweetheart,' she said. 'There's a lovely fire in the parlour. You'll soon warm up.' Taking Rebecca's hand, she straightened. Lydia swallowed hard. Her instinct was to grab Rebecca and get as far away from that place as possible.

'I'm sorry,' she said, with more confidence than she felt. 'There's been a misunderstanding. Come along, Becky.'

As she reached for Rebecca, Mickey's hand closed over her wrist like a vice. 'I don't think so,' he said coldly. 'You belong to me now.'

Lydia's pulse began to race. 'You brought me here under false pretences, Mr Fox,' she said. 'I don't believe this is a . . .' she glanced around her, breathing deeply to calm her nerves '. . . a reputable business.'

'Unless you can repay what you owe me right now, I'm afraid I can't let you leave.' He smiled. 'As soon as you've earned enough to pay me back, you're free to go.' He nodded at Nora, who shot Lydia a look of sympathy.

'Mum?' Rebecca whimpered, straining against Nora's grip.

'Let my daughter go!' Lydia said, grabbing Rebecca's arm.

'You're upsetting the girl, Mrs Wheeler,' Mickey said mildly. 'Don't make this more difficult than it needs to be.'

Lydia swallowed. Cursing herself for her naivety and real-izing she had inadvertently put herself and her daughter in grave danger – she could see something lurking in Mickey's eyes, something dark – she forced a smile. 'Go with Nora,

Becky,' she said. 'Mr Fox and I need to discuss the terms of my employment.' She paused, her mouth dry. 'I – I won't be long.'

Rebecca bowed her head. Avoiding Lydia's gaze, Nora pulled her into the parlour, closing the door firmly behind them.

'Mother, a glass of brandy for Mrs Wheeler, please,' Mickey said.

'No,' Lydia snapped.

'It will relax you,' Mickey said, and pointed to the stairs. 'This way, Mrs Wheeler.'

Lydia followed his gaze, her insides turning to water at the thought of what might lie ahead. Light flickered from a wall sconce at the top of the stairs. From somewhere above she heard muffled laughter. She swallowed hard, her throat constricting with fear.

Tina returned from the kitchen with a tumbler of brandy.

'Drink it,' Mickey instructed.

'I don't—'

'I said, drink it,' Mickey said, his voice dangerously low.

Lydia stared at him, fear rising in her. With a shaking hand, she gulped the brandy, grimacing as it burned her throat. She handed the empty glass to Tina, who smirked unpleasantly.

'Upstairs,' Mickey said. On legs that felt weighed down by lead, Lydia made her way up the stairs. Despite the poor lighting given off by a single wall lamp, she could see four doors. Two were closed. There was a further staircase at the far end of the landing.

'In here,' Mickey said, indicating the nearest open door. Her heart beating wildly, Lydia preceded him into the room. A lamp burned on the night table, its warm glow lending a cosy feel to the room. The room was dominated by a large, four-poster bed, its gossamer-thin curtains tied to the wooden posts with red ribbons. It was covered with satin sheets, and a thick comforter was folded neatly at the foot. A full-length mirror and a small dark-wood wardrobe stood against one wall. A chaise longue was positioned opposite, a pink silk robe draped across its back. A rattan screen was folded in one corner.

'I'm sure you can have no complaints regarding your accommodation?' Mickey said, with a sarcastic grin, closing the door behind him. Lydia ignored him.

'The child can sleep in the kitchen. It's warm enough in there.'

'Why can't she be in here with me?' Lydia asked hoarsely, fully aware of what Mickey's reply would be.

'You'll be hard at work.' He moved towards her, smiling wolfishly as he removed his jacket and began to unbutton his shirt. 'Now, Mrs Wheeler, you were a married woman. I'm sure you know how to please a man.'

'Please, Mr Fox,' Lydia said, pulling herself to her full height of five foot five. 'I'll do anything but this. Please don't make me.' She was close to tears. 'I'd rather die first.' She made to move towards the door, but Mickey quickly blocked her path.

'You're going nowhere,' he growled. 'And if you resist me, your little girl will take the brunt of my wrath.'

'You can't do this,' hissed Lydia, her stomach churning. 'Please, let us go. I'll find a job and pay you back what I owe you, I promise.'

Mickey shrugged. 'It's you or the kid.'

'What?' Lydia froze, her blood turning to ice in her veins. 'You wouldn't dare?' she whispered.

'Try me. There are plenty of punters whose tastes are . . . slightly against the norm. A pretty little thing like her will fetch a good price.' He splayed his hands. 'It's up to you.'

Lydia stared at him in horror. How could she have misread him so badly? She felt so angry with herself for putting herself and Rebecca in this position. Tears pricked her eyes. She'd let down her beloved Ivan too He'd be turning in his grave, she thought, tears of shame streaming down her cheeks.

'I'm glad we've got that settled,' Mickey said, with a leer. 'And now I'm going to show you exactly what our customers will expect. Take your clothes off and get on the bed.'

In the quiet parlour, Rebecca watched as Nora expertly shuffled the deck of playing cards.

'Have you ever played Rummy?' Nora asked, as she laid the cards on the small table in front of them. Rebecca shook her head. Her father had played cards with Mr Ford and Mr Willis but, though her brothers had occasionally joined them, her mother had always said card games were not a suitable pastime for a young lady. She glanced up at Nora under her lashes, noting how she chewed her tongue thoughtfully as she dealt out the cards.

'Will you play, Miss Tina?' Nora asked the older woman, who was seated closest to the fireplace.

'No,' she replied, regarding Rebecca with a sour expression that made her shiver. She glanced towards the ceiling. She hoped her mother wouldn't be too long. Nora was all right, but Miss Tina frightened her.

'I'll explain as we go along,' Nora said, drawing Rebecca's attention back to the game. Suddenly they heard a blood-curdling scream overhead. Rebecca jumped and even Nora flinched. 'Come on, love,' she said, with forced jollity. 'It's your turn.'

Rebecca stared at Nora. That scream had come from her

mother, she was sure. It was followed by another, chilling Rebecca to the bone. She leaped to her feet, almost upsetting the card table. Nora grabbed her arm. 'Come on, love, sit down. Let's get on with our game.'

'Mama!' Rebecca shrieked. 'He's hurting her!'

Nora glanced helplessly at Miss Tina, who got to her feet, reaching for the poker. 'Sit down,' she said sternly, raising it. Rebecca was rooted to the spot in terror.

'Please, love,' Nora said quietly. 'Sit down. Your mama will be fine, I promise you.'

Rebecca was trembling so violently that her legs gave way and she fell back into her chair. 'Why don't we go to the kitchen and have a nice cup of cocoa?' Nora suggested, deftly gathering up the cards. 'Come.' She held out her hand.

After a short hesitation, Rebecca allowed herself to be hauled out of the chair and ushered down the chilly corridor to the kitchen at the back of the house. She sat on a stool, listening to the wind rattling the window frames while Nora set a pan of milk on the stove to heat. It had gone quiet upstairs and Rebecca was beside herself with worry. Was her mother dead? Why didn't she come downstairs? Her mind churned with these anxious thoughts, while Nora kept up a string of chatter.

'Here you are, love.' Rebecca raised her head as Nora set the cocoa on the table in front of her. 'Drink up. You'll feel better.' Rebecca stared at the steam rising from her mug. The sweet aroma made her feel sick.

She heard a noise outside the door and turned her head. 'Mama!' Quick as a flash, she was off the stool and flying across the room into her mother's waiting arms. Lydia sank to her knees, and pulled Rebecca close, burying her face against her daughter.

'Mama, I heard you scream,' Rebecca said, drawing back and regarding her mother tearfully. 'Did Mr Fox hurt you?' she whispered as she glanced anxiously behind her just in case he or Miss Tina was lurking nearby.

'Oh, no, no,' her mother replied emphatically, shaking her head. 'You're mistaken sweetheart. Perhaps you heard a noise from the street.'

To Rebecca, her mother's bright smile seemed strained and, young as she was, the look that passed between her mother and Nora didn't go unnoticed. 'Come, drink up your cocoa. Mr Fox has agreed that you may sleep upstairs with me tonight.'

Rebecca drained her mug quickly and licked the foamy residue from her upper lip.

'Goodnight,' Nora said. She laid her hand on Lydia's arm. 'It'll all seem better in the morning.'

Lydia nodded. Taking Rebecca's hand, she led her out of the kitchen. They climbed the stairs in silence. Every step seemed to make her mother wince. Suddenly, a shadow appeared on the landing above them, causing Lydia to flinch. Rebecca shrank against the wall. In the light of the sconce, their benefactor no longer appeared the generous man of just a few hours earlier.

'I'm allowing you to sleep with your mother for tonight,' Mickey said, resting one hand on the banister as he peered down at them. 'From tomorrow you'll be sleeping in the kitchen. You'll find it comfortable enough, I'm sure.' He grinned. 'Sleep well, Lydia,' he said, as he made his way to the top of the stairs. 'You'll need all your stamina, come tomorrow evening.'

Lydia looked away, her cheeks flaming, and hurried Rebecca up the stairs.

*

A short while later, huddled under the sheets, Lydia listened to her daughter's breathing and planned her escape. Surely Mickey and Miss Tina couldn't watch them all the time. She'd bide her time and, at the first opportunity, she would get herself and Rebecca as far away from Mickey Fox as possible.

CHAPTER SIX

'Welcome.' The tall, brassy-blonde beamed at Rebecca over her mug of tea. 'We haven't never had a kid living here before, have we, Maddy?'

An older girl, with raven-black hair and dark, almond-shaped eyes, turned from the stove where she was stirring a pan of porridge. 'Mickey must really like you if he lets you keep your kid,' she said, giving Lydia a friendly smile. She tugged at the collar of her lace-frilled gown, but not before Rebecca caught sight of the purple bruise on her collar bone. 'Two of the girls, Jessie and Belinda, have kids, but Mickey insisted they live with relatives. I don't think Belinda sees hers any more.' The pan lid clattered. 'You got no family who'll take your girl in?'

Rebecca had woken with a sick feeling of dread in her stomach, which had only grown more intense when Miss Tina had hammered on the bedroom door, demanding she and her mother come down to the kitchen. Now she sat on a stool close to Lydia, her eyes darting between the two young women.

'Morning, ladies.' Rebecca straightened as Nora came in. She trusted the pleasant redhead and felt safer when she was around. Nora poured herself a mug of tea and came to stand beside Lydia. 'How are you?' she asked gently.

Lydia shrugged.

'It'll get easier, you'll see,' Nora said, close to Lydia's ear. 'Now,' she said brightly, turning to Rebecca, 'I expect you're starving?'

Rebecca nodded.

'Porridge is coming right up,' Maddy said, taking a bowl from the dresser. 'There's no cream but there's milk and sugar,' she said, placing the bowl on the table in front of Rebecca. 'Eat up.'

Despite the knot in her stomach, Rebecca realized she was very hungry, and ate quickly. Beside her, her mother stared into space, her fingers curled around her mug of tea as it slowly grew cold.

'I shall speak to Miss Tina about Rebecca attending the local school,' Nora told Lydia, as they washed up the breakfast things.

For the first time that morning, Lydia's face lost its vacant look.

'Do you think she'll allow it?' she asked hopefully.

'I think she'd prefer it to having her hanging about all day getting underfoot.'

'Then please ask her,' Lydia said, a flame of hope igniting in her chest. If she could leave this place to take Rebecca to school, they could escape. Suddenly her situation didn't seem quite as bad as it had a few minutes before.

Over breakfast, Lydia and Rebecca had been introduced to Belinda and Jessie. They were several years younger than Lydia, with blonde hair and blue eyes. They spoke kindly to Rebecca, and Jessie told Lydia about her two boys who lived with their grandmother in Totnes. She saw them twice a year.

Now the four ladies had disappeared either to the parlour or their rooms, leaving Nora and Lydia to the washing-up. Rebecca sat at the kitchen table, playing cat's cradle with a bit of wool Nora had fished out of her dressing-gown pocket. 'I knit a lot,' she'd said, by way of explanation. 'It helps pass the time between customers.'

Her words tightened the knot in Lydia's stomach. She was dreading what the day held.

The doorbell jangled, bringing Miss Tina scurrying from the parlour. Rebecca heard the door being opened, followed by a voice she recognized. She glanced at her mother. Lydia had turned from the sink, confusion written across her face as the voice of Erastus Mead carried clearly down the passage.

'My dear Mrs Wheeler,' he said, standing in the kitchen doorway. Miss Tina stood beside him, a peculiar expression on her unpleasant face. 'How lovely to see you again,' he said, extending his hands. 'And your pretty daughter.'

'Mr Mead,' Lydia choked out. 'Please, you must help us. Mr Fox is keeping us here against our will and . . .' Behind her she heard Nora's sharp intake of breath.

'Lydia, don't,' she hissed, as Miss Tina chuckled.

Erastus's smile broadened. 'Lydia,' he simpered, 'May I call you Lydia? Let's not be difficult. Mr Fox has given you a place to live and a job.' The smile slipped from his face. 'You should be grateful.'

Lydia tried to swallow but her throat was dry. She stared at the man who just the night before she'd believed was trying to help her.

'Go on, Mr Mead,' Tina said, smiling nastily. 'It's on the house. A thank-you, if you like.'

'No!' Lydia clutched the back of the nearest chair, debating whether she could make a run for it. On her own, possibly, but by the time she'd grabbed Rebecca, the element of surprise would have been lost. Her shoulders slumped as tears pricked her eyes.

'Rebecca,' she whispered hoarsely.

'I'll watch her,' Nora said, reaching for Rebecca's hand.

Lydia walked slowly out of the room, Erastus following. She could feel his hot breath on the back of her neck. Somehow, she made it up the stairs and into the room.

'I've been looking forward to this all night.' Erastus grinned as he bolted the door firmly behind them.

'I believe you wish your daughter to attend school,' Mickey Fox said, barging into Lydia's room later that morning. Although Erastus had left more than an hour ago, Lydia hadn't been able to summon the courage to leave her bed. How could she face Rebecca after what she'd just done? Instead of going downstairs, she'd curled into a ball and pulled the sheets over her head. She could smell Erastus on her skin, and her stomach recoiled, bile rising in her throat.

Now she peered gingerly out from under the bedclothes, terrified she might be subjected to another of Mickey's 'lessons'. He strode towards the bed, and she tensed, as he perched on the edge, his hands clasped around one knee.

'That can be arranged. There's a school about a ten-minute walk from here. My mother will enrol her.'

'But . . .' Lydia sat up, dragging the rumpled sheets up to her chin.

'I'm not a fool, Lydia,' he said. 'I know the minute you set foot out of this house with the kid you'll be gone. No, I've invested a lot of money in you. You'll bring me a tidy profit with your posh way of speaking and your looks. I can charge much more for you than I can for any of the other common trollops round here.' He gave her a hard stare. 'My friend Erastus was a little disappointed, by all accounts. I expect you to treat my clients with courtesy and to give them exactly what they want. They pay good money for an exceptional service. If they wanted anything less, they'd settle for the poxy dock dollies down by the harbour. I run a high-class establishment. Policemen, lawyers, doctors, they all make use of my services and they've come to expect a certain standard. Any girl who doesn't live up to my expectations will find herself on the receiving end of my wrath.' He grinned. His uneven teeth gleamed in the darkened room. 'And, believe me, you do not want to make me angry.'

'I don't care what you do to me,' Lydia said, her eyes flashing defiantly. 'I'm not a whore and I shan't behave like one.'

Mickey's grin widened. 'But you do care what happens to your daughter,' he reminded her, with a coldness that sent icy fingers running down Lydia's spine. 'There's no point in being coy,' he said. 'You know what's expected of you. I've been lenient long enough. Pull your weight or the kid will suffer.' He got to his feet as Lydia stared at him, unable to comprehend that anyone could be so cold-hearted, so cruel as to hurt an innocent child. 'I shall expect to see you washed, dressed and ready for business in half an hour. In the meantime, my mother will take the kid to school and get her enrolled.'

Rebecca hurried to keep up with Miss Tina as they traversed the narrow streets. The cobbles were greasy underfoot and several times she slipped. The air was cold and smelt of rotting fish and sewage.

She'd felt uneasy leaving her mother behind, but Lydia had

insisted she accompany Miss Tina and, knowing how much her father would have wanted her to continue her schooling, Rebecca had reluctantly acquiesced.

'Hurry up, child,' Miss Tina said, glaring at Rebecca over her shoulder. 'I haven't got all day.' She waited until Rebecca came alongside her, then gave her a shove, propelling her forwards. She would have fallen, had she not careered into a barrel someone had left outside an open doorway. 'Why I have to play nursemaid to a brat, I don't know,' Miss Tina muttered, grabbing Rebecca's arm and pushing her ahead. 'Turn right at the end of the alley.'

A few minutes later the stinking alleyway gave onto a wider street. Directly opposite Rebecca saw a large, red-brick building with a paved yard and iron railings that ran the length of the street. A clock tower rose from its sloping roof, the grey slate tiles glistening in the wet. 'Bayards Cove School' was spelled out in different-coloured bricks across the front.

'Up you go.' Miss Tina ushered Rebecca through the open gateway and across the yard to the entrance marked 'Girls' in faded lettering.

From somewhere nearby she could hear children reciting the six-times table. A door opened to her left and a tall, stern-looking woman looked into the corridor. 'May I help you?'

'Good morning,' Miss Tina said, pushing Rebecca ahead of her. 'I'm here to enrol my niece in your school.' Rebecca's head jerked round. She opened her mouth to contradict the woman but, at the warning look on Miss Tina's face, thought better of it.

'This way, please,' the woman said, heading back into her office. 'You'll need to fill in her details.' Settling herself behind a tidy desk, she opened a large book and dipped her pen into the inkwell. 'Name and address?'

'Rebecca Wheeler. Fourteen Angel Terrace.'

The woman paused; her pen poised above the page. She raised her eyes, thin lips pursed in a line of disapproval.

'Yes, you heard that right,' Miss Tina said, with a smirk as two spots of colour appeared on the other woman's cheeks. The secretary coughed and lowered her head. The only sound was the rhythmic tick of the mantelpiece clock and the scratch of the nib on the paper.

At that moment an adjoining door opened and a middle-aged man with greying light brown hair and a paunch entered the small, cosy office. At the sight of Miss Tina standing in his secretary's office, his cheeks turned a vivid crimson.

The secretary cleared her throat. 'Mr Williams, this lady wishes to enrol her . . . niece.' Her brow lifted.

'Yes, well, very good, excellent,' Mr Williams stammered, rubbing his hands together.

Standing motionless, her hands clasped behind her back, Rebecca watched him, puzzled, wondering why he appeared so flustered. Miss Tina, on the other hand, smiled slyly. Mr Williams was a frequent visitor to 14 Angel Terrace, every Thursday evening from half past seven to eight, regular as clockwork, while his wife attended her Ladies Aid committee meeting at the church around the corner.

'Miss Jackson will escort you to your classroom,' Mr Williams said, studiously avoiding Miss Tina's eyes as he nodded at Rebecca.

'I'll be waiting at the gate for you at half past three,' Miss Tina said, her tone devoid of emotion as she bade Rebecca goodbye. 'Mind you behave yourself, or you'll feel the weight of my hand.'

'This way, girl,' Miss Jackson said, as Miss Tina left the room.

Mr Williams coughed loudly and disappeared into his office, shutting the door firmly behind him.

Miss Jackson's fingers clamped firmly on Rebecca's shoulder as she steered her out into the draughty corridor. Their footsteps echoed as they walked the length of it and halted outside a closed door. Behind it, children were reciting the Lord's Prayer. Miss Jackson waited until they'd finished before rapping loudly and turning the handle.

'Forgive the interruption, Miss Clavering,' Miss Jackson said, poking her head around the door. 'I have a new pupil for you.'

'Turn to page eleven in your readers, children,' Rebecca heard the teacher say. The door opened wider, and Miss Clavering appeared. She was a tall, angular woman. Her fair hair was scraped back in a tight bun, which served to accentuate her sharp features. She gazed at Rebecca down her long nose.

'This is Rebecca Wheeler,' Miss Jackson said.

'Go and find a seat, child,' Miss Clavering said, stepping aside to allow Rebecca into the classroom. Rebecca faltered her eyes searching the sea of curious faces for an empty seat.

A pale-faced girl with blonde pigtails raised her hand. Smiling shyly, she patted the empty place beside her. With a rush of relief, Rebecca started towards her.

'She lives at that Gentlemen's Club in Angel Terrace,' she heard Miss Jackson whisper.

'Oh, my,' Miss Clavering breathed. She lowered her voice an octave, but Rebecca could clearly hear her words. 'I've heard such rumours about that place.'

Sweat prickling her skin, Rebecca made her way slowly down the aisle to the vacant space, her cheeks burning. She sat down, not daring to look at her seatmate. Shame bubbled inside her, but she didn't know why. For some reason she felt dirty. Tears pricked her eyelids.

Miss Clavering shut the door and turned to face the class. 'Peter, please read the first paragraph.'

As a plump boy got to his feet, Rebecca felt a hand close over hers. The pretty blonde girl beside her gave her a warm smile. Rebecca managed to smile back.

'Penny and, you, new girl,' Miss Clavering's voice rang out, cutting Peter off in mid-sentence, 'pay attention, or the pair of you will spend the rest of the morning outside Mr Williams's office.'

Out of sight beneath the desk, Penny gave Rebecca's hand another squeeze and the two girls turned their attention to their reading books.

CHAPTER SEVEN

1878

Lydia tugged her satin gown around her pale shoulders and leaned back against the rumpled pillows, watching the fat, middle-aged man buttoning his trousers. He smiled at her, his bald head gleaming in the lamplight. As her regulars went, Fred Ellis was a decent sort. He treated her kindly, unlike a lot of the others. He was nice to Rebecca, too, on the rare occasions their paths crossed, and would often bring one of his home-made meat pies for Lydia to give to her. At first she'd viewed his generosity towards her daughter with suspicion, but over time she'd learned that Fred was just a nice, if very lonely, man.

'If it wasn't for my missus, I'd take you away from all this and make an honest woman of you,' Fred said, sitting down heavily on the chaise longue and lacing his boots. His wife was an invalid and practically bedridden, but she seemed quite the harridan, though that might have been his justification for his weekly visits, Lydia acknowledged. Still, she couldn't help but feel sorry for him.

'I'll be off, then,' he said, his words laced with regret. He opened his wallet and peeled off a note. 'A little extra for yourself,' he said, as he always did, placing the money on the bedside cabinet.

'Thank you, Fred,' Lydia said. 'See you next week.'

'Until then.' Fred nodded, picking up his hat. Folding his coat over his arm, he opened the door. Blowing Lydia a kiss, he stepped out onto the dingy landing. From the bedroom next door came the loud squeak of bedsprings. His florid cheeks turning an even darker shade of red, Fred scurried by and down the stairs.

Rebecca was letting herself in at the front door as Fred descended the last of the stairs. Her thin face lit up at the sight of him. 'Mr Fred, hello.'

'Hello, Becky.' Fred grinned at her, tugging on his coat. 'How was school?'

'It was all right. I got full marks for my maths test.'

'Excellent.' Fred patted her head. 'Here's a little something as a reward,' he said, delving into the deep pocket of his black wool coat and pulling out a bar of Fry's chocolate cream.

'Thank you, Mr Fred!' Rebecca exclaimed in delight.

'You're welcome. Don't eat it all at once,' he chuckled, 'or you'll spoil your tea.' He winked, touched the brim of his hat and stepped out into the frosty February evening.

Three weeks later, Rebecca made her way up Angel Terrace, her head bowed against the brisk March wind. It had been blowing a gale all day, shaking the classroom windows and whipping the nearby trees into a frenzy. Clouds chased each other across a pale blue sky and the intermittent sunshine did little to take the edge off the bitter cold. She pulled her hands from her coat pocket and pushed open the front door. The hallway was warm, a welcome relief from the icy wind. She unwound her scarf, her gaze falling immediately on the red ribbon tied to the banister. She felt a stab of disappointment. She was desperate to tell her mother her exciting news but the red ribbon was the signal that Lydia was working and was not to be disturbed.

Sighing impatiently, Rebecca went into the kitchen. Finding herself alone, she took off her coat and hung it up. She checked the teapot and, finding it still warm, poured herself a mug and settled herself at the table.

The tea was tepid and stewed, but it warmed her as she got out her schoolbooks and made a start on her homework. The screaming wind battering the windowpane and shaking the door on its hinges brought back painful memories of the storm that had claimed the lives of her father and brothers. She chewed the end of her pencil, her chest tightening in a sudden rush of grief. Sometimes she felt as though it had had happened only yesterday. Had it really been sixteen months? Sixteen months of missing them every minute of every day. Sixteen months of living under Mickey Fox's menacing presence. The thought of him made her shudder with revulsion.

In the early days her mother had kept promising Rebecca they would leave as soon as she'd earned enough money to pay Mickey back what she owed him, but weeks had drifted into months and her mother didn't talk about leaving any more.

Rebecca spent much of her time in the kitchen. She slept beside the range, and in the morning, as she was usually up before anyone else, she started making the porridge. She was a favourite with the other women, apart from Miss Tina. Hardly a day went by when Rebecca didn't feel the sharp edge of her tongue. Thankfully, she seldom came into the kitchen. Rebecca did her best to avoid Mickey, making herself scarce whenever he was around.

Over time, she'd grown used to the steady stream of men who frequented the house. Lydia was adamant that Rebecca keep out of their way and she was only too happy to comply. The way some of them looked at her made her skin crawl. If only they were all as nice as Mr Fred, she mused, turning the page of her exercise book.

She glanced towards the hallway, willing her mother to appear. She was brimming with the urge to share her news.

To her dismay, school had not been the happy escape she'd hoped it would be. Three days after she'd started, Penny had come up to her, eyes red and swollen from crying, and announced that she was no longer allowed to be her friend. Several of the other girls who'd made tentative overtures of friendship in those early days had, too, withdrawn. Her mother had held her while she cried, rocking her as she stroked her hair, and telling her to take no notice of what people said.

The only one at school who treated her with any kindness was Mr Williams. She'd spotted him at the house once. He'd been bundled up in a hat, scarf and coat but she'd recognized him and had called after him, earning herself a slapping from Miss Tina, who had been coming out of the parlour.

Nora had comforted her, sitting by the fire, as Rebecca sobbed into her shoulder, her red cheek smarting, while Nora explained that, whoever she saw, she must never call them by name. 'It doesn't matter who it is, sweetheart,' Nora said, stroking Rebecca's long hair. 'The men who come here need to know they're safe. Most of them use aliases and if you start shouting their real names, they'll take their custom elsewhere and Mickey won't like that one bit.'

The following evening, Mickey had turned up in a foul mood. Giving Rebecca a withering look, he'd stormed upstairs to her mother's room. Rebecca had no idea what Mickey said to Lydia, and her mother refused to tell her what had happened, but when Lydia came down later that day, she was subdued and sporting a livid bruise across her throat.

The incident had left Rebecca feeling sick and, not for the first time, she'd begged her mother to leave. She couldn't understand why they stayed there when they were both so clearly unhappy, but she was too young to understand that her mother had given up hope.

Now, as Rebecca bent over her books, she heard the front door slam. She straightened, hopeful that, if her mother's visitor had just left, she might come down to the kitchen and she could share her news. She had been dreading leaving school that coming summer and, today, Mr Williams had offered her a chance to stay on.

She scraped back her chair and filled the kettle. Her mother would want a cup of tea when she came down.

Instead, it was Nora who appeared. 'Hello, Becky,' she said pleasantly, reaching for the tea caddy. 'How was school?'

Rebecca smiled. 'Good, thank you,' she replied, only just managing not to blurt out her news. Much as she loved Nora, she wanted her mother to be the first to know.

'It's a shame you'll be leaving soon,' Nora said, biting her lower lip as the kettle came to the boil. 'You're a clever girl. Unlike me.' She grinned, spooning tea leaves into the pot. 'I can barely write my name.' She made the tea and set the teapot on the table.

'I'm waiting for Mum,' Rebecca said, impatience making her restless.

'She shouldn't be much longer,' Nora said, giving Rebecca's arm a pat as she joined her at the table. 'That was her gentleman leaving just now.' She smiled at Rebecca across the scrubbed-pine table. 'She probably just needs a few minutes.'

Rebecca tried to concentrate on her books, but her mind was racing. She wasn't quite sure what her mother did with the men who visited her room, something they couldn't get at home, according to Maddy, who'd tried to explain one evening when she'd had too much gin. Lydia had been furious when Rebecca had recounted the conversation and had given Maddy a good telling-off, which had left Rebecca even more confused than before.

'I think there might be some biscuits in the tin,' Nora said, interrupting Rebecca's thoughts. 'From Dora's mum.'

As if on cue, Rebecca's stomach growled. Her mother had overslept that morning and, in the rush to leave for school on time, Lydia had forgotten to give Rebecca dinner money. She fetched the battered tin from the shelf and brought it back to the table. She lifted the lid and took out a biscuit, then slid the tin across to Nora.

She'd just taken a bite when they heard a bloodcurdling scream.

'What on earth? Stay here.' Nora leapt to her feet, and hurried to the hallway. One of the doors along the corridor opened and Dora peered out, her face white.

'What's happened?' she asked, as Nora ran past her. Nora waved a hand dismissively and, hoisting her skirt above her ankles, raced up the stairs. Rebecca came to stand by the kitchen door. The screaming had given way to hysterical wailing.

'What the heck's all that racket?' Miss Tina grumbled, bustling through the front door. 'You can hear it halfway down the street.' She untied the ribbons on her black bonnet, scowling up towards the landing. 'What is it, Nora?' she snapped in exasperation, as Nora's ashen face peered over the banister.

'Miss Tina, would you come up here, please?' Nora said, her voice shaking.

Fear gnawed at Rebecca's stomach. Something bad had happened. Why didn't her mother come to her? On legs that felt like jelly, she made her way along the hall as Miss Tina climbed the stairs, muttering in irritation. 'For Heaven's sake, Nora, will you tell Dora to stop that caterwauling!'

Rebecca stood at the foot of the stairs and peered up into the gloom. Nora and Dora were huddled on the landing, arms around each other. Dora was sobbing. Heart pounding, Rebecca inched her way up the stairs. Miss Tina emerged from Rebecca's mother's room, her mouth set in a grim line. Rebecca uttered a strangled cry and ran the last few steps to the landing.

Nora caught her wrist. 'I thought I told you to stay in the kitchen,' she said, fear making her tone harsh.

'Is Mama all right?' Rebecca pleaded.

Nora's face softened. 'Go back to the kitchen, Becky,' she said. 'I'll be down in a minute. Dora, go with her.' Dora stopped sniffing and gazed at Rebecca with red-rimmed eyes. She opened her mouth to speak but Nora shook her head vehemently.

'Come on, Becky.' Wiping her face with the back of her hand, Dora took Rebecca's hand and led her downstairs. Rebecca sat on a stool, her head bowed. She felt as if a giant fist was squeezing her chest and she could scarcely breathe. Dora was slumped over the table, her shoulders heaving as she fought to control herself. No matter how many times Rebecca asked about her mother, Dora refused to answer.

After what felt like hours, but was little more than ten minutes, voices sounded in the hallway, followed by the slam of the front door. A moment later, Nora appeared in the kitchen doorway. At the sight of her red-rimmed eyes in her chalk-white face, Rebecca burst into tears. Pushing back her stool, she flung herself into Nora's arms.

'Oh, Becky,' she whispered, her voice breaking. 'Your dear mama has gone to Heaven. I'm so sorry.' Nora slumped to the floor, Rebecca cradled in her lap, sobbing into Nora's chest, her own tears streaming unashamedly down her cheeks.

'What a mess.' Miss Tina snorted, coming into the kitchen sometime later. 'Has someone gone for Mickey?'

'Jessie,' mumbled Maddy, her hands shaking.

Miss Tina pulled a face. 'He'll be in a filthy mood. One of his best earners going and getting herself murdered.'

'Miss Tina!' Nora hissed, glancing anxiously across the table at Rebecca, who was sitting at the table, head bowed, her fingers curled around a mug of sweet tea. 'Have a heart. The child has just lost her mother.'

Miss Tina made a disparaging noise in her throat but she said no more. The other girls had gathered in the kitchen as word of Lydia's murder spread.

'Was he one of her regulars?' Nora whispered, drawing Miss Tina aside, out of Rebecca's hearing.

Miss Tina shook her head, her expression grim. 'Never seen him before. He was a sailor, by the look of him,' she said, reaching for the glass of gin in front of her. She gulped it down and motioned for Dora to refill her glass.

'You didn't get his name?' Nora frowned.

Miss Tina raised her eyebrows mockingly. 'As if he'd tell me,' she said, quailing at the sound of the front door opening and shutting. The women fell silent, as heavy footsteps echoed in the hallway and Mickey's broad frame filled the door.

'Is somebody going to tell me what the bloody hell happened here?' Mickey growled, his voice dangerously quiet as he scanned the room.

Jessie slunk round him, shooting Rebecca a sympathetic glance as she squatted on the hearth in front of the fire.

'I only wanted to ask if I could borrow her rouge,' Maddy said, her voice trembling. 'I waited until I heard her customer leave before I knocked. When she didn't answer, I tried the handle and—' She broke off with a sob. 'Oh, God, it was horrible.' She wept. 'There was blood everywhere.'

Nora made a noise in her throat. Seeing her warning glare, Maddy checked herself. 'I'm sorry, Becky,' she said, dissolving into tears again.

Mickey scowled. 'Did no one hear anything?' he demanded, glaring round the shell-shocked women. The women cast furtive looks at each other and shook their heads.

'Her room's next to mine,' Nora said tearfully. 'Surely I should have heard something.' She wiped at her eyes angrily. 'When will the police be here?' she asked Mickey.

He ignored her. 'I'd better go and see the damage for myself. You girls sort yourselves out. You've got customers.'

Nora balked. 'You don't expect us to work tonight?'

'Why not?' Mickey replied, glaring at her. 'I'm a girl down. You'll all have to work that much harder tonight to make up the shortfall. Right, Mother, you come with me.'

Turning on his heels, he stalked from the room, leaving Nora and the others staring after him in shock. Miss Tina drained her glass and scurried after her stepson.

Rebecca listened to the whispered conversations through a fog of grief and disbelief. Her mother couldn't be dead. She gripped her mug tighter, her knuckles whitening as hot tears ran down her cheeks.

Staring at the carnage that confronted him, Mickey cursed loudly. 'How could you let this happen?' he demanded angrily, turning to his stepmother.

'It's not my fault,' Miss Tina retorted, bristling defensively. 'I only see them in. What they get up to with the girls is their own business. You've always said that's why our establishment is so popular. We don't ask questions, and if the punters like to play a little rough, the girls know to put up and shut up. After all, you pay their medical expenses if things get out of hand.'

'This is more than out of hand, wouldn't you say?' Mickey snapped, waving to where Lydia's bruised and battered body lay sprawled across the bed. 'It would have to be my best earner too. That lot downstairs aren't a patch on her, and the punters know it.' His nostrils flared in disgust. With her refined ways and posh voice, he'd been able to charge top rate for Lydia. He usually reserved her for his more upmarket clientele. How the hell had she ended up murdered by a common sailor?

'What are you going to do?' Miss Tina asked nervously. 'We can't have the police sniffing round here. It'll be bad for business.'

'I've got contacts who deal with this sort of thing,' Mickey replied. While most of the local constabulary were happy to turn a blind eye to what went on inside his establishment, there was bound to be the odd copper who'd insist on a proper investigation and, his best earner or not, he wasn't prepared to let the death of a whore ruin his livelihood.

He shut the bedroom door and followed his stepmother down to the kitchen. No one had moved. Someone was sniffing softly, and several of the women had tears streaming down their cheeks. They kept their eyes downcast. Only Nora stared at him, her eyes flashing defiantly. Mickey frowned. He hoped he wasn't going to have trouble with her. He gave her his cold-eyed stare. She returned it with one of her own, reaching out to place a protective arm around Rebecca's shoulders. The girl stirred, turning her tear-swollen face in his direction, causing Mickey to gasp in surprise. He'd barely taken notice of the kid. He recalled that she'd been a pretty thing but now . . . He swallowed, licking his lips. She was beautiful. He wondered how old she was. Eleven, twelve? He couldn't remember. No matter. He knew plenty of punters who'd pay good money for a girl her age, no questions asked. Perhaps he didn't need to search for a replacement for Lydia after all, he mused, rubbing his hands in anticipation of the money he would be raking in.

'Right, ladies,' he said. 'Back to work.'

'What about Lydia?' Nora asked. 'Have you called the police? And we need to arrange for the coroner.'

'It's all in hand,' Mickey said, holding up a hand. 'Let me worry about the details.' He gave Rebecca a nod. 'I'm sorry for your loss.'

'Unfeeling bastard!' Nora spat, as he retreated down the hallway, Miss Tina following swiftly behind him. 'You'd think he'd have some compassion. Lydia was our friend.'

'Mickey doesn't have a compassionate bone in him,' said Maddy, wiping her nose. She was still shaking. The image of Lydia's broken body kept coming into her head. In a way it would be a relief to work. At least it might keep the nightmares away.

'Nor does Miss Tina,' Jessica retorted. 'Evil cow.'

In the parlour they could hear Mickey and her having a heated discussion about what to do with Rebecca. Rebecca looked at Nora with large, frightened eyes. 'I don't want to go to the orphanage, Nora,' she whispered.

'Now, love,' Nora said, folding her into an embrace, 'you can't stay here, not now. You'll be well looked after there. It won't be for long. You'll be leaving school in the summer, and they'll find you a nice position.'

At the mention of school, Rebecca's eyes filled with fresh tears. Now she would never share her exciting news with her mother.

'Mr Williams wants me to apply for a scholarship,' she said, in a small voice. 'He said I'm clever enough to go to the high school. I was waiting to tell Mama.'

'Oh, love,' Nora sighed, 'she would have been so proud. I'm proud of you, but I'm afraid you can't apply for the scholarship, love. Not now. Even if you got it, which I don't doubt you would, a clever girl like you, there'd be the cost of your uniform, and your tram fare every day. The parish couldn't afford it, love.'

'I don't want to go to the orphanage,' Rebecca said, her arms reaching around Nora's neck. 'Why can't I stay with you?' In the time she'd lived in Dartmouth, Nora and the girls had become like family to her. They all took turns to look after her, keeping her out of Mickey's way, when her mother was otherwise engaged, and they did their best to protect her from Miss Tina's spite.

'I'm sorry, love,' Nora said, prising off Rebecca's arms. 'You can't stay here. Not now your mum's . . . It's for the best. And it'll only be for a few months. They'll find you a nice live-in position and, once you're settled, we can meet up on your day off.'

Rebecca looked at her doubtfully. As heavy as her heart felt now, the prospect of leaving Nora was more than she could bear. 'Do you promise?' she asked, in a small voice.

'Of course,' Nora replied, knowing that once Rebecca left the house, it was unlikely she'd see her again.

The front door opened, and a gentleman entered, shaking his black umbrella and showering the hallway with droplets of water.

Miss Tina emerged from the parlour. 'Maddy,' she called, smiling sweetly. 'A gentleman for you.'

Maddy shot Nora a look and got wearily to her feet. He was swiftly followed by another client, and the girls drifted back to work. The evening's business had begun.

CHAPTER EIGHT

Nora opened her eyes. For one blissful second, she lay still, enjoying the early-morning silence as her eyes adjusted to the gloom. Then the events of the previous day came crashing in on her. She sat up with a jerk. Rebecca.

Flinging the bedclothes aside, she grabbed her dressing-gown, tugging it over her shoulders as she opened the door. The landing was deserted, but she noticed immediately that Lydia's door was ajar. She crept towards it and gently pushed it open, exhaling quietly at the sight of Rebecca curled up on the bare mattress.

Careful not to wake the sleeping child, Nora tiptoed across the room. The soiled bedding had been taken away to be burned, but even in the dim light she could make out the dark stain on the mattress. She stood beside the bed, gazing down at Rebecca's tear-stained face. She'd clearly cried herself to sleep. Nora sighed inwardly. Poor little mite. She debated waking her but decided against it. Let her enjoy oblivion for a while longer.

Straightening, she surveyed the room. Everything was as Lydia had left it, Nora realized, her throat constricting painfully. Her pink satin gown was slung over the Chinese screen, her lotions and face creams in neat rows on the vanity unit. Nora walked over to the washstand, tears welling as she trailed her fingertips through the cold, clear water. A small cake of scented soap lay in the rose-patterned dish beside a neatly folded flannel. Rebecca stirred and mumbled something incoherent but didn't wake. As Nora turned, she caught sight of something glinting under the bed. Curious, she crouched to retrieve it, her fingers closing over something cold and hard. It was Lydia's locket. She drew it out into the dim light and held it in the palm of her hand, letting the thin chain run through her fingers. The clasp was broken, she noticed. It must have fallen off while Lydia was being attacked and got tangled in the bedclothes, then dropped to the floor when the bed was stripped. Thankfully, neither Miss Tina nor Mickey had spotted it. She had an idea it was worth a tidy sum. If either of them had found it, they'd have pawned it straight away. She turned the locket over, admiring the intricate pattern engraved into the silver. Lydia had told her once that it had belonged to her mother. Nora slipped it into her pocket. It belonged to Rebecca now. She would give it to her as soon as she woke up. It would be a precious reminder of her mother.

The door opened, making her jump.

'What are you doing in here?' Miss Tina asked, her eyes narrowing suspiciously. 'And why's the kid in here?'

'Mama?' Rebecca sat up, rubbing her eyes. Then she remembered. Her face crumpled as she burst into tears.

'Oh, sweetheart,' Nora said, hurrying to comfort her. 'The door was open,' Nora told Miss Tina, as she rocked Rebecca in her arms. 'I saw Becky was in here, so I stayed with her. I knew she'd be upset once she woke up.'

'Stop snivelling, girl, and get downstairs,' Miss Tina said, with a derisive sniff. 'You're not going to school today.'

'I should think not,' Nora retorted, giving Rebecca's hand a squeeze as the girl wiped her eyes. 'She's just lost her mother.'

'Downstairs,' Tina repeated, tilting her head towards the door.

'Come on, love,' Nora said, getting up and taking Rebecca by the hand. 'I'll make you some cocoa.'

'Not you, Nora,' Miss Tina interjected. 'I want to talk to you.' Rebecca looked at Nora uncertainly.

'It's all right, love,' Nora assured her. 'I'll be down in a minute.'

Her shoulders convulsing with silent sobs, Rebecca reluctantly left the room.

'Where's Lydia?' Nora demanded, as soon as she was sure Rebecca was out of earshot. 'When was she taken away?'

'Last night,' replied Tina, closing the door and walking over to the bed, her lip curling in distaste as she noticed the bloodstain. 'Mickey sorted it.'

'Will there be an inquest?' Nora asked, with a frown. 'What are the police saying? Do they have any clues?'

'The police are not involved,' Tina said, her voice heavy with warning. 'And there won't be a funeral.'

'But . . .' Nora began.

'I told you, Mickey's sorted it. Leave it now, if you know what's good for you.'

Nora sank back in angry silence. She was fuming at the thought that her dear friend's murder would go unreported. No one to be held accountable. Poor Lydia was even to be denied a funeral. She clenched and unclenched her fists, forcing herself to remain calm. 'It's so unfair,' she muttered.

'Who ever said life was fair?' scoffed Miss Tina, picking lint from her black skirt.

'Poor Becky.' Nora sighed, her heart aching for the poor motherless girl. She wouldn't even have the comfort of seeing her mother laid to rest. She wondered what Mickey had done with Lydia's body. She hoped to God he hadn't had her dumped in the harbour. She deserved better than that.

'Have you spoken to the orphanage?'

'The girl isn't going to the orphanage,' Miss Tina said, with a sly smile. She picked up a jar of face cream, unscrewed the lid and sniffed the contents.

'She can't stay here,' objected Nora. 'Not without Lydia to protect her.'

'Mickey's keen to put her to work.' Tina replaced the jar on the dressing-table and turned to face Nora, who stared at her with growing horror, as the cold reality of the woman's words became clear.

'She's twelve years old,' Nora remonstrated. 'A child.'

Tina shrugged. 'Mickey says there are men out there who'll pay good money for her.'

'You can't agree to that, surely,' Nora said. 'It's morally wrong, not to mention illegal. Mickey could go to prison.'

'He's prepared to take the risk.'

'What about her schooling?'

'She's finished with that,' snapped Miss Tina, with a dismissive gesture.

'They'll ask questions,' Nora fired back. 'You'll have the truant officer round. Once he finds out what's going on . . .'

'You know old Williams is unlikely to cause a fuss, Nora.' MissTina interrupted her. 'She'd be leaving in a few months, anyway.'

'But Mr Williams wants Becky to apply for a scholarship . . . Yes, I know.' Nora raised her hands in supplication. 'I know her staying on at school is out of the question but, come the end of term, the orphanage would find her a good position. I'm begging you, Miss Tina.' Nora grabbed Tina's hands, hoping to inject some compassion into the woman. 'Don't let Mickey do this to our Becky. Please.'

'Once Mickey's decided, there's no changing his mind,' Tina said, shaking herself free of Nora's grip. 'You know that. She can have today off on compassionate grounds. From tomorrow she starts to earn her living. I'll leave it to you to tell her what's what.'

'No, you can't. It's immoral!'

Miss Tina shook her head, a smile tugging at her lips.

'You don't care, do you?' Nora whispered. 'You're sick in the head, both of you. Ow!' she shrieked, as Miss Tina slapped her hard across the face.

'You mind who you're talking to, Nora Lee,' Miss Tina snarled.

Holding her cheek, Nora swallowed, forcing down the bile that burned the back of her throat.

'How Mickey and I do things around here is nothing to do with you,' continued Miss Tina, with a toss of her head. 'All you need to concern yourself with is making sure the kid knows what's expected of her.'

She stalked from the room, skirts rustling, pulling the door shut behind her. Nora sank down on the edge of the mattress, her heart racing. She had to do something. She owed it to her friend to keep her daughter safe. Somehow she had to get Rebecca out of the clutches of Miss Tina and her morally deficient stepson.

Rebecca sat at the kitchen table, her forehead resting on her arms. Her insides felt hollow, and her chest ached. Everyone she loved left her. First her father and beloved brothers. Now her mother, her dearest mama, was gone, too. She raised her face, looking to where Maddy and Dora stood by the stove, talking in low voices. These women had become her family. Now she was losing them as well. Once she was sent to the orphanage, she would be truly alone.

Maddy glanced up from stirring the porridge, her pale face pinched with worry. Her eyes met Rebecca's and she gave her a sympathetic smile. The brutal attack on Lydia had sent shockwaves through the house. All the women were wary and on their guard. If this could happen to someone like Lydia, it could certainly happen to them.

Footsteps sounded in the hall and Nora entered the kitchen, her mouth set in a grim line. She threw Rebecca a tired smile and, raising her hand to indicate that she should stay where she was, she joined Maddy and Dora at the stove. She laid a hand on Dora's arm and, lowering her head, spoke quietly into the ears of the two girls.

Rebecca heard Dora's sharp intake of breath, and Maddy turned to look at her, a queer expression on her face that set Rebecca's stomach churning.

'Leave that a minute,' Nora said sharply.

Maddy lifted the porridge off the heat and Nora ushered them out into the yard.

'How are you feeling this morning, love?' asked Jessie, coming into the kitchen in her dressing-gown.

Rebecca said nothing but her stricken expression said more than any words could.

'You poor thing,' Jessie murmured, wandering to the cupboard to take a mug off the hook. 'I was very fond of your mum. She'll be much missed.' She sniffed and wiped her nose

71

on the back of her hand, as she tested the warmth of the teapot. 'Where is everyone?'

As if in answer to her question, the back door opened.

'It's perishing out there,' Nora said, coming into the kitchen ahead of Dora and Maddy. 'That wind goes right through you.'

'What were you doing out there, anyway?' asked Jessie, shivering in the cold draught.

'I needed the privy,' Nora said.

'What – all of you?' Jessie raised her brows. 'Together?'

'Mind your own business, Jessie Parker,' Maddy snapped, peering into the porridge pan. 'Right, Becky,' she said, turning on the heat. 'Breakfast will be ready in a jiffy.'

'I'm not hungry,' Rebecca said morosely.

'You need to keep your strength up,' Nora said sternly. She pulled out the chair next to Rebecca's and sat down, reaching into her pocket. 'Here, I found this in your mother's room.'

'Mama's locket,' Rebecca exclaimed, her expression brightening briefly, before tears welled again. She took it, letting the long chain run through her fingers. She opened the locket, a sob rising in her throat as she studied the miniature paintings of her mother and father.

'The catch is broken,' Nora told her, 'So keep it hidden in your pocket. For goodness' sake, don't let Miss Tina or Mickey know you've got it.'

Rebecca nodded.

'I can fix the catch for you,' Dora said, joining them at the table. 'My dad's a silversmith,' she explained, in response to Nora's raised eyebrow. 'I used to help him in his workshop before he took up with his fancy woman and kicked me out.' She smiled at Rebecca and held out her hand. 'Here, hand it over. I'll have it done in no time.'

'It's all right, love,' Nora said, when Rebecca hesitated. 'You know you can trust Dora.'

Rebecca reluctantly handed it to Dora, who slipped it into her pocket.

'Where's Miss Tina?' Nora asked Jessie, as Maddy dished up bowls of steaming porridge.

'In her room,' Jessie replied. 'I'm to take her up a pot of tea and a crumpet at eleven. She's got a migraine coming on.'

'Oh, good.' Nora grinned unsympathetically. 'That means she'll be incapacitated for most of the day.'

'As long as Mickey doesn't hang around,' grumbled Maddy, pouring milk onto her porridge. 'After what's happened, he might decide to be here more.' She passed the jug to Rebecca, who poured some onto her porridge but made no move to pick up her spoon. She had no appetite and, in any case, she wouldn't be able to swallow, with the huge lump in her throat.

'I doubt it,' Nora snorted. 'He's never bothered about our safety before. No, I reckon we'll have the place to ourselves until mid-afternoon, at least.' Rebecca caught the looks exchanged between Maddy, Dora and Nora, and wondered what they were up to. Not that she cared. She missed her mum so much, and she was terrified of leaving everything familiar to go to the orphanage. Perhaps if Miss Tina's migraine was particularly bad, she'd forget about sending Rebecca away and she'd get a reprieve, at least for a few days.

'Eat up,' Nora said, breaking into Rebecca's thoughts.

She shook her head. 'I'm not hungry.'

'Be that as it may,' Nora said kindly, 'you need to keep your strength up. You don't want to go making yourself ill now, do you?'

'Look, Becky,' Dora said, 'I know you're going through a

tough time, but you need to eat. Your mum wouldn't want you to get sick, would she?'

Rebecca picked up her spoon and swirled it around her bowl.

'Good girl.' Nora gave her arm a gentle nudge. 'Just a few spoonfuls, for your mum's sake?'

Rebecca forced down a mouthful of porridge.

'Good girl,' Nora said again. 'When you've finished that, we can go up to my room. I've got a couple of hours before my first customer.'

Rebecca bowed her head over her bowl.

A short while later Nora ushered Rebecca into her bedroom. Although Rebecca had been in Nora's room many times, she never failed to be awed by its abundance of silk, lace and feathers. She perched on the edge of the burgundy-red velvet bedspread that covered the large four-poster, her fingers brushing the pink feather boa that was entwined around one of the posts.

'I need to talk to you, love,' Nora said. Closing the door firmly, she leaned against it, regarding Rebecca with a frown before she came to sit beside her on the bed. She slid her arm around Rebecca's shoulders.

'Am I going to the orphanage today?' Rebecca asked, her bottom lip trembling.

Nora cleared her throat. 'You're not going to the orphanage.' She felt a stab of despair at the sheer relief on Rebecca's face. 'Look, love, I'm not sure how much you know about what goes on here, but it's no place for a kid. Mickey wants you to stay here, and if I take you to the orphanage, he'll only think of a ploy to get you back.' She inhaled deeply as she gathered her thoughts. 'I think you'd be better off away from here. I've got a plan. I'm just waiting for Maddy and Dora.'

'But if Mickey says I can stay, then that's good,' Rebecca said, her relief on her face.

'No, Becky,' Nora said. 'Mickey's not saying that out of the kindness of his heart. He . . . Look, all you need to know is that he means you harm and we need to get you as far away from him as we can.'

'But . . .' Rebecca frowned '. . . where will I go?'

'I've an idea. If it works out as I hope, you'll be well cared for.'

'Can't you come with me?' Rebecca asked, the hope in her voice breaking Nora's heart.

'I can't, love. I'm sorry,' Nora said, jumping as someone tapped softly on the door.

'It's only me,' hissed Dora, opening the door and poking her head into the room. She held out the locket.

Rebecca's eyes lit up. 'You mended it.'

'I said I would.' Dora beamed, as Rebecca bent forward to let her clasp the delicate silver chain around her slender neck.

'I think Jessie was a bit suspicious,' she said, joining them on the bed, leaning back on her elbows.

'Much as I like Jessie,' Nora said, 'she's very much in fear of Mickey. It's better she doesn't know anything, for her sake as well as ours.'

CHAPTER NINE

Rebecca sniffed pitifully as Nora hurried her along the street. Her outfit of trousers, shirt and jacket that Maddy had procured from the rag-and-bone man offered little protection from the bitter March wind. Her boots were too big and, though Nora had stuffed the toes with newspaper, she stumbled frequently, and she could feel the start of a blister on her heel. Her long hair was piled under her cap. It was a disguise that would never hold up under close scrutiny, but Nora was confident that, from a distance, Rebecca would be taken for a boy.

Somewhere nearby a clock chimed ten. Nora bit her lip in consternation. It had taken longer to get Rebecca ready than she'd expected. She had to be back by a quarter to eleven for her first customer. The last thing she wanted was for the man to complain to Miss Tina and rouse Mickey's suspicions. She uttered a silent prayer that Fred would be at his usual pitch, and that he'd go along with her plan. He was a kind-hearted man and he'd been very fond of Lydia. He was good to Becky as well, so she was fairly hopeful she could persuade him.

The cold wind whipped Rebecca's damp face as they rounded the corner into Market Square. The air was thick with the smell of animals and the briny odour of the sea. The stiff wind blew clouds of swirling chaff into the air. Animals bleated and bellowed in their pens, the noise competing with the shouts of the stallholders.

Gripping Rebecca's hand tightly, Nora wove in and out of the crowds, relief surging as she spotted Fred's rotund form. She dragged Rebecca to the edge of the small crowd gathered in front of the stall.

Despite her lack of appetite earlier, the rich, meaty aroma made Rebecca's mouth water. The stallholder's voice sounded vaguely familiar to her as he exchanged banter with his customers. As one woman thanked him and moved away, clutching her purchase under her arm, Rebecca caught a glimpse of the round, florid face and shining bald pate.

'It's Mr Fred,' she whispered to Nora. Nora shushed her, glancing around nervously. She could see no one she recognized but that didn't mean no one was watching her. As Mickey was always telling them, he had eyes everywhere.

As the mid-morning rush eased, and the crowd of housewives and domestic servants began to dwindle, Fred caught sight of Nora hovering behind the woman he was serving. His blue eyes widened in surprise, but he kept his attention focused on his customer, his double chins wobbling as he bantered with her.

'There you are, madam,' he said, handing the woman two pies wrapped neatly in brown paper. 'Thank you for your custom. Be sure to remember me to your husband,' he called, as she moved away.

Nora swiftly took the woman's place in front of the stall. Rebecca stood at her side, gazing up at Fred from under her too-large cap.

'Nora? Becky, is that you?' He frowned at Nora. 'What're you up to? Why's she dressed like a lad?' He scanned the crowed milling about the marketplace. 'Where's her mother?'

'Lydia's dead, Fred,' Nora said bluntly.

'What?' Fred rocked back on his heels, clearly stricken. 'I don't believe it. When? How?'

'She was killed yesterday afternoon.' She lowered her voice. 'Murdered.'

Fred reeled back in horror. 'Murdered!' he exclaimed, catching the interest of several passers-by. A soberly dressed young woman handing out Temperance Society tracts outside the Methodist church behind Fred's stall glanced over in alarm.

'Shush!' Nora hissed, looking around nervously.

'Sorry.' Fred lowered his voice. 'Poor Lydia.' He shook his head. 'She was a good woman. She didn't deserve that.' He looked down at Rebecca. 'I'm sorry for your loss, Becky.'

'The thing is,' Nora said, her voice dropping even lower, 'I was hoping you'd be able to help.'

'Anything, you know that,' Fred replied solemnly.

'I've got to get the child away from Mickey,' Nora said quietly. 'If you get my meaning.'

'He wouldn't . . .' Fred's rosy cheeks turned a darker shade of red, his blue eyes glittering angrily as he gazed at Rebecca. She felt ashamed, though she didn't understand why.

'The man's a—' He broke off, cursing under his breath. 'I know I'm . . . but kids?' He shuddered. 'Hanging's too good for the likes of him. What is it you want me to do?' he asked, outrage giving way to puzzlement.

'I know you were fond of Lydia, Fred, and, as punters go, she thought you were all right. You're fond of Becky, too. I know you are. She's a good girl. She'll be no trouble.'

'Are you suggesting I take her in?' exclaimed Fred, as

comprehension dawned. 'Are you mad? How would I explain her presence to Mrs Ellis?'

'Oh, come on, Fred,' Nora cajoled. 'You can't let Mickey get her into his clutches.. You can keep her safe. Please, Fred,' she added urgently, as two women approached the stall.

He hesitated. 'Oh, all right,' he muttered, looking less than pleased to find himself saddled with a twelve-year-old child. 'I won't be packing up until mid-afternoon,' he grumbled. 'She'll have to hang about until then.'

'That's fine.' Nora smiled in relief. 'Give us one of your pies,' she said. 'She can eat it while she waits.'

Sighing again, Fred wrapped up a meat pie and handed it to Nora. She thanked him and dragged Rebecca down a narrow alley just off the square. 'I need you to stay here, Becky. Keep this for your dinner. Fred will come for you when he's ready to go, all right?'

Rebecca gave a hesitant nod, glancing along the alleyway. It was narrow and damp, and it stank. Water trickled down the discoloured brickwork, splashing into a small puddle in which floated a dead rat.

'Do you hear me, Becky?' Nora said, giving her shoulder a gentle shake. Rebecca gave another nod. 'Stay here. Promise me? It's important that you do as you're told.'

'I promise.'

Nora smiled. 'Good girl.' She straightened up. 'I've got to go, love.' She planted a kiss on Rebecca's forehead. 'Fred will see you right. He's a good man. You like him, don't you?'

Tears filled Rebecca's eyes, but she nodded, before flinging herself against Nora.

Nora held her close for a moment, then disentangled herself from Rebecca's embrace.

'I've really got to go, love.' Her tone was firm, though her eyes glistened with tears. Giving Rebecca one final squeeze, she turned on her heel and hurried around the corner, leaving Rebecca staring after her, tears streaming down her face.

CHAPTER TEN

'You'll be all right with me, Becky,' Fred said, giving the girl slumped on the seat beside him a sideways glance. She looked up at him with big, tear-filled eyes and he sighed. What did he know about taking care of a young girl? He and his wife, Letty, had never been blessed with children. Which was just as well, he snorted quietly, considering how his marriage had turned out. Pushing aside thoughts of his miserable home life, he shook the reins urging the pony onwards.

'Not too far now, kiddie,' he said. more cheerfully than he felt. News of Lydia's murder had hit him hard, and he wasn't sure how he'd cope now he didn't have his weekly visits to look forward to.

Rebecca wiped her eyes. Her chest ached with crying and her eyes felt sandy and rough, but she lifted her gaze enough to take in her surroundings. The purple sea was just visible above the budding hedgerows, the last rays of sunlight shimmering on the western horizon. On her other side, through the trees, she could see rolling green fields, dotted with small farms and clusters of cottages. The pony whinnied and the cart picked up speed as the road dipped and they rounded a bend, coming to a halt outside a small stone cottage. It was set back from the lane, an uneven path leading through an overgrown garden to a front door in need of painting. Smoke curled from chimney pots at either end of the sagging tiled roof.

'Now,' said Fred, the cart creaking in protest under his weight, 'my lady wife isn't going to take kindly to me bringing you home.' He glanced at the upstairs window. Rebecca followed his gaze. Despite the early hour, the curtains were tightly drawn, the glass filthy.

'Mrs Ellis is an invalid,' continued Fred, as Rebecca looked at him anxiously. 'She's seldom well enough to leave her bed, but if you're careful and quiet, you shouldn't bother her too much. Come on.' He engaged the brake. 'I'll show you where you can sleep.' He climbed down, the cart rocking precariously.

Rebecca scrambled after him, following him around the side of the cottage. Like the front garden, the back was an overgrown tangle of weeds and brambles. Fred strode purposefully along the path to where a small shed stood in the corner of the garden, the door hanging open, creaking on its hinge in the wind.

'Here we are,' he said, stooping to enter. He beckoned to Rebecca. She stood in the doorway, breathing in the damp, musty air as her eyes adjusted to the dimness. 'You can share the stable with our Peggy. You'll need to clean it out every morning, I'm afraid, but you'll get used to the smell. Some fresh straw and a few blankets, you'll be proper cosy.'

Gazing at the dirty straw scattered across the damp wood floor, Rebecca was doubtful. She blinked back more tears. She didn't want to cry in front of Fred any more. She understood he was doing his best. She managed a weak smile in reply.

'That's the spirit.' Fred exhaled in relief. 'Farmer Tucker

delivered a load of fresh straw this morning. It's around the back. So's the pitchfork. You make a nice bed for yourself and our Peggy while I make us a cup of tea. Mrs Ellis will be needing one.'

As he began to leave, Rebecca caught his sleeve. He gazed down at her, his eyes kind, despite the furrow across his brow. 'Thank you, Mr Fred.' Fred's smile broadened.

'You're welcome, pet.'

Rebecca hugged herself as she watched him walk across the garden. Darkness was coming on quickly now, so she roused herself and, finding the pitchfork and the pile of straw behind the shed, she got to work.

She'd just finished spreading the straw in Peggy's stall when Fred returned, leading the sweet-natured pony behind him. She snorted softly, her tail flicking her hindquarters as Fred settled her.

'You've done a fine job, girl,' Fred said, holding the lantern aloft and glancing round appreciatively. He gave Peggy an affectionate slap on her neck, and she nuzzled his pockets. He laughed. 'Yes, you can.' Taking out a crumpled paper bag, he fished out a misshapen lump of sugar. 'You want to give it to her?' Rebecca recoiled and drew back. 'Don't be scared. She won't hurt you, will you, Peggy, love? Here, hold your hand flat, like this.'

Nervously, Rebecca did as he showed her. Peggy guzzled greedily, her hairy lips tickling her palm.

'Right, I'll fetch that cup of tea,' Fred said, as Rebecca wiped her hand on her trousers. 'We can use that crate as a table.' He ducked out into the growing twilight, leaving Rebecca alone with the mare, who whickered gently as she buried her face in the feeding trough. Fred returned moments later carrying two mugs of tea, which he set down on the crate. With much grunting, he lowered himself onto an old three-legged stool. Rebecca sank into the sweet-smelling straw. Her stomach rumbled and she blushed, embarrassed. Fred grinned in the lamplight. 'Here,' he said, reaching into his coat pocket and drawing out a meat pie, which he handed to her. 'Eat up,' he said, lifting his mug to his lips and slurping noisily. Rebecca hesitated, then bit into the delicious pie, chewing hungrily.

'I've told Mrs Ellis you're my new apprentice,' he said, as she ate. 'Stay out of the house and you'll be all right. She won't bother you here.' He drained his mug. 'The privy is behind the kitchen. On Friday nights I play dominoes at the King's Arms. You can have your weekly bath then. I'll fill it for you before I go and leave it in front of the fire. You'll find a bar of soap in the pantry and a towel hanging on the back of the door. Be sure to wash behind your ears.' He grinned. 'That's what my mother always told me. I'll fetch you some blankets,' he said, grunting noisily as he got to his feet. 'Then I think it's bedtime. You've had a long day, and we'll be up early tomorrow.'

While Fred fetched the blankets, Rebecca finished her tea. Fred took her mug on his return, wished her goodnight and left her to it.

Alone in the all-consuming dark, the events of the last two days crashed over her. Loneliness weighed heavily on her heart and there was an ache in her chest that made it hard to breathe. She missed her mother so much. She curled up in the straw, tugging the blankets over her shoulders, and let the tears fall. Peggy whickered softly in the darkness, her breath fanning Rebecca's wet cheek. Despite her grief, Rebecca found Peggy's presence strangely comforting. The straw rustled and she stiffened, holding her breath, listening to the sound of something small scurrying about. Peggy snorted and pawed the ground. Rebecca inched herself closer to the pony. She felt Peggy's nose nudge her head. The pony's breath was warm on her bare neck. With Peggy's soft whickering in her ears, Rebecca finally fell asleep.

Fred woke her the following morning before daybreak. 'This is the last time you get preferential treatment,' Fred said, with mock sternness, as he handed her a freshly baked meat pie and a mug of hot tea. 'From tomorrow you'll be getting up at three with me. I'm going to teach you how to make the best meat pies this side of the River Dart.'

Rebecca bit into the pie hungrily. Still warm from the oven, it oozed rich gravy.

'How did you sleep?' he asked, hanging the lantern on its hook and placing the feed bucket on the floor.

Rebecca swallowed. 'All right, thank you.'

'Good.' Fred nodded. 'I know you've had a rough couple of days,' he said, laying a large, shovel-like hand on Rebecca's shoulder. 'But you'll be all right with me, you hear? I promised Nora I'll look out for you, and I will.' He coughed, clearing his throat. 'Right. As soon as Madam here's had her breakfast I'll be hitching up.'

'Are we going back to Dartmouth?' asked Rebecca, gulping her tea and almost choking in her haste.

'Steady on, girl,' Fred chided her, slapping her between the shoulder-blades as she coughed and spluttered. 'We'll be giving Dartmouth a miss for a week or two,' he said, almost to himself. 'No, we're off to Brixham so we need to get going. We've a long road ahead of us.'

Fifteen minutes later they were on their way. A bitter wind blew across the fields, rustling the trees that formed shadowy canopies across the lane. Rebecca's nostrils were filled with the pungent scent of wild garlic. It was dark still but for the pool of yellow lantern light. From far away came the faint pounding of waves on rocks.

The sun was rising an hour later as they neared the town of Brixham. The roads were busier, the winding lanes clogged with sheep and cattle, wagons and carts. Dust swirled in the air, coating the back of Rebecca's throat and stinging her eyes. As beautiful as the surrounding countryside was, Rebecca took little notice. Her grief had settled like a rock behind her ribcage, and even Fred's cheerful chat had failed to raise her spirits. He'd eventually given up, lapsing into silence.

'Market day in Brixham,' he said now, rousing himself as he steered the pony towards the main street. 'My most lucrative day of the week.'

Rebecca looked along the road, which was crammed with stalls and animal pens. Horse-drawn vehicles lined the kerb. A cockerel crowed, joining the cacophony of bellowing cattle and bleating sheep. A yellow cloud hovered over the market where a hundred stamping hoofs churned the dust. Merchants were touting their wares and the street teemed with people.

Fred pulled on the reins and Peggy slowed to a halt outside the Thirsty Mariner public house. The plump blonde woman sweeping the pavement paused in her work, and smiled at them. 'Morning, Fred,' she called cheerfully. 'Who's your new friend?' She leaned on her broom and smiled up at Rebecca.

'Morning, Celeste,' replied Fred, in an equally cheerful manner. 'This is my niece, Becky,' he said, giving Rebecca a wink. He'd been pondering how to explain the girl's sudden appearance all the way to town. 'She's staying with me and the missus for a while,' he explained, wheezing as he eased his heavy frame from the seat. 'Come on, kid.' He tapped Rebecca's arm. 'Let's get these pies round the back.'

'I'll have a jug of ale ready for you, once you've unloaded.' Celeste grinned, getting back to her sweeping.

Rebecca scrambled from the cart and, taking the box of delicious-smelling meat pies, followed Fred to the back of the pub. The aroma of ale drifted from the open door where a heavily built man with a shaven head was manoeuvring a wooden barrel across the worn stone floor.

'Morning, Seth,' Fred called.

'Fred.' Seth set the barrel on its end, straightened and held out his hands.

'Barely been out the oven more than an hour,' Fred said, as Seth took both boxes. His shirt sleeves were rolled to the elbow and Rebecca stared in amazement at his intricately tattooed forearms.

Seth grinned at her. 'I ran away to sea when I was just a lad of fourteen,' he explained. 'Saves me buying postcards. I've got mementoes from all round the world.' He jerked his head. 'Come through.'

They passed through the cluttered storeroom into the dim saloon bar. The air was heavy with stale tobacco smoke, ale and fresh sawdust, the furniture dark and heavy.

'Here's your ale, Fred,' said Celeste, emerging from behind the polished bar. The row of glasses shone in the flickering lamplight and the large mirror gave the illusion that the room was much larger than it was.

'So, what's your name, then, lad?' asked Seth, sliding a glass of weak ale across the table to Rebecca. Rebecca shot Fred a worried glance. Celeste snorted, coming over to join them at the bar.

'Haven't you got eyes in your head, Seth Mathews? You can

clearly see she's a lass.' She gave Rebecca an apologetic smile. 'This is Fred's niece, Becky.'

'The girl lost her mother a couple of days ago,' Fred explained soberly, licking froth off his upper lip. 'She's staying with me and the missus.'

'Sorry to hear about your mum, Becky,' Seth said, lifting his glass in salute. 'Lost mine ten years ago and I still miss her.'

'Heart of gold Seth's mum had,' Celeste said. 'I expect you miss your mum a lot?'

Rebecca nodded, feeling the sting of tears at the back of her throat.

Celeste patted her shoulder. 'Sorry for your loss, too, Fred,' she said. 'I didn't realize you had any family, other than Mrs Ellis. Is she your brother or sister's child?'

'Sister,' Fred spluttered, his cheeks darkening. 'We weren't close.'

'Well, Becky, I've known your uncle Fred a long time. He's a good 'un. He'll look after you all right, won't you, Fred?'

'I'll do my best.' Having regained his composure, Fred smiled. 'Thanks for the ale, Celeste, but we'd best be going. Can't keep the customers waiting.'

'See you next week,' Seth said, as the two men shook hands. 'Good to meet you, Becky,' he called after Rebecca, as she followed Fred out into the chilly sunshine.

Fred took the reins and led the pony through the crowds towards the harbour.

'Why did you tell those people I was your niece?' Rebecca asked, as she helped Fred unload the pies from the back of the cart.

'It makes life simpler,' Fred replied, handing her the oilskin tablecloth. 'And it'll stop folk asking awkward questions. Now, pass me that peg, and we're ready for business.'

*

Business was brisk. Fred's pies were clearly in demand and, listening to his easy chat with his customers, Rebecca could tell he was well respected in the town. On being introduced as his recently orphaned niece, most of the housewives and servants queuing for meat pies addressed her with friendly sympathy. She was glad to be busy. The morning flew by and she almost made it to dinner time before being overwhelmed once more by a tidal wave of grief. Her happy mood evaporated immediately as tears welled. 'I miss my mama so much,' she sobbed, as Fred gave her shoulders a comforting squeeze.

'Poor lamb,' muttered a motherly woman, taking her wrapped pie and slipping it into her basket.

'Do you want to go and sit down for a moment?' asked Fred, deftly wrapping two pies in brown paper.

Rebecca shook her head. Taking a shuddering breath, she wiped her eyes and, plastering a bright smile on her face, turned to the next customer waiting in line. 'Good morning, madam. What can I get you?'

By early afternoon they had sold out. Fred treated them both to a late dinner of cockles, which they ate sitting on the quayside, watching the gulls wheeling and diving among the boats rocking in the harbour. The wind had dropped, and the early spring sunshine felt warm on Rebecca's face. She took off her cap, shaking her long, cornfield-blonde hair free. It tumbled down her back in a shimmering wave.

The roads back to the tiny hamlet where Fred lived were clogged with animals, pedestrians and traffic, so it was late in the afternoon by the time they drew up in front of his ramshackle cottage. Fred employed the brake as a sharp rapping sound drew their gaze to one of the upstairs windows. The face peering through the grime-streaked glass was red and angry. Rebecca glanced anxiously at Fred, before her eyes were drawn back to the window.

Fred sighed. 'Mrs Ellis. See to Peggy, will you, Becky?' he said, his broad shoulders sagging in resignation. 'I'll go and see to the missus.'

Holding the pony's reins, Rebecca watched Fred trudge wearily up the path. She glanced up at the window. The woman was gone. Swallowing hard, she led Peggy into the shed. She had no experience with horses, but remembering how Fred had rubbed Peggy down yesterday, she did the same. She refilled the water bucket from the well and filled the trough. Grabbing her blanket, she huddled in a corner of the stable, listening to Peggy's gentle munching, and waited for Fred. She hoped and prayed he wouldn't send her away.

After what seemed ages, she heard the cottage door bang. Getting quickly to her feet, she hurried to the stable door, careful to keep to the shadows, as Fred walked towards her. At the expression on his face, Rebecca's shoulders relaxed. It wasn't the expression of someone about to tell her to go – at least, she hoped not.

'It's all right,' he said, as he drew within earshot. 'I've put my foot down.' He swallowed. He wasn't about to tell the girl how his wife had shrieked at him that she'd not put up with the shame of having the daughter of his favourite whore in her home. In a rare flash of anger, Fred had told Letty in no uncertain terms that, if it wasn't for him, she'd be in the workhouse, what with her being bedridden and all. 'I should have just told her about you from the off,' he said, with a rueful shrug. 'No matter. Mrs Ellis needs a lot of nursing. You can help around the house, too, and sleep under the stairs. It'll be a bit more comfortable and warmer than sharing with old Peggy here.' He smiled.

'Your wife won't mind?' Rebecca asked, in a small voice. She remembered the look of pure loathing she'd seen on the woman's face and a tremor ran through her body.

'She'll like it or lump it,' Fred muttered. 'Come on. I'll show you around.'

The cottage smelt of damp and neglect. The only part of the kitchen that was spotless was the area where Fred baked his pies. Clothes were tossed over the back of chairs and dust covered every available surface. The floor was filthy, and dirty dishes were piled in the sink.

Rebecca looked about in amazement, thinking how appalled her mother would have been to see such slovenly housekeeping.

'If you could make a start cleaning up?' Fred suggested.

Rebecca nodded. 'I used to help Mama with the housework.'

He glanced around the cluttered house. 'You'll find everything you need in the cupboard. First, though, put the kettle on. You can take Mrs Ellis a cup of tea. The sooner you make her acquaintance, the better.' He pulled a face. 'Her bark's much worse than her bite. Remember that.'

'What do you want?'

Rebecca stood in the doorway of the small bedroom, the unpleasant smell wafting from the bed making her stomach heave. Letty Ellis sat propped against a mound of pillows, regarding Rebecca with a cold stare, her lips pursed in a disapproving line. 'I told him he was to send you packing,' she said shrilly.

'I – I brought you a cup of tea,' Rebecca stammered. The window was shut tight, the curtains pulled back so that the pale early spring sun shone directly into the room.

Letty eyed her belligerently. 'Put it there,' she said, indicating the cluttered table beside the bed.

Rebecca did as she was told, retreating quickly to the doorway. 'Is there anything else I can get for you?' she asked politely.

Letty's eyes narrowed. 'Don't try ingratiating yourself with me. That imbecile I married might think I was born yesterday but I'm not daft. I know your mum was the one my Fred's been sneaking off to see. Oh.' At the look of shock on Rebecca's face, Letty grinned. 'He talks in his sleep, does Fred. Oh, I know all about your mother, the whore. You're a chip off the old block too, I shouldn't wonder.' She stretched her thin lips over her rotting teeth in a macabre parody of a smile. 'Is that why he's brought you here?' she asked slyly. 'I suppose he's a man, after all and—'

She broke off as heavy footsteps sounded on the stairs. Fred burst through the door, breathing heavily, his cheeks crimson. 'I thought by telling you about Becky's situation you might show some compassion,' he said quietly. 'I should have known better.' His lips curled in a disgusted sneer. 'You don't have a compassionate bone in your body.' Rebecca shrank against the doorframe, her heart pounding. What were they saying about her mama? 'Lydia might have been a . . .' He caught sight of Rebecca's face and his jaw snapped shut with a loud clack.

'A whore?' his wife sneered. 'You can say it in front of the kid, Fred.'

'She was worth ten of you.' Fred's nostrils flared angrily. He took a deep breath to calm himself. 'The reason I brought the girl here,' he continued, his voice low, leaning in close until he and Letty were almost nose to nose, 'is that that pervert, Mickey, was all for selling her off to the highest bidder.'

'So what?' Letty hissed. 'She's not your problem.' Her eyes widened. 'Or is she? Is the brat yours, Fred Ellis?'

'Don't be daft, woman.' He drew back from the bed, his fleshy features twisted in disgust. 'At least with me she'll have a chance in life. I'm going to teach her the trade. She'll be able to get decent employment.'

Letty waved her gnarled hand. 'You're such a soft touch, Fred,' she said, with a mocking laugh.

'Better than being a cold-hearted bi—' Again, he caught himself before the word left his lips. What sort of behaviour was this for the girl to witness? He smiled at Rebecca. 'Come on, your tea's getting cold.' As he made to usher her from the room, he glanced back over his shoulder. 'Rebecca's going to help look after you now,' he said, ignoring the girl's look of alarm. 'See you treat her right, or you'll have me to answer to.'

The woman's tart reply was lost by the slam of the door behind them.

'My mama wasn't one of those women, was she, Fred?' Rebecca asked, as he ushered her down the rickety staircase. Her cheeks grew hot, remembering the sneers she'd received at school from pupils and staff alike.

Fred sighed deeply. 'Look, Becky, your mum was the nicest, kindest person I ever met,' he said. 'Let that be enough.'

CHAPTER ELEVEN

1879

Rebecca set the mug of tea and plate of toast on Letty's bedside table and crept quietly from the room, grateful that the woman was asleep and she was spared her acid tongue. In the fifteen months she'd been living with Fred, Rebecca had taken on the sole responsibility for Letty's day-to-day care, an arrangement that wasn't agreeable to either of them. But after he'd seen Mickey out and about in Dartmouth on several occasions, Fred had decided it would be safer for Rebecca to remain at home as much as possible. She still occasionally travelled with him to Brixham and some of the other towns, which she enjoyed. Even manning the stall in the face of a bracing gale was better than being at Letty's constant beck and call.

In the small kitchen, she prepared her own breakfast, gazing round the small cottage in satisfaction. It was a far cry from the untidy, filthy place she'd come to more than a year before. Despite their limited circumstances, her mother had always been houseproud, and Rebecca was determined to follow her example. The windows sparkled in the sunlight, and, during the spring and summer, she always made sure there was a jug of flowers on the table. Fred had been amazed the first time he'd come home to find his cottage bright and shining as a new pin. Rebecca had blushed at his effusive praise. Now she understood exactly what had gone on in the house on Angel Terrace, she was even more grateful to Fred for taking her in, and Nora for organizing her escape. She thought of her old friends often, hoping they were all right and that somehow they, too, might find a way to free themselves of Mickey.

True to his word, Fred had taught Rebecca how to make meat pies and had proclaimed them as good as, if not better than, his own. With the vegetables she grew in the garden, they ate well.

Now she carried her breakfast to the table. A warm breeze wafted in through the open back door. The air was alive with birdsong and from further away the bleating of sheep was carried to her on the summer breeze. As she picked up her mug of tea, she became aware of a horse whinnying. She set down her mug and listened, frowning. It couldn't be Peggy, surely. Fred had set off an hour ago.

She went to the door, wondering if the whinnying was coming from the lane. She frowned. It was definitely Peggy. With a growing sense of unease, she hurried down the garden path towards the stable, calling Fred's name. Peggy whinnied louder, hoofs banging on the floor.

'Fred?' Rebecca rounded a large redcurrant bush to find him sprawled across the path, one arm flung out into the grass, the other clutching his chest. His eyes were open, staring skywards, his face ashen.

'Oh, no!' Rebecca wailed, sinking to her knees beside him. 'Fred, wake up,' she whispered, taking his hand in hers. His skin was waxy and cold to the touch. 'Fred!' She shook his shoulder. 'Fred!' His free hand fell limply to his side. Rebecca rocked back on her heels, letting out an anguished sob. She glanced about in wild panic, searching for help. A cock crowed nearby, and her shoulders sagged in relief. Farmer Tucker. She scrambled to her feet and ran out into the lane. Her luck was in: she had only just set off in the direction of the farm when she heard whistling and Horatio Tucker appeared, leading his prize bull. His dog, Jack, gave a short bark and ran up to Rebecca, sniffing at her skirt, his tail wagging.

'Becky?' farmer Tucker exclaimed, the sight of Rebecca's tearstained face stopping him in his tracks. 'Whatever is the matter?' he asked, as the bull pawed the ground impatiently.

'It's Mr Fred,' Rebecca panted. 'I can't wake him up. Please come.'

'Run and get Mrs Tucker,' Horatio said. 'You'll find her in the dairy. I'll just tie old Sam up and I'll go over and see to Fred.'

Leaving the farmer to deal with his bull, Rebecca flew down the lane. She found Mrs Tucker in the dairy straining the milk. She looked up in alarm as Rebecca almost fell through the open door. 'Mr Fred won't wake up,' she panted, tearfully. 'Farmer Tucker says please will you come?'

'Oh, gracious, child,' Irene Tucker said, blowing out her plump cheeks in consternation. 'Mavis, Ginny,' she said to the two red-cheeked girls stirring the curds and whey to make cheese. 'I'll be back as quick as I can.' Ushering Rebecca out of the cool dairy, she hurried across the yard, calling, 'Abel, Martin, Mr Ellis has been taken ill. Bring the cart.'

'Be right there, Mrs T,' a voice shouted from inside the barn.

Rebecca ran back down the lane, Irene Tucker hurrying after her and calling on her to wait. She skidded to a halt at the sight of Farmer Tucker standing over Fred's prone form, his expression grave. 'I'm sorry, girl,' he said, scratching his chin. 'I'm afraid he's gone.'

'Ah, poor old Fred,' Irene said, coming up behind Rebecca and pulling her into her motherly embrace. 'Ah, it's a shock for you, love,' she said, as Rebecca started to cry. 'You'd better send for the doctor, Horatio.' She sighed. 'And I suppose I shall have to tell his wife.' She glanced up at the bedroom window. She certainly wasn't relishing the prospect.

'Better coming from a woman,' her husband agreed, turning towards the sound of an approaching cart. 'Abel, go for the doctor. Tell him . . .' he shot Rebecca an apologetic glance '. . . tell him there's no hurry.'

The young farmhand looked over to where Fred lay in the grass. He blanched.

'Is he . . .?'

Farmer Tucker nodded. 'Martin,' he instructed the other young farmhand, as Abel drove away. 'Fetch a coat or blanket, something to cover him with.'

Martin ran off towards the house.

'Come on, Becky,' Irene said, her hand between Rebecca's shoulder-blades. 'I'd better give your aunt the sad news. Be a good girl and put the kettle on. We'll all need a cup of tea after this.'

When Rebecca carried up the tea tray a short while later, she was surprised to hear Letty speaking in her normal tone. She had expected some weeping, at least. Pushing open the door, she was even more surprised to see Fred's widow sitting up in bed, perfectly composed. She was dry-eyed, her mouth a thin, angry slash in her pale face.

'Put it over there,' she snapped, barely affording Rebecca a glance. 'As I was saying, Mrs Tucker,' she said, turning back to Irene, who was perched uncomfortably on a small stool beside the bed, 'my sister lives in Dartmouth. I shall give you the address and you can send her a telegram. She could be here by late this afternoon.'

'Are you sure she'll come, Mrs Ellis?' enquired Irene, doubtfully. 'If you say you're estranged . . .? But if she doesn't want to come, at least you've still got Becky.' She gave Rebecca an encouraging smile, thinking that the poor girl's burden had suddenly got a whole lot heavier.

'I want that little trollop out of the house right now,' Letty spat.

'Mrs Ellis!' Irene exclaimed. 'I'm shocked that you could speak so about the girl when she's just lost her uncle.'

'Uncle!' Letty shrieked with laughter. 'He wasn't her uncle. She's nothing but the daughter of Fred's whore!'

Irene blanched. Unable to meet her gaze, Rebecca bowed her head in shame.

'Now, you send that telegram to our Susan,' Letty said, pointing at Irene. 'The sooner you do that, the sooner she can be here. And as for you,' her venomous gaze swivelled to Rebecca, 'I want you gone. Now.'

'I've nowhere to go,' Rebecca said. She didn't dare raise her head, lest she see the shock and disgust in Irene Tucker's face. It pained her that the woman, who had always had a kind word for Rebecca in passing, would be thinking ill of her. 'Where am I to go?'

'I don't care where you go,' Letty snapped. 'Just so long as you're not here.'

'You can stay with us for tonight,' Irene said, abruptly getting up from the stool. 'Pack your belongings.'

'You'd better watch she doesn't take anything that don't belong to her,' Letty snarled.

'You run along, Becky,' Irene said, regarding Letty with intense dislike. 'I'll wait for you outside.'

'Don't forget to send my telegram,' Letty called after her belligerently. 'Mrs Archibald Pike, seven Victoria Terrace.'

In no time at all, Rebecca had gathered together her few belongings. She fastened her locket around her neck, tucking it safely under her shirt before leaving the house. Irene was in the garden talking to the doctor. She broke off at the sight of Rebecca and held out her hand. 'Come on, let's get you home.'

Averting her gaze so she wouldn't have to see poor Fred being loaded onto the back of the cart, Rebecca followed Irene out into the lane. Misery had formed a thick lump in the back of her throat. She would miss Fred so much, she thought, blinking back the tears.

If Irene was curious about what Letty had told her of Rebecca, she didn't mention it. Instead, she ushered her indoors, settled her at the large kitchen table and poured her a glass of milk. 'Now,' she said, leaning against a Welsh dresser crammed with crockery, arms folded across her chest, 'you can help the girls in the dairy for the rest of the day. It'll do you good to keep busy. Once Mr Tucker comes home, we can decide what to do with you.'

'Can't I stay here?' Rebecca asked, biting her lip anxiously.

Irene gave a snort. 'Lordy, no, child!' she exclaimed, throwing up her hands. 'I've enough on my plate without another mouth to feed.' At the sight of Rebecca's woebegone expression, her tone softened. 'You're a hard worker. We'll find you a good position. Now, run along to the dairy. I'll call you at dinner time.'

*

Rebecca spent the rest of the morning working alongside Mavis and Ginny in the dairy. Towards midday she heard barking, followed by the sound of a pony cart entering the yard. A few minutes later, Abel appeared in the doorway to tell Rebecca she was wanted in the parlour.

Hastily taking off the apron Ginny had given her, Rebecca made her way to the house, her heart pounding in trepidation. Hearing voices as she entered the kitchen, she hesitated.

'If we can't find her a position, it'll be the workhouse,' Horatio Tucker was saying. Rebecca cowered against the wall and held her breath.

'There's bound to be somebody round here who's looking for help,' replied Irene. 'I don't like to think of the girl in the workhouse. Whatever her relationship was with Mr Ellis, she's barely more than a child and she deserves a chance in life.'

'I can't promise anything more than to try my best,' Farmer Tucker answered her gruffly. The floorboard under Rebecca's feet creaked. The voices fell silent, and the parlour door swung open. 'Ah, Becky,' declared Farmer Tucker, heartily. 'Come in. Mrs Tucker and I were just discussing your situation and I'm going to do my best to secure you a position at one of the surrounding farms.'

'Please, sir,' Rebecca said, a little breathlessly. She'd been pondering her future all morning while working in the dairy and she'd suddenly thought of Seth and Celeste. They had been fond of Fred. Surely they wouldn't turn her away. 'I have friends in Brixham. Mr and Mrs Mathews at the Thirsty Mariner. Would you be able to take me to them?'

Irene pursed her lips. 'A public house?' she said, the tone of her voice conveying exactly what she thought of such an establishment. She looked to her husband. 'Horatio, I don't think . . .'

'It's an option.' Horatio nodded, stroking his beard thought-fully. 'It's worth a visit. We'll leave immediately after dinner,' he said, smiling at Rebecca's obvious relief.

'I'm not sure a public house is a suitable place for the girl,' Irene protested, frowning.

'I won't abandon her there,' Horatio promised. 'If I'm not comfortable with the situation, I shall bring Becky back here and we'll try the local farms.'

It was just gone two o'clock when the cart rolled to a halt outside the Thirsty Mariner. The door was open, the smell of stale beer mingling with the salty air. A few men loitering outside watched Rebecca alight with mild interest. Farmer Tucker gave them a curt nod and they moved aside, allowing him and Rebecca to pass through the doorway. The men sitting at a nearby table gave them barely a glance.

'Becky!' Seth exclaimed in surprise, from behind the bar.

'Mr Mathews, I presume?' Horatio said.

'That's me,' Seth replied. He put down the glass he was polishing and held out his hand. 'Call me Seth. Is everything all right?'

'Fred's dead,' Rebecca cried.

Seth stared at her, clearly shocked. 'What? When?' he blurted. 'What happened?'

'Just dropped dead this morning,' Horatio said, shortly. 'Doc thinks it might have been his heart.'

Seth nodded slowly. 'Poor Fred.'

'Yes, poor Fred,' Horatio agreed, clearing his throat. 'Thing is, Mrs Ellis doesn't want the girl and Becky here is under the impression you'd be happy to offer her employment.'

Before Seth could reply, the curtains behind the bar were

swept aside and Celeste appeared, hair coiffed and face carefully made up ready for the afternoon ahead. 'Becky! What are you doing here?' She frowned, regarding the farmer with open suspicion.

'Fred passed away this morning,' Seth told her.

'Fred?' Celeste's eyes widened. 'Oh, my. Poor man. I'm so sorry, Becky. I know you were very fond of your uncle.'

'Can I stay here?' Rebecca asked. 'You did say I could always come and work for you when I was older.'

Celeste hesitated. 'I'm not sure the Thirsty Mariner is the place for a young girl, Becky,' she said gently.

'Please, Celeste,' Rebecca begged.

Celeste and Seth exchanged glances. Seth gave a slight shrug of his broad shoulders. Celeste smiled. 'All right. But I don't want you hanging around the bar. We get all sorts in here. If you keep out the back, I suppose it'll work. Are you all right with that, Seth?'

'Goes without saying,' her husband replied, going back to his polishing.

'If you're certain?' Horatio said cautiously.

'Positive,' Celeste assured him, placing a motherly arm around Rebecca's shoulders. 'She'll be fine with us, won't you, love?'

Rebecca nodded.

'Have you got any baggage?'

'I'll fetch it,' replied Horatio, giving Seth a nod. He ducked out of the door to return a moment later with the bag that contained Rebecca's few belongings. 'Good luck to you, girl,' he said, setting it on the floor at Rebecca's feet. Tipping his hat, he bade her goodbye and took his leave.

'Right, then,' said Celeste, smoothing the skirt of her red

velvet dress. 'I suppose I should show you where you'll be sleeping. This way.' She led Rebecca up two flights of stairs to a small attic that contained a narrow bed pushed under the sloping ceiling and a small washstand. 'Before I knew you, we used to have a barmaid who lived in,' Celeste said, walking over to the small wardrobe. 'She left a few of her clothes behind.' She opened the door and took out a plain dress of dark blue. 'You look about the same size. I'm surprised your aunt didn't see to it that you were better clothed,' she added, casting a disparaging glance at Rebecca's attire. Rebecca blushed. She'd grown quite a bit in the last year since Fred had bought her the skirt and blouse she now wore. Celeste held out the dress. 'What do you think?'

'It's beautiful,' cried Rebecca, blinking back tears of gratitude. 'Thank you so much,' she said shyly.

'You're welcome, I'm sure,' Celeste replied. 'I'll bring you up a jug of hot water. Once you've had a wash and changed your clothes, you can join me in the kitchen. You can make a list of all the ingredients you need to make your pies, then pop out and get them.'

Rebecca's eyes widened. 'You want me to bake pies?'

'Fred said you beat him hands down at pie-making,' grinned Celeste. 'And my regulars are going to be clamouring for them come tomorrow dinner time, so, yes, love, I want you to bake pies.'

CHAPTER TWELVE

'Once the next batch of pies is in the oven, I'd like to make a start on cleaning the kitchen shelves,' Celeste said, breezing into the kitchen where Rebecca was elbow deep in soapy water. 'I've been putting it off for ages. You can give me a hand.'

'Of course,' Rebecca replied quickly. Wiping her hands on her apron, she lifted the tray of unbaked pies and slid them into the oven. She had been living at the pub for three weeks now and her pies were gaining a reputation with the locals. She certainly earned her keep, she mused ruefully, shutting the oven door. She was up before dawn and seldom went to bed before nine, but Celeste and Seth treated her fairly and she was growing more comfortable with them as the days progressed.

'Use these to line the shelves,' Celeste said now, laying a bundle of newspapers on the table. 'I heard you crying last night,' she said, after a moment's pause, resting one hand on the tabletop. 'Were you thinking of your uncle Fred?'

Rebecca nodded. 'I miss him.'

'We all do,' Celeste said, with a sad smile. 'You make a start in that cupboard over there and I'll do these. If we crack on, we'll be done by opening time.'

While Celeste heated the water, Rebecca began emptying the shelves,

She removed the yellowed newspaper lining the first and was about to crumple it up when a picture caught her eye. She froze. She smoothed it in front of her, her hands trembling as she recognized Nora's face staring back at her. It was a drawing, faded with time, but there was no mistaking the subject. The likeness was uncanny. 'DO YOU KNOW THIS WOMAN?' screamed the words in bold type above Nora's face. Her eyes were closed, as if she were sleeping, and she was bareheaded, her hair smoothed back from her face. Rebecca scanned the short paragraph below, her blood turning to ice in her veins: 'The body of an unidentified woman was pulled from the harbour on Tuesday evening. She had significant bruising to the throat, suggesting foul play. Police are appealing for anyone who recognizes this woman to contact them without delay.'

'What's the matter, Becky?' Celeste asked, rocking back on her heels and frowning over her shoulder at Rebecca.

Wordlessly, Rebecca passed Celeste the sheet of newspaper. She was visibly shaking. Who would want to harm dear, sweet Nora?

'Do you know her?' asked Celeste, scanning the article.

'She was a friend of my mum's,' Rebecca said.

'Oh, love, I'm sorry,' Celeste said, with a sympathetic sigh. 'It's dated the tenth of April last year. That wasn't long after your mum died, and you went to live with your uncle Fred.' She pulled a face. 'Poor woman. Let's hope the police caught the culprit.' She crumpled the sheet of paper into a ball and threw it on the fire where it shrivelled in the flames. 'You've had a shock. I'll get you a drink.' She disappeared, returning a few minutes later with a small amount of brandy in a glass. 'Here.'

Rebecca swallowed the liquid, wrinkling her nose in disgust.

She shuddered as the warm brandy slid down her throat and coughed.

'Have a break if you need one,' said Celeste, taking the empty glass from her.

Rebecca shook her head. 'I'm all right,' she mumbled. She bent her head and chose another sheet of newspaper. Her insides felt icy cold. Though she'd tried to hide it, Nora had been terrified that morning she'd taken Rebecca to the market. Had someone seen them and reported back to Mickey or Miss Tina? If so, Mickey would have been furious. Now the idea that he might have been responsible for Nora's death had lodged itself in her head, she couldn't shake it.

'You're very quiet, Becky,' Celeste said, later that afternoon, coming into the kitchen where Rebecca was putting everything back on the newly papered shelves. 'Are you still worrying about your old friend?'

Rebecca nodded. Climbing down from the stool, she leaned her palms on the table.

'I'm scared that whoever hurt Nora will come after me,' she said.

Celeste smiled. 'Oh, Becky. That was such a long time ago. I'm sure you've nothing to worry about. Anyway, it happened in Dartmouth, though I suppose it could happen anywhere. Every town has its fair share of ruffians, especially down near the harbour, which is why I don't allow you out after dark. It's not sensible for a young girl to be out at night, but even so, I don't think you need worry about something that happened well over a year ago.'

'I think Mickey Fox killed Nora,' Rebecca whispered.

'Who's he when he's at home?' Celeste frowned, arms folded across her chest as she leaned against the dresser.

'The man Mum and Nora worked for. That's why Nora took me to Fred.' She looked down at her shoes. 'Fred wasn't my uncle. He visited Mum at the house. It was work, Mum said. After she died . . .' Rebecca swallowed, her mouth dry '. . . after she died, Nora said Mickey wanted me to work for him, too,' she explained, her cheeks burning with shame. 'That was why she took me to Fred.'

'What?' Celeste paled. 'Are you saying . . .? Exactly what are you saying? Fred came to visit your mum at this establishment? She was a . . .?' She threw up her hands in amazement. 'Well, that's a turn-up for the books,' she said drily. 'He was a dark horse, old Fred, wasn't he?' She laughed mirthlessly. 'Cheer up, love. I'm not judging them. Lord knows I've not lived like a saint.' She sighed. 'So, this Mickey Fox, he ran the place, did he?'

Rebecca nodded.

'Hmm, all right. I'll get Seth to see what he can find out about him. I doubt you have anything to worry about, though. It's been months. If he was so keen on finding you, he'd have done so by now. Thank God your friend had the foresight to get you away from him.' She shuddered. She gave Rebecca's shoulder an affectionate squeeze. 'Once you've finished that, there's some glasses need washing. I'll bring them through.'

Despite Celeste's reassurances, after she'd found the newspaper article Rebecca never felt safe away from the pub. If she ever had to run an errand for Celeste or Seth, she made sure to cover her hair and face with a shawl, whatever the weather.

Seth had done a bit of investigating and Rebecca had overheard him telling Celeste that, from all accounts, Mickey Fox was a man to be feared. While he could appear charming, and had friends in high places, the word on the street was that he was ruthless when crossed. While Celeste didn't repeat any of this to Rebecca, she and Seth were convinced that it was likely Mickey Fox had been responsible for Nora's death. However, neither of them was overly concerned about him coming after Becky. She'd been away from him for well over a year. It was unlikely he'd waste his time chasing round the countryside looking for a young girl, even one as striking as Becky.

A fortnight later, as Becky was setting a tray of freshly baked pies on the rack to cool, Seth wandered into the kitchen, carrying the accounts ledger and looking perplexed. 'Is Celeste about?' he asked, gazing around the steam-filled kitchen as if she might appear.

'She's gone to the market,' replied Rebecca, wringing out a cloth and wiping down the table. 'Is everything all right?'

'I can't make head or tail of these accounts,' Seth said, tapping his chin with his pencil. 'I've spent the best part of an hour going over them, and I can't get the figures to add up. I thought Celeste might be able to see where I've gone wrong.'

'May I have a look?' Rebecca asked shyly.

Seth glowered at her. 'No, you cannot,' came the brusque reply. 'What does a slip of a girl like you know about figures?'

Rebecca blushed. 'I'm good at sums,' she murmured.

'Sums?' Seth gave her a sceptical smile. 'All right. Have a go. Can't do any harm, I suppose.' He dropped the ledger onto the table. 'I've got customers to serve. I'll be back in a bit.'

Once he'd gone, Rebecca dried her hands and opened the ledger. She sighed and began to sort through the handful of receipts tucked between the pages. She'd helped Fred with his household accounts, but they had been straightforward compared to the complicated columns of numbers dancing before her eyes right now. Once she'd familiarized herself with Seth's untidy handwriting, though, she soon discovered where the problem lay. The man couldn't read his own writing and had obviously mistaken certain numbers for others, as well as getting some of his debits and credits confused. By the time Celeste returned from the market twenty minutes later, Rebecca had the accounts perfectly balanced.

'Seth can't add up to save his life,' Celeste said, setting her basket on the table and peering over Rebecca's shoulder. 'And I can't abide doing the accounts. If you're willing, and you've got the time, I'd be more than happy for you to take over the books.'

'Won't Seth mind?' Rebecca asked.

'He might bluster a bit,' Celeste said, as she unpacked the shopping. 'Not good for his pride to admit you're cleverer than he is, but underneath he'll be more than pleased, you'll see.'

Celeste was proved right, and as well as being kept busy with her baking, Rebecca was now in charge of keeping the books.

As summer drifted into autumn, Rebecca settled into a comfortable routine and Mickey Fox no longer loomed so large in her thoughts.

September brought an abrupt change in the weather. A cold wind blew off the sea and the grey waters were flecked with white horses as rainclouds gathered on the horizon. The salty wind whipped at Rebecca's skirt and tugged tendrils of fair hair free from beneath her bonnet. Shivering, she tugged her shawl tighter around her shoulders.

'We should get back,' Celeste said, shouting to be heard above the clamour of the gulls wheeling overhead. Boats rocked on the swell as water lapped against the sea wall, sending a shower of spray into the air. 'Seth will be wondering what's keeping us.'

Rebecca exhaled in relief. Although her anxiety over Mickey had subsided somewhat, she still wasn't comfortable leaving the sanctity of the Thirsty Mariner for too long, but it had been nice to get some fresh air, and she was pleased Celeste had insisted she accompany her on her errands. She tucked her hand through Celeste's arm as they made their way along the path back to the pub.

'The sea air has put some colour in your cheeks,' Celeste said, holding on to her hat with her free hand. Her charge was blossoming into an attractive woman, she mused, as they turned the corner. Even more reason to keep her well away from the punters, she thought, with a wry tug of her lips.

As they approached the entrance to the pub, Rebecca felt a tingle down her spine. Glancing behind her, she caught sight of a man standing by the harbour wall. He was too far away for her to see his features clearly but as he reached up and touched the brim of his hat, her heart lurched. She stood still, rooted to the spot.

'What is it, Becky?' asked Celeste. 'You're shaking.' She followed Rebecca's gaze.

'It's Mickey Fox,' Rebecca whispered, her dry tongue barely able to form the words.

'Are you sure?' Celeste asked, squinting into the pale light. The man raised a hand in a semblance of greeting before turning and walking away.

'Come on,' Celeste said, her brows knitted in a worried frown. 'Let's get you indoors.' She bustled Rebecca into the pub as the first drops of rain started falling.

'Did you enjoy your walk?' Seth asked from behind the counter where he was polishing glasses while chatting to two fishermen perched on stools at the bar.

'Go through to the kitchen, Becky,' said Celeste, ignoring Seth's question as she peered out of the window.

'What's wrong?' Rebecca heard Seth ask as she went into the kitchen. She took off her shawl, swapping it for the apron hanging on the peg. The customers would be coming in for their dinner soon and she needed to get busy heating the pies she'd baked earlier, but fear had rendered her immobile. She was certain it had been Mickey she'd seen. How had he found her? Fear dried her throat.

'Are you certain that was Mickey Fox?' Celeste asked, her expression grim as she entered the kitchen a few minutes later.

Rebecca nodded, and Celeste sighed. 'What's his game?' She went over to the back door and locked it. 'Just stay out the back here,' she said, biting her bottom lip anxiously. 'Seth got another compliment on your pies,' she said, perhaps to cheer Rebecca. 'Even better than Fred's, according to the customer. You should be very proud of yourself. Fred would be, God rest him.' She patted Rebecca's arm. 'Try not to worry, love,' she said, as she left the kitchen to get back to work.

Rebecca tried to push her fears to the back of her mind as she set to work heating pies and making pans of creamy mashed potato, but every loud noise set her heart racing, terrified that at any moment Mickey would barge through the curtain.

It was gone nine by the time she served the last plate of food. As she washed the dishes, she could hear the dulcet tones of Molly, the singer employed to provide the evening's entertainment, mingling with the clink of glasses, and the rise and fall of deep, masculine voices. As she reached for the tea-towel the curtain was drawn aside and Celeste came into the kitchen, her face white beneath her make-up. 'I think it's him,' she hissed,

111

with a jerk of her head. 'The man we saw this morning. He's at the bar.'

'Mickey Fox is here?' Rebecca blanched, her chest tightening painfully. She looked at Celeste, wild-eyed with fright.

'If you're right and it was Mickey Fox we saw this morning, then, yes, he's here.' She held a finger to her lips. 'Go upstairs and barricade yourself into your room. Quickly.'

Once she was sure Rebecca was safely upstairs, Celeste returned to where the man they assumed to be Mickey Fox was leaning against the bar, nursing a pint of ale. 'You just passing through, sir?' she asked, leaning on the bar top.

'Just here to reclaim something that belongs to me,' Mickey drawled, his lazy smile not reflected in his cold-eyed stare.

Celeste swallowed. 'And what would that be, sir?' she asked nonchalantly.

'I think we both know the answer to that, don't we?' he said, draining his glass.

'Look, we don't want any trouble,' Seth said in a low voice. 'Just give me the girl and I'll be on my way.'

Seth raised an eyebrow, feigning surprise. 'What girl would that be?'

'The girl I saw you with this morning,' Mickey said, directing his gaze towards Celeste.

'You must be mistaken, sir,' Seth said sternly. 'That was our ward. She's the niece of a dear friend who sadly passed away a few months back.'

Mickey grinned. 'Ah, yes, fat Fred Ellis. That stupid Nora thought she could pull a fast one. She should have known better than to try and get one over on me,' he said, pushing his face close to Seth's, all traces of mirth slipping away. 'As for old

Fred, he was on borrowed time. Luckily for me, his dodgy ticker saved me a job.'

Celeste exchanged glances with her husband. Her heart was pounding but she refused to be intimidated by this man. 'I'd like you to leave,' she said hoarsely.

Mickey grinned. 'All right. I'm spending the night at the Green Dragon and heading back to Dartmouth at first light tomorrow. The girl had better be ready to go with me, or else.' He pushed himself off the bar, flashing Seth and Celeste a menacing smile as he turned and walked away. The door slammed shut behind him and Celeste leaned on the bar for support.

'Where is she?' Seth whispered.

'I sent her upstairs. Told her to barricade herself in.'

Seth nodded. 'We need to get her away from here. He's a ruthless bastard. It's clear he'll stop at nothing to get what he wants, and for some reason he wants our Becky.' He scratched his head. 'I mean, he practically admitted murdering that Nora.'

Celeste recalled the newspaper article Rebecca had shown her. Much as it would pain her to let Becky go, she had to put the girl's safety first.

Huddled in the corner of her room, Rebecca stiffened at the sound of footsteps on the other side of her door.

'Becky? It's me, Celeste. It's all right. He's gone. You can unlock the door.'

For a moment, fear paralysed her but when Celeste called her name again, she got stiffly to her feet. Pushing aside the chest of drawers she'd used to barricade the door, Rebecca turned the key. The door sprang open, and she fell sobbing into Celeste's arms.

'Seth and I have agreed that you're not safe here,' Celeste

said, a few minutes later, once Rebecca's terrified sobs had subsided and they were sitting on the edge of her narrow bed. 'That Mickey Fox appears to have some sort of dangerous obsession with you. He won't give up, Becky. You need to get far away from here.'

'I don't want to leave,' Rebecca said, wiping her eyes on her sleeves.

'I know, love,' Celeste murmured. 'And it'll be a wrench seeing you go, but we need to keep you safe. Now, I've got a bit of money saved. It's not much but it'll get you a train ticket to Gillingham. Seth's got family over that way. Seymour, their name is. I'll write it all down for you. Someone will be able to direct you. Tell them Seth sent you. They'll take you on.' She patted Rebecca's hand. 'Pack a few things, then get some sleep. You'll be leaving well before dawn.'

CHAPTER THIRTEEN

Rebecca felt as though she'd barely closed her eyes before Celeste was shaking her awake. 'Seth's going to take you to Paignton,' she said, handing Rebecca a cup of tea. 'I wouldn't be surprised if Mickey's got someone watching the railway station. Seth's checked outside and there doesn't seem to be anyone about, but you'll go out the back way. The cart's already down the street.'

Reaching under her bodice for her locket, Rebecca squeezed it, gaining courage from the feel of the cool metal in her shaking fingers.

'Oh, girl, I shall miss you,' Celeste said, a few minutes later, as she embraced Rebecca in the cold kitchen. Rebecca glanced at the bare table. She would have been getting up to make a start on her pies, had this been a normal day, she thought sadly.

'Thankfully, there's a lot of cloud,' Seth said, donning his heavy coat. 'Come on. I don't want to risk missing the first train.'

Giving Rebecca a final hug, Celeste ushered her out into the darkness. Seth pulled his hat low over his face and motioned to Rebecca to do the same with her shawl. It took her eyes a moment to adjust to the darkness but even then it was hard, with no moonlight to guide their steps. Finally they reached the spot where Seth had tethered the horse. He helped her onto the seat of the cart, and they set off. They travelled in silence, the horse's hoofs echoing in the deserted streets. Rebecca held on to the edge of the narrow wooden seat, misery weighing heavily on her young shoulders. Once again she was contemplating an uncertain future.

It was still dark when they pulled up outside the railway station in Paignton. Several carriages lined the kerb, their lanterns spilling pools of light onto the cobbled street. A horse whinnied softly, pawing the ground, its breath billowing in the chill morning air.

'You've got the piece of paper Celeste gave you?' Seth asked, as they made their way to the ticket office. Rebecca held it up and nodded. 'Good. I haven't seen my cousin Holly in years, but I know she'll see you right.'

Once Seth had paid for Rebecca's ticket, they found a seat in the small waiting room. There were three other passengers, all older gentlemen, who didn't give Rebecca and Seth a second glance. Hunched on the seat beside Seth, again Rebecca clasped her locket, the feel of it against her skin giving her the strength she needed.

'What if Mickey hurts you or Celeste?' She voiced the thought that had been on her mind since Mickey's visit the previous evening.

Seth shuffled in his seat. The same thought had crossed his mind several times during the long journey. The man clearly had no scruples when it came to getting his own way, and he wouldn't put it past him to cause a commotion when he turned up at the pub to find Rebecca gone. He'd given Celeste strict instructions not to unlock the doors until he returned.

'Don't you worry about us,' he assured Rebecca now, with a wry smile. 'Ah, here she comes,' he said, as they heard the shrill whistle of the approaching train. He got to his feet, his hat in his hands. 'Well,' he said awkwardly, 'I wish you all the best, Becky. Maybe you could let us know you're all right, once in a while.'

'I will,' Rebecca promised, her words drowned by the train as it rushed into the station, enveloping them both in a cloud of swirling steam.

Seth held out his hand. 'Goodbye, Becky. God speed.'

They shook hands and, picking up her bag, Rebecca boarded the train. Trying to ignore the dull ache of loss, she went into the first carriage she came to, dumped her bag on the overhead rack and slid into the seat, peering out onto the platform. Through the dissipating steam, she saw Seth walking to the exit. He paused in the doorway, turning towards the train. Their eyes met and he raised his hat, then turned away and disappeared. Rebecca sank back in her seat and unfolded the piece of paper she was still clutching. Holly and Jeremiah Seymour, Elm Tree Farm, Shaftesbury. Seth had seemed confident his cousin would take her in, but what if she didn't? Anxiety gnawed at her insides. What would become of her, alone in a strange place? Blinking back tears, Rebecca took off her locket, opened it and studied the tiny paintings of her parents. Tears filled her eyes. She missed them so much. Her mother would want her to be brave, and she would be, she thought, with a defiant thrust of her chin. She would make a life for herself away from the malevolent shadow of Mickey Fox. She just hoped Seth and Celeste would be all right. She couldn't help but worry.

*

It was just after midday when the train pulled into Gillingham. Rebecca looked out at the tiny station. Only a handful of passengers were waiting to board the London-bound train. The stationmaster strode up and down, waving his red flag.

Rebecca got stiffly to her feet and picked up her bag. She'd had the carriage to herself for most of the journey, for which she was grateful, so now she joined the passengers on their way to the door. She jumped down onto the platform. The late September air was cool after the warmth of the train and she shivered. The stationmaster blew his whistle, signalling that the train was ready to depart. The door to the waiting room flew open and two young men in top hats and tails ran out, hopping aboard just in time.

The train whistled and the stationmaster was enveloped in a cloud of steam. By the time it had cleared, Rebecca was alone on the platform but for the stationmaster. He glanced at his pocket watch. 'Right on time,' he said, flashing Rebecca a smile, as he tucked the watch into his breast pocket. 'Are you all right, miss?' he asked. 'May I be of assistance?'

'I need to get to Elm Tree Farm,' Rebecca replied, holding out her slip of paper.

'Shaftesbury's about five miles from here,' he said, scanning the address and handing it back to her. 'It's straightforward enough. Just follow the road. You'll see the signpost. It's about an hour and a half's walk. This time of day, you're bound to get a lot of passing traffic. Someone'll offer you a ride.' He grinned. 'It's quite a steep climb, once you get closer.'

Thanking him, Rebecca went out onto the busy street. The pavement was teeming with pedestrians and a small black and tan dog ran in and out of the line of wagons and carts driving slowly along the wide road. A woman was sweeping the steps outside the hotel opposite. She nodded at Rebecca, who managed a shy smile in return. She spotted a signpost on the corner and crossed the street. 'Shaftesbury, 5 miles,' it proclaimed.

Her stomach rumbled noisily. She'd eaten the last of the pies Celeste had packed for her. Ignoring her hunger pangs, she set off at a brisk pace, the bustling town soon giving way to a winding tree-lined lane. Leaves tinged with red and gold, the trees resounded with birdsong. She passed cottages and farms along the way, and the occasional grand house. At first the incline was gradual but within minutes she was panting heavily, and perspiration trickled down her spine. Wiping beads of sweat from her brow with the back of her hand, she took a moment to catch her breath, leaning against a sturdy tree trunk to gaze up the steep hill rising in front of her. Above the trees she could make out roof tops and a church spire. Dispirited at the prospect of the climb ahead of her, she started on her weary way. At the sound of a cart coming up behind her, she moved to the side, stepping onto the dusty verge as a dapper little piebald pony came alongside her.

'You need a ride?' called a voice. Turning, she saw a dark-haired, broad-shouldered lad, a couple of years older than herself, grinning down at her from the seat on the cart. 'I don't bite,' he added, when she hesitated. 'Ben Troke.' He thrust out a large, workworn hand.

After a moment, Rebecca reached up and shook it. 'Becky Wheeler.'

'I'm pleased to meet you, Becky Wheeler,' Ben said. 'Hop up.' Rebecca grasped his outstretched hand, and he hauled her up beside him. 'You thirsty?' he asked, reaching under the seat to retrieve a stone jug.

Thanking him, Rebecca pulled out the stopper and swallowed several mouthfuls of warm, sweet cider, then handed it back to him. Ben gulped a mouthful, replaced the stopper and shoved it back under the seat. 'Whereabouts are you headed?' he asked, urging the pony onwards.

'Elm Tree Farm,' Rebecca replied.

Ben gave her a quizzical look. ' I live there. It's where I work. I'm on my way back now.' His brows dipped. 'Aunt Holly didn't say they were expecting anyone.'

'Mrs Seymour is your aunt?' she exclaimed in excitement. 'Do you know Seth and Celeste Mathews?'

To her disappointment, Ben was shaking his head. 'I can't say I do. And she's not my real aunt. I'm a workhouse boy. Aunt Holly and her husband, Uncle Jerry, took me on when I was twelve. Three years I've been with them now. They're good people. So, how do you know the Seymours?'

'I don't,' Rebecca admitted. 'They're relatives or friends of Seth and Celeste Mathews. Seth, my friend, said they'd make me welcome.'

'He's right there,' Ben said, leaning forward to give the pony's neck an encouraging pat as the road climbed even steeper. 'Hearts of gold, they have, especially Aunt Holly. They'll see you right.'

Ben echoing Seth's words acted as a balm to Rebecca's troubled thoughts. 'Were you a long time in the workhouse?' she asked, after a few minutes of silence had passed between them.

'I was born there. My mother died when I was two. I never knew my father,' Ben said, with a rueful smile. 'Don't even know his name.'

'I'm sorry,' responded Rebecca. 'I lost my parents, too, and my two brothers. I'm the only one left.'

'As we're both orphans, we'd better stick together, hadn't we?' Ben said, giving her a lopsided smile.

She was still reeling at how quickly her life had changed yet again, but Ben's cheerfulness was infectious and Rebecca smiled back.

It was market day in Shaftesbury, the streets crammed with livestock and stalls. The stench of animal dung hung on the dusty air as Ben manoeuvred the pony and cart along the crowded street. He turned into a wide avenue lined with terraced cottages and down a winding road, which led back to open farmland. After the bellowing and bleating of penned animals, the relative tranquillity was welcome.

'Elm Tree Farm is just along here,' Ben said, as they turned onto a narrow tree-lined track. A breeze ruffled the branches, sending a flurry of early autumn leaves floating onto the grass verge. The entrance to Elm Tree Farm was just a few yards further on.

With a whinny of joy, the pony trotted through the open gateway and along a wide track lined on either side by hawthorn bushes. As they approached the red-brick farmhouse, Rebecca's apprehension grew. What if, despite what Seth and Ben had told her, the Seymours didn't like her? Where would she go? The knot of anxiety in her stomach tightened as they pulled up in front of the house. Smoke curled from its two chimneys, and the six windows reflected the clouds chasing across the afternoon sky. Chickens clucked and scratched in the dirt and two medium-sized dogs came bounding around the corner of the house, barking and wagging their tails. They circled the cart, leaping up at Rebecca as a woman came to the door, wiping her hands on her apron. She was of medium height with light brown hair, pinned back in a bun, and a weathered complexion. 'Hello,' she said, giving Rebecca a friendly smile as Ben hushed the dogs.

'Aunt Holly, this is Becky Wheeler,' Ben said, engaging the

brake. 'She's a friend of your cousin Seth.' He leaped to the ground, pushing the dogs away good-naturedly.

'You know Seth?' Holly smiled. 'Then you are very welcome. How is my cousin?' she asked, as Rebecca jumped to the ground.

'He and Celeste are very well,' Rebecca replied, hoping fervently that that was still the truth.

'That's good to know. So, what brings you up here?' she asked. 'Not my business,' she added, seeing Rebecca's hesitation. 'Come inside. I've just made a fresh pot of tea. Oh, Ned, Jim,' she chastised the two dogs, which were dancing around Rebecca, tongues protruding comically, 'leave the girl alone. Just give them a pat and they'll be happy.' Rebecca did so and the dogs fell into step behind Holly, as she ushered Rebecca into the kitchen. 'After you've seen to Dolly,' she said to Ben over her shoulder, 'fetch Uncle Jerry, would you? Tell him we've got company.'

'Yes, ma'am.' Ben gave Rebecca a wink.

'Have a seat,' Holly said, fetching three mugs from the dresser. Rebecca pulled out a chair and sat down at the large table, tucking her bag between her feet. There was a gleaming range at one end of the room, an armchair at either side. A pipe and battered tobacco tin rested on the arm of one, which Rebecca assumed to belong to Holly's husband. She felt a twinge of anxiety at the thought of meeting him, but Holly's warm welcome had comforted her. While Holly poured the tea, chatting amiably about nothing in particular, Rebecca took in her surroundings. Handwoven rugs were scattered over the slate floor and bunches of dried herbs hung from the low ceiling. There was a vase of lavender on one of the broad window-sills, its heady perfume filling the room. On the other, a large ginger cat snoozed in the sunlight. It seemed to Rebecca that the kitchen exuded warmth and ease.

The dogs had settled in the doorway where they were snoring softly, noses resting on their large paws.

'Are your parents alive?' Holly asked, pushing a mug of tea to Rebecca as she joined her at the table.

'No, ma'am,' Rebecca replied.

'I'm sorry to hear that. How old are you?'

'Thirteen, ma'am.'

'Well, I must say, your arrival is quite providential.' Holly smiled. 'The girl we had working for us recently left to be married. If you want it, the job's yours. You'll get your board and lodging and a small wage. Can you read and write?'

'Yes, ma'am, and I can reckon figures.'

Holly's smile widened. 'That's good to know. I could do with someone to help with the household accounts. And you can call me Aunt Holly. Ah, that'll be Jeremiah, my husband,' she said, as the dogs leaped to their feet, barking.

Moments later a broad-shouldered man appeared in the doorway.

'Hello, Jerry,' Holly said, getting to her feet. 'Come and meet Becky.'

'Pleasure to meet you, Becky,' Jeremiah said, giving his wife an affectionate kiss on the cheek and removing his hat as he turned his attention to Rebecca. His eyes reflected his smile, and Rebecca felt the last of her unease slip away.

'Have you time for a cup of tea?' Holly asked, picking up the teapot.

'I have. I've left Kenneth and Ben mending the fence in the far field.' He laid his hat on the table and pulled out a chair. 'So, you know old Seth, then?' he said.

Rebecca nodded. 'Yes, sir.'

'He's got a good heart, has Seth.' Jeremiah smiled. 'I expect you've a story to tell but you can do that in your own time.'

'I've offered her Millie's old job,' Holly told him, passing Jeremiah a mug of tea.

'Thank you, my dear. You'll find us a decent lot,' he said, as Holly disappeared into the pantry, returning a moment later with a fruit cake. She cut Rebecca a large slice and put it on a plate, sliding it towards her.

It was only as she inhaled the rich fruity aroma that Rebecca remembered how hungry she was. She bit into the cake with relish.

'You've already met Ben, of course,' Jeremiah said, stirring sugar into his mug. 'Then, there's our boy, Kenneth. He's fifteen, same as Ben.' Jeremiah grinned at Rebecca over the rim of his mug. 'That taste good?'

She swallowed quickly. 'Yes, sir,' she replied, wiping crumbs from her mouth with the back of her hand.

'She makes the best fruit cake, don't you, Holly, my love?' Jeremiah chuckled.

'It's what made you fall in love with me in the first place,' Holly said, joining them at the table. 'I was working as a cook in the big house not far from here. Jeremiah came to deliver the milk and I offered him a slice of my fruit cake and he was smitten.' Holly laughed.

She had a pleasant laugh, Rebecca decided. She felt more relaxed than she had for a long time. She was far enough away that Mickey would never find her, and the Seymours seemed kind people. If their son, Kenneth, was as nice as Ben, they'd get on like a house on fire.

'Can you cook?' Holly asked.

'I make a good meat pie,' replied Rebecca, modestly.

'Do you now?' Jeremiah smiled. 'Well, we'll have to put you to the test some time. I love a good pie.' He patted his rounded stomach. 'You'll have to be a master pie maker to top my Holly. Her pastry is second to none.'

'Don't tease the girl,' Holly chided him mildly. 'Take no notice of him, Becky. I'm sure we can rustle up a tasty meat pie between us. Now, would you like another slice of cake to tide you over until supper time?'

CHAPTER FOURTEEN

'I'd better get back to work,' Jeremiah said, draining his mug of the last drop of tea. 'I'll see you ladies at supper time.'

'It'll be on the table when you're ready,' Holly assured him. She turned to Rebecca. 'Come, I'll show you around.' She led Rebecca through a doorway into a cosy parlour. Framed photographs and paintings adorned the rose-patterned walls, and the window looked out onto barns and outbuildings. 'The stairs are through here,' she said, opening a door beside a large dresser crammed with trinkets. 'Through there is the dining room,' she added, indicating a closed door at the foot of the stairs. 'We only use it at Christmas or if the vicar comes to dinner.'

Rebecca followed Holly up the steep staircase and through the door she held open.

'This is my room?' she asked, in amazement, looking at Holly for confirmation.

'Yes,' replied Holly, smiling at Rebecca's obvious delight.

Rebecca took in the bed tucked under the sloping ceiling and covered with a patchwork quilt in various shades of blue, the white-painted wardrobe, and the chest of drawers that stood under a window, affording her a view of rolling hills and fields. 'It's lovely,' she breathed.

'Millie, our maid, made the quilt,' Holly said, walking to the wardrobe. 'I said she should take it with her but she wanted to leave it as a gift. She made a similar one for her bottom drawer. You've plenty of space for your things,' she added, opening the wardrobe.

Rebecca blushed. Her bag contained a change of underwear and her spare dress.

Seeing her discomfort, Holly smiled. 'Leave your bag here – you can unpack later – and we'll make a start on the supper. Once we've eaten I'll show you around the farm. We work hard here, but we have fun too. I hope you'll be happy with us, Becky, for as long as you decide to stay.'

Rebecca couldn't think of anywhere else she'd rather be, except back at Leonard's Bay with her parents and brothers. Her chest tightened at the thought of them, but she forced away her sadness, and smiled.

Holly and Rebecca spent a happy couple of hours in the kitchen preparing the evening meal. Just before six, as the low sun cast long shadows across the yard, the dogs bounded into the yard, their arrival heralding the return of the men. Jeremiah and Ben came into the kitchen, laughing. They were followed by a tall, lanky young man with a shock of dark brown hair. He leaned against the doorframe, regarding Rebecca with his dark, brooding gaze.

'This is our son, Kenneth,' Jeremiah said, sitting down to unlace his boots. 'Kenny, this is Becky, who I told you about.'

'Hello, Kenny,' Rebecca said shyly, from the other side of the table.

'Becky.' Kenneth nodded. 'Welcome,' he said, shuffling his feet awkwardly. He didn't exude the same warmth and friendliness as his parents, but Rebecca assumed he was shy.

A few minutes later, after Ben and Kenneth had disappeared into the scullery to wash their hands, Jeremiah confirmed her suspicion: 'Don't mind Kenny if he's a bit uncomfortable around you,' he said, with a reassuring smile. 'He's a bit gawky around girls, especially pretty ones,' he added, as Rebecca flushed.

'We had a bit of trouble with him and Millie,' Holly confided in a whisper. 'He developed a liking for her,' she said, picking up the bowl of steaming potatoes and dumping it on the table. 'It was difficult, especially as Millie was engaged. It was a relief to everyone when she left. Kenneth's a good boy. A bit too sensitive. Wears his heart on his sleeve,' she continued, lifting the roasted rabbit from the oven and placing it on an iron trivet as the three men came back into the kitchen.

Conversation and laughter abounded around the supper table. The food was delicious and, despite the two slices of cake, Rebecca managed a second helping.

'I like to see a girl who enjoys her food,' Jeremiah remarked, nodding at Rebecca's clean plate. He pushed his aside. 'What's for pud?'

After the apple pie and custard had been served and eaten, Jeremiah and the boys went out to the barn to see to the animals, leaving Holly and Rebecca to deal with the dishes.

Once everything was clean and had been put away, Holly took off her apron and suggested to Rebecca that they might go outside for a little fresh air. It was a mild evening and the moon was bright, a million stars twinkling overhead as they walked across the yard, passing the barn where the chickens were roosting. Dolly shifted in her stall as they walked past and whinnied in the hope of a treat.

'Ah, sweet Dolly,' Holly said, running her hands up and down the pony's long nose while ferreting a sugar lump from her skirt pocket. 'You're a love, aren't you?' The pony whickered softly and bent her head to her manger.

They left Dolly to her grazing and continued their walk. Holly showed Rebecca the dairy and milking shed. Cows lowed in the distance. 'In Jerry's grandfather's day, they had a host of people working on the farm. Several families lived in those cottages along there.' In the ghostly moonlight, Rebecca could just make out a row of stone houses beyond the trees. 'Then his fortunes took a turn for the worse, and he had to lay people off. It was a terrible time, by all accounts. We run the farm on a much smaller scale now.' Holly smiled.

'I would have liked a daughter,' Holly continued, as they strolled along a track that led to woodland. 'I hoped we'd have a houseful of babies but, sadly, it never happened.' She gave Rebecca a wistful smile. 'I think that's why we like to help those less fortunate. What Kenneth calls my waifs and strays.' She turned to Rebecca, her gaze earnest. 'I want you to feel that this is your home, Becky. You're welcome to stay for as long as you like.'

'Thank you, ma'am . . . Aunt Holly.'

'Good girl.' Holly shivered. 'It's turning chilly. I think we should head back. I'll make us a nice mug of cocoa before we retire for the night.'

'You look exhausted, girl,' Holly said, fifteen minutes later, as she handed Rebecca her cocoa. 'Why don't you take it up with you?'

Hardly able to keep her eyes open, Rebecca did as Holly suggested. As she set the mug on the nightstand, she heard voices outside. Crossing to the window, she peered out. The moon was bright, illuminating the yard as though it were daylight.

'Goodnight, Ben,' she heard Uncle Jerry say, as he reached down to scratch one of the dogs behind the ear. Ben's reply was lost in the sigh of the breeze rustling the ivy that clung to the ancient stonework, but she watched him cross the yard, the dogs following at his heels. Holly had told Rebecca that Ben had a room above the stable, and that the dogs preferred to sleep in the straw near Dolly. She heard the door to the house shut and the heavy tread of footsteps on the stairs, then Jeremiah and Kenneth whispering their goodnights. She crept back to bed. She pulled the covers under her chin, listening to the house creak and settle. Then all was silent. Tired as she was, sleep eluded her. She wondered about Seth and Celeste and sent up a fervent prayer for their safety as her thoughts turned to Nora, Fred, and her family. She was overcome by an overwhelming sense of loss. Blinking back tears, she reached under the patched nightdress Aunt Holly had given her and clasped her locket. Just having it in her hand made her feel closer to her parents. She missed them and her brothers so much . . .

CHAPTER FIFTEEN

1883

'Becky? Becky, where are you?' Rebecca bit her lip to stop herself laughing at Ben's growing frustration. Leaning back on her elbows, she peered up at the sunlight streaming through the willow fronds. The clump of trees offered welcome relief from the heat of the day. She rolled onto her side, wriggling her fingers in the cool water of the stream. Dappled sunlight danced on the water burbling over sun-bleached pebbles.

'Come on, Becky. We're going to be late back,' she heard Ben grumble. 'It's all right for you. You can't do anything wrong in the Seymours' eyes. I'm the one who'll get a flea in my ear from Uncle Jerry if I'm late for work.'

Deciding she'd teased him long enough, Rebecca got to her feet. What Ben said was true. She'd been at Elm Tree Farm for almost four years and was treated like one of the family. Both Jeremiah and Holly doted on her, and Aunt Holly had told her on numerous occasions that she loved Rebecca as the daughter she'd never had.

Getting to her feet, Rebecca dried her hand on the grass,

and pushed through the curtain of green fronds, smiling at Ben, who was standing, hands on hips, beside the pony and cart. 'Come on,' he said, with an air of exasperation. 'I'll get what-for if I'm late.'

'Uncle Jerry only pretends to be harder on you because Kenneth's jealous,' Rebecca said, falling into step beside him, as they made their way along the rugged track. He had no need to hold Dolly's reins for the pony knew her way home. The cart creaked as its wheels jolted over the uneven ground. Nettles and cow parsley brushed Rebecca's skirt. The meadow was awash with buttercups as high as her knees and the June sun was warm on her face.

'I don't know what Kenneth has to be jealous about.' Ben snorted, pulling a face. 'I don't know what's come over him lately. He's changed such a lot. We used to be such good friends but now, well . . .' he shrugged '. . . we're almost like strangers.'

'I know,' Rebecca agreed. 'He never wants to come out with us any more.' She sighed, lifting her heavy plait to allow what little breeze there was to cool the back of her neck. After a wet May, June was turning out to be a scorcher. 'We used to have such fun,' she said, thinking how, until recently, the three of them had always spent their free time together.

As they reached the fork in the road, Rebecca paused to gaze back over the rolling hills shimmering in the hazy light, totally unaware of how striking she looked with her flaxen hair framing a face tanned the colour of honey, blue eyes sparkling with fun. Ben found himself having to look away: the sight of her stirred a longing deep inside him. For some time now, he'd been fighting a growing attraction towards Rebecca. She was like a sister to him, he reminded himself, and was his employer's ward. As such, she was out of bounds. Though he hadn't said as much to Rebecca, he had an inkling that Kenneth's sudden aversion to spending time in their company and his sudden jealousy of Ben was down to the fact that he, too, was developing feelings for Rebecca. The way Kenneth watched her hadn't gone unnoticed by Ben and the realization that he and Kenneth might be rivals for Rebecca's affections gave him a hollow feeling in his stomach. It stood to reason that Kenneth would be a fairer prospect for Rebecca than himself. After all, Kenneth would inherit the farm one day.

'Penny for them.' Rebecca slapped his arm.

'Save your money.' Ben grinned. 'My thoughts aren't worth a penny.' He ran his hand through his thick, dark hair and Rebecca's stomach did a little flip.

'Come on,' she said, glancing away so Ben wouldn't notice her confusion. 'I promised Aunt Holly I'd prepare supper tonight, seeing as she's a bit under the weather.'

'We can't go any faster than Dolly.' Ben laughed, urging the pony onwards. 'Come on, old girl. There'll be a carrot for you at the end of it.'

'You're a good girl, Becky,' Holly said, as Rebecca adjusted her pillows. 'Thank you.' She coughed, gasping as she fought to draw breath between the spasms.

'Rest now, Aunt Holly,' Rebecca said, her face creased in a worried frown. 'I'll bring you up some supper in a bit. Would you like another cup of tea in the meantime?'

Holly shook her head. 'A sip of water, please,' she croaked.

Rebecca filled the glass from the jug beside the bed and held it to her lips.

'Thank you. My throat gets so dry,' Holly wheezed.

'I hope you feel better soon,' Rebecca said. She perched on the edge of the bed, stroking the pink and white patchwork quilt. A soft breeze stirred the floral-patterned curtains. It was a pretty room, light and airy. The walls were covered with large pink cabbage roses and the bare floorboards hidden beneath a thick cream rug.

Holly shrugged. 'You know how I get, Becky,' she said, leaning back against the pillows with a sigh. 'I'll be right as rain in a day or so.'

'You'd better be.' Rebecca stood up. 'You won't want to miss the summer ball.'

'I shall be perfectly well by then,' Holly promised, managing a weak smile.

Rebecca kissed her forehead, picked up the cup and saucer and carried them downstairs to the kitchen. A fly buzzed lazily along the windowsill, and the gentle lowing of the cows making their way to the milking shed drifted through the open window.

'How is she?' Jeremiah asked, looking up from lacing his boots.

'I believe she's over the worst,' Rebecca replied, putting the dirty crockery into the sink.

'That's good to hear,' Jeremiah said, with a sigh of relief, running his hand through his thick hair. 'She hasn't been this bad for a while,' he said, standing up. 'I wish she'd let me call the doctor, but you know Holly.' He flashed Rebecca a rueful grin. 'She's a stubborn old mare and can't abide spending money on herself. If it was you or one of the boys, no expense would be spared.'

'She's determined to be able to attend the summer ball,' Rebecca assured him.

Jeremiah smiled. 'I expect she's told you we used to attend the ball when we were courting.'

'More than once.'

'She was the prettiest girl in the district,' he continued dreamily, as his mind travelled back through the mists of time. 'Her father was a clockmaker, and I was just a clumsy, bashful farmer's son. In my wildest dreams, I never imagined she'd look at me twice, but she did, and I've thanked my lucky stars ever since.' He gave a nostalgic sigh and picked up his hat. 'Right, I'm off to do the milking.'

'Supper will be ready by the time you get back,' Rebecca promised. She took her apron from its hook and tied it around her waist. Shooing away a fly, she went into the pantry to retrieve the meat and potato pie she'd made earlier and popped it into the oven. Her life had certainly changed for the better since she'd come to live at Elm Tree Farm, she mused, standing in the open doorway and savouring the quiet tranquillity of the Sunday afternoon. She wrote to Celeste and Seth regularly and, to her relief, they seemed well. If there had been any trouble with Mickey Fox after she had left the pub, they'd never mentioned it, and as time passed, she'd finally let go of her fear of the man.

Before any thoughts of Mickey Fox could take root in her mind, she forced them away. It was too beautiful a day to be spoiled by the ghosts of her past. She fingered the locket around her neck. She still missed her family, but her grief wasn't as sharp as it had been, and she found comfort in the thought that, had her mother and Aunt Holly ever met, they would have been friends. Her mother would certainly be very grateful for the way in which Holly and Jeremiah had welcomed Rebecca into their family.

Her thoughtful meanderings were broken by the sound of approaching voices. Beyond the hedge, the cows were returning to their field, their hoofs churning up clouds of dust.

'Becky.' Kenneth hailed her. He pushed open the gate and loped towards her, his cheeks flushed. 'This is for you,' he said, pulling a small package from his trouser pocket.

'Oh, thank you,' Rebecca said, with pleasure, unwrapping the brown paper to reveal a length of royal-blue velvet ribbon. 'It's very pretty.'

'I thought it would go well with your fair hair,' he said, his cheeks turning a darker shade of red.

'I shall wear it to the summer ball,' she said, running the ribbon through her fingers. 'It will match my new dress.'

Kenneth cleared his throat. He looked at his feet, his fingers tugging his shirt collar as he shuffled awkwardly. 'Will you be my partner at the ball this year?'

Rebecca frowned in confusion. 'Aren't we all going together as usual?'

Kenneth kicked at a stone, sending it skittering across the ground. 'I thought you might like to go with me,' he mumbled. 'As a couple.'

Heat rose to Rebecca's cheeks. 'You mean like courting?' she said, with a twinge of discomfort. Kenneth was like a big brother to her. She looked up to him but she'd never considered him as anything other than a friend.

'Look, if you're not interested, just say so,' he snapped, as Rebecca continued to hesitate. 'I suppose you're going with Ben. Is that it?'

'No.' Rebecca's frowned. 'Ben and I are friends. Kenny, what has got into you, lately? We used to have such fun together and—'

They were interrupted by the dogs bounding through the gate, followed by Jeremiah and Ben, who were laughing together. Rebecca's eyes lit up at the sight of Ben.

'Oh, forget it,' Kenneth snapped, fists clenching in angry disappointment. Barely acknowledging his father, he turned abruptly and stalked back to the house.

'I'm starving,' Jeremiah said, rubbing his hands together.

'Me, too,' Ben concurred, flashing Rebecca a grin.

Kenneth's behaviour had unsettled her, but she pulled herself together, smiling at the two men. 'It's just about ready,' she said. 'I've got to drain the potatoes, so it should be on the table by the time you've washed.'

CHAPTER SIXTEEN

Rebecca held the dress up to the light. Jeremiah had arrived home from market one afternoon with yards of the beautiful royal-blue material, and before Holly had become ill, she and Rebecca had worked on it every evening. Not being adept with a needle, Rebecca had had to wait until Holly was better before they could finish the dress. True to her hopeful prediction, Holly had recovered with days to spare and, though she'd been weak, she'd been determined to complete Rebecca's dress in time for the ball. Rebecca couldn't wait to wear it in a week's time. With a sigh, she folded it back into its tissue wrapping, and laid it in the wardrobe.

She was about to hurry downstairs when she heard voices coming from Holly and Jeremiah's bedroom.

'I asked Becky if she'd accompany me to the ball,' she heard Kenneth say. She hadn't meant to eavesdrop but, hearing her own name, she couldn't help but hover outside the slightly open door to hear Holly's response.

'Did she say yes?'

'No,' Kenneth replied sulkily.

'I won't pretend I haven't entertained the notion of you and

Becky marrying one day,' Holly said, causing Rebecca to catch her breath. 'Give her time, Kenny. She's still young.'

'She's old enough to start courting,' Kenneth protested sullenly. 'You and Father were courting when you were her age. She'll end up an old maid if she's not careful.'

'She's seventeen, Kenny, hardly an old maid,' Holly said, with a smile in her voice. 'Give her time. Let's all go to the ball together, as we always do. See what transpires on the night.'

Kenneth's reply was lost in the banging of the back door. The dogs started barking, and Rebecca took the opportunity to slip past the bedroom and hurry down the stairs, grateful for the cacophony covering her footsteps.

Ben was on his knees on the kitchen floor, hastily gathering up the logs that were scattered around him. 'I dropped the firewood.'

'And set the dogs off,' Rebecca said, with a mock-stern glare in his direction. She helped Ben gather up the wood, her mind reeling over what she'd heard. The idea that Aunt Holly nurtured hopes about her and Kenneth only added to the discomfort she felt about Kenneth's invitation a few days earlier.

Quiet now, the dogs flopped on the stone doorstep, sighing heavily as they laid their noses on their paws.

'Is everything all right?' Holly called from upstairs.

'Yes. I'm sorry, Aunt Holly,' Ben called back, winking at Rebecca.

Footsteps sounded overhead and Kenneth came down the stairs.

'Kenny,' Ben said, 'you could have given me a hand with the wood. Where were you?'

Kenneth scowled. 'I was talking to Mother,' he said, 'not that it's any of your business.' Rebecca and Ben exchanged glances. Ben opened his mouth, as if he were about to say something, but before he could speak, Kenneth turned to Rebecca. 'Shouldn't you be in the dairy?'

'I'm on my way,' replied Rebecca, ducking her head to disguise her blushes. She didn't want Kenneth to know she'd been listening to his and Holly's conversation.

'Come on.' Kenneth nudged Ben with his shoulder. He grinned, some of his old good humour returning. 'You need to get that milk up to town. Can't have it hanging around for too long in this heat.' He reached for his boots.

'I'm on my way,' replied Ben. He looked across at Rebecca. 'Do you fancy coming up with me? We could make a day of it.'

'I'd like that.' Rebecca smiled. 'If Aunt Holly gives me permission, then, yes, please. We could have dinner at the Knowle Arms.'

'Hey, that's not fair,' blurted Kenneth, pouting like a petulant child.

'Come with us,' Rebecca felt obliged to say, though she was looking forward to spending time alone with Ben.

'I can't.' Kenneth scowled. 'Father wants me to mend the fence. Old Whitcher's been complaining about our cows getting into his field.' His expression darkened as he stood up. 'Are you sure you can be spared from the dairy?' he said, glowering at Rebecca. 'Mother hasn't long recovered. We don't want her to fall ill again.'

'Oh, I didn't think,' Rebecca said. 'Perhaps I should stay,' she told Ben.

'It wouldn't hurt to ask Aunt Holly,' Ben said.

'Ask me what?' Holly said, descending the stairs.

She looked so much better, Rebecca reflected. She had some colour in her cheeks, though the dark circles under her eyes remained.

'Would it be all right if Becky came to market with me?' Ben asked. Holly's gaze flitted between the three of them, coming to rest on Kenneth. Her brow puckered. 'You're not going?'

'Father needs me in the fields,' Kenneth replied reluctantly.

His mother gave him a sympathetic glance. 'I suppose I can manage,' she said, pursing her lips. The recent tension between the three young people hadn't gone unnoticed by Holly and she was astute enough to know that Becky was at the centre of it. She did hope that being rivals for the girl's affections wouldn't destroy Kenneth and Ben's friendship. Of course she hoped Becky would choose her Kenneth. She'd love nothing more than to welcome Becky as a daughter-in-law, but the girl must choose her own path. She sighed, consoling herself that Becky was still young. There was plenty of time for her to make up her mind.

'Are you sure?' Rebecca asked now, her brow crumpled in concern. 'I'd hate you to have a relapse.'

'I shall manage,' Holly assured her with a smile. 'In fact, you'll be doing me a favour. There are some things I need,' she added, going into the parlour. 'I'll write you a list while you change into something more suitable.' Rebecca looked at her in surprise. 'Well,' Aunt Holly said, smiling at her over her shoulder, 'that dress might be suitable for working in the dairy, but for town? I don't think so. Run along and change.'

'I'll load up in the meantime,' Ben said, putting on his hat as he went out of the door, Kenneth close behind him.

From her bedroom window, Rebecca watched the two young men cross the yard. Jeremiah was hitching Dolly to the cart. Ben and Kenneth began to load the milk churns onto it. While she found unsettling Aunt Holly's hope that she and Kenny might one day marry, she couldn't help feeling sorry for him. She didn't often accompany the boys to Shaftesbury on market

141

day, but when she had gone with them, they'd always had such a great time. It was such a shame that their relationships seemed to be altering in a way she didn't understand. Why couldn't things stay the same? she pondered, opening her wardrobe and taking out a blue and white sprigged dress she and Aunt Holly had made last summer. She shrugged off her faded work dress and pulled the other over her head, twisting this way and that as she buttoned it up the back. She took the ribbon Kenneth had given her and tied it into her hair, standing back to admire her reflection in the mirror. She looked quite the young lady, she thought, with a smile. She washed her hands and face in the small bowl on the dresser and hurried back downstairs.

'Ben's waiting with the cart,' Holly said, shoving the list at her and shooing her out of the door. 'Have a lovely time.'

'I will.' Rebecca snatched her straw hat from the hook by the door.

'You look very nice,' Jeremiah said, helping her into the cart with one hand as he held on to Dolly's reins with the other. The milk churns were in the back. The dogs milled about, tails wagging, tongues lolling. It was early but the day promised to be hot. Already the sun was burning through the misty haze that shrouded the nearby hills. Rebecca didn't really need her shawl. She unwound it from around her shoulders and laid it across her lap. Dolly pawed the ground impatiently, the chickens clucking indignantly as they scurried out of her way. Swifts dived and swooped across the yard, watched benignly by the cat, lurking in the shadows.

'Get the best price you can,' Jeremiah said, handing the reins to Ben as he climbed up onto the seat beside Rebecca. 'We'll see you back this afternoon.'

'Well, this is nice,' said Ben, as they pulled into the narrow lane. The verges were thick with cow parsley, nettles and fox-gloves as high as the hedges. The air smelt sweet and earthy, the morning dew sparkling in the early-morning sunlight. 'I'm pleased you decided to come. I was hoping you would.'

'Like old times,' Rebecca said, picking at a small thread in her shawl. She must remember to darn it later, she thought, before it became a hole. 'It's a shame Kenneth couldn't come.'

Ben couldn't help but think that, given the way things had been between them lately, Kenneth's presence would have spoiled the day. He smiled. He was certainly relishing spending time alone with Rebecca again.

They chatted amiably as the cart made its way slowly up the winding hill. They were held up several times by flocks of sheep and cattle being driven to market, and the stench of animal dung hung heavily on the air.

Rebecca held her shawl to her nose as they entered the town, joining the throng of carts, wagons and animals processing ahead of them. 'I'd forgotten how noisy and smelly it is on market day,' Rebecca said ruefully as Ben pulled up alongside the kerb. He tied Dolly to a hitching post and Rebecca helped him unload the churns. It was heavy work, and she was perspiring profusely by the time the last was off the cart.

Dust and chaff swirled in clouds above the pens of cows, sheep and pigs, the air full of grunting, bellowing and squealing. Chickens clucked in their baskets and truckles of yellow-skinned cheese sweated in the heat. Market day was when people from the outlying farms and villages could socialize and people sat around on bales of straw, sipping mugs of cider as they caught up on the latest news or haggled over prices.

'Come on.' Ben held out his hand. 'We've a while before the auction starts. Let's have a wander around the stalls.'

Rebecca took his hand as they made for the stalls lining the high street. Shopkeepers were out sweeping the pavements and shovelling horse manure from in front of their doorsteps. Wending their way between the horse-drawn traffic in the street, Rebecca and Ben surveyed the many stalls. 'Bet they don't taste as good as yours,' Ben whispered, as they passed a stall selling meat pies. Rebecca gave his hand a squeeze. Dear Fred. He'd have been proud to know her pies were so praised. He'd certainly taught her well.

'Perhaps I might bring some to sell next month,' Rebecca said, only half joking, as they paused to inspect a display of lace in the window of the haberdashery.

'You'd make a killing,' Ben said. 'See what Aunt Holly thinks. I'm sure she'd be all for the idea.'

'A pretty trinket for your sweetheart, young man?' an elderly woman with wiry silver-grey hair leaned across a stall crammed with knick-knacks.

'Oh,' Rebecca said, feeling herself blush. 'We're not—'

'I'll take a closer look at that brooch, please,' Ben interrupted, leaning closer to the old woman. She beamed, displaying a mouthful of crooked, blackened teeth.

'Ben,' Rebecca hissed, as the woman ferreted the brooch from its nest of blue satin and handed it to him.

'Hush,' Ben murmured, inspecting it, his thick brows meeting across the bridge of his nose as he frowned in concentration. 'I'll take it, thank you.'

The woman cackled, her fingers reaching out to snatch the coins Ben dropped into her palm. 'Pleasure doing business with you, sir.'

'Ben, you shouldn't have.' Rebecca frowned as Ben gave it to her. She held it in her hand. It was a cheap trinket, tin that had been beaten and fashioned into an intricate rose-pattern. 'I'm not your sweetheart.'

'No,' Ben pursed his lips. 'Would you like to be?'

Rebecca blushed.

'You must know how I feel about you, Becky,' Ben said, his dark eyes regarding her hopefully. He took her hand, drawing her away from the busy stall. 'Could you be interested in me?' he asked. 'Or does your heart belong to Kenneth? I know he likes you.' He tried to smile but failed. 'I'm sorry, Becky. I'd like us to start courting but if you prefer Kenneth, then tell me so.'

'I overheard Aunt Holly and Kenny talking this morning,' Rebecca said, after a pause. 'She's hoping Kenny and I will marry . . . Oh.' She groaned. 'Why do things have to change? We were so happy as we were, the three of us.'

'It's called growing up,' Ben said, stony-faced. 'What about you? Would you like to marry Kenny and be mistress of Elm Tree?'

'I don't care about that at all,' Rebecca said, indignant. 'I look upon Kenneth as a friend, nothing more,'

'And me?' Ben asked earnestly. 'Do you think you can ever look upon me as anything more than a friend?'

'I . . . um . . .' Rebecca stammered, embarrassed to have been put on the spot. She looked away. To be truthful, she wasn't sure how she felt about Ben. She was fond of him, of course, but recently she'd found herself taking more care over her appearance and her stomach did funny little flutters whenever she saw him. And on Sundays of late, it had been just herself and Ben and she'd enjoyed it.

'Your hesitation gives me hope,' he said. 'I shall spend the rest of today trying to win your heart. After all, faint heart never won fair maiden.'

'You're daft.' Rebecca smiled. 'Here.' She held out the brooch. 'Pin this on, then.'

Ben obliged, his hands steady as he placed the brooch just above her left breast. 'It looks nice on you,' he said, standing back to admire it.

Rebecca thanked him. It was a pretty piece of costume jewellery and, whatever happened between her and Ben, she knew she would treasure it always.

The sun beat down, the heat growing more intense as the day progressed, and Rebecca was grateful for her straw hat. The clouds of dust grew thicker, and the growing mounds of dung steamed in the heat. They got a good price for the milk and it was a relief to escape the busy marketplace for the pub where they enjoyed a meal of bread and cheese washed down with jugs of light ale.

They spent the afternoon wandering round the shops, until it was time to return to the cart. Dolly whickered softly when she spotted them, tossing her head in welcome.

'I really think you should give some serious thought to supplying pies to the local hostelries,' Ben said, as they started for home. 'Aunt Holly would appreciate the extra income, I'm sure.'

'I'll speak to them this evening,' Rebecca promised.

'And have I persuaded you I'm a good bet when it comes to courting?' he asked, staring straight ahead.

Rebecca laughed. 'You've been very patient,' she said. 'Not one complaint about how long I was browsing.'

'That's not an answer.' Ben grimaced.

Rebecca leaned back on her hands, tilting her face to the

afternoon sun. 'I think I'll wait to find out whether your dancing's improved. After all, I couldn't possibly court someone with two left feet. I don't think I can cope with bruised toes again this year.'

'I didn't stand on your feet on purpose,' Ben objected, looking wounded. 'And the ball's less than a week away. That doesn't give me much time to practise.'

Rebecca just smiled.

CHAPTER SEVENTEEN

Rebecca loaded the last of the pies into the cart and covered them with a cloth.

'Are you sure you don't want me to come with you?' Ben asked, stroking Dolly's nose.

Rebecca shook her head. 'Uncle Jerry needs you,' she said. 'I'll be fine.' Taking Ben's hand, she climbed up into the cart and he handed her the reins. 'I'll be back as soon as I can.'

She smiled down at him fondly. 'I'm really looking forward to the ball tonight.'

Ben grinned. 'I've been practising my steps. You'll be impressed, to say the least.' His smile faded a little.

Rebecca laughed. 'I can hardly wait.' She shook the reins and Dolly started her slow plod out of the yard and onto the lane. The hedgerows were a riot of purple foxgloves, pink dog roses, red campions and creamy hawthorn. Rebecca breathed in the scent of sweet meadow grass. In the two weeks since her trip to town with Ben, she had visited several of the town's eating establishments, all of which had agreed to try her pies. After such a busy fortnight, she was glad to be alone to gather her thoughts. As she negotiated the narrow lane, she found herself thinking of Ben. She'd thought of him a lot, lately. No longer did she see him as just one of her dearest friends: now she was noticing the way the skin crinkled around his eyes when he smiled, and how his muscles rippled under his shirt as he wielded the pitchfork. Holly and Jeremiah had been supportive of her idea to try to sell her pies and, not one to let the grass grow under her feet, Rebecca had baked her first batch that evening.

She sighed, a shiver of anticipation running down her spine. The only fly in the ointment was Kenneth's continued sullenness. She hoped he wouldn't spoil the evening. She was looking forward to it so much.

Dolly heaved a heavy sigh as she hauled the cart up the steep, winding hill. Rebecca leaned forward and patted her neck. 'Almost there, girl,' she coaxed, relaxing her grip on the reins as the sturdy pony tossed her head and they made their way into town. A handsome coach, complete with liveried footman, waited outside the Grosvenor Coaching Inn. The driver, seated high on his box, nodded to Rebecca as she pulled up in front of him and engaged the brake. Of all the hostelries in town that had agreed to buy her pies, the grand hotel was her most prestigious customer. Heart beating erratically, Rebecca jumped down and, reaching under the cover, drew out the large basket of pies destined for the hotel's diners.

Drawing a deep breath, she carried it around the side of the building to the kitchen.

'Morning, Miss Wheeler,' Mr Duke, the manager said, glancing up from a thick ledger.

'Good morning, Mr Duke,' Rebecca stammered, her cheeks turning crimson with nerves. This was only her second delivery to the hotel and she was anxious to hear how her pies had been received by the customers. If they'd been found wanting, there would be no more orders. She held her breath as the manager lifted the crisp cloth covering the basket. He smiled. He was a thin man with oiled dark brown hair and a monocle, which he kept tucked into the breast pocket of his brown suit jacket. He pulled it out now, holding it over his right eye.

'These look delicious,' he said, raising his gaze to Rebecca. 'I must say,' he continued, straightening and tucking his monocle back into his pocket. 'We've had some excellent compliments on your pies. I believe the chef was quite disappointed he couldn't claim the credit for himself. Isn't that right, Mr Clewitt?'

'It is indeed,' Raymond Clewitt, replied, from where he was supervising a young kitchen boy slicing bacon. He was a large man, with a ruddy complexion and beady blue eyes. Beneath his white chef's hat, he was as bald as a billiard ball. He had been dubious of Rebecca when she'd first called in to see him. He'd studied under the best chefs at the smartest of London's hotels, he'd told her haughtily, while she'd stood quaking in her boots, feeling hopelessly out of her depth. It was one thing to sell her pies to the pubs around the town, but a hotel as grand as the Grosvenor? She'd hung her head, awaiting his derision, but instead he'd surprised her. 'My pies are good, Miss Wheeler, but yours are magnificent.' He'd smiled. 'Your pastry!' he'd exclaimed. 'It's so light and airy, you'd believe it was made by fairies.'

There and then he'd placed a large order and Rebecca had returned to the farm feeling as though she were walking on air.

Holly and Jeremiah were pleased that her endeavour was proving fruitful, and she was happy that she could repay them for their generosity and kindness by contributing to the household bills.

'We may be looking to increase our order, Miss Wheeler,' Mr Duke said now, letting the cloth fall back into place. 'Would you be able to make another dozen, do you think?'

'Yes, sir.' Rebecca nodded, her quick mind already reckoning how much more she would need of her ingredients. 'Thank you, sir.'

'Thank you, Miss Wheeler,' Mr Duke said, walking her out. 'It's a pleasure doing business with you.'

Rebecca delivered the rest of her pies to the various establishments around the town and, having received compliments from each of her customers, she returned home bursting with pride.

'I'm pleased your pies are so well received,' Holly said, once Rebecca had joined her in the cool dairy.

Tucking a strand of hair behind her ear, Rebecca grabbed a paddle and beat the cream in the large vat. The air was filled with the rich, creamy smell. 'So am I,' she replied, wiping sweat from her brow with the back of her hand. 'I was so nervous.'

'You had no need to be.' Holly smiled. 'I can vouch for the quality of your pies. They're delicious.' Her brow furrowed. 'Will you manage the extra workload, though, what with working in the dairy and the household?'

'I'm sure I shall.' Rebecca nodded. 'I don't mind getting up even earlier if need be.'

'Jeremiah and I are very proud of you, Becky,' Holly said, leaning over the vat with a ladle to lift out the mounds of yellow butter. She drained it, then pressed it into wooden moulds, setting them on the shelf to cool and set. 'I hope you have a good time at the ball tonight. You certainly deserve it after all your hard work.'

'Thank you. I intend to. Ben's been practising his dance steps.'

Holly tutted loudly. 'That's a relief.' She chuckled. 'I don't

151

think my poor feet could cope again after last year. Bless him, he's not a natural dancer, is he? Not like our Kenneth,' she added, giving Rebecca a pointed look.

Supper was a hurried affair, and while the men went back out to finish their work , Holly and Rebecca took their baths. The men would take theirs in the barn. Lying back in the warm water, Rebecca closed her eyes, her fingers playing with the locket that hung around her neck. Her stomach fluttered with anticipation of the evening ahead. The ball was held on a neighbouring farm and people came from miles around to enjoy the music, the dancing and the local cider.

She washed quickly, and left Holly to enjoy her own bath in peace while she changed into her dress. She smoothed the soft material over her hips, turning this way and that as she admired her reflection in the mirror.

'You look beautiful, my dear,' Holly said, standing in the doorway.

Rebecca turned, blushing. She hadn't heard Holly come up the stairs. 'Thank you. It is a beautiful dress. The stitching is barely noticeable at all.'

'My mother was a seamstress before she married my father.' Holly smiled. 'I inherited her flair for sewing. Would you like me to do your hair?' Coming to stand behind her, Holly picked up the hairbrush. 'I know your mother should be doing this,' she said, causing Rebecca to experience a rush of emotion. 'I like to believe she's somewhere looking down on you.' She drew the brush gently through Rebecca's glossy blonde hair. Her throat constricted by emotion, Rebecca could only manage a trembling smile. Her reflection blurred as tears welled.

'Don't be sad,' Holly said, resting her chin on Rebecca's

shoulder as their eyes met in the mirror. 'Today is a time for joy. Your mother would want you to enjoy yourself, wouldn't she?'

Rebecca nodded. Reaching under the bodice of her gown, she took out her silver locket and undid the delicate clasp.

'She was a beautiful woman,' Holly said, tilting her head to admire the tiny portrait. 'You look like her.'

'Do I?' Rebecca asked, eagerly.

'In your features, and colouring, yes. Definitely. Though I can see something of your father in you, too.' Taking comfort from Holly's words, Rebecca smiled. Though her grief was no longer as raw as it had once been, there were times, such as now, when she felt an overwhelming sense of loss. How she would have loved to have her mother brushing her hair, like Holly was doing. She sighed quietly, wondering what her father would have thought of Ben. Her brothers had been easy-going and friendly. She had no doubt Simeon and Robert would have got on with him. He was very similar to them in character.

'There,' Holly said, breaking into Rebecca's reverie. She put down the brush and stood back. Rebecca smiled at her reflection. Her hair shimmered like sun-ripened wheat in the mellow light streaming through the open window. Holly had gathered the hair at the sides of her head and tied it back with the blue ribbon. Now Rebecca pinned the brooch Ben had bought her to her dress.

'Pretty as a picture,' Holly said, her eyes shining with unshed tears. 'You'll be the belle of the ball.'

Rebecca laughed. 'You look very pretty too, Aunt Holly,' she said. 'That colour suits you.'

'Why, thank you,' Holly replied, smoothing the skirt of her red-rose-sprigged dress. 'These buttons are quite fiddly, though. I should have used larger ones but they're all Mrs Bloom had that were the exact colour I wanted.' She smiled. 'I think I can hear the men returning. We'd better get downstairs.'

With one last critical glance in the mirror, Rebecca followed Holly down the stairs to the airy kitchen just as the three men entered through the back door, looking very dapper in their Sunday best.

'You look very pretty,' Ben whispered, grinning at Rebecca. He was handsome in his slightly-too-big suit, his damp hair slicked back.

'What lucky chaps we are to be stepping out with two of the prettiest girls in the Vale.' Jeremiah grinned, slipping his arm around Holly's waist. 'What do you say, lads? Are we fitting escorts for two such pretty ladies?'

'No, sir.' Ben beamed, offering Rebecca his arm. 'But it's an honour to be allowed to accompany them to the ball.'

Rebecca slapped his arm. 'You're silly, Ben Troke.' Seeing Kenneth standing awkwardly to the side, she offered him her other arm. His initial reaction was to scowl, but he quickly re-arranged his features into a smile and took it.

The sun was still warm as the five set off. The dogs followed as far as the lane, before flopping down in the dust to await their return. The hedgerows were full of birdsong and there was only the faintest of breezes. The sky was an azure blue, flecked with feathery-white clouds, tinged with pink. The distant hills shimmered golden in the early-evening sunlight. The sound of music drifted across the fields, and as they caught up with friends and neighbours heading towards Manor Farm, the lane became a hub of conversation as people caught up on news and gossip.

Rebecca was conscious of Ben's arm in hers. Though Kenneth had kept up a steady stream of conversation, it was Ben she was concentrating on. He hadn't spoken much, but he kept giving her sideways looks, making her want to burst out laughing. She clamped her lips together and pretended to give Kenneth her full attention, making sure she nodded in the appropriate places. She hadn't realized until just now, she thought, as they neared the entrance to Manor Farm, how much Kenneth's conversation revolved around himself.

The wooden arch was adorned with pastel-coloured bunting. The music was louder now, a cheerful melody drifting across a field of golden wheat. The balmy evening air was filled with laughter and the hum of conversation.

'The dancing's already begun,' Ben said, inclining his head towards the makeshift dance-floor. People sat on bales of hay, sipping mugs of cider and watching the dancing. The three-piece band played in the shade of a flowering horse-chestnut tree. 'Come on, Becky.' Dropping Kenneth's arm, Rebecca allowed Ben to lead her onto the dance-floor. She smiled up at him as one arm circled her slender waist and the other took her hand.

'Your practising has certainly paid off,' she whispered, as they whirled across the floor. She was so swept away by the music and laughter that she failed to notice Kenneth staring at her, his expression grim. After a few moments, with a toss of his head, he headed to the refreshment stand.

CHAPTER EIGHTEEN

The first stars had appeared in the damson-coloured sky. A solitary blackbird had sung its last note and the ball was in full swing. Panting, Rebecca sank onto a bale of straw and leaned down to rub her throbbing foot. Ben had trodden on her feet only twice, a definite improvement on previous years, she mused, reaching up to accept a mug of cider. It was a balmy night and the gentle breeze rustling through the trees did little to alleviate the humidity.

She leaned back on one hand, watching the dancers as she sipped the sweet cider, relishing its coolness as it slid down her parched throat.

'I'm just going to have a word with Arthur over there,' Ben said, leaning close so she could hear him over the music. Giving her a quick kiss on the cheek, he sauntered off to where a tall, wiry young man, with a pencil-thin moustache and unkempt hair, was standing self-consciously under a sycamore tree nursing a tankard of ale.

Rebecca drained her mug. Nocturnal insects hummed in the long grass at the edge of the clearing, and the hauntingly beautiful call of an owl drifted across the valley. Babies and children slept on their mother's laps. A young man, more than a little worse for wear, tripped over a hay bale, to the raucous amusement of his friends. Rebecca looked away from the spectacle and, spotting Holly near the refreshment stand, got up to make her way over. She was edging her way past the dancers when a hand grabbed at her elbow and jerked her around. She found herself face to face with Kenneth, his face flushed and shiny with sweat. He glared at her with unfocused eyes and she was shocked to realize that it had been Kenneth who had just made a fool of himself in front of them all.

'I think you need to sit down, Kenny,' she said, a nervous edge to her voice. She'd seen enough during her time at the Thirsty Mariner to know how unpredictable a drunk man could be.

'Dance with me,' he slurred. 'Please?'

'You're in no fit state to dance,' Rebecca said evenly, trying not to let her disappointment show.

'Come on,' he said petulantly, tugging at her arm. 'You've danced with every fellow here but me.'

'Kenny, I'm not dancing with you. You're drunk.' Pulling herself free of his grip, she turned away from him. Quick as a flash, Kenneth's hand snaked around the back of her neck, pulling her face close to his. She could smell the cider on his breath and the odour of his sweat as he pressed his lips against hers. She pushed at his chest, trying to turn her face away. She felt his lips press against her cheek until, suddenly, he was on the ground, blood gushing from his nose. Ben stood over him, clenching and unclenching his fists, his cheeks flaming with fury. Conversation had dried up as people stopped to stare. Rebecca caught Holly's shocked expression as she stared at them across the dance-floor.

'What the . . .?' Kenneth sat up with a groan. He ran his

hand across his face, staring in astonishment as it came away crimson.

'Kenneth.' Holly pushed her way through the gawping crowd, shooting Ben a pained look as she pressed a clean tea-towel to her son's face,

'Sorry, Kenneth,' Ben mumbled, kicking a loose stone with the tip of his shoe. 'I didn't mean to hit you so hard.'

'There was no need to hit him at all,' Holly snapped, turning to glare at Ben. 'What on earth possessed you?'

'He was taking liberties with Becky,' mumbled Ben, shamefaced.

'It was just a kiss,' Kenneth mumbled, attempting to get to his feet. He stumbled and Holly caught his arm, steadying him.

'Are you all right, Becky?' she asked, her expression softening. 'No harm done?' Her eyes begged Rebecca to agree.

'No harm done,' Rebecca muttered, eyes downcast.

'Leave me alone.' Kenneth snatched the bloodied tea-towel from his mother and flung it to the ground. 'I'll get you for this. Ben Troke,' he snarled, spraying blood over Ben's shirt. 'You too, Becky Wheeler. No one humiliates me. No one.'

'I think you need to go home and sober up,' Ben said, by way of reply.

'Kenneth,' Holly chided him, spots of pink blossoming on her cheeks. 'Let me see to your nose . . .'

Kenneth ducked out of her way and, shoving his way through the small crowd of onlookers, staggered off in the direction of the lane.

'I hope he'll be all right,' Holly said to Rebecca, as she bent down to pick up the discarded tea-towel, shaking it free of grass. 'Should I go after him, do you think?'

'I think he feels humiliated enough, Aunt Holly,' Ben said,

massaging his bruised knuckles. 'Give him time to sober up a bit.'

'I think Aunt Holly blames me,' Rebecca whispered, watching her moving through the crowd.

'It's understandable,' Ben whispered in her ear. People had drifted away, rejoining the dancing, and they were alone now. 'Kenneth's her son. She's hurting for him.' He sighed. 'I honestly didn't mean to hit him as hard as I did. I'll apologize to him tomorrow.'

'Where do you think he's gone?' Rebecca whispered back.

'Taken my advice and gone somewhere to sober up, I hope,' Ben replied drily.

'Do you think he'll be all right?'

'He'll be right as rain tomorrow.' He grinned. 'He'll have a bit of a sore head, and a couple of black eyes, no doubt, but otherwise he'll be fine. His pride is dented more than anything.' He tilted Rebecca's face towards his. 'How are you, more to the point?'

'I'm all right.' Rebecca gave a hollow laugh. 'It was the shock, really. I never thought he'd behave like that.'

'And he wouldn't normally,' Ben said charitably. 'I blame the scrumpy. It's a particularly potent batch. It probably affected his judgement. No doubt, he'll feel a right idiot in the morning and be apologizing to you.'

'I hope so,' Rebecca said, with a sigh. 'I hate Aunt Holly being annoyed with us, though.'

Ben slipped his arm around her shoulders. 'She'll get over it. Knowing how fond Aunt Holly is of you, I can't see her staying cross for very long.'

CHAPTER NINETEEN

To Rebecca's immense relief, Holly's annoyance was short-lived. By the time the ball was winding to a close, she was back to her cheerful self, and had even joined Rebecca and some of the other girls in a country dance. Rebecca didn't know the steps, but she gamely followed the others, enjoying herself immensely as she skipped and linked arms. No one appeared to mind if she turned the wrong way or made a misstep.

'That was fun.' Holly fanned her hot cheeks as they sank onto a bale of straw, gratefully accepting a glass of warm lemonade from Jeremiah. He'd made no mention of the incident and appeared to be his usual amiable self, though Rebecca did notice he kept scanning the edge of the clearing, presumably wondering whether Kenneth had gone home or was sleeping off his inebriation closer by.

The following morning Ben made good on his promise and sought out Kenneth.

'It didn't go well,' he told Rebecca ruefully, later. She was in the dairy, churning the milk. She wiped a sheen of sweat from her brow and set the paddle to one side.

'He wouldn't accept your apology?' she asked.

'Wouldn't even acknowledge me,' Ben replied, with a shrug. 'Just brushed me off and went off to work at the far end of the field.'

'Could Uncle Jerry not have a word?' Rebecca wondered.

'He won't get involved,' Ben said. 'As far as he's concerned, we're grown men. We need to sort it out ourselves.'

'He's probably still feeling a bit embarrassed,' Rebecca said. 'He did look a sorry sight this morning, what with his black eyes and swollen nose.'

'I heard him retching in the yard first thing this morning, too. I reckon he's feeling like he's been kicked by a horse.' Ben pulled a face. 'I'm not proud of what I did, Becky, but I couldn't let him take liberties with you.'

'I know that.' Rebecca touched his arm. 'It's just unfortunate it happened in public.'

Changing the subject, Ben said, 'It looks like it's going to stay fine. Do you fancy a walk later?'

'I can't,' Rebecca declined wistfully. 'I have baking to do. The Grosvenor sent word that they want to triple their order this week so I shall be rushed off my feet.'

'Another time.' Ben smiled. 'I'll see you at supper, then.'

Rebecca watched him leave. She had barely slept the night before, worrying about Kenneth and what had happened. She hoped they would be able to repair their friendship but, given Kenneth's moodiness of late, she couldn't help but worry that this latest incident had been the final nail in its coffin.

As the days drifted into months, the rift between the three seemed to widen, but Rebecca was so busy she had little time to worry about it. Demand for her pies had grown at such a rate that, during the month of October, Holly and Jeremiah made the decision to hire a girl to replace Rebecca in the dairy, releasing her to concentrate on her baking.

Hearing the dogs start to bark, Rebecca wiped her hands and opened the door just as Dolly came round the corner of the house, pulling the cart. Jeremiah brought it to a halt close to the house and engaged the brake, the dogs prancing around it in a show of exuberant welcome. The pale-faced girl seated between Holly and Jeremiah, wearing a coat two sizes too large for her, looked down at the dogs in terror.

'This is Ella McMullen,' Jeremiah said, as Rebecca approached the cart.

Mindful of her own nerves as a newcomer to the farm, she smiled at the girl in a way she hoped would put her at her ease. 'Hello, Ella. I'm Becky.'

Ben strode from the barn, followed by a sullen-faced Kenneth. 'Welcome, Miss McMullen,' Ben said, extending his hand to Ella as Jeremiah assisted Holly. Managing only a quick smile and a muttered greeting, Ella allowed him to help her down. The dogs milled about her, sniffing at her dress, and she pressed herself against the cart.

'They won't hurt you,' Jeremiah said. 'Just give them a pat and they'll leave you alone.' Ella tucked her hands behind her back, shrinking even further away as one of the dogs pushed its snout up against her. Realizing the girl seemed genuinely scared of the dogs, Jeremiah shooed them away and they slunk off, their soulful eyes heavy with reproach.

'You'll soon get used to them,' Holly said. 'Let's get out of this wind,' she added, once she'd introduced Ella to Kenneth as well. 'Put the kettle on, Becky, would you?' she said, ushering Ella towards the house.

The kitchen was warm and filled with the aroma of warm meat pies. Rebecca noticed how Ella licked her lips at the sight of them cooling on the windowsill, gravy bubbling through the slits on the top. There was another tray on the table, waiting to go into the oven, and one already inside it.

'Our Becky is a master baker,' Holly said, with a smile. 'Her pies are in demand in most of the eating houses around the town.'

'You exaggerate, Aunt Holly.' Rebecca laughed, crouching to open the oven and peer in. 'A few more minutes yet, I think,' she said, straightening.

'Why don't you show Ella where she'll be sleeping while I make the tea?' Holly suggested, giving the timid girl a reassuring smile. 'Afterwards, I'll show you the dairy.'

Rebecca led Ella up to the front bedroom where Jeremiah had already assembled the new iron bedstead. Ella stood in the doorway, as awestruck as Rebecca had once been as she took in the pretty wallpaper and matching bedspreads. 'I've never seen anything so lovely,' she whispered.

'Here,' Rebecca said, opening the wardrobe and taking out a rose-pink and white checked dress. 'You can wear this. It's too tight on me now but it looks like it should fit you nicely.'

'For me?' Ella's cheeks flushed with pleasure. 'I've never had a new dress in my life.'

'Well, it's not new exactly. It was one that Aunt Holly altered for me when I first arrived. It's very serviceable material, though, so it should last you a while. Aunt Holly and Uncle Jerry are very kind,' she said, as she helped Ella out of her shapeless grey tunic and into the dress. 'I'm sure you'll be very happy here.'

*

163

'The warden assured us you were familiar with dairy work?' Holly said, passing Ella a mug of tea.

'Yes, ma'am,' Ella nodded, blushing furiously. 'I've been in the workhouse dairy since I left school, ma'am.'

'Excellent.' Holly beamed, sipping her tea. 'And please call me Aunt Holly.' She picked up her mug and took a sip. 'We have a small herd. The milk is taken up to Shaftesbury to be sold on market day, or it goes by train to Salisbury. The shops take our butter and cheese. Ben or Kenneth used to take it up in the cart but now that Becky goes into town most days, she usually takes it, don't you?' She turned to Rebecca, who was lifting a tray of pies from the oven.

'Yes, I do,' Rebecca replied, grunting with effort as she carefully set it on the rack to cool. 'You could come with me sometimes,' she said to Ella, shaking out the thick tea towel she'd used to lift the tray and hanging it on the hook. 'You can acquaint yourself with the town. Market day is particularly festive.'

'If I can be spared, then I would very much like to,' replied Ella, shyly.

'There's always time to enjoy ourselves,' Aunt Holly said. She nodded at Ella's mug. 'If you're done, I'll show you the dairy.'

'I'll make a start on the dinner,' Rebecca said, giving Ella an encouraging smile. She hoped Ella would soon lose her nerves. She couldn't have asked for a better family to work for, or a nicer place to live than Elm Tree Farm.

Ella soon settled into her new life and Rebecca enjoyed having another girl to talk to. The days were growing shorter, and the cosy autumn evenings were spent in the parlour, where Holly might play the piano, or Jeremiah would read out interesting facts from his newspaper while the girls knitted or tackled their mending. Kenneth was seldom home in the evenings and, while no one said as much, Rebecca couldn't help but feel the evenings were more pleasant for his absence. According to his mother, Kenneth had started seeing the daughter of a neighbouring farmer.

To Rebecca's delight, Ben seemed to enjoy the cosy fireside evenings. Though he and Jeremiah spent a lot of time discussing the price of milk or other farming matters, Rebecca just enjoyed having him close by. She would watch him as she pretended to concentrate on her knitting, her ears attuned to every word he said. Every now and then he would catch her eye and treat her to one of his smiles.

One evening, to Rebecca's dismay, Kenneth declared that he would join them after supper. She tried to concentrate on her mending, but the atmosphere felt heavy and claustrophobic. Ben made several attempts to draw Kenneth into the conversation but, if he deigned to reply at all, his responses were short, indifferent at best but downright rude at worst, earning him a stern glance from his father. Finally, it appeared Jeremiah had heard enough.

'If you're determined to be unpleasant, Kenneth,' he remonstrated, folding his newspaper and laying it aside, 'I'll thank you to take yourself off to bed.'

Rebecca kept her gaze averted but out of the corner of her eye, she saw the crimson flush that flooded Kenneth's cheeks and neck. She sighed inwardly. This would be just another humiliation for him to add to his list of grievances.

'I should have known I wouldn't be welcome,' he said, getting angrily to his feet. 'You've got your little band of waifs and strays. Why should you want me?'

'Kenny!' Holly leaped to her feet. 'Of course, you're welcome,' she cried, as Kenneth stormed from the room, slamming the door shut behind him.

'Leave him!' commanded Jeremiah, as Holly made to go after him. Rebecca and Ben exchanged worried glances. Kenneth wouldn't let this go.

'Likely he's had a bit of a falling out with his lady friend,' Holly ventured, breaking the heavy silence.

'He needs to grow up,' Jeremiah said, returning to his newspaper. 'I feel sorry for the poor Weeks girl if he treats her so.' He glowered at his wife over the top of the paper. 'I didn't raise my son to speak to people like that.'

'I'll talk to him in the morning,' Holly said. She tried to smile but her voice sounded strained. Rebecca and Ben exchanged another look. Ben's shoulders rose in a surreptitious shrug. Rebecca gave him a wry smile of understanding. They were both doubtful Holly would remonstrate too much with Kenneth. If she had any fault, it was her apparent blindness to her son's shortcomings.

CHAPTER TWENTY

1885

Rebecca leaned on the gate, shielding her eyes against the August sunshine. The air smelt of warm grass and sunbaked earth as the countryside shimmered in the midday heat.

'Becky!' Ben jumped over the low dry-stone wall and strode across the field towards her, running a hand through his sweat-damp hair. Rebecca pushed open the gate and went to meet him.

'I've missed you,' Ben said, greeting her with a kiss as they met in the middle of the meadow.

'It's only been a couple of hours.' Rebecca laughed, tucking her arm through his.

'A couple of hours too long.' Ben grinned, untying his necker-chief and mopping his damp forehead. 'I always miss you when you go into town.' He balled up the neckerchief and stuffed it into his trouser pocket. 'How did you get on?'

'Busy,' Rebecca replied, pausing to gather a handful of flowers. 'Mr Wilcox at that new restaurant on Bell Street has increased his order again.'

'Your nest egg must be looking quite healthy by now,' Ben said.

'Aunt Holly suggested I start buying things for my bottom drawer,' she said, her cheeks colouring.

'I think Aunt Holly is right,' replied Ben, giving Rebecca a sideways glance. He pulled her into an embrace and kissed her tenderly. Still clutching her posy, Rebecca slid her arms around his neck, surrendering herself to his kisses. She could feel the beat of his heart through the fabric of his shirt, in tune with her own.

They broke apart, flushed and breathing hard.

'Oh, Becky,' Ben sighed. 'I know we've talked about getting married and, well . . .' Letting go of Rebecca's hand, Ben dropped onto one knee. Rebecca regarded him with mounting excitement as he looked up at her, his eyes watering in the sunlight. 'My dearest Becky, would you do me the honour of becoming my wife?' He cleared his throat, nervously. 'I've been carrying this around with me for ages trying to find the perfect moment,' he continued, holding up a ring. It was a simple gold band set with a single garnet. 'It belonged to my mother. They gave it to me when I left the workhouse.' He looked up at her, his eyes pleading.

'I don't know what to say,' Rebecca whispered.

'Yes?' Ben suggested hoarsely.

'I've been dreaming of this day for so long,' Rebecca murmured. 'Yes, Ben, yes,' she breathed. 'I would love to marry you.'

The rest of her words were lost in Ben's whoop of delight as he leaped to his feet and swung her into his embrace. He kissed her long and hard on the mouth before slipping the ring on to the fourth finger of her left hand. 'It fits perfectly,' Rebecca said, holding out her hand to admire the way it caught the light.

'I thought we might be married the last Saturday of September,' Ben said, as they walked slowly back to the farmhouse hand in hand. 'The harvest will be behind us, and we'll have plenty of time to have our banns read.'

'That gives us six weeks,' Rebecca said.

'Is it enough time?' Ben asked. 'We can delay a few weeks, if not.'

'Certainly not,' responded Rebecca. 'I would be happy with a small wedding, but I'm sure Aunt Holly will want a celebration with our neighbours and friends. Oh, I must tell her. She'll be so happy for us. Oh! You didn't mention anything to her already, did you?'

Ben shook his head. 'I asked Uncle Jerry's permission, of course, and he gave me his blessing, but I thought you'd want to tell Aunt Holly yourself.'

'She'll be thrilled,' Rebecca said. 'So will Ella. Perhaps we could ask her to be my bridesmaid.' Her smile faded. 'Will you ask Kenneth to be best man?'

'At one time he'd have been my obvious choice.' Ben frowned. 'I think I will, anyway. Perhaps that will go some way to building bridges between us. I hate us being at odds. He used to be my best friend, after all.'

'It's such a shame the way things have turned out,' Rebecca said, shaking her head sorrowfully. Over the past two years she and Ben had tried several times to reconcile with Kenneth. Though the memory of his attempt to kiss her still rankled, she'd been prepared to overlook it as a drunken mistake, but he'd shunned them every time.

'It's his loss,' Ben said cheerfully, caressing Rebecca's cheek with his fingertips. 'Let's not spoil today by thinking about him.'

'You're right.' Rebecca smiled. 'It's his loss.'

Hand in hand they made their way across the fields towards the farmhouse. The light brown thatch was bathed in sunlight and the windows reflected the sapphire-blue sky. A cockerel crowed throatily as they entered the yard.

They found Aunt Holly and Ella in the kitchen, preparing the evening meal.

'You two look like the cats that got the cream,' Holly remarked, slicing potatoes into a pan. 'What're you up to?'

'Aunt Holly, Ella,' Rebecca looked at Ben. He smiled back, encouraging her to go on. 'Ben has asked me to marry him,' she said.

'Oh, Becky,' Holly exclaimed in delight. 'I'm guessing you said yes?'

Rebecca and Ben laughed.

'I did.' Rebecca blushed.

'Oh, I'm so happy for you both,' Holly cried, dropping the knife onto the table. Wiping her hands on her apron, she pulled Rebecca close and reached out an arm to draw Ben into the embrace. 'Oh, what wonderful news,' she said, wiping her eye with a corner of her apron. 'Jeremiah will be pleased. He thinks the world of you both, as you know.'

At Ben's sheepish expression, she gave him a mock scowl. 'Does he already know?' she demanded, grabbing a nearby tea-towel and flicking him with it.

'Only that I intended to propose to Rebecca,' he explained apologetically. 'I thought it only right to ask his permission first.'

'Of course you did,' Holly conceded. 'I wouldn't have expected anything less. Oh, Becky.' She threw her arms around Rebecca again.

'I'm pleased for you, too, Becky,' Ella said, with a smile. She was midway through plucking a pheasant. Feathers drifted

170

across the slate floor, wafted along by the warm breeze blowing through the open doorway. A cat sat on the windowsill, its yellow-eyed gaze fixed on the dead bird in Ella's hands. 'Have you set a date?'

'We were thinking the last Saturday in September,' Ben said.

'That doesn't give us much time to plan,' Holly said, turning her attention back to the potatoes. 'We'll go up to town on Saturday morning and see Miss Pickup about making you a wedding dress, Becky. Ben, you'll need to make an appointment to see the vicar. We can have the reception here. The barn is large enough to accommodate a decent number of people. Oh, you'll have to work out a guest list. The printers in Salisbury Street can do the invitations, but I'll need to know how many to order . . . Oh, my goodness,' she threw up her hands, beaming at Rebecca and Ben, 'so much to do! I'm giddy with excitement, I really am.'

'What's all the commotion?' Jeremiah came into the kitchen.

'Becky and Ben are betrothed,' Ella blurted, wiping her hands down her apron.

'You asked her, then?' Jeremiah clapped Ben on the back. 'Well done, lad,' he said, shaking his hand heartily. 'You've done well for yourself.' He turned to Rebecca. 'Congratulations, my girl. I truly wish you both all the happiness in the world.'

'Thank you,' Rebecca said, blushing.

'I will need to go to town on Saturday,' his wife told him, setting the pan on the stove. 'They've set the date for the end of September. That only gives us six weeks.'

'That's plenty of time,' Jeremiah teased. He sat down to unlace his boots. 'All you need is a cup of tea and a piece of cake to wish them on their way.'

'Nonsense,' Holly retorted sharply. 'We're giving these two

the best wedding we can afford. Ella's going to be bridesmaid, I take it?'

'Oh, yes.' Rebecca nodded. 'If you'd like to? She met Ella's gaze across the feather-strewn table.

'Oh, yes, please,' Ella breathed in delight. 'Will I wear a new dress, too?'

'Of course.' Holly smiled. 'Pale pink, or blue, perhaps,' she said, sizing Ella up. 'Something that complements your colouring. We'll all go to town on Saturday. Jeremiah, you can take the boys to the gentlemen's outfitters and organize their suits. You need a new one, too. Your old one has seen better days, and I couldn't help noticing it was a little snug the last time you wore it.' She gave her husband's stomach a fond pat.

'I blame our Becky's pies,' Jeremiah said, with a rueful grin. 'They're too good to resist.' He stretched his braces, letting them go with a sharp twang. 'Will you be asking Kenneth to be best man?' He gave Ben an enquiring look.

'Oh, Ben, you must.' Holly gave him a look full of reproach. 'He'd be so hurt if you didn't.'

Ben shuffled his feet uncomfortably. 'Of course.' He mustered a smile. 'I'll ask him as soon as I see him.'

'Good.' Holly beamed. 'Isn't it exciting, Jerry?' She slid her hand around his waist. 'Maybe Kenneth will follow suit and propose to Polly soon.'

'I don't think Kenneth's in any particular hurry to wed,' Jeremiah said, with a regretful shake of his head.

'Well, he should get a move on,' said Holly, grabbing the broom to sweep up the errant feathers. 'A girl like Polly won't wait around for ever. Where is he, anyway?' she asked, glancing out of the window.

'He's just unhitching the cart,' Jeremiah replied. 'If this

weather holds, we should have all the silage in by the end of next week. Then we can make a start on the ploughing. Which reminds me, when we're in town on Saturday, I need a new tooth for the plough. Kenneth broke it on a rock the other day.'

'What am I being blamed for now?' Kenneth stamped his boots on the mat, brushing bits of straw from his shirt sleeves.

'Do that outside, would you, love?' Holly chided him. 'I've just swept the floor.'

With a tut of annoyance, Kenneth took a few steps backwards.

'Your father was just saying the plough needs a new tooth,' Holly said, apologetically.

'It wasn't my fault,' snapped Kenneth, shooting his father a glare. 'I didn't see the rock.'

'No one is saying it was, Kenny,' Holly said, to pacify him. 'Will Polly be joining us for supper?' she asked, changing the subject.

'No.' He frowned. 'Why?'

'Ben and Becky have some good news to share. I thought we could make supper a bit of a celebration and it would have been nice if Polly could join us.'

'She's busy,' Kenneth replied shortly. He glowered at Rebecca, then at Ben. 'So?' he challenged, arms crossed belligerently across his chest. 'What is it?'

'They're betrothed,' Ella squeaked. 'Isn't it exciting?'

'Betrothed?' Kenneth's brows dipped low as his eyes narrowed. He uncrossed his arms, running a hand through his thick, dark hair.

'Isn't it exciting news?' Holly smiled. Though she couldn't help wishing it was Kenneth that Rebecca was marrying, she would never begrudge the pair their happiness. And she was hopeful that it wouldn't be too long before her son and Polly, too, were joined in matrimony.

'Am I to congratulate you?' Kenneth scowled.

'That is the usual polite response,' Jeremiah said sternly.

'Ben has something he'd like to ask, haven't you, Ben?' Holly said, when Kenneth remained silent. She gave Ben a nudge.

Ben cast Rebecca a pained look. She shrugged. There were other young men working on the neighbouring farms whom she would have preferred to act as Ben's best man, but it wasn't up to her and, perhaps, as Ben said, it might begin the reconciliation they were hoping for.

Ben cleared his throat. 'If you're willing, I'd like you to stand up as my best man.'

Kenneth slowly raised his head. 'Me?' he asked sardonically.

Ben nodded. 'Yes.' He stuck out his hand. 'Come on, Kenneth. I know we've had our differences, but can't we let bygones be bygones?'

Kenneth stared at Ben's hand as if it were a snake.

'Kenneth,' his father said, a clear warning note in his tone. 'What Ben's asked of you is an honour.'

Kenneth's lip rose in a sneer. 'Yes,' he said, ignoring Ben's outstretched hand. 'Why not?' He slumped in the chair recently vacated by his father. 'What's for supper?' he asked. 'I'm starving.'

CHAPTER TWENTY-ONE

'We can get everything you need for your bottom drawer here,' Holly said, running her fingers across the glass-topped counter at the haberdasher's.

'We have some lovely handmade lace.' May Pickup slung her tape measure around her slender neck as she bustled over. She was a pleasant-faced woman with dark brown hair, pulled back in a bun, and blue eyes that exuded friendliness and warmth.

'Oh, that's lovely,' Holly said, as May unwrapped a length of delicate lace. 'Come and have a look, Becky.'

Closing the book of dress patterns she'd been leafing through, Rebecca wandered over for a closer look.

'Handmade by a local woman,' May told them, draping a length of the lace over Rebecca's hand.

'It would look very pretty on the hem of a petticoat,' suggested Holly, as Rebecca fingered the soft lace. 'Shall we take a yard?'

'Yes, please.' Rebecca nodded.

'I'll wrap it for you,' May said, laying the lace flat on the counter and reaching for her scissors. 'Have you decided on a pattern?'

'I can't make up my mind,' replied Rebecca, and returned to the books. 'You'll have to help me decide, Aunt Holly.'

'This one is my favourite.' Holly turned a couple of pages. 'What do you think?'

'It's beautiful,' Ella said, peering over Rebecca's shoulder.

Rebecca leafed back and forth between the patterns she particularly liked, finally settling on a modern one with a ruffled skirt and ruffled three-quarter-length sleeves. 'I think it will suit you very well,' Aunt Holly said. 'The bodice has a great deal of beadwork. Do you have artificial pearls in stock, Miss Pickup?'

'I haven't any at the moment, Mrs Seymour,' May apologized, 'but I shall endeavour to have them in by the end of the week. Miss Wheeler, please follow me, and I can take your measurements.'

Leaving Aunt Holly and Ella thumbing through the pattern books in search of a dress for Ella, Rebecca followed May Pickup into the back room.

'You'll need a serviceable black dress, as well,' May said, holding the tape measure between two fingers and scribbling Rebecca's waist measurement in her notebook. 'And what about some new day dresses? Arms up, please.'

'Oh, I don't . . .' Rebecca faltered. Aunt Holly and Uncle Jerry had already been more than generous. She didn't want to take advantage. Nor did she want to be an expense to Ben, before they were even married. She had her own savings, of course, but she was keeping them for a rainy day.

'Two new day dresses, I think, May,' Aunt Holly said, pulling back the curtain. She smiled at Rebecca's look of consternation. 'Jeremiah and I have discussed it, Becky, and we're in agreement that you deserve a few treats.' She patted Rebecca's arm. 'We were never blessed with a daughter of our own, so let us

have the joy of treating you on the occasion of your marriage.'
Holly smiled.

'Thank you.' Rebecca's smile wobbled. She really didn't
deserve such kindness, especially as she knew how much Aunt
Holly had nurtured the hope that she would marry Kenneth.

'I've got all your measurements,' May said, hanging the tape
measure around her neck again. 'Shall we choose the material?
Mrs Seymour, have you selected a pattern?'

The three women trooped back onto the shop floor where
Ella was still looking through the pattern book, unable to make
up her mind.

'I'm torn between this one,' she told Rebecca, pointing to a
pretty, scallop-necked dress with a flowing skirt and long sleeves,
'or . . .' she flipped over a few pages '. . . this.'

'I prefer this one,' Rebecca told her, with a smile. 'But it's
your decision.'

'Oh, I can't decide,' Ella wailed. She flicked back to the previous pattern, her brow furrowed in a frown of indecision.

'In the meantime, why don't you ladies choose your material?' May beamed, bustling behind the counter. 'This calico is
very serviceable.' She pointed it out, fingering the edge of a bolt
of red and white sprigged cloth. 'It will last you years.'

Rebecca scanned the rows of cloth. 'I think I prefer the blue,'
she said, pointing to a white and blue flower-patterned material. 'And perhaps the brown and orange? It reminds me of
autumn leaves.'

'That's very pretty,' Holly agreed, from where she was trying
to decide between a pale blue silk or a mauve satin. 'It will suit
your colouring.'

'A very wise choice,' May agreed, pulling the bolt of cloth off
the shelf and laying it aside. 'And now for the wedding dress,'

she said, indicating the bolts of silk satin ranging from purest white to dark ivory.

After a lot of consideration, Rebecca finally settled on a cream silk satin.

'That would have been my choice.' May beamed. She carried the bolt of cloth to the counter, glancing at Ella, still dithering between the two patterns. 'Have you made a decision, miss?'

'We'll come back in an hour or so,' Holly said, as Ella miserably shook her head. 'We're meeting my husband in town. Perhaps Ella will make up her mind over dinner,' she added, with a wry smile.

'I'm sorry, Aunt Holly,' Ella apologized, as they left the shop. 'I've never had such a pretty dress before. I want to make sure I choose the exact right one.'

'Of course you do, sweetheart.' Holly smiled. 'Come,' she said, glancing up at the clock tower. 'Jeremiah and the boys will be waiting for us.'

The high street was bustling with pedestrians and horse-drawn traffic. A barking dog raced down the wide road, chasing three lads with hoops. A policeman stood to attention beside a lamppost, watching the busy scene with mild interest. The public house next to the church was heaving. Rebecca glanced through the window. There was a crush of men around the bar, but the dining area looked less busy, and she spotted Ben as she followed Holly through the door. The smell of stale beer and tobacco smoke sent her right back to the Thirsty Mariner and she shivered.

'Are you all right, Becky?' asked Ella.

'Someone walked over my grave,' Rebecca whispered. She hadn't thought of Mickey in ages, and she certainly wasn't going to let bad memories ruin the life she had now.

'Hello, ladies.' As the women approached the table Jeremiah got to his feet and leaned over to kiss Aunt Holly's cheek. 'I hope you've had fun spending all my money,' he teased, pulling out a chair for his wife.

'I don't think we're destined for the poorhouse just yet,' Holly teased back, arranging her packages on the floor beneath the table. 'How did the suit fittings go?'

'Very well,' Jeremiah replied, waving to attract the attention of the young barmaid who was clearing a nearby table.

'You boys will look so handsome,' Holly said, smiling at Ben and Kenneth.

'I'm sincerely grateful to you and Uncle Jerry,' Ben said, reaching across the table to clasp Rebecca's hand. 'We both are.'

Kenneth made a soft noise in his throat. He was slouched on the bench, his expression sullen as he regarded Rebecca with his hooded gaze.

'Everything all right, Kenneth?' Jeremiah said, turning to his son once he'd given the order for three mugs of sweet cider and bowls of mutton stew.

'Yes, sir,' Kenneth muttered. He continued to stare at Rebecca, his jaw working as he chewed the side of his mouth. Rebecca ignored him, concentrating instead on listening to Jeremiah and Ben as they brought the women up to date on the renovations for the old cowman's cottage Ben and Rebecca would move into after they were married.

'I'll take you to see it this afternoon,' Ben promised Rebecca. 'You'll be amazed at how different it looks now.'

'I hope so.' Holly unfolded her napkin as the barmaid appeared carrying a tray of steaming mutton stew. Rebecca was pleased to see two of her pies on the tray as well, destined for another table. She and Ben had agreed that she would continue to bake after they were married, at least until the babies came along. And Holly had already dropped many hints that she was more than happy to mind the children, should Rebecca wish to carry on with her baking.

'That cottage was little more than a hovel the last time I looked at it,' Holly continued, picking up her spoon.

'It was in quite a bad state of disrepair,' her husband agreed. 'But you'll be amazed at the work Ben's put into it. You can be proud of yourself, lad,' he said, turning to Ben.

'Thank you, sir.'

Beside him, Kenneth grimaced. He adjusted his position, his expression stony.

'The cottage next door to that one will be yours when you marry, Kenneth,' Holly said, her voice over-bright as she smiled at her only son.

'Live in a cowman's hovel?' Kenneth sneered. 'No, thank you.' He picked up his tankard, glowering at the contents. 'Old man Weeks has already promised Polly he'll move in with his sister so we can have the farmhouse.'

'That's very generous of him,' Jeremiah remarked, his spoon poised midway to his lips. 'Have you set a date, then?'

'I didn't know you'd proposed?' Aunt Holly said, looking hurt.

'I haven't,' Kenneth said, picking up his spoon and attacking his stew with the gusto of a man who hadn't eaten for days. 'We've discussed marriage, of course,' he said, reaching for a hunk of bread. 'Well, Polly has.' He took a bite of bread, chewing slowly. 'I'm in no rush,' he said, his mouth full. 'Plenty of time for settling down.'

'Polly might not feel so,' Aunt Holly warned him mildly. 'If you keep her waiting too long, she may find someone else.'

Kenneth snorted. 'So be it,' he said, with an indifferent shrug.

'I'd like to get married,' Ella piped up.

'You've plenty of time yet.' Ben grinned at her.

'I'm sixteen.' Ella pouted. 'Old enough to start courting.'

'And have any of the local boys caught your eye?' Aunt Holly asked, with a smile. 'You certainly weren't at a loss for partners at the summer ball.'

Ella shrugged. 'The boys were very attentive,' she said, a blush colouring her cheeks as she focused her gaze on her stew. 'There is someone . . .' she said, with a shy smile. 'But he's already spoken for,' she added, a wistful note to her voice.

'You'll meet someone in good time,' Holly assured her. 'Hmm, this stew is delicious.' She took a sip of cider before turning back to Ella. 'Are you any closer to deciding which dress pattern you prefer?'

Ella pulled a face. 'No.' She groaned. 'It's so difficult. I like them both.'

'Then you may have both dresses,' Jeremiah said, waving his hand expansively. 'You've proved yourself a hard worker and you deserve a treat.'

Ella's mouth fell open in surprise. She looked at Holly and Rebecca, who smiled indulgently. They were used to Jeremiah's generous nature.

'Thank you, Uncle Jerry,' Ella breathed, her cheeks turning crimson. 'Thank you so much.'

Jeremiah grinned. 'It's my pleasure, Ella. You're a good girl.' He pushed his empty bowl aside. 'If we've all finished, you ladies may go and conclude your business with the dressmaker. The lads and I will sup another pint and we'll meet you on the corner. I can smell rain in the air, and I'd like to get home before the heavens open.'

*

'That was good timing,' Holly said, as they let themselves into the house half an hour later, and the first drops of rain fell. Lightning forked the sky and a peal of thunder rolled across the valley, setting off the dogs as a gust of wind rattled the window frames.

'Goodness.' Rebecca laughed, dropping her parcels on the kitchen table as rain lashed the glass. 'That came on suddenly.'

'Just a brief summer storm,' Holly said, peering out of the window at the swirling black clouds. 'I hope it doesn't do too much damage.'

'Thankfully most of the silage is under cover,' Rebecca reminded her. She picked up the kettle. 'Will you have tea?'

'Before you do that,' Holly said, turning away from the window, 'there is something I'd like to give you. Come.' Puzzled, Rebecca left the kettle and followed her into the little-used parlour. Already patches of blue were visible among the grey through the parlour window. 'Come in.' Aunt Holly beckoned to Rebecca and Ella, who were hovering in the doorway. She crouched in front of the large mahogany sideboard that took up most of one wall. A collection of silver-framed photographs, Jeremiah's family members, was neatly arranged on a hand-made lace-edged cloth, which had once been white but had discoloured with age.

'Give me a hand, would you, Becky?' Rebecca hurried to help her lift a large wooden box from the bottom of the sideboard. 'Put it on the table.' Ella moved the vase of freshly cut roses from the highly polished side table and replaced it with the box. It was old, the wood faded and warped, with metal edges. The name of a company was stamped in black across the top.

'Jeremiah's mother gave me this when he and I were married,' Holly said, lifting the lid, 'and I'd like you and Ben to have it.'

182

Rebecca moved closer. Nestled in a bed of straw was a pale blue and white patterned teapot, a matching sugar bowl, milk jug and two cups and saucers. 'I've never used them,' Holly said, lifting out one of the teacups. 'I was always so afraid I might break one of the pieces.' She brushed away a strand of straw and handed Rebecca one of the cups.

'It's beautiful,' breathed Rebecca, running her index finger over the delicate porcelain. 'It's too much, Aunt Holly.'

'Nonsense,' Holly chided her. 'I considered giving them to Kenneth's wife one day but I'd much rather you had them. I know you will treasure them, as I have.'

'Thank you.' Rebecca gently replaced the cup in its straw nest.

Holly gestured towards the window. 'The rain's easing. It'll be stopping soon, and you can go to look at the cottage. Ella, put the kettle on, love. We'll have that cup of tea now.'

CHAPTER TWENTY-TWO

Pulling a shawl around her shoulders, Rebecca took her basket and crossed the muddy yard. The surrounding trees dripped from the recent shower and her hem was soon soaked by the wet grass. The September sky was clear, a small bank of clouds over the nearby hills the only evidence of the earlier rain.

She followed the well-worn path across the field, pausing to pick a handful of the last of the season's blackberries, careful to avoid the myriad rabbit holes that dotted the sloping edges of the field. Ahead, the old farm cottages gleamed in the hazy sunshine. There were two, standing together, nestled at the foot of a low hill upon which two piebald horses grazed peacefully. Dark, weathered stone, sloping slate-tile roof, the cottages looked out over the farm. The second was still in a state of disrepair. Loose shutters hung at odd angles, and it had a gaping hole in its roof.

'Hello,' Rebecca called, peering in at the open doorway. 'Ben?' The only reply was the resounding thud of a hammer. Ducking under the lintel, Rebecca stepped inside the empty parlour. The cottage comprised four rooms: a parlour, kitchen and two bedrooms upstairs. Following the sound of the hammering, she made her way up the stairs, finding Ben on his hands and knees in the doorway of the master bedroom.

'Becky.' Ben let out an exclamation of pleasure. He laid down his hammer and got to his feet, sweeping Rebecca into his embrace.

'I called, but I suppose you didn't hear me above all the hammering.' She grinned as he released her. 'It's coming along nicely, though, isn't it?' She crouched, running her fingers over the newly laid floorboards.

'Just got these last few to do,' Ben said, indicating the boards propped up against the uneven wall. 'Then I'm done. We can start bringing our belongings here this week.'

'I can't wait.' She wandered over to the window. 'It really will start to feel like a home then,' she said, gazing out over the meadow. A female deer emerged from the bank of trees to nibble the soft grass at the edge of the field, her ears twitching nervously. Rebecca watched her, listening to the thud of Ben's hammer.

'Could you hand me some more nails, please, Becky?' he said, silence settling on the room.

Rebecca crossed back to where he was working and handed him the nails. 'I brought a picnic,' she said, settling herself on the step between the bedroom and the landing, 'as you said you wouldn't be back for your dinner.'

'I wanted to get this finished.' Ben grunted, fitting a board into place. 'Our wedding is in two weeks and I won't have my wife moving into an unfinished house.'

'As long as the roof doesn't leak and I'm not going to fall through a hole in the floor and break my neck, I don't care about the rest,' Rebecca told him. She folded her arms around her knees, drawing them to her chest.

'Well, I do,' Ben said firmly. 'But once this is done, there's only a few bits and pieces outside that need fixing up. A lick of paint here and there.' He reached over to take Rebecca's hand. 'You go and set up our picnic while I finish off. I'll be down in a jiffy.'

'Don't be too long,' Rebecca said. Planting a kiss on his cheek and holding up her skirt so she didn't trip on the stairs, she made her way down to the kitchen.

Taking the basket, she rounded the side of the cottage, where she had an uninterrupted view of the surrounding hills and fields. She spread the blanket under the horse chestnuts, and began to unpack the food, glancing up every so often to enjoy the view. The doe had disappeared but several rabbits had emerged from their burrows to enjoy the sunshine. Rebecca watched their playful antics for a while, the warm breeze tugging at her hair. In two weeks' time she would be Mrs Ben Troke, mistress of her own home. She fingered the silver locket around her throat. If only her mother and father were here to share her joy, she thought, her eyes misting as she thought how much her mother would have enjoyed the wedding preparations. Much as she loved Aunt Holly and Uncle Jerry, it should be her father walking her down the aisle. It should be her mother accompanying her to her weekly dress fittings.

'Penny for them.'

At the sound of Ben's voice, she jumped. She turned her head, laughing sheepishly. 'Sorry, I was a bit melancholy.'

Picking up an apple, Ben stretched out on the blanket. 'What's caused you to be melancholy on such a lovely day?' he asked, taking out his pocketknife and peeling the apple.

'I was thinking about my parents,' Rebecca said, sitting close to him, 'and how I wish they could be at our wedding.'

Ben nodded his understanding. 'I feel the same about my mother. I wish you could have met her. You would have loved each other.' He handed Rebecca the perfectly coiled apple skin.

'It's a shame Celeste and Seth can't come to the wedding,' she said, as she nibbled the sweet-tasting peel. 'They sent their congratulations and a postal order for a shilling.'

'That's kind of them,' Ben said, putting his arm around Rebecca's shoulders as she handed him one of her pies. 'At least we have Uncle Jerry and Aunt Holly. They couldn't have been more generous if we were their own flesh and blood.'

'They certainly go out of their way to make us feel like a part of the family,' Rebecca agreed.

'They do,' Ben said. 'And,' he added, with a mischievous grin, 'all being well, we'll be starting our own little family soon.'

Without warning, the dark clouds returned, scurrying across the sky, blotting out the sun and leaching the colour from the landscape. The rabbits disappeared back underground.

'You'd better go before you get soaked,' Ben said, as Rebecca packed up the leftover picnic. He kissed her warmly on the mouth. 'I'll be home in time for supper,' he promised, as Rebecca started down the sloping meadow. The billowing clouds had brought a drop in the temperature and she shivered, tugging her shawl tighter around her shoulders. She glanced back, ready to wave, but Ben had gone. She smiled at the memory of his kisses. Fortune had indeed smiled on her in bringing her a man like Ben, she mused. She glanced up at the sky. It was dark and foreboding, the threat of more rain hanging heavily in the damp air.

The wind whipped the trees, as she quickened her pace. Large raindrops hit the ground in front of her and she ducked her head, tugging her shawl over her head as she rounded the barn. A few more steps and she'd be home and dry . . . She let out a startled shriek as someone grabbed her wrist, yanking her into the barn.

Heart beating wildly, she wrestled against her assailant in the dim barn. 'Kenny?' she squeaked in surprise, as her eyes adjusted to the gloom. 'What are you playing at? Let me go.' She tried to snatch away her arm but he tightened his grip. 'What are you— Ow!' Rebecca scowled. 'Kenneth? Let go. You're hurting me.'

'Hold your tongue!' snarled Kenneth, pulling her further into the barn.

'Kenneth!' Rebecca snapped. 'Stop being silly. Let me go. I've got work to do.'

'I said, hold your tongue!' Kenneth hissed.

She remembered how he'd tried to kiss her at the summer ball, and she wondered briefly whether he'd been drinking, but she couldn't smell alcohol on his breath. She was starting to feel alarmed.

'Kenny,' she said, forcing herself to remain calm, 'let go of me. I'll – I'll scream.'

Before she realized what was happening, she was on the ground, and Kenneth was on top of her. 'Scream all you like. No one will hear you.'

With a sinking heart Rebecca remembered that Jeremiah and Holly had gone to town for Ella's final dress fitting. The air smelt musty and stale, and the ground was hard beneath her, as Kenneth fumbled with her skirts. 'Kenneth, don't,' she pleaded, tears of humiliation and anger streaming down her face. She clawed at his face but he grabbed her hands, holding them tightly as he used his other to undo his trousers. Rebecca screamed.

'Shut up, bitch!' The back of his hand connected with her cheek, knocking her head sideways. Rebecca swallowed, tasting blood. She screwed her eyes shut, unable to bear the sight of Kenneth's face above her as he scrabbled between her legs. She felt them being stretched apart and then a sharp stab of pain. She turned her face away, hating the touch of his breath on her skin. She felt sick. She clenched her fists, vaguely aware of the sensation of dusty chaff beneath her fingernails. Suddenly she heard Kenneth groan. He shuddered and went limp, his face buried in her neck. She held her breath, listening to his ragged breathing.

After what seemed an age, he rolled off her. 'Get up,' he said, nudging her none too gently with the toe of his boot. 'You need to get cleaned up before Mother and Father return.' Rebecca turned onto her side, drawing her knees to her chest, hot, bitter tears rolling down her cheeks. There was a moment of silence. All she could hear was the all-too-normal sound of the chickens scratching in the dirt outside the barn door.

'Now you know what a real man is like,' Kenneth said, with a humourless chuckle, as he buttoned his trousers. 'Have a happy marriage.' He laughed. 'If Ben still wants you now you're soiled goods.' Through the slit in her eyelashes, Rebecca saw him bend down and pick up her shawl. 'Cover yourself,' he said disparagingly. 'You're disgusting.' He threw the shawl at her head. Blinded by it, Rebecca could only listen as he walked away. Once she was sure he wasn't coming back, she pulled the shawl from her face, clasping it to her chest as if it were a barrier between herself and the world.

How long she lay there, she didn't know. She was shivering with cold, and her throat was bone dry. Her body ached and she couldn't stop her teeth chattering. She just wanted to lie there and never move.

The chime of the church clock surprised her. Three. Had she lain here for almost two hours? Holly and Jeremiah would be home in another two hours. They couldn't see her like this. Nor could Ben. The thought of her dear, sweet fiancé brought a fresh flood of hot, angry tears. She couldn't let him find her like this. Fear brought her to her feet. She arranged her skirts, wincing at the pain of her bruised thighs, and stumbled to her feet. Clutching her shawl, she staggered across the yard to the pump, oblivious to the pouring rain. Glancing around to make sure no one was about, least of all Kenneth, she washed quickly, shivering as her skin met the cold water. Rain lashed at her as she picked straw from her hair and clothes. She was shivering violently now, whether from the cold or shock, she didn't know or care.

She dragged herself upstairs. She knew she should move faster, but it was as if her body was refusing to obey her. She stood at the doorway, tears streaming down her face as her gaze fell on her trunk. Inside were her new dresses and the things she'd bought for her bottom drawer. Over the next few days Ben would be moving them to the cottage. She shed her wet clothes and sank onto the bed, sobbing bitterly as she thought of her wedding dress. It was still on the mannequin in May Pickup's workroom. She was due to go for her final fitting tomorrow. 'Oh, Ben,' she cried. What would she say to him? How could she marry him now? She was soiled, ruined. With his one evil act, Kenneth had destroyed everything good in her life. She could never tell Ben what he had done. Ben would kill him, of that she had no doubt. And then Ben would hang. She had to protect him. And she couldn't marry him. Not now. Not after what Kenneth had done. Having such a dark, ugly secret between them would erode their happiness as sure as a cancer, eating away at them until nothing remained of their love but an empty shell. Rebecca bunched up the counterpane, holding it tightly in her fist, and wishing it was Kenneth's neck she was squeezing.

Suddenly overcome by nausea she only just made it to the chamber pot before her stomach emptied itself. Rocking back on her heels, she clutched her throat in horror as she was hit by the chilling realization that Kenneth might have left his baby inside her. The thought sent goosebumps erupting all over her body. She vomited again until there was nothing left in her stomach.

She sank onto the bed, clutching the blanket around her shivering body. She must have fallen asleep for when she opened her eyes, the rain had stopped and white clouds scudded across a pale blue sky. She sat up in alarm, terrified that at any minute Jeremiah and Holly would return or, worse, Ben would come home.

She had to leave Elm Tree Farm, and she had to leave now. Stiffening her resolve, Rebecca climbed wearily off the bed and, with shaking fingers, opened her trunk. For a moment she could only stare at her new clothes, each item wrapped in tissue paper. Taking a deep breath, her eyes smarting, she unfolded the neatly wrapped parcels until she found her black dress. She pulled on a new petticoat and underwear and tugged the black dress over her head. Not even taking time to look at her reflection, she packed her other new things into the small carpet bag she'd brought with her when she'd left Dartmouth and closed the trunk. From her bedside cabinet, she took her savings, and slipped the money into her pocket. On tiptoe, she crept to the window. There was no sign of Kenneth.

Picking up her bag, she was about to leave the room, when

she hesitated, glancing down at her hand. Her betrothal ring glinted in the fading light. Crying, she slid it off her finger and placed it on the dressing-table. The brooch Ben had bought her lay in a small dish. She picked it up, remembering the day he had given it to her. Choking back a sob, she pinned it to the collar of her dress and hurried downstairs. She paused on the bottom step, listening. All she could hear was the beating of her heart and the rush of blood in her ears. As she waited, she became aware of the church clock chiming a quarter past three.

She made her way cautiously to the parlour where she opened Jeremiah's desk, drew out a sheet of paper and wrote a note, saying how sorry she was that she had to leave. She apologized to Ben, saying she would always love him but that she couldn't marry him. She promised Jeremiah she would repay him every penny he'd spent on her wedding. With tears blurring her vision, she folded the note in half and, propping it against the mantelpiece clock, picked up her bag and let herself silently out of the house. Glancing round nervously in case Kenneth might be lurking nearby, she set off down the track.

CHAPTER TWENTY-THREE

She avoided the main road, not wanting to risk running into Holly and Jeremiah returning early. Instead, she took the lane leading in the opposite direction. She had barely gone half a mile before it started to rain again. Within minutes she was soaked to the bone.

Above the howl of the wind in the trees and the rain, she became aware of an approaching cart. She glanced over her shoulder, preparing to move onto the verge and let it pass, when she realized it was slowing. Swallowing her mounting terror that Kenneth had come after her, she felt faint with relief when a grizzled old man peered at her from beneath the tarpaulin cover. 'Where you headed, miss?'

'The station,' Rebecca said, blurting out the first thing that came into her head.

The man frowned. 'Which train do you want?'

'I'm trying to get to London,' Rebecca said, again off the top of her head. She had no idea how far London was from Shaftesbury or what she would do when she got there.

'All right.' The man coughed. 'Hop up.' He lifted the cover enough to allow Rebecca to scramble onto the cart. Despite the uncomfortable jolting and the hard, narrow seat, it was a relief to be out of the rain. Once they were on their way, the man lapsed into silence. Rebecca was in no mood for conversation either. She felt numb. She wondered if Holly was home yet. Had Jeremiah found her note? As she imagined Ben's shock and disbelief when Holly told him she was gone, she felt as if a vice were tightening around her heart. He would come looking for her, of that she had no doubt. That was why she had decided on London. She would be able to disappear.

Holly spotted the note the minute she'd come into the parlour to wind the clock. As she'd read it the colour had left her world. She'd sunk onto the nearest chair, calling for Jeremiah. He and Ella had come running. 'She's left us,' she'd wailed, thrusting the note under her husband's nose.

Jeremiah had read it in grim silence, then passed it to Ella and run his hands through his hair. 'I'd better tell Ben,' he said, exhaling deeply.

'Oh, Ben,' Holly wailed. 'Poor, poor Ben.'

'What about the wedding?' Ella whispered.

Holly shushed her. 'Go and see if she's taken her things,' she told Ella. Ella had just left the room when Ben stormed in. Jeremiah followed, looking broken. Ben faced Holly, red-faced, not caring that he was dripping water on the carpet.

'Uncle Jerry said Becky's gone,' he asked, his eyes begging her to deny it, to tell him it was a mistake, a cruel joke.

Unable to speak, Holly could only nod.

Now she handed Ben the note. He scanned it, the paper trembling in his shaking hand. 'But we were together just this afternoon.' His heartbroken expression tore Holly's heart and she reached out to embrace him but a loud sob from the doorway caught her attention.

194

Three pairs of eyes turned towards Ella, who was sobbing uncontrollably in the doorway. 'Her new clothes have all gone,' she choked out, between sobs. 'I found what she was wearing today, wet through, in the laundry basket.'

'She can't have gone,' Ben said, his brow furrowed. 'Where would she go?' He looked at Jeremiah. 'I have to find her.'

'Of course,' Jeremiah agreed, spurred into action. 'She can't have got far in this weather. We'll call in at Jack's place and borrow a couple of horses. They'll be quicker than old Dolly.'

'What's going on?' Kenneth asked, almost crashing into his father in the doorway.

'Becky's gone missing,' his mother told him gently. 'You didn't happen to see her this afternoon, did you?'

'No, not since this morning,' Kenneth replied. 'I thought she was going to see you,' he said to Ben.

'She did,' he replied, frowning. 'She left me just after one. You're sure you didn't see her when she came back to the house?'

'I've just said, haven't I?' Kenneth snapped.

Holly bit her lip. 'What could have possessed her? Do you think she's got cold feet about the wedding?' She looked at her husband hopefully.

'Becky wouldn't just walk out on me,' Ben said forcefully, before Jeremiah could reply. 'I have to find her.'

'We will, lad,' Jeremiah said firmly. 'Come on, let's get going. Kenneth, you too.'

'What about the cows? They need milking.'

'I'll ask Carter to send a couple of his lads over. Please?'

Kenneth hesitated. 'All right,' he said reluctantly. Then he slapped Ben on the shoulder. 'We'll find her,' he said, pulling his hat low over his eyes.

Ben nodded, his expression bleak.

On hearing what had happened, Jack Carter was only too happy to lend them his horses. He readily agreed to send a couple of his cowmen to see to the milking, and five minutes later, their faces set in grim determination, the three men set out.

'Which way?' Ben shouted above the torrent. Rain dripped from the brim of his hat, almost blinding him. The wind lashed at his mount as she whinnied and pawed the ground. Water was pouring off the fields in muddy streams.

'Let's split up,' Jeremiah suggested. 'I'll go this way.' He pointed with his crop. 'You boys take one of the other lanes.' He locked eyes with Ben. 'Chin up, lad,' he said. 'She's bound to have taken shelter in this weather. Search every barn, hut, hedgerow. We'll find her.'

Ben nodded. He scanned the windswept, rain-lashed fields. Apart from a handful of mournful sheep huddled beneath a large tree, there was no sign of life. With mounting despair, he nudged his horse forward, and started down the road.

'Here you are, miss.' The owner of the cart, whose name Rebecca had learned was Elijah, halted outside the railway station. 'Good luck.' He engaged the brake and lifted the edge of the tarpaulin. Thanking him, Rebecca grabbed her bag and scrambled to the ground, wincing as her feet sank deep into a puddle of brown water. Rain drummed on the station roof, pouring from the gutter and spilling down the station steps as she made her way onto the almost deserted platform.

'You're just in time,' the stationmaster said, glancing at his pocket watch as she paid for her ticket. 'The train's due in three minutes.'

Thanking him, Rebecca pocketed her ticket and went to sit in the waiting room, sliding down in her seat in despair as the enormity of her situation crashed over her. The thought that she would never see Ben again sat like a heavy rock in her chest. Grief settled over her, crushing her, and for a moment, she could hardly draw breath. She clamped her hand to her mouth to prevent herself crying out as silent tears slid down her cheeks.

'Five-fifteen to London, Waterloo,' called the stationmaster, waving his red flag. A porter came hurrying onto the platform, trolley at the ready. The bags waiting to be loaded sat in a neat row along the edge of the platform.

Rebecca got stiffly to her feet. She felt bruised inside and out. Her thighs throbbed, but the pain in her heart was far worse, and she was crying softly as she slowly boarded the train. She found a seat in an empty compartment and, placing her bag on the seat next to her, she rested her forehead against the window, raindrops blurring her view of the brown and green scrubland on the other side of the tracks.

By now, Ben would know she had gone. He would be so confused. She'd broken his heart, of that she had no doubt, but how could she have stayed? She couldn't. It was as simple as that. Ben would fall in love again. The thought caused a small sob to escape from her throat. He would be happy again, one day. And Kenneth . . . She tried to dispel the memory of Kenneth forcing himself on her. She felt sick. Nausea rose in her throat, and she swallowed it. To her relief no one entered her compartment. The doors closed, the guard blew his whistle, and the train pulled out of the station. Rebecca leaned back in her seat, staring unseeingly at the rainswept countryside drifting past the window, her sense of loss overwhelming. As the train neared Tisbury, she was overcome by the urge to get off and make her way back to Shaftesbury, but as it drew to a halt, she stayed where she was, frozen to her seat. She couldn't go back. Not now, not ever. She couldn't bear to see the disgust in Ben's eyes when he realized what had happened to her. Oh, he'd pretend. He was a good man, a kind and compassionate man. He'd marry her anyway, but what Kenneth had done would place a wedge between them. The train set off again, the small village slipping into the mist. As it snaked its way towards Salisbury, Rebecca closed her eyes and sobbed.

'She's left her ring,' Ella said, as Ben strode into the kitchen just after first light. He stared at her with incomprehension, his eyes red-rimmed and bloodshot from lack of sleep and grief.

'What?' he said brusquely, accepting the mug of tea Holly handed him. Jeremiah and Kenneth were sitting at the table, bleak-faced as they sipped their tea.

'Her betrothal ring,' Ella repeated slowly. 'Becky left it on the dressing-table. She must have taken it off before she left.'

Visibly deflating, Ben sank onto the nearest chair. 'I don't believe it,' he whispered. 'Why would she do that? We were so happy. She was so excited about the cottage. We were looking forward to married life.'

'She's duped you,' Kenneth said, hardly able to believe his luck. He'd had his story prepared. Becky had seduced him. But now, with her sneaking off, she'd played into his hands. Leaning back in his chair, he stretched his feet towards the range. The rain had stopped overnight, and the coming day promised to be fine, the dawn sky streaked with a blush of pink. 'She's taken you all for fools,' he said, giving his parents a disparaging look. 'Got you to spend all that money on her, and for what? We're better off without her, as far as I'm concerned.'

'You shut your mouth!' Ben was on his feet.

'Careful, Ben,' Jeremiah cautioned him, laying a restraining hand on Ben's arm.

'Kenneth, that's enough,' Holly said, shaking her head. 'We're all hoping Becky will come back, Ben,' she said, turning to him.

'Sit down, lad,' Jeremiah said gently.

Ben sat, his jaw clenched. His fingers tightened around his mug, his knuckles white. 'She wouldn't leave without a good reason,' Ben muttered, glowering at Kenneth, who glared back, his expression insolent.

'We searched everywhere,' Jeremiah said, with a weary sigh, rubbing the back of his neck. 'Kenneth checked the station at Gillingham, didn't you, lad?'

Kenneth nodded. 'The stationmaster said he hadn't seen anyone of Becky's description,' he lied. In truth, he hadn't bothered to ask. Wet and cold, he'd popped into the Red Lion for a pint of ale instead.

'I asked at Sturminster Newton.' Ben sighed. 'I got there just as the last train left and no one fitting her description had been seen.' He banged his fist on the table, making Holly and Ella jump. 'Where *is* she?'

'You searched the barns, outbuildings?' Holly bit her lip. 'What if she was sheltering somewhere? Did you ask at the neighbouring farms?'

Her husband shot her a look of exasperation. 'What do you take me for, Holly? Of course we did.' He shrugged. 'Unless she's gone across country, but that would be hard in the weather we've had. The fields are like bogs.' He exhaled loudly and rubbed his hand across his face. 'I don't know where else we can search,' he said.

'Should we tell the police?' asked Holly, getting up to refill the teapot.

'Becky left of her own accord.' Jeremiah pushed his empty mug aside, scraping back his chair. 'They won't be interested.' He put a hand on Ben's shoulder. 'The cows will want milking.'

Ben's heart was in tatters. He pushed back his chair and got to his feet. 'No breakfast for me,' he told Holly, as he grabbed his hat from where he'd hung it to dry in front of the range. 'I've no appetite.' With that he ducked out of the door, striding angrily across the yard.

Kenneth followed. Leaning on the gate of the milking parlour, Ben watched the other man through narrowed eyes as he went silently about his work, gathering the milking stool and pail. He was half hopeful Kenneth would do something to annoy him. He'd relish nothing more than smashing a fist into his smug face.

CHAPTER TWENTY-FOUR

Rebecca opened her eyes, blinking in the grey light filtering into the cavernous railway station. She swallowed, disoriented by her surroundings. Her mouth was dry, her eyes gritty and sore. She could smell bacon frying and her stomach rumbled. Ignoring her hunger, she sat up, heaviness settling inside her as the events of the previous day returned to her. She stifled a sob. She felt stiff and sore after a night on the wooden bench. Fighting back the tears, she scanned the station. The concourse was bustling with early-morning travellers. Pigeons roosted on the thick metal girders overhead, their incessant cooing echoing above the hustle and bustle. It was just gone six, according to the station clock. She rubbed her eyes.

Gripped by sudden panic, she reached under the bench, exhaling in relief as her hand closed over the handle of her bag. She touched her bodice, relieved to feel the comforting shape of her purse tucked close to her skin.

The first train from the south-west came steaming into the station, sending the pigeons swooping into the air, a flurry of feathers drifting like snowflakes. Shrinking back against the wall, Rebecca pulled her shawl over her face. She held her breath, scrutinizing the alighting passengers. Ben. His name formed silently on her lips even as her brain refuted what her eyes thought they'd seen. The man had a similar build and colouring, but he was shorter and dressed for the city. Her disappointment was tempered by relief: if Ben had come looking for her, she wasn't sure she would have the courage to send him away. And she refused to ruin his life as hers had been ruined. He deserved better. He deserved a wife unsullied by another man. The memory of Kenneth's brutal attack brought a fresh wave of bile racing up her throat and she reached the cloakroom just in time. She rocked back on her heels on the sawdust-strewn floor, the foul stench of the public convenience filling her nostrils. She rested a hand on her stomach, sending up a silent prayer that her ordeal hadn't left her in the family way. Her situation was dire enough. How would she cope as an unmarried mother? On shaky legs, she made her way slowly back to the platform where vendors were setting up stalls selling food. Despite her earlier hunger, her appetite had deserted her. She scanned the station for the exit and, with the aroma of frying food turning her stomach, she followed the tide of humanity heading for the street.

Once outside, she inhaled deeply, breathing in the damp, smoky air. The cobbled street was congested with omnibuses, horse-drawn carriages, carts and wagons. Ragged children, barefoot and dirty, darted between vehicles, and the pavements were bustling with pedestrians and street vendors plying their wares.

Having no idea where to go or what to do, Rebecca found a nearby café. The windows were fogged with condensation, the air thick with cigar smoke and the smell of fried food, but she was desperately thirsty so, gritting her teeth against the wave of nausea, she made her way to an empty table. A harassed-looking woman bustled over as she was pulling up her chair. 'What can I get you, love?'

'Just a pot of tea, please.'

'Anything else?' Rebecca shook her head. 'Pot of tea over here,' the woman shouted.

The tea was hot and strong, and seemed to settle her stomach. She sipped it slowly, watching the blur of passers-by through the fogged-up window. At this time of the morning, the clientele was predominantly factory workers, filling up on coffee and bread and dripping before a long, twelve-hour shift. Finding a job was her priority. Deciding that she couldn't waste any more time, she drained her mug and approached the counter.

'Have you any jobs?' she asked the proprietor, as she paid for her tea.

'Sorry, love.' The woman shook her head. 'We took on a new girl last week. You could try over the road, or the factories hereabouts are always on the lookout.'

Thanking her, Rebecca hefted her bag onto her shoulder and stepped out onto the busy street. It was growing warm, the sun cresting the station roof and catching the windows of the buildings opposite. During a brief lull in the traffic, she crossed to the café on the corner. It was busy. A woman carrying two steaming bowls emerged from the back.

'I was wondering whether you might have any jobs?' Rebecca blurted, as the woman hurried past her.

'Sorry, love. Nothing here. Try the canning factory around the corner. They may be hiring.'

Rebecca returned to the street. She found the canning factory easily enough. A large crowd of men and women had gathered in front of the gates. The smell of boiled meat hung heavily on the air, and a tall chimney belched clouds of black smoke into the sky. A large rat scurried across the top of the high wall. Another ran across her foot, making her flinch.

'All right, love?' a toothless old woman asked, edging closer to Rebecca. She was short and wrinkled, a threadbare shawl pulled over lank grey hair. She clutched it with gnarled fingers, her fingernails long and encrusted with dirt. 'Been waiting long?'

'I've just arrived,' Rebecca replied, almost recoiling at the woman's pungent smell.

'You're not from around here?' the woman said, her sharp eyes regarding Rebecca with open curiosity.

Rebecca shook her head, her hand moving automatically to the locket hidden beneath her bodice.

'Mrs Chubb.' A stern voice spoke out of the crowd. 'Stop pestering the girl.' A tall, heavily built woman with flaming auburn hair and piercing green eyes pushed her way through the crowd. 'You want to watch her,' she warned Rebecca, as the old crone shuffled away, muttering to herself. 'Give her an inch and she'll take a yard. She'll have the shirt off your back if you let her. Chrissie Flemming.' The woman thrust out a large, calloused hand.

'Becky Wheeler.'

'Nice to meet you, Becky.' Chrissie's handshake was firm and hearty. 'You new in town?'

Rebecca nodded.

'I thought so. You need to have your wits about you round here, pet,' she said, folding her arms across her chest. 'I've lost count of the number of country girls I've seen arrive in town and get themselves fleeced by some unscrupulous individual. Green as they come, most of them.' She smiled at Rebecca's discomfort. 'I don't mean to scare you,' she said kindly. 'Keep a sensible head on your shoulders and you'll do all right.'

'Will they open the gates soon?' Rebecca asked.

Chrissie shrugged. 'Most of this lot have been here since before dawn. They'll have taken in a quota already. Depends how many more they need. They often take people in at various times during the day.' She inhaled. 'I was late getting here this morning. My old man came home in a bit of a state last night. Lost his job on the docks, didn't he? So the fool decided to spend his wages on drink. No matter he's a wife and three kids at home needing to be fed.' She scowled. 'The rent's due tomorrow, so I need to earn enough today to make up the short-fall and get me and the kids some supper.'

Rebecca shifted her feet uncomfortably, her hand moving subconsciously to the bulk beneath her skirt. If she was frugal, she had enough savings to see her through several weeks. 'I need to find accommodation. Do you know of anywhere?'

Chrissie shook her head. 'There are lodgings all over the place,' she said. 'Depends how fussy you are and how much you can afford. I'd avoid the doss houses.' She pulled a face. 'And there are some unscrupulous landlords. And if you've got any valuables on you, sleep with them under your clothes. I've heard stories of people being robbed while they slept.'

A sudden sense of expectation rippled through the crowd. Rebecca stood on tiptoe to see above the heads of those crowding round the tall iron gate. A stocky, mean-faced man jangled a bunch of keys. 'Stand back,' he snarled, slotting a key into the lock. 'Don't crowd me.' He opened the gate a crack. 'You, you, you,' he said, motioning to five men and a woman. The chosen few hurried into the yard. 'Move back!' the man shouted, shoving away a young man who tried to push through the gate. A collective groan rose from the crowd as the gates slammed with a resounding clang.

'That's another couple of hours to wait,' Chrissie muttered. Her stomach gave a loud rumble and Rebecca guessed that she probably hadn't eaten a decent meal in days.

'Look,' she said, delving into her pocket. 'I've got a bit of money. Buy some food for you and your children.' She pulled out a handful of coins and held them out.

Chrissie snatched her hand, pushing it out of sight. 'Are you daft?' she hissed, glancing round to see if anyone was paying them attention. 'You're going to get yourself robbed. Did you not heed a single word I said earlier?'

Rebecca blushed. 'I'm sorry. I thought . . .'

'It's kind of you,' Chrissie said, her tone softening. 'And I appreciate it. If I don't get work, I may take you up on your offer, but you must be careful, love. If some of these lot know you've got money about you, they'll be on you like a pack of wolves.'

Rebecca felt foolish.

'Don't take it to heart.' Chrissie grinned. 'Look, have you had anything to eat?' Rebecca shook her head. 'If you keep my place in the queue, I'll nip over to one of the street vendors and get us a pie.'

'I'm not really hungry,' Rebecca said, 'but you're welcome to one.'

'You need to keep your strength up,' Chrissie told her sternly, taking the handful of coins Rebecca had offered her. 'No one will take you on if you look half starved.'

Rebecca smiled weakly. How could she tell her new friend that she wasn't abstaining from worry over money, but that her broken heart had robbed her of her appetite? She watched

Chrissie pick her way across the congested street. A young boy in rags hurtled across the road, almost getting run over by a horse-drawn carriage. He leaped onto the pavement just in time. The driver raised his whip, yelling at the boy, who made a rude gesture in return and disappeared down a nearby alley. A scuffle broke out between three men queuing at the gates, drawing the attention of a nearby policeman.

'Happens all the time,' Chrissie said, as one of the men was led away by the constable. She handed Rebecca a greasy paper-wrapped parcel. The fatty aroma turned her stomach as she unwrapped it and bit into the soggy pastry. The filling was sparse, stringy and more gristle than meat. She pulled a face. Fred would have been disgusted by such an inferior-quality pie and would have tossed the offending article into the gutter to be devoured by one of the many stray dogs that seemed to inhabit the area. 'Not good,' Chrissie said, swallowing hard.

'I can make better pies than this,' Rebecca said, without thinking.

'You're a pie maker?' Chrissie looked at her, interested. Rebecca nodded. She folded the remains of her pie into its wrapping and shoved it into her pocket to give to some passing street urchin later.

Chrissie raised a questioning eyebrow. 'Then why are you queuing outside Campbell's canning factory? Why aren't you applying to pie shops?'

'I only arrived here last night,' Rebecca explained. 'I asked at a couple of cafés, and they suggested I try the factories.'

'Tell you what,' Chrissie said, brushing pie crumbs from the bodice of her plain brown dress. 'You come back to mine tonight. I've got an idea.' She leaned in close. 'Forgive my impertinence, but how much money have you got?'

Rebecca had known Chrissie for approximately an hour but something told her she could trust her. Chrissie's eyes widened slightly when Rebecca told her. 'I sold my pies to several hotels and eating houses in my local area,' Rebecca said, by way of explanation. 'Aunt Holly was insistent I keep most of what I earned.'

'Aunt Holly?'

'She's not my real aunt,' Rebecca said, with a pang of loss. She wondered what Holly and Jeremiah thought of her sudden disappearance. And Ben. Her chest tightened and she pushed aside thoughts of him. There would be time for tears later, when she was alone. 'She and her husband were my employers, but they treated me like a member of the family.'

'It sounds like you were living the good life,' said Chrissie. 'Why did you leave?'

Rebecca said, her words laden with regret, 'Something happened. I couldn't stay.' She looked at her feet.

Clearly sensing she didn't want to talk about her situation, Chrissie changed the subject. 'It's about an hour's walk to mine. There's five of us in two rooms, but you're welcome to squeeze in with the kids for tonight.'

'That's very kind of you,' Rebecca said. 'I'm able to afford lodgings, though. You don't need to put yourself out.'

'To be honest, I don't feel like being in the house with my old man by myself. He'll have a heck of a hangover after what he drank last night, so he'll be like a bear with a sore head.'

'All right,' Rebecca acquiesced. 'But you must let me pay towards my keep and buy dinner.'

Chrissie's face brightened. 'That would be a help.'

The sun climbed above the rooftops, the shadows shortening as it reached its zenith. The city steamed and boiled beneath the September sun. The air was a thick stew of rotting rubbish, horse manure and the cloying, sickly stench emanating from the tanning factory.

As the day wore on, Rebecca and Chrissie took turns to go to the water pump and slake their thirst. The water tasted foul, quite unlike what she'd enjoyed on the farm, pumped from the spring. Rebecca wiped her mouth on her hand and straightened. Was it only yesterday she'd left? Yesterday afternoon she'd been happily betrothed to the love of her life, her whole life mapped out before her, yet just twenty-four hours later she was in a strange town, drinking foul-tasting water with no clue as to what her future held.

Bone-weary, her back aching from standing around all day, she made her way to Chrissie. The gates had opened twice more, with only a handful of people being ushered into the factory yard each time. From various parts of the city clocks chimed, counting down the hours. The shadows were lengthening, the sun sinking below the rooftops. Gulls wheeled overhead, while pigeons and crows squabbled over scraps in the gutters. The taverns began to fill as whistles signalled the end of the working day.

'Come on.' Chrissie tucked her hand through Rebecca's arm. 'Let's go home.'

Rebecca gave her a grateful smile. She was desperately tired. She had slept little the night before. The bench had been uncomfortable, the railway station noisy but, as well as that, she'd been too overcome by sadness to sleep. As they made their way through the narrow streets, she was conscious of a knot of anxiety building in her stomach. Chrissie had been less than complimentary about her husband, Joe, over the course of the day and Rebecca couldn't help but fret about what he would say to his wife bringing home a stranger.

They called in at a small grocery shop where, ignoring Chrissie's protest, Rebecca bought enough food to last the family a few days. 'Just until you or your husband find work,' she told Chrissie firmly, as she settled up.

'I'll pay you back, I promise,' Chrissie said, shame colouring her pale cheeks. 'I hate being indebted to a friend.'

'I'm in your debt more,' Rebecca replied. 'You're opening up your home to me.'

Chrissie gave a snort. 'You might wish you'd decided to look for lodgings elsewhere when you see it,' she said drily, as they rounded the corner into a narrow street of tall, soot-blackened brick buildings, each with grimy windows at pavement level. Smoke billowed from chimneys and the smell of cooking hung heavy on the air. Grimy windows were thrown open to the cool evening breeze, voices drifting and mingling with the shouts of the children playing. Grubby-faced toddlers crawled in the gutters.

Two small boys, their trousers patched at the knees, shirts untucked, cuffs frayed and edged with dirt, hurtled towards the two women.

'Mama,' shouted the taller of the two, a gangly lad of about six with strawberry-blond hair and his mother's green eyes, as he flung his arms around Chrissie's ample waist.

'I'm hungry, Mama,' whined the smaller child. He was stockier, his dark blond hair flopping in his dark brown eyes.

'Hello, Sidney, hello, Harry.' Chrissie kissed both boys on the top of their heads, as they pressed themselves into the folds of her skirt. 'We've brought food.' She held both boys at arm's length, her expression serious. 'Have you had nothing to eat all day?'

'Mrs Fisher gave us some bread and dripping at dinner time,' the older boy said.

'That was kind of her. Where's your father, Sidney?'

The taller of them gave a shrug. 'Sleeping. He told us not to come into the house cos we'd wake him up.'

Chrissie exhaled slowly, her lips pressed into a thin line of annoyance. 'Perhaps we should wake him up,' she said grimly, placing an arm around her boy's shoulders.

'Maybe I should go,' Rebecca said nervously. 'I'll find somewhere . . .'

'I'm not letting you wander these streets on your own,' Chrissie said firmly. 'You'll be eaten alive. Come on. You're more than welcome. And don't mind my old man. I can handle him. Boys, this is Mama's new friend, Miss Wheeler. What do you say?'

'Good afternoon, Miss Wheeler,' Sidney said politely.

'How do you do?' intoned Harry, solemnly.

'I do very well, thank you.' Rebecca smiled. 'I'm pleased to meet you both.'

'I'm six,' Sidney told her proudly. 'Harry's only four.'

'I'm almost five,' Harry protested fiercely, scowling at his brother.

'No, you're not,' scoffed Sidney. 'He's not, is he, Mama?'

'Well, not for another ten months.' She smiled. 'Now, don't quarrel. We have a guest. Whatever will Miss Wheeler think of you both?'

Rebecca smiled. 'They're lovely boys,' she said, watching them as they ran off to join their friends, many of whom had paused in their play to stare at the strange woman walking up their street. Chrissie seemed to know everyone, waving and exchanging a few words with the groups of housewives huddled in their doorways or enjoying a few moments' respite in the street before returning to the endless round of chores.

'We've a good community around here,' Chrissie said, with a grin, as they stopped outside a narrow, dark-brick house midway along the terrace. 'Everyone looks out for each other.' She motioned to a short flight of steps leading below street level. 'We're down here,' she said.

Trying not to give in to the temptation to hold her nose, for there was an overpowering smell of tom cat in the dank air, Rebecca followed Chrissie into a small, cramped parlour where a man was dozing on a threadbare settee.

'Joe!' Chrissie said loudly, letting the door bang shut behind her. 'Wake up. We've got company.'

The man opened his eyes, squinting up at his wife in the dim light. 'Oh, my head.' He groaned, dragging a hand over his chin, the two-day-old stubble rasping against his rough palm. He swung his feet to the floor, pushing a lock of black hair out of his bloodshot eyes.

'You'll get no sympathy from me,' Chrissie said sharply. 'This is my friend, Becky. Becky,' she said drily, 'my husband, Joe.'

'Good evening, Mr Flemming,' said Rebecca, eyeing him nervously.

Joe nodded and mumbled a reply.

'Becky paid for our supper,' Chrissie said, dumping the bag of provisions on the table, 'seeing as you decided drink was more important than filling your kids' bellies.'

'Thanks,' Joe muttered sheepishly, getting to his feet.

'And where do you think you're going?' Chrissie snapped, as he reached for his coat. 'You're not leaving this house unless it's to look for work, and you're not going to get anything at this hour, are you?'

'Bob next door said they were looking for a night watchman at his place,' Joe responded sullenly. 'He said he'd put in a word for me.' He glanced at the clock. 'I need to go now if I'm to be in with a chance.'

Noticing Chrissie's eyes narrow, Rebecca had a feeling her new friend's husband couldn't always be relied upon to tell the truth.

'If you're pulling a fast one,' Chrissie said, confirming Rebecca's suspicion, 'and you come home rolling drunk again, I'll swing for you, I swear.'

Joe held up his hands in supplication. 'I'm telling the truth, promise.'

Chrissie snorted. 'Off you go, then,' she said. 'Here.' She shoved a parcel into his hands. 'I expect you haven't had anything to eat all day either, have you?'

'Thanks, love,' Joe said, leaning in for a kiss.

'Get away with you,' grumbled Chrissie, wrinkling her nose in distaste. 'You stink of drink.' She let out a long-suffering sigh. 'Go on, then. You don't want to be late and miss your chance.'

As the door banged shut behind him, she said, 'Don't ever get married, Rebecca.' Then she caught sight of Rebecca's stricken face. 'Oh, Becky, love, what is it?' she cried.

The tears began to fall and before she could stop herself, Rebecca was sobbing uncontrollably.

'Come and sit down.' With obvious dismay, Chrissie ushered Rebecca to the sofa. 'I'll put the kettle on.'

'Do you want to tell me what that was all about?' Chrissie asked a few minutes later, handing Rebecca a mug of sweet, milky tea. 'You don't have to if you don't want to,' she added, as Rebecca wiped her eyes.

'I'm sorry,' she mumbled, blowing her nose.

'Please don't be,' Chrissie said soothingly, as she perched

next to Rebecca on the settee. 'My grandmother always said a good cry does a person the world of good.' She sipped her tea. 'You're obviously very upset. Has it to do with the reason you left your aunt's?'

Rebecca nodded. 'I was engaged to be married,' she said, so quietly Chrissie had to strain to hear her. Rebecca absently stroked the brooch pinned to her collar.

'What happened?' Chrissie sipped her tea.

Rebecca's eyes clouded. 'Yesterday Aunt Holly's son, Kenneth . . . he forced himself on me.' She heard Chrissie gasp as her own mind struggled to process what she had just said. Was it only yesterday that she had been looking forward to her wedding in just two weeks' time? Only yesterday that Ben had kissed her? Grief tightened her chest until she could hardly breathe.

'Your fiancé broke off the betrothal?' Chrissie asked, clearly affronted on Rebecca's behalf.

'I didn't tell him,' Rebecca replied. 'Ben would have married me anyway, of course he would. He's an honourable man.' A single tear trickled down her cheek. Her expression softened. 'But it would always be between us. He'd grow to hate me. And what if I'm with child? We'd never have known if it was his or . . .'

'Oh, you poor girl,' Chrissie crooned sympathetically.

Rebecca stared at the tea in her mug. She hoped to God she wasn't carrying Kenneth's child. 'I was also scared Ben would fight him,' she whispered. 'I couldn't risk him going to prison, or worse.'

'I'm sorry, Becky,' Chrissie said sorrowfully. 'It's unfair but I can understand why you had to leave.'

'Mama, we're hungry,' shouted Sidney, barrelling into the parlour, his younger brother close behind him.

'Just a minute,' Chrissie said, as Rebecca turned away so the children wouldn't notice her tear-stained face. 'Go out the back and wash. Mama and Miss Wheeler are just talking.'

The two boys trooped out of the back door through which Rebecca caught a glimpse of a lichen-speckled wall and damp flagstones.

'What was it you wanted to discuss with me?' Rebecca asked, suddenly remembering the reason Chrissie had invited her home in the first place.

'It can wait until tomorrow,' Chrissie said, giving Rebecca's hand a squeeze. 'I'll get supper on the table. Thanks again for your generosity. I shall repay you.'

'You're offering me a bed for the night,' Rebecca said. 'That's payment enough.' She smiled gratefully. The idea of spending a night in a boarding house, alone and knowing no one, had terrified her.

They ate supper at the table with the back door open to the breeze, allowing Rebecca a view of the yard. There was a privy, which, she learned, was shared with the rest of the tenants, and a coal bunker. It was surrounded by tenement buildings so the yard only got light when the sun was at its zenith. The flagstones were green and slippery from the perpetual damp. She spotted a large black and white cat washing itself on top of the wall, and wondered if it was responsible for the stench she'd noticed earlier.

'No sign of Joe,' Chrissie remarked, mopping up the last of her gravy with a hunk of dry bread. 'He's either got the job or he's in the Three Bells.'

Stifling a yawn, Rebecca set her knife and fork to one side. She had little appetite. Noticing Sidney and Harry eyeing her untouched food, she passed them the plate.

'You look shattered, Becky,' Chrissie said sympathetically. 'We'll have an early night. I'm afraid we've only got the one bedroom, but you can go in with me. Joe's used to the settee. He'll be fine.'

'Are you sure?' Rebecca asked. 'I don't mind taking the settee.'

'I wouldn't hear of it. You're our guest.' She grinned at the boys. 'Right, you two. If you've finished you can get ready for bed.' The boys scampered into the next room. Chrissie smiled. 'They're good lads,' she said, beaming with maternal pride. 'I think we'll have a last cup of tea once we've tackled the washing-up, and then get off ourselves. It's been a long, tiring day.'

CHAPTER TWENTY-FIVE

'Do you think there's a market for another pie seller?' Rebecca stared at Chrissie across the breakfast table. Loud snores reverberated from the bedroom where Joe was fast asleep. He'd arrived home just before six o'clock, after a full night's work, and to Chrissie's obvious relief, they'd offered him the position full time.

'I certainly do, if your pies taste as good as you say they do,' Chrissie said, nodding emphatically in response to Rebecca's questioning gaze. 'You can bake them here and hawk them around the factory gates.'

'I'm not sure.' Rebecca looked doubtfully around the cramped room. After Holly's spacious kitchen, there was barely room to swing a cat in Chrissie's. Not to mention the tiny oven.

'We'll manage,' Chrissie assured her. 'Eventually we could move to bigger premises.'

'Let's not get ahead of ourselves,' laughed Rebecca. She bit her lip. She hadn't slept well again, thoughts of Ben keeping her awake much of the night. When she'd finally cried herself to sleep in the early hours, she'd been haunted by memories of her ordeal.

'It's hard work,' she said, unable to muster any enthusiasm. 'And it'll be an early start.'

'I'll be working alongside you,' Chrissie insisted. 'At least consider it, Becky,' she pleaded. 'You'd be doing me a favour. I can be at home to keep an eye on the boys and earning at the same time. Now Joe's back in work, we'll soon be on our feet again.'

Rebecca felt herself weakening. Chrissie's enthusiasm was infectious, and she certainly wasn't relishing the thought of factory work. She glanced around the kitchen area again. 'I suppose we could give it a go,' she said, at length.

'Good.' Chrissie sat back; arms folded triumphantly across her chest. 'Give me a list of ingredients and I'll send Sid down to Mason's. He'll put it on the slate and we can pay him back at the end of the week.'

'I can afford to pay up front,' Rebecca reminded her.

'That's your money. Hold on to it for the time being,' Chrissie told her. She rubbed her hands together. 'Oh, I haven't felt this excited about anything for a long time.' She scraped back her chair. 'I'll get a pencil and paper.'

'Mmm, it smells so good in here, Mama,' said Sidney, flopping onto the sofa. It was just gone ten o'clock in the morning and the aroma of stewing meat filled the small room. 'We could smell it all the way up the street. Mrs Jones from upstairs wants to know what's cooking.'

'You can tell Mrs Jones she's welcome to buy one of our delicious pies for her supper.' Chrissie flapped at a large bluebottle with a tea-towel.

'I'm so hungry, Mama,' whined Harry, tugging at his mother's skirts.

'Here you are, boys,' Rebecca said, ladling a spoonful of the gently simmering stew into bowls. 'You can be our official tasters.'

'Not too much, now,' Chrissie cautioned.

Rebecca grinned. 'There's plenty more and I'm curious to see what the boys think.' She raised her brows expectantly as the children each swallowed a spoonful of the rich, meaty stew.

'I like this!' declared Harry.

'Me too,' echoed his brother.

Rebecca and Chrissie exchanged smiles. For a moment the only sound was the scraping of spoons in bowls.

'That was so good,' Sidney said, with a sigh. 'I'd like some more,' he added hopefully.

'There'll be a pie for you at dinner time,' Rebecca promised, as Chrissie chased them out into the street.

'What are you cooking in there, Chrissie Flemming?' shouted a woman from across the street.

'Ah, you'll see,' Chrissie called back, with a grin. 'I think we're the talk of the street,' she said, poking the potatoes boiling rapidly on the stove. 'Almost done,' she said, laying the knife on the table. She glanced at the clock. 'Will we be ready for the dinner-time trade, do you think?'

'Oh, yes,' replied Rebecca, as she rolled out the pastry. 'Tomorrow we'll be up earlier. What time is your neighbour bringing the trays round?'

'Within the next fifteen minutes, his wife said.'

Rebecca nodded. As always when she was introducing her pies to new customers she felt anxious, but so far, she'd never had a bad word so she was hopeful the workers of Whitechapel would feel the same.

'I never knew just how heavy these trays are,' she said, an hour later as she and Chrissie set off down the street. They each held a large wooden tray laden with freshly baked meat and potato pies. The thick leather strap rubbed along the back of her neck and dug into her shoulders.

'The discomfort will be worth it,' Chrissie remarked cheerfully. 'You certainly weren't exaggerating. I've never tasted pies this good.'

Rebecca smiled at the compliment but couldn't help thinking regretfully of all the customers she was letting down in Shaftesbury. If her pies sold well today, she would start putting money aside to send back to Jeremiah. She was determined to repay him for all the expense he'd gone to for the wedding.

They were followed down the street by a gaggle of children, Sidney and Harry among them. 'Pies for sale!' Sidney yelled. 'Delicious pies for sale!'

Despite her overwhelming misery, Rebecca couldn't help but laugh at the boy's enthusiastic sales pitch.

They turned the corner and made their way through narrow, shadowy streets. Men stood in groups, smoking and talking. They paid the two women no notice. Rebecca began to feel anxious and vulnerable, and she was glad of Chrissie's presence. Her friend was certainly more worldly wise than Rebecca.

The air smelt acrid and foul. Tall chimneys belched great columns of thick smoke into a gunmetal grey sky. Pigeons cooed from where they perched on the factory windowsills and the pavements reverberated with the sound of heavy machinery.

'Pies!' Chrissie yelled, making Rebecca jump as they approached a group of desperate-looking men and women huddled in front of the locked gates of a meat canning factory. 'Freshly baked meat and potato pies. Best you've ever tasted.'

'Oh, yeah?' sneered a burly man with a shaven head. 'Says who?'

'My six-year-old son, that's who,' Chrissie responded

cheerfully, lifting the corner of her tray-cloth and allowing the aroma of the rich gravy to waft towards the crowd.

'Smells all right,' the man said grudgingly. 'How much?' Chrissie told him. 'Give us one, then,' he said, delving into his trouser pocket and coming up with a handful of coins. Rebecca took his money and gave him one of the warm pies. Her first sale. She watched hopefully as the man bit into the crisp pastry, his eyes widening with pleasure as he chewed. He swallowed. 'Not bad,' he said, nodding appreciatively. 'Not bad at all.' Chrissie gave Rebecca an I-told-you-so smile.

Within the hour, they had sold out. They walked back to Chrissie's, counting the money, and were soon hard at work on the next batch.

As the days passed, Rebecca's reputation grew. By the end of the first week there wasn't a family in the street who hadn't tried her pies, and by the end of the following week, the factory workers were actively watching out for the two women. Rebecca and Chrissie were kept busy from morning until dusk. Joe borrowed a small handcart from his new employer and delivered pies to the local public houses every evening on his way to work.

On the last Saturday of September, which should have been her wedding day, Rebecca woke up feeling physically ill. Somehow she'd managed to bake the required number of pies but, unable to face going out, she'd remained at home while Chrissie and the boys had taken the pies round the factories. Joe had given them use of the handcart while he caught up on his sleep. While they were gone, Rebecca sat huddled in a chair, fingering the brooch Ben had bought her at the market. She wore it every day and, though it had no value, it was as precious to her as her mother's silver locket.

Mercifully, Kenneth's attack hadn't left her in the family way, but while the bruises had faded, the trauma remained. She still flinched at the sound of male voices raised in anger. Joe was the only man whose presence she could tolerate. Even when they were buying her pies, she held herself tense, ready to flee at the slightest provocation, panic rising inside her if they crowded her or got too close, and she was eternally grateful for Chrissie's forceful presence.

'I think we need to talk about where the business is going,' Chrissie said through chattering teeth as they walked home one evening in early February.

'I see,' Rebecca said slowly, with a flutter of anxiety. She hoped Chrissie wasn't going to say she'd had enough. Demand for their pies had increased to such a degree that making them was taking over the small space and she'd been thinking for a while that the situation wasn't ideal. She and Chrissie still shared the double bed at night, while Joe was at work. He'd been at the factory for five months now, a record according to Chrissie.

'I think we need to consider moving to bigger premises,' Chrissie said, as they neared her house. The street was deserted, but for a group of bigger boys playing football at the end of the road. A cold wind howled between the tenement buildings, whistling under the eaves and tossing debris in its wake.

'I've been thinking that myself,' Rebecca said. The wind scoured her cheeks, its cold fingers tugging at her hair. 'Do you know of somewhere?'

'The woman who runs the fish stall outside the station said there's a place come up in Tannery Lane.' Chrissie grinned. 'We could go and view it now, if you like. It's not far.'

'Yes, let's.'

They dropped off the heavy trays at home. The boys were playing quietly in front of the stove with their toy soldiers so as not to disturb their sleeping father.

'We won't be long,' Chrissie told them, closing the door softly behind her. She tucked her arm through Rebecca's and they walked quickly up the street, their footsteps echoing on the cobbles as they rounded the corner into Tannery Lane. The road sloping down towards the blackened arches of the railway bridge was lined with shops. A few still had their awnings out but most were shutting for the evening.

'It must be that one, there,' Chrissie said, pointing at the 'To Let' sign pasted across the window of a shop situated towards the end of the row, between a butcher's and a haberdashery.

'Are we ready to take on a café, do you think?' mused Rebecca, peering through the grimy window.

'It'll mean no more lugging those heavy pie trays about,' replied Chrissie. 'Our customers will come to us.'

'But what about the factory workers?' Rebecca protested. 'They've supported us so well and I'd hate to disappoint them.'

'We'll hire a couple of lads to cover the factory trade,' Chrissie said, waving away Rebecca's concern. 'What do you think?'

Rebecca felt excitement stir deep inside her, as she took in the tables and chairs stacked along one wall.

'Shall we enquire?' Chrissie asked.

Rebecca smiled and nodded. They made their way along the passageway between the café and the butcher's to the backyard and climbed the metal staircase to the upstairs flat.

'I hope someone's in,' remarked Rebecca, hanging on to her hat, the cold wind whipping at her skirts as she knocked on the door with a gloved hand. From inside came the sound of children squabbling. A man's voice shouted at them to be still, as heavy footsteps approached the door. It was opened by a heavily built man with dark hair. He had shadows under his eyes, and he exuded a weary air.

'We're sorry to bother you,' Rebecca said, as the sound of a child's crying rose to a crescendo somewhere behind the man, 'but we've come about the café you have to rent.'

'You're interested?' the man exclaimed, his demeanour brightening.

'We are,' replied Chrissie, as a small girl of about eighteen months with a dirty nose and tear-stained face squeezed herself between the man's legs.

'Thomas, Christopher,' the man said, whirling round. 'Look after your sister. I'll be back in a minute.' Steering the toddler down the hallway, the man grabbed a handful of keys from a hook by his head and stepped onto the narrow walkway, shutting the door firmly on the now snivelling child. 'Sorry about that,' he said, with a weary smile. 'They miss their mother. I'm Gordon – Gordon Graham.' He ran a hand through his unruly hair.

'Mrs Flemming and Miss Wheeler.' Chrissie made the introductions.

Gordon indicated the stairs. 'After you, ladies. It's been in my family for generations,' he said, unlocking the back door and standing aside for Rebecca and Chrissie to enter. The air smelt musty, as if no one had been inside for a long time, and dust clung to every surface. The floor was covered with old sawdust, and cobwebs swayed in the disturbed air.

'Until my wife fell ill last year, we ran a successful tea shop. I closed it to care for her and look after the children. Sadly, she passed away last September.'

'I'm sorry to hear that,' Rebecca murmured.

'Thank you.' Gordon gave her a wry smile. 'It's been hard.' He cleared his throat. 'Taking care of the children is a full-time job in itself. How my dear late wife managed to look after the three of them and find time to help me in the tea shop, I'll never know. She was a wonderful woman.' He ran a hand through his hair. 'The ovens are all in perfect working order, and there's plenty of workspace.'

'Miss Wheeler bakes the most excellent meat pies,' Chrissie said, walking slowly round the room, inspecting every nook and cranny.

'Is that so, Miss Wheeler?' Gordon asked, seeming genuinely interested.

'They do seem popular,' Rebecca replied modestly, feeling a flush creep up her neck.

'Wait until you taste one, Mr Graham,' Chrissie said. 'What do you think of the place, Becky?' she asked, her eyes dancing with excitement.

'It does seem ideal,' agreed Rebecca.

Gordon beamed. 'I'd better go back to the children. They've been particularly quarrelsome today. I'll return shortly and you can let me know what you've decided.'

As soon as Gordon was out of earshot, the two women flung their arms around each other.

'I'm so excited,' Chrissie squeaked, as they hugged each other hard. 'Me, Chrissie Flemming, a business owner. Who'd have thought?'

'I need to pinch myself,' Rebecca said, anxiety twisting a knot in her stomach. 'You don't think we've bitten off more than we can chew, do you?'

'Becky Wheeler,' Chrissie said sternly, holding her friend at arm's length. 'You are the best pie maker for miles around. This venture will be a huge success, you mark my words.'

'I hope so,' Rebecca said, walking over to the window and looking out onto the dark street. The lamplighter was doing the rounds and the flickering yellow light of the lamp outside the shop cast a warm glow over the dirty floor.

Her fingers clasped her locket and, as always, her thoughts turned to Ben, and the family she'd left behind. What would they think of her having her own shop? Had things been different, Holly would have been so proud. The thought brought tears to her eyes. She'd sent a postal order repaying all the money Jeremiah had spent on her wedding dress and the new clothes she'd brought with her to London. She'd posted it from nearby Hatfield, to throw anyone off the scent, should they come looking for her. By 'anyone', she meant Ben. She knew he would never give up his search for her, and it broke her heart.

She stood in front of the window, looking out at the darkness, her reflection staring back at her. The lamp sputtered in the draught, sending shadows darting up the walls. She missed Ben with every fibre of her being, every minute of every day.

Footsteps sounded on the metal staircase and the back door opened, letting in a gust of icy air. 'Have you ladies come to a decision?' Gordon asked, rubbing his cold hands together.

Turning from the window, Rebecca and Chrissie exchanged excited glances. At Chrissie's nod, Rebecca smiled and said, 'We'd like to take it, Mr Graham.'

'Congratulations,' said Gordon, as he handed over the keys. 'I look forward to seeing what you do with the place. It's been neglected for far too long.'

CHAPTER TWENTY-SIX

Ben stood in the windswept churchyard, his mood as bleak as the grey March sky. In the six months since Rebecca had walked out on him, his life had fallen apart. He'd been out of his mind with grief as he'd travelled the length and breadth of the county in search of her, to no avail. There had been a few weeks of hope, just before Christmas, when a postal order had arrived, with a brief note explaining it was to repay Jeremiah and Holly for their expense. The envelope was postmarked Hatfield and Ben had spent ten days scouring the area without success.

Holly and Jeremiah had been patient with him. They'd understood his heartbreak. After all, they were dealing with their own grief, as well as feeling betrayed and let down by Rebecca, whom they'd loved and trusted.

In the new year, Ben had made the painful decision to leave Elm Tree Farm. Memories of Rebecca were everywhere. He'd have gone completely mad had he stayed. Jeremiah had shaken his hand and said he understood. Holly had held him close, trying hard not to cry, while Ella had openly sobbed. Even Kenneth had shaken his hand.

He'd been taken on by a neighbouring farmer, Angus Nichols.

Angus was a taciturn man, with a reputation for working his labourers hard, which suited Ben perfectly. He had no need of friends, and the hard work and long hours kept his mind from straying where he didn't want it to go.

In the two and a half months he'd been at Cherwell Farm, he'd not seen anything of the Seymours or Ella, so it had come as a surprise when Kenneth came to see him, and an even greater surprise when he asked him to be best man at his upcoming wedding. So here he was, standing in the cold churchyard, summoning the courage to go back into the church. He knew Kenneth would be wondering what he was doing, but sitting in the front pew, knowing it was where he and Rebecca should have been married six months earlier, was almost unbearable, and he'd had to get out.

He leaned against the stone wall of the church, scanning the lane. A gust of wind shook the trees, sending a flurry of pink blossom drifting to the damp ground. The gate creaked and Ben nodded to a middle-aged couple hurrying down the gravel path, the woman clutching at her hat as the wind threatened to whip it off her head. They ducked into the porch as the vicar, a tall, angular man with a long, thin nose and receding dark hair, emerged, his robes billowing in the wind.

'No sign of the bride yet,' Reverend Gray observed.

'No, sir,' replied Ben, straightening his cuffs. He took a deep breath. He could prevaricate no longer. Not for the first time, he wished he hadn't agreed to stand up with Kenneth. How would he get through the ceremony without thinking about Rebecca and what should have been?

'Ah, here they come.' The vicar smiled. He patted Ben's shoulder. 'You can let the lucky man know his bride has arrived.'

It was dim inside the church, the flickering candles doing little to penetrate the gloom. The stained-glass windows gleamed dully in the muted light. Heads turned at the sound of Ben's footsteps on the scuffed stone floor, and he kept his gaze fixed on the altar. He had time only to give Kenneth a reassuring nod before the vicar was inviting them to be upstanding for the arrival of the bride.

'It's lovely to see you again, Ben. I was so pleased Kenneth asked you to be his best man. I always hoped you two would become friends again,' Holly said, slipping her hand through the crook of Ben's arm.

Ben nodded noncommittally. While he held no grudge towards his old friend, he doubted they would ever regain the ease of their former relationship.

'You promised you'd visit,' Holly added, eyeing him reproachfully.

'I'm sorry. I did intend to but I'm so busy. How's the new lad coming along?'

'Will's settled in very well. He's a hard worker. He and Ella get on well. I think he looks upon her as an older sister. Speaking of Ella, you should go over and say hello. She misses you.' Ben followed Holly's gaze. Ella was standing beneath one of the cherry trees. A few pink petals had settled on the brim of her hat.

As if sensing their gaze, she turned towards them, and Ben couldn't help but notice how her face lit up at the sight of him. Excusing herself from the woman she was talking to, Ella hurried over, the hem of her pink dress brushing the daisy-strewn grass. 'Ben,' she breathed, a faint blush colouring her cheeks. 'How lovely to see you.'

229

'You too, Ella,' Ben replied, with genuine warmth. He'd always been fond of her, and he'd missed her cheerful presence. 'You're looking very well.'

'So are you,' Ella said, her blush deepening.

'I must have a quick word with Mrs Judd,' Holly said, with a smile. 'Don't leave without saying goodbye,' she added to Ben.

'I won't,' he promised.

'Are you coming to the wedding breakfast?' Ella asked hopefully.

'I told Kenneth I would.' He patted his breast pocket. 'I have my speech prepared.'

'I'm sure you'll do very well,' Ella said, as they moved towards the gate.

The bride and groom were already walking along the lane, thronged by well-wishers. The wedding breakfast was being held at the Weeks family's home, a mere five-minute walk along Foyle Hill. Ben offered Ella his arm, and she took it with a smile. She was as chatty and cheerful as he remembered, and it struck him how bereft of female company he had been. Angus's wife was as reticent as her husband, as was Peggy, who worked in the kitchen and dairy. For the first time in months, Ben felt himself relax. He was enjoying Ella's company and was almost disappointed when they reached their destination and he had to leave her to join Kenneth and Polly at the top table in the draughty barn, which had been scrubbed and decorated with freshly cut green boughs and garlands of early spring flowers.

'I suppose you haven't heard from Becky?' he asked Holly casually, as they waited for their meal.

Holly shook her head, her expression wistful. 'Nothing since we received that postal order. I would have told you, if I had,' she replied, placing her hand over his. 'Surely, she must know it's not about the money . . . I just wish we knew why she left. It makes no sense. Why didn't she say something to you if she was unhappy?'

'Mother,' Kenneth hissed. 'It's my wedding. Can we not talk about Becky for just one day?'

'I'm sorry,' Holly apologized, flushing. She smiled brightly. 'Kenneth's quite touchy about Becky,' she whispered to Ben, once her son had turned his attention back to his new wife and in-laws. 'I know her heart belonged to you, but I think Kenny still carries a torch for her. I'm sure that was why he proposed and married Polly so quickly.' Her lips quivered. 'I do hope they'll be happy together.'

Ben didn't reply. Kenneth had turned into a sullen, morose young man, prone to bouts of temper, so he doubted he could make a bubbly, outgoing girl like Polly Weeks happy for long. He hoped he was wrong, for Holly's sake. Becky had broken her heart and she deserved some happiness. Perhaps it wouldn't be too long before they made her a grandmother. He knew Holly would like nothing more than a baby to fuss over. Jeremiah too. Although the latter didn't wear his heart on his sleeve like his wife, Ben was astute enough to know that he'd been very upset at Becky's departure. He watched him now, seated next to his wife. He was turned slightly away, talking to a tall, gangly young man Ben assumed to be the new farmhand, Will. They seemed to be at ease with each other and Ben was pleased. He'd felt bad at leaving Jeremiah in the lurch, but he'd had no choice. He could never have stayed where memories of Rebecca lurked in every corner. He wondered what had become of the cottage but couldn't bring himself to ask. It was a relief when the food arrived and he could concentrate on eating instead of making small-talk.

His speech went well. It was short, to the point and witty, and he sat down to resounding applause as Kenneth clapped him on the shoulder. To his relief, people were beginning to leave. As promised, he sought out Holly and Jeremiah, who were talking to Polly's parents, Tom and Jenny Weeks.

'I'm sorry to interrupt,' Ben butted in politely, 'but I must be off now, Aunt Holly.'

'Oh, Ben,' Holly held him by the shoulders, 'it's been so lovely to see you again. You must visit, please.' Her eyes were sorrowful. 'It will only be hard the first time,' she said softly. 'It will get easier after that.'

'I know, and I will. I promise. Goodbye, Uncle Jerry. Mr and Mrs Weeks, thank you for your hospitality. Good afternoon.'

He was heading up the lane when he heard someone call his name. Turning, he frowned to see Ella hurrying after him, her skirts bunched in one hand, her hat in the other.

'You didn't say goodbye,' she panted, coming to a halt beside him.

'I'm sorry. You were with your friends. I didn't want to intrude.'

'Oh, them,' she said dismissively. 'They're relatives of Polly's, cousins or something. I don't know any of them from Adam.' She let her skirt fall to the ground and set her hat back on her head.

'You look very pretty,' Ben said truthfully.

Ella beamed. 'May I walk along with you?' she asked.

'Of course.' Ben offered her his arm. 'I enjoyed your company earlier.'

The sun was breaking through the clouds, bathing the landscape in shards of pale light. The wind had dropped so it was pleasant strolling along the lane, the bleating of newborn lambs filling the air.

'I used to think Kenneth was the handsomest man I'd ever known,' Ella blurted out, taking Ben by surprise.

'I can see how he would turn a girl's head,' he replied.

Ella took a deep breath. The skin above her high collar had turned a shade of bright crimson. 'But that was when I was young and silly. Now I think you are, Ben.' The colour raced from her neck to her cheeks.

'Ella . . .' Ben smiled sheepishly. He turned to face her, taking both her hands in his. 'Look . . .'

'I'm not a child any more, Ben,' Ella said. 'I know how much you loved Becky, but she's gone now and . . .'

'I'm sorry, Ella,' Ben said gently. Ella lowered her gaze. He continued to hold one of her hands and with the other he gently tilted her chin so she was looking at him. Tears shimmered on her lashes. 'I'm very fond of you, Ella. You know that, don't you?' Ella nodded, dislodging a tear. It rolled down her flushed cheek and onto Ben's hand. 'And if I was wanting to court anyone, it would be you.'

'Really?' Ella asked, her lip trembling.

Ben nodded. 'Yes. You're a lovely girl but I'm still in love with Becky. I think I always will be. It wouldn't be fair to you. Do you see?' He squeezed her hand. 'Friends?'

'Friends,' whispered Ella, puce with mortification. 'I'd better go,' she muttered, snatching her hand from Ben's. Head bowed, she set off at a quick pace.

Ben watched her go. He felt sad that she was clearly so upset but he couldn't offer her what she wanted. Not now, maybe never. He shoved his hands into his trouser pockets and kicked angrily at a pebble. It skittered across the lane, disappearing

233

into the grass verge. 'Damn you, Becky Wheeler,' he muttered, under his breath. She'd ruined every other girl for him. Taking off his jacket, he swung it over his shoulder and continued down the lane, misery descending on him like a heavy shroud.

CHAPTER TWENTY-SEVEN

1887

Rebecca propped the broom against the wall and opened the door, allowing the warm August breeze to waft inside. She wiped sweat from her brow. It was just before nine o'clock, yet the humidity was already uncomfortably high. Above the belching chimneys, the sky was a hazy blue. The smell of the latrines at the end of the street hung heavily on the still air. Sighing, she wedged the door open with a sliver of wood she kept for that purpose and unhooked the awning, nodding to Mr Carpenter, the butcher. Over the past eighteen months the two had built up a good business relationship. Rebecca bought all her meat from him and, in return, he recommended Rebecca's pies to his customers. Not that Rebecca needed much in the way of recommendations. Her reputation spoke for itself.

She and Chrissie had been astounded by the speed with which their pie shop had become a success. There was never a day when they failed to sell out. They'd employed two young lads who hawked their pies around the factories and offices of Whitechapel and further afield. 'Morning, Miss Wheeler.'

'Good morning, Mary.' Rebecca smiled. Mary Tucker was fifteen and lived in a small, overcrowded cottage a few streets away. Rebecca and Chrissie had recently employed her to serve in the shop, which freed them to spend their days in the bakery. Under Rebecca's patient tutelage, Chrissie could now bake pies to a standard of which Fred would have approved.

'It's going to be a hot one today,' Mary said, unrolling her apron. She was an attractive girl with fair hair tied in a long plait down her back and an engaging personality that made her a favourite with the customers. Perspiration glistened on her heat-flushed face. 'Ma said to tell you thanks for the pies,' she said, tying the apron around her slender waist.

Rebecca ran a finger along the windowsill. She prided herself on keeping a clean and tidy shop, never settling for the evening until she'd scrubbed and swept every inch of the place. 'You may take some more today. I can imagine how difficult it must be feeding five growing boys.'

'Each one of them eats like a horse.' Mary grinned. 'We really appreciate your kindness, Miss Wheeler.'

'Consider it part of your wages,' Rebecca told her. 'You certainly earn it.'

'So sorry I'm late,' Chrissie said, bursting in through the door, red-faced and sweating profusely. 'I couldn't get the baby to settle.'

'How is little Jimmy?' Rebecca asked, leading the way through the shop to the bakery. 'Has he recovered from the sickness?'

'He seems to have,' Chrissie replied, with a relieved smile. 'He's got some more teeth come through, so Mother-in-law thinks that's what caused it.'

'Has Joe been behaving himself?' she asked, in an undertone. Since she'd moved into the back room adjacent to the bakery, Rebecca had seldom gone to Chrissie's house. By the time she'd closed the shop and cleaned up, she was usually too exhausted to do anything except fall into her narrow little bed and sleep until four when she got up to start the morning's baking. Chrissie usually arrived about half an hour later, once her mother-in-law had arrived to look after the boys. She would get the two older ones up and ready for school, then take Jimmy to her house so as not to disturb Joe, who would come home from work and sleep most of the day. It was a difficult life for them all, but Rebecca and Chrissie were saving as much as they could in the hope that, eventually, they could step back and employ others to do most of the work. That dream was a long way off yet, Rebecca mused, as she lifted a tray of freshly baked pies out of the oven to cool.

'Joe's still working, so that's something,' Chrissie replied drily. 'I told him if he keeps drinking on the job, he'll get himself sacked.' She shook her head. 'He won't listen, though.'

'Can't you ask his mother to have a word?'

Chrissie shrugged. 'He can't do anything wrong in her eyes. If he's lacking as a husband, she tells me it's my fault for not being a proper wife.' She straightened up, arms akimbo. 'She says I should be at home looking after him instead of out working all day.'

'What does Joe have to say about that?' Rebecca asked, peering into the second oven where a tray of pies was just turning a golden brown.

'He sleeps all day, so he doesn't even notice I'm not there. As long as his tea's on the table on time and his uniform is washed and pressed, he's not bothered. Right, where are those two lads? These pies are just about ready to go.'

As if on cue, they heard voices on the shop floor, followed by the sound of footsteps on the flagstone steps.

'Morning, Miss Wheeler, morning, Mrs Flemming,' chorused the boys, snatching their caps from their heads. Brothers, they were thin with fair hair and green eyes, bony wrists protruding from too-short jacket sleeves. Rebecca and Chrissie paid a fair wage but their widowed mother had nine mouths to feed, so new clothes were an unaffordable luxury.

'Good morning, boys.' Rebecca grinned. 'Have you had any breakfast?'

'No, miss,' Alex, the older of the two, replied.

'Nor any supper last night,' piped up his younger sibling.

'Oh, Simon, why not?' Rebecca frowned. Over the past few months, she'd come to realize that Queenie Robbins, the boys' mother, wasn't good at budgeting. Not for the first time, she found herself wondering what the woman did with the wages the boys faithfully handed over every Saturday night.

'There's porridge on the stove, boys,' she said now. 'Help yourselves.'

Alex and Simon disappeared behind the curtain that separated Rebecca's living quarters from the rest of downstairs. She glanced up at the sound of footsteps overhead. Gordon occasionally popped in for a chat once he'd got the older children off to school. Only three-year-old Betty was at home during the day and, if the back door was left open to allow in the breeze, Rebecca would often look up from rolling pastry or crimping the pie edges to find the little girl's elfin face peeping in at her. She'd grown fond of her, as had Chrissie, having had only boys herself.

Rebecca carried the tray of pies into the shop, where a queue of customers had already formed at the counter, and slid them under the glass-topped counter. She spent a few minutes talking to her regulars, then set to work laying the tables in preparation for the dinner trade.

A shrill whistle split the air and a train thundered across the bridge at the end of the cobbled street, shaking the shop's foundations. Rebecca went to the window. The street shimmered in the heat, intensifying the stench of sewage, raw meat and fermenting rubbish. The smell used to make her stomach turn but she'd got used to it over time. The same as the trains. At first they'd kept her awake at night, but now that she went to bed so exhausted she was barely aware of them.

The street was congested with horse-drawn traffic, the pavement bustling with passers-by. A tramp limped by, his beard lank and unkempt. He leaned heavily on a stick, dragging his left leg. Catching sight of Rebecca watching, he raised his stick in recognition, his dry, sun-cracked lips parting briefly to reveal a row of blackened teeth. Feeling a surge of pity for the man, she hailed him. Motioning for him to wait, she rounded the counter and took out a pie, which she wrapped in brown paper.

'You shouldn't encourage him, dear,' one of her customers said, her lip curling in disdain. 'If you're not careful, you'll have every tramp in the city knocking at your door.'

Rebecca gave a thin smile. She had a fair amount of money put by and, as long as she could afford it, she was determined to help others less fortunate than herself, if she could. 'There you are,' she said to the man. He gripped the parcel with grime-encrusted fingers, the nails torn and black. 'Thank you, ma'am,' he mumbled, his eyes brimming with tears of gratitude. Rebecca had to steel herself not to recoil from his foetid breath.

He shuffled away. Watching him go, Rebecca was filled with a sudden longing for the green fields of Elm Tree Farm. How long had it been since she'd felt the soft grass beneath her feet? She thought back to a rare Sunday afternoon when she'd accompanied Chrissie and the boys to Hyde Park. It must have been in the spring, she recalled, for the trees were in bud, and there had been clumps of daffodils and crocuses on the lawns. Little Jimmy had been a few weeks old. It must have been four months ago, at least. The memory made her sad. She seldom allowed herself to dwell on what she had lost. She had her life in London. She was earning good money but her dream was one day to buy a small cottage somewhere in the country. She doubted it would ever happen, but it kept her going when painful memories surfaced and threatened to overwhelm her. She still thought of Ben, though she tried not to. It was almost two years since she'd left the farm. She supposed he had met someone else by now. It had been a long time. He might even be married, she mused regretfully, as she fingered the brooch pinned to her grey blouse. She tried not to think of Kenneth but the memory of that fateful day still rose in her at unguarded moments, and she would have to run out the back to compose herself.

'Are you all right, miss?' Mary asked, interrupting Rebecca's meanderings. 'You look sad.'

'Just lost in thought,' Rebecca replied, with a smile. 'Though I do find this heat quite oppressive. I may just take a moment.'

'You look a bit pale,' a customer said, overhearing. 'You work too hard, love.'

It was even hotter in the back room where the ovens were blazing.

'The lads got off about five minutes ago,' Chrissie said, glancing up at Rebecca.

'It's stifling in here,' she said, wiping her forehead with the back of her hand. 'I'm just stepping out for some fresh air.'

'You do that,' Chrissie said, wiping floury hands on her apron. 'I'll make us a cup of tea in a minute and join you. Mary's perfectly able to cope on her own for a bit.'

It was marginally cooler in the shaded yard. The stench of the neighbourhood notwithstanding, it was a refreshing change from the heat of the café kitchen. Perching on an upturned crate, and trying to ignore the coppery scent of blood wafting from next door, she leaned her head against the wall and closed her eyes. Hearing footsteps on the metal staircase, she opened them as Gordon and Betty descended the last few steps. 'Good morning, Miss Wheeler,' Gordon said, as Betty scampered to Rebecca and gave her a hug.

'Good morning, Mr Graham. Hello, sweetheart.'

'How's business?' Gordon asked, pulling up a nearby crate and sitting down.

'It's good,' Rebecca replied. 'How are you both keeping?'

'Oh, we're doing all right, aren't we, Betty?' The little girl nodded. She was a pretty child with golden hair that tumbled in ringlets around her thin face. Gordon had once mentioned to Rebecca how much Betty resembled her late mother.

'I wonder, might I ask you something,' Gordon said, looking uncharacteristically bashful.

'Of course.' Rebecca smiled.

'There's this concert, you see, . . . on Sunday afternoon and I was wondering whether you might like to accompany me.'

'Oh,' Rebecca said, somewhat taken aback.

'It's just that I have two tickets,' Gordon said in a rush. 'My sister-in-law has offered to take the children for the day so I thought you might . . . I shall understand if you say no. I know you're very busy . . .' He trailed off, his large hands hanging limply at his sides in the awkward silence.

Seeing his discomfort, Rebecca smiled. What was the harm? 'Thank you,' she said. 'I would like to go.'

'You would? Excellent.' Gordon snapped his braces. 'Right.'

He grinned, rubbing his hands together. 'The concert starts at half past two. Shall I call for you at about one o'clock? We could have dinner first. Abram's on Jewry Street is very popular, I've heard.'

'Thank you. That would be a nice treat.'

'Tea's up,' Chrissie said, as she came outside carrying two steaming mugs. 'Oh, good morning, Mr Graham. I'd have made you a brew if I'd known you were down here. Hello, precious,' she added, giving Betty a warm smile.

'I was just heading back upstairs,' Gordon said, waving away Chrissie's apology. 'Thanks, anyway.'

'Look here, miss.' Betty tugged at Chrissie's skirt and pointed at a woodlouse scurrying across the flagstones.

'Urgh.' Chrissie grimaced, handing Rebecca her mug. 'I'm not keen on insects, sweetheart.'

'Come on, Betty.' Gordon held out his hand.

'I want to stay.' Betty looked hopefully at the two women.

'It's all right, Mr Graham.' Rebecca smiled. 'We'll keep an eye on her.'

'Very well.' Gordon smiled fondly at his youngest child. 'Mind you do as you're told and don't give the ladies any trouble.'

'I won't,' promised the little girl, crouching to follow the woodlouse on its epic journey across the yard.

Rebecca waited until she heard Gordon enter his flat before she told Chrissie about his invitation.

'You're walking out with Mr Graham?' she asked, her brows lifting in surprise.

'We're not walking out,' objected Rebecca. 'It's just a concert . . . and a meal.'

'Goodness, a meal too!' Chrissie grinned.

'It's nothing fancy,' Rebecca said. 'We're just going to the pie and mash place on Jewry Street.'

'Still,' Chrissie said, a hint of envy in her voice, 'it's more than I get from my old man.' She sipped her tea, idly watching Betty, who was now halfway across the yard, crouched so low that the woodlouse was almost at eye level. 'You could do a lot worse than Gordon, you know.'

'I'm attending a concert with our landlord, Chrissie,' Rebecca responded. 'He knows I don't get out much. He probably feels sorry for me.'

'Hmm.' Chrissie smiled knowingly. 'We'll see.'

Rebecca sighed. 'Please don't read anything into it. He's our landlord and a friend. He's lonely, obviously, and missing his wife. He's only invited me for a bit of company. No one likes going to concerts alone, do they?'

A sudden shriek from Betty brought them both to their feet, Rebecca almost spilling her tea in her haste to get to the little girl. 'What's the matter, love?' Betty was hopping from one foot to the other, shrieking as hundreds of woodlice scurried about her feet. An upturned log lay to one side.

'Oh, pet, you've unearthed a woodlouse nest.' Rebecca laughed. 'They won't hurt you.' Taking the little girl's hand, she led her away. 'Come, why don't you help me bake a nice pie for your father? Would you like that?'

Betty nodded. With one final glance over her shoulder at the insects, which were hurrying back to the dark, shady damp of the woodpile, Betty happily followed the two women inside.

CHAPTER TWENTY-EIGHT

'Hello,' called Gordon, at promptly one o'clock that Sunday afternoon, rapping gently on the doorframe with his knuckles.

'Mr Graham, good afternoon.' Rebecca smiled as she stepped out from behind the curtain. Having worked herself up into a state of nerves throughout the morning and having deliberated for hours over what to wear, she was pleasantly pleased by Gordon's reaction.

'You look . . . very nice,' he said lamely, his mouth all but hanging open in surprise.

'Thank you.' She had finally settled on a blue and white sprigged skirt and a plain white blouse with lace-edged cuffs and a high lace collar, to which she had pinned Ben's brooch. Putting on her hat, she took Gordon's arm and they made their way along the narrow passageway that led out onto the street. Gordon had made an effort to dress up, Rebecca noticed. He was wearing a dark suit, his hair neatly combed and dampened down.

A brief storm during the night had broken the oppressive heat, leaving the air pleasantly warm, and quite a few people were about, mostly couples walking arm in arm along the sunny side of the street. Rebecca had always found Gordon pleasant company and easy to talk to, and they chatted amiably as they walked the few short blocks to Abram's. The door was wedged open, and Rebecca could smell the meaty aroma wafting up the street.

'The salt beef is very popular,' Gordon told her, as they seated themselves at one of the few empty tables. 'As are the eels.'

'I can't abide eels,' Rebecca said, 'so I shall try the salt beef.' She glanced at the adjacent table where the proprietor, a large, raw-boned man with lamb-chop sideburns, was delivering two plates of pie and mash, swimming in green liquid, to two Hassidic gentlemen. Rebecca had become quite partial to the parsley liquor that was so popular with Londoners, so much so that she had added it to her own menu, a decision that had proved very popular with her regulars.

While they ate, Rebecca found herself relaxing. She'd always looked upon Gordon as her landlord first and a friend second, but by the time they vacated Abram's, she found she was thinking of him more as a friend than a landlord. He was a fount of knowledge when it came to local history. His family had lived and worked in the area for generations.

'My parents left me comfortably off,' he told Rebecca, as they queued to get inside the guildhall, 'so I can afford to stay at home with the children.'

'You seem to be doing an excellent job,' Rebecca told him, as they moved forward in the queue. From inside the hall came the sound of instruments being tuned.

'That's kind of you to say, but children need a mother, don't you think?'

'Well,' Rebecca said, somewhat taken aback, 'ideally, yes, but as you and I have both learned through tragic circumstances,

we do not live in an ideal world. Life is seldom fair or kind.'
Rebecca felt for her locket beneath her blouse. How different
might her life have been if her parents had lived? She would
most likely still have been living in Leonard's Bay, married to
one of the local fishermen. The idea made her smile. But then
she would never have met Ben.

She wished more than anything right now that she had
her mother to talk to. The way Gordon was looking at her
was making her feel quite unsettled, her earlier ease vanish-
ing like the dew in the morning sun. She studied the printed
programme self-consciously. She'd noticed from the queue
of concertgoers thronging around her that they were mostly
middle and upper class, and she couldn't help feeling out of
place in her second-best outfit among the smartly dressed
couples' braying laughter as they found their seats. As if reading her mind, Gordon leaned close to her ear. 'Don't let them
intimidate you,' he whispered, laying a comforting hand on her
arm. Rebecca flashed him a grateful smile.

Up front, the musicians had finished tuning their instruments
and appeared to be talking quietly among themselves. Out of
the corner of her eye, Rebecca caught sight of an elderly man
who appeared to be staring at her with a scrutiny that unsettled her. She turned away quickly. It had been a long time since
she'd thought of Mickey Fox but the way the man was looking
at her brought all her old fears racing to the surface. She risked
a glance to where he was standing, confirming her suspicions
that he was, indeed, watching her. She pretended to study her
programme.

'Are you all right?' Gordon asked, with concern. 'You look
a little flushed.'

'It's quite warm in here,' Rebecca said. She fanned her face with her programme, hoping it would obscure her from the stranger's view. It was a relief when the lights dimmed, signalling the start of the concert.

The music was uplifting and emotional in turn, allowing Rebecca momentarily to forget about the staring stranger. When the lights came on, she risked an anxious glance in his direction, and was startled to discover that his seat was empty. She craned her neck, scanning the people getting out of their seats and thronging the aisle, but there was no sign of him. By the time she and Gordon made their way out onto the street, she had convinced herself that her imagination had run away with her.

The sun was hovering above the rooftops, the buildings silhouetted against pink-tinged clouds. Towards Whitechapel a haze of smoke and smog hung over the tanneries, breweries and foundries, growing more oppressive as they drew closer.

'I have very much enjoyed your company today,' Gordon said, as they turned into Tannery Lane. 'I was wondering whether next Sunday you might fancy a trip to Regent's Park Zoological Gardens with the children and me.'

'Oh, I'm sure you wouldn't want me intruding on your family outing,' Rebecca protested.

'Quite the contrary. The children would much prefer your company to mine, especially Betty. She is so very fond of you.'

'As I am of her.' Rebecca smiled. 'If you'd like me to come, I will.'

'I've enjoyed today,' Gordon said, as they parted company in the yard. 'Thank you.' He tipped his hat. 'Good evening, Miss Wheeler.'

Rebecca hurried inside and closed the door. She leaned against it, inhaling deeply. She couldn't deny that she'd had a pleasant time with Gordon, but she hoped he wasn't planning to court her.

'Of course he is,' said Chrissie, when she voiced her concerns the following morning. 'I've seen the way he looks at you lately. You could do a lot worse.'

'He's a lovely man,' Rebecca said, rolling up her sleeves. 'But I'm not interested in courting anyone.'

'I know you still have feelings for Ben, Becky,' said Chrissie, gently. Rebecca flinched and Chrissie reached over to give her arm a squeeze. 'You're young. You don't want to remain a spinster all your life, surely. Despite the age gap, Gordon is a good catch. You'd be set up for life.' She smiled. 'You may find yourself changing your mind about him. I wasn't keen on my Joe to begin with.' She pulled a face. 'Though the way things have turned out, I should have trusted my initial feelings.' She lowered her voice so that Mary, singing softly to herself as she swept the shop floor in readiness for opening, would not overhear. 'He's had his second warning at work,' she whispered. 'The fool was drunk on duty, again. Next time he's out on his ear. I'm so grateful for this job, Becky, you've no idea.'

'I couldn't run this place without you, Chrissie. I'll happily increase your share of the wages.'

'No,' Chrissie said firmly, shaking her head. 'We agreed, we take a fair amount as wages and the rest goes into our nest egg.'

'It's there for emergencies,' Rebecca reminded her. Her expression turned serious. 'Honestly, Chrissie, if you ever need a bit extra, let me know, please. I mean it. I don't want you or the boys going short.'

'I will,' Chrissie smiled, 'but we're managing.'

'Promise?' Rebecca raised an eyebrow.

'I promise. Now, where are those two lads? Alex, Simon,' she called.

'Just finishing our breakfast, Mrs Flemming,' Alex replied, peering out from behind the curtain.

'Well, get a move on,' Chrissie chided him. 'Those pies will be stone cold by the time you get out the door.'

Once the boys had left, Rebecca joined Mary in the shop, leaving Chrissie to keep an eye on the pies browning in the oven. She spent a pleasant couple of hours helping Mary serve the continuous stream of customers.

'It's a disgrace,' a woman in a purple hat was saying to her companion, as Rebecca set meat pies in front of them both. 'I don't know why the police can't move them on.'

'It's shocking,' her companion murmured. 'Thank you, my dear.' She smiled up at Rebecca. 'We're just discussing the situation regarding the . . .' her voice dropped so low that Rebecca had to lean closer to hear what the woman said '. . . ladies of ill repute,' she hissed, drawing back with a look of horror on her face.

'They're all over the place,' the lady in the purple hat said, with a nod. 'Why, one can hardly walk home from the railway station of an evening without seeing them everywhere.'

Rebecca gave the ladies a wan smile. She'd noticed the prostitutes, had walked by them as they huddled in pairs on the street corners, with their haunted expressions and sad eyes. Returning to the kitchen, she couldn't help feeling uneasy. In her limited experience, she doubted any woman became a prostitute out of choice. Her own dear mother, God rest her soul, would never have resorted to such a trade if it hadn't been for Mickey Fox. Just thinking his name sent a shiver of revulsion down her spine.

Her thoughts turned back to the man at the theatre. Thinking about him in broad daylight, she was positive she had imagined his interest in her.

She filled the kettle, wondering at her sudden sense of fore-boding. She pushed it away, chiding herself for being silly. Clearly the man at the theatre had unsettled her more than she had realized. A knock on the window startled her, making her jump.

'I didn't mean to scare you,' Gordon said, when she opened the window. 'I just wanted to say once again what a nice time I had yesterday.'

'I did too.' Rebecca smiled.

Gordon appeared to be about to say something, then changed his mind. 'I'll let you get on, then. I can see you're busy.'

'I've time for a cup of tea, if you'd like to join me,' she said kindly, her heart sinking at the sight of Gordon's delighted expression.

'Thank you. I'll be round in a minute.'

'Our Mr Graham is definitely sweet on you,' Chrissie said, once Gordon had gone back upstairs.

Rebecca glanced out of the window to where the Grahams were playing in the street with the other children. Betty sat on the kerb with a little girl of similar age. It worried Rebecca that the children dashed in and out of the traffic. She was terrified that one would be struck by a horse or wagon wheel, but it was too hot to keep them confined upstairs. She kept a keen eye on them, satisfying herself with the knowledge that the mothers who lived in Tannery Lane would be doing likewise.

'He's lonely, that's all.'

'Lonely for a wife to warm his bed.'

'Chrissie!' Rebecca gasped, shocked.

Her friend shrugged. 'It's true. He wants a wife and a mother for his little 'uns.'

'Did you hear those women complaining about the prostitutes earlier?' Rebecca asked, eager to change the subject. 'That Mrs Andrews got right on her high horse.'

'They are a nuisance, though,' Chrissie stated. 'Joe said he's been propositioned so many times. They're soliciting under the railway bridge, and on every corner.' She leaned against the bakery wall, arms folded across her chest. 'Word is, there's a new brothel opened over Smithfield way. I've warned Joe to give it a wide berth. If I ever get wind he's been anywhere near, he'll be out on his ear.'

This was said with such vehemence that Rebecca couldn't help wondering if Joe had strayed before. He wasn't a bad man, but he had a weak character. She doubted hc'd be able to say no if it was handed to him on a plate. She hoped for Chrissie's sake that he behaved himself, and that went for drinking on the job, too.

'Likely the authorities will get it shut down,' Rebecca said, wiping the tabletop.

'I doubt it,' sneered Chrissie. 'I heard most of their clients are important people in high places. And they haven't done a good job ridding the streets of them, have they?'

Rebecca looked away. She knew her and Chrissie's views differed but, then, Chrissie had probably never even spoken to a prostitute. Nora and Dora, her mum, Maddie, they'd been nice people who'd been handed a rotten deal in life. Pain pierced her heart as she thought of her mother and Nora. So far as she knew, neither of their killers had been brought to justice. She had no doubt Mickey had killed Nora but to Rebecca he was just as responsible for her mother's murder. If there was an afterlife, she hoped he'd burn in Hell. He certainly deserved nothing less.

CHAPTER TWENTY-NINE

1888

Rebecca slipped out of bed, shivering in the frigid air as she groped in the darkness for the matches. With shaking fingers, she lit the candle and dressed quickly by its feeble light. After an unseasonably mild December, winter had arrived with a vengeance in the first week of the new year. Every morning Tannery Lane was blanketed by a fresh fall of snow, though its pristine whiteness was brief. All too soon it was churned up by the constant passage of hoofs and wheels, leaving huge mounds of grey sludge piled along the kerb. By midday the road was a quagmire of melted snow and mud, and Rebecca faced the continual task of wiping windowpanes and mopping up puddles.

Now she set the kettle to boil and prepared the porridge. Alex and Simon would no doubt be blue with cold and starving hungry when they arrived later. Rebecca had bought new winter coats for them to replace their thin jackets, which were totally inadequate for the sharp dip in temperature.

While she waited for the kettle to boil, she lit the ovens in the bakery, holding her hands out to the warmth. There wasn't a sound overhead and she felt a flash of envy for Gordon and his children, still snug and warm in their beds. He'd recently started coming down to lend a hand in the shop once the two older children had gone to school.

The stoves soon took the edge off the chill and she drank her tea sitting at her small table, her hands wrapped around the mug, savouring the comforting warmth. She liked this time to herself, before the hustle and bustle of the day began. It was her time to plan for the coming week and reflect on what had been. She smiled. She'd spent Christmas Day with Gordon and the children. Normally she would have declined, spending the day with Chrissie and her family, but this year Joe had insisted they go to his mother for the day. Chrissie had told Rebecca she was welcome to join them but, as she didn't particularly like Chrissie's mother-in-law, she'd politely declined. She had been intending to spend the day quietly alone until Gordon issued his invitation. And she'd enjoyed the day immensely. She'd woken early to get the goose into the oven. By the time they'd returned from church, the bird was roasted to perfection. Gordon had carried it upstairs, where they dined in his cosy kitchen, the children exuberant and over-excited. They had taken a walk in the afternoon, stopping at a nearby park so the boys could fly their new kites, followed by supper at the home of Gordon's sister and her husband. Though Elizabeth was a decade older, Rebecca enjoyed her company and could see why the children were so fond of her and her husband, Cyril.

'It's so nice to see Gordon happy again,' Elizabeth had said, in an aside to Rebecca as they prepared to leave. 'He's been such a lost soul since Clara passed away.' The way she'd looked at Rebecca had left her disconcerted and she wondered what Gordon had told her. Had he intimated that they were walking out together? Rebecca had arrived home that evening with a growing sense of disquiet that hadn't gone unnoticed by her landlord.

'Are you feeling unwell, Miss Wheeler?' Gordon asked, his brow furrowed in concern as he saw her to her door. 'Only you seem a little withdrawn.'

'I'm well, thank you,' she said, forcing a smile. Gordon was a kind, sensitive man and she was loath to upset him, but she couldn't allow him to foster the false hope that there could be anything between them other than friendship. Sensing he was about to say more, she had lifted the latch and, bidding him a pleasant goodnight, slipped inside, closing the door firmly behind her.

Since that night, at least a week ago, he had given her no cause to believe that he considered her anything more than his friend and tenant, and their easy relationship appeared to be restored.

The bell jangled as another couple of workmen entered, stamping frozen feet and rubbing their gloved hands together, cheeks red raw from the scouring wind. The windows were fogged with steam, the warm, damp air filled with the aroma of freshly baked pies. Wielding the mop, Rebecca couldn't help a surge of pride as she surveyed the full tables, and the queue at the counter.

She squeezed the mop into the bucket. The pools of melting snow were proving a full-time job to clear this morning, she mused wryly. She could hear Chrissie humming to herself in the bakery, followed by the heavy thud of one of the oven doors being slammed. Leaning the mop against the wall, Rebecca hurried to the back. Chrissie had just lifted a tray of pies from the oven, her face flushed from the heat.

'They're just about queuing out of the door,' Rebecca told her. Picking up a tea-towel, she opened the second oven and peered at the pies. 'These need a few more minutes.' She glanced at the stove where the potatoes were boiling furiously, throwing up great clouds of steam, a pot of green parsley gravy simmering gently beside them.

'We didn't get our vegetable delivery this morning,' Rebecca said, stirring the pale green liquor with a wooden spoon. 'I'll go to the market in a bit.' She was interrupted by a knock on the back door. 'Oh, Mr Graham,' she said, as Gordon pushed the door just wide enough to peer round it, letting in a blast of Arctic air. 'Come in.'

Gordon stepped into the bakery, brushing snow from his shoulders as he shut the door, stamping more snow from his boots. 'Morning, ladies,' he said, unwinding his scarf.

'Good morning, Mr Graham,' Chrissie replied, grunting with effort as she slid a tray of pies into the oven to bake. 'How are the children?'

'Better,' Gordon replied, unbuttoning his coat. 'I've just been to the chemist for more cough linctus, and kept the boys off school again today.'

'My Sid's had a bad cough all week, and Harry started with it last night.'

'Oh, Chrissie,' Rebecca said, slightly exasperated. 'Why didn't you say? You shouldn't have come in today. Mary and I would have managed.'

'It's all right,' replied Chrissie, wiping her hands on her apron. 'My mother-in-law is looking after them.'

'There's a lot of coughs and colds about,' Gordon said, draping his coat over the back of a chair. 'This weather doesn't help.'

'You should get back to your children,' Rebecca told him. 'They need you more than we do.'

'I will, in a minute,' Gordon said. The sudden change in temperature had brought a rosy hue to his cheeks, and he ran his hand through his hair. 'I wondered if I might have a word, Miss Wheeler.'

'Of course,' replied Rebecca, folding the tea-towel and laying it on the table, with a sudden twinge of unease. She looked at him expectantly, wondering if he might be about to increase their rent.

'Um, would you mind, Mrs Flemming . . .?' Gordon said, in a somewhat strangled voice.

Rebecca frowned. She cast Chrissie a puzzled look.

'I'll take these out to Mary,' said Chrissie, cheerfully, carefully avoiding Rebecca's eye. She ladled green liquor over the plates waiting to go out and, picking up the tray, carefully mounted the steps to the café.

Rebecca turned back to Gordon, wondering what he might possibly want to say that couldn't be said in front of Chrissie.

'Mr Graham,' she gasped, in alarm, as he lowered himself clumsily onto one knee.

'Miss Wheeler,' he began, his voice high-pitched with nerves, 'would you do me the honour of agreeing to be my wife? I know we've only been courting for a short while,' he blustered, before Rebecca could formulate a reply, 'and I realize I'm considerably older than you, but you must see how fond I am of you. I . . . I am in love with you.' He gave her a wry grin. 'I know you are not in love me, but I'm hopeful that, in time, you will come to regard me with fondness.'

'Mr Graham . . .' Rebecca stammered '. . . I don't know what to say. I am very fond of you, of course, but . . .'

'Don't reply straight away,' Gordon said, getting to his feet. 'Think about it, please. Take as long as you need.' He reached for his coat. 'I would just ask that you give my proposal serious consideration.'

'I will,' promised Rebecca. She touched his arm. 'Thank you. I'm honoured.'

Gordon nodded. Picking up his hat and scarf, he tugged open the door and stepped out into the swirling snow.

Rebecca sank onto the nearest stool, her hand pressed to her chest, her heart beating wildly.

'Well?' asked Chrissie, on her return, her smile fading as she saw her friend's distress.

'Mr Graham proposed to me,' Rebecca said, sounding dazed.

'How exciting!' squeaked Chrissie. 'I had a feeling that was what he was about.'

'You did?' Rebecca frowned.

'Oh, Becky,' Chrissie said, crouching beside her friend. 'Mr Graham has been in love with you for ages, possibly even from the moment we took on the lease. Surely you must have realized, with all the attention he pays you.'

'Well, yes,' Rebecca replied slowly. 'I'd started to believe that his feelings for me were deeper than mere friendship and I was working myself up to set him straight . . .'

'You turned him down?' Chrissie's disappointment was obvious.

'He didn't give me a chance,' Rebecca explained. 'He asked me to take time to consider my answer.' She sighed. 'I'm fond of him, and I adore the children, but . . .' She shrugged. How could she explain to Chrissie that her heart would always belong to Ben? She doubted she could ever love another man in the way she'd loved him. 'It wouldn't be fair on Mr Graham. He deserves a wife who loves him.'

'It's a shame,' Chrissie said, getting to her feet. 'I love a good wedding.'

'Chrissie Flemming!' Rebecca laughed. 'I'm not getting married just because you fancy a knees-up.' The church clock chimed a quarter past nine. 'I need to get going to the market before all the good produce has sold out,' she said, grabbing her coat from its peg. 'I won't be long.'

'Take your time,' Chrissie replied, as Rebecca wound her knitted scarf around her throat and pulled on her hat. 'You've got Mr Graham's proposal to consider.'

Rebecca shot her a wry grin. Picking up her basket, she tugged on her soft, rabbit-skin gloves. For some reason, they made her think of Ben. Pushing thoughts of him out of her head, she bade Chrissie and Mary goodbye, and set off for Spitalfields.

The deep snow made it hard going and she was sweating by the time she reached the market. The cold, crisp air was heavy with the sounds and smells of the market. Chickens squawked in wooden cages and glassy-eyed fish stared up at her from their icy beds. Canvas awnings snapped in the cold draught whistling down the rows. Rebecca made her purchases and was about to head home when she caught sight of a man selling hot chestnuts. She smiled. She'd buy a penny's worth to take home for Alex and Simon. Her smile broadened as she imagined their pleasure when they returned from selling their pies, nearly frozen stiff. She joined the short queue and was handing over her money when, out of the corner of her eye, she spotted a dark figure leaning against the corner of the bank. Her breath caught in her throat. Her imagination must be playing tricks on her again. What on earth would Mickey Fox be doing here, in London? She shrank behind the nearest stall, watching the figure surreptitiously, her scarf pulled high up her face. The figure turned, and her legs turned to water. He was older, of course, and fatter, but there was no denying that it was Mickey Fox and he was standing a mere ten feet away from her.

'Here you go, miss.' Rebecca jumped in fright.

'Whoa, miss, are you all right?' The hot-chestnut vendor regarded her curiously. 'Your chestnuts?'

Muttering her thanks, Rebecca took the bag with a shaking hand and shoved it into her basket. She moved to the side where she was half hidden by a pillar box. Dry-mouthed, she peered round. He was still there. In his dark suit, he looked every bit the wealthy gentleman. What was he doing here? She backed away, the rest of her errands forgotten. Keeping her gaze on him, she wasn't looking where she was going and collided with a passer-by. 'I beg your pardon . . .' she began, her words petering out as she found herself face to face with Tina Fox.

'Look where you're going,' Mickey's stepmother snapped. She was about to move away when she turned back to Rebecca, her eyes narrowed in recognition. 'I know you,' she said, leaning closer.

'No,' Rebecca blurted quickly. 'I don't think so.'

'You look familiar . . .' Tina persisted, making a grab for Rebecca as she started to walk away.

'I'm sorry. You're mistaken,' Rebecca blurted in panic. Almost spilling her purchases in her haste, she turned away, pushing through the throngs of shoppers. She felt as though a vice was tightening around her chest, gasping painfully for breath as panic threatened to overwhelm her. She ploughed through the snow, sweat trickling down her spine, her breath coming in great, gasping clouds.

'Whatever's the matter?' Mary cried, as she fell through the door into the pie shop. 'You look like you've seen a ghost.'

Rebecca sank onto the nearest empty chair, her customers eyeing her curiously.

'I'll get you a cup of water,' Mary said, hurrying out the back.

'Are you all right, love?' one of the customers asked, concern creasing her brow.

Rebecca nodded. 'Thank you, yes,' she said.

Mary returned with the water, followed by an anxious-looking Chrissie. 'What's happened?' Chrissie demanded, crouching down beside Rebecca. 'Are you ill?'

Rebecca shook her head. 'I'm all right,' she said, gratefully accepting the cup of water from Mary and gulping it down as the two women exchanged puzzled glances.

'Are you sure?' Chrissie persisted.

Rebecca nodded. 'I walked too quickly, that's all,' she said, forcing a smile. She nodded at a customer. 'Hello, Mrs Wilkins. How's your Barry getting on?'

'He's much better now, thank you for asking,' the woman replied, scraping back her chair as she got to her feet. 'Excellent pie, as always,' she said. 'You work too hard, love,' she said, nodding at Mary and Chrissie. 'Make sure she has a rest, poor love. You look done in.'

'I'm fine, really,' Rebecca protested, as Chrissie insisted she go for a lie-down.

'Mrs Wilkins is right,' Chrissie said firmly, ushering Rebecca out the back. 'You're exhausted. Go and put your feet up for an hour. Mary and I will manage. The lads can help if we're busy, though we're unlikely to be run off our feet in this weather.'

'I got the boys some chestnuts.' Rebecca handed the warm bag to Mary.

She was shaking as she shed her wraps. She hung them up and sank onto her narrow bed, drawing her knees under her chin. She knew she would never sleep. Her mind was racing. What were Mickey and Tina Fox doing in London? And in her neighbourhood? The thought of how close she had come to bumping into him made her blood run cold. Had Tina realized who she was? She could only hope and pray that she hadn't. After all, she'd been a child when she'd last set eyes on the woman.

Fear curdled her stomach, the memory of the artist's impression of Nora's poor bloated face filling her mind. She shivered. A snippet of conversation drifted into her mind. Hadn't a customer mentioned something about a new brothel in Spitalfields? Icy cold fingers of dread ran down Rebecca's spine. Was it Mickey who had opened the new brothel that had got everyone's backs up? She pressed her fingers to her throbbing temples. It was the most dreadful of coincidences that he should end up here, where she was so happy. She didn't want to leave but how could stay here with Mickey down the road? It had been ten years since he'd come looking for her at the Thirsty Mariner. She was a grown woman now. Surely she had nothing to fear from him. Her mind reeled with the shock of her past catching up with her out of the blue. She knew Tina was shrewd. It wouldn't take her long to work out why Rebecca seemed so familiar. Worry clawed at her chest. She took a deep breath. She wasn't going to allow someone like Mickey Fox to drive her from her home. There had to be a solution.

Once Chrissie and Mary had left for the night, Rebecca crawled into bed, pulling the covers up to her chin. Sleep eluded her and she tossed and turned until the early hours. Finally, giving up on sleep, she got up and made a mug of cocoa, which she drank, seated in a chair, watching the swirling flakes of snow drifting past the dark window. A plan was forming in her mind. A plan that could keep her safe and free of Mickey's clutches. With a new resolve, she hurried to dress. As soon as she heard movements overhead, she threw on her shawl and let herself out into the cold, snowy morning.

CHAPTER THIRTY

'Miss Wheeler!' Gordon's face registered his surprise on opening his door to find Rebecca shivering on the icy landing. He lifted the lamp higher, casting a pool of yellow light over the pristine snow covering the yard below. 'Don't stand there catching your death,' he exclaimed, stepping aside. 'Come in. The children are still in their beds. I thought I'd let them have another day off to recover fully.' Rebecca followed him into the warm kitchen where a fire crackled in the grate. 'Tea?' he asked, rubbing his hands. 'I've just brewed a pot.'

'Thank you.' Rebecca pulled out a chair and sat down. Her heart was beating so loudly she was sure Gordon must be able to hear it. She wiped her sweaty palms on her skirt and smiled as Gordon kept up a stream of chatter while he made the tea. He appeared as nervous as she was. He clearly expected, correctly, that she and come in response to his marriage proposal.

'So, what brings you here so early?' he asked, his expression wary as he handed Rebecca her tea. The cup rattled in its saucer, his hand shook so wildly.

Rebecca took a deep breath. 'I've come about your proposal,' she began, also overcome with nerves.

'Yes?' Gordon took the chair opposite. 'Dare I hope you're here to accept?' He grinned in a self-deprecating manner.

'There's something I must say first,' Rebecca said.

'Go on,' Gordon said slowly, after a short pause.

Rebecca inhaled deeply. 'I do not love you. I'm very fond of you, and I believe I can be a good wife to you. I will be a good wife to you,' she amended. 'If you still wish to marry me, then my answer is yes. I would very much like to marry you.'

'I see.' Gordon sat forward in his chair, his fingers steepled together. 'I thank you for your honesty,' he said, after a short silence. 'I knew you did not love me. I hope you may, in time, come to feel a genuine affection for me, but in the meantime, I'm happy you will consent to be my wife.'

'I would prefer a quiet wedding,' Rebecca said, not wanting to draw attention to herself with any lavish plans.

'Whatever you wish, my dear,' Gordon said. 'We must set a date.'

'As soon as possible,' Rebecca said quickly, startling Gordon. He blinked in surprise.

'Very well,' he said, recovering fast. 'I shall speak to the vicar this afternoon and see how soon we can have the banns read.' He leaned over and took Rebecca's hands in his. 'You have made me a very happy man, Miss Wheeler.'

'Becky.' Rebecca smiled.

'Then you must call me Gordon, my dearest Becky,' he said, regarding her with such affection that she wished with all her heart she could love him back. Perhaps love would come in time. She hoped so. Gordon was a good man. He deserved a wife who loved him.

'You and Mr Graham are engaged? You accepted? But I thought . . .'

'You were right,' Rebecca said, turning her face so Chrissie wouldn't see the telltale blush creep up her cheeks. How could she explain to her friend that she was marrying Gordon for his protection? On so many occasions she had been tempted to tell Chrissie about her past, but she'd always felt too ashamed and, seeing how disparaging Chrissie was about the local prostitutes, she knew she would never tell her. She couldn't bear Chrissie thinking ill of her mother.

'Gordon is a kind man. He will be a fine husband. I'm sure I shall grow to love him, in time.'

'Oh, Becky,' Chrissie threw her arms around her friend's neck. 'I'm so happy for you. You deserve a good life and Mr Graham will be a good husband to you. I know it.'

'Will you carry on working here once you're wed?' Mary asked, anxiously chewing her lip. It was just after closing time and she was putting on her wraps in readiness to brave the bitter cold. Rebecca smiled. 'It will depend on Mr Grah— Gordon, though I expect I shall be too busy taking care of the home and the children,' she replied, trying to ignore the churning anxiety in her stomach. She knew that, as her husband, Gordon would expect certain things. Kenneth had been brutal and rough, and she couldn't help but fear that part of the marriage contract. She forced her worries aside.

'You won't shut the pie shop, will you? I love working here.'

'I'm sure we will come to an arrangement that suits all of us,' she assured the younger girl, with more confidence than she felt. She had been an independent woman for so long. Was she ready to give up her freedom? But her fear of Mickey Fox far outweighed any misgivings.

'There will always be a job for you here, Mary,' she said, placing a reassuring hand on the girl's arm. 'I guarantee it.'

Once Chrissie and Mary had left for their respective homes, Rebecca put on her coat and hat and climbed the stairs to Gordon's flat. He must have seen her coming for he had the door open before she reached it.

'Becky.' He smiled. 'What a pleasant surprise,' he said, standing aside to allow her into the small hallway.

'May we talk?' she asked, hanging up her coat as the children appeared in the parlour doorway, noses red from the effects of their colds.

'Of course.' Gordon frowned. 'Is everything all right? You haven't changed your mind?' he added, with a nervous laugh.

Rebecca gave him a reassuring smile. She spent a few minutes with the children, who were all thrilled at the idea of Rebecca becoming their stepmother, before Gordon sent them back to the parlour. Pulling out a chair in the kitchen, he invited Rebecca to sit. 'There's tea in the pot, if you'd like a cup?' he said, sitting down opposite her, looking worried.

Refusing the offer of tea, Rebecca folded her hands on the table in front of her. She took a deep breath. 'There are just a few things I'd like to clear up before we are wed.'

'Yes?' Gordon said slowly.

'Would you be willing for me to continue working in the shop? I understand that I shall have duties in the home and, of course, I wish to be a proper mother to the children but—' She broke off as Gordon reached across and took her hands in his.

'Whatever makes you happy,' he assured her. 'As you can see,' he said, with a wry smile, indicating the kitchen with a wave of his hand, 'I do my best, but the housekeeping has been very slapdash. It lacks a woman's touch, and the children need a mother, but now that Betty's at school, I have no objection to you carrying on in the café, at least until the babies come along.' At the mention of babies, Rebecca felt herself flush beetroot red. Flustered, she lowered her gaze. Gordon gave her hand a squeeze. 'I promise I will be the best husband I can be,' he said gently. 'And I have news,' he said, releasing her hands and sitting back in his chair. 'I spoke to the vicar this afternoon. We can be married the first Saturday in March, if that suits you?'

Rebecca nodded. The sooner the better, as far as she was concerned. Once she was Rebecca Graham, she would feel safer.

'Remember I said I bumped into someone yesterday and she looked familiar?' Tina said, raising her glass of port to her crimson lips. Mickey grunted.

'Well, I've just realized who she reminded me of.' Tina grinned. 'You remember that posh woman?' she smirked. 'Lydia.'

Mickey lowered his newspaper with a weary sigh. 'You seeing ghosts now, Mother?' he drawled mockingly, reaching for his pint.

They were in a tavern across the street from the market. It was a spit-and-sawdust place, frequented by dockers, prostitutes and the morally dubious. Someone was attempting to play the piano, which hadn't been tuned in years. A fire roared in the grate, the acrid smell of smoke mingling with the stink of stale ale, damp sawdust and wet cloth.

Mickey surveyed his surroundings with a disparaging sneer. He was used to frequenting the best clubs in town, usually on the invitation of his wealthy clients, those who would not wish

268

their wives or employees to know how they spent their evenings. But an unfortunate incident back in Dartmouth had put a stop to all that. A wealthy, well-known judge had been found dead with one of Mickey's girls. The resulting scandal and threat of arrest had sent him scuttling to London. It would take time to build himself up again, but he would do it. He already had a few members of the local constabulary in his pocket, willing to take a bribe to turn a blind eye. It wouldn't be long before he was back in with the city's elite.

'I know it's not her,' Tina snapped in irritation. 'I said she reminded me of her, that's all.' She sank back in her seat, scowling as she nursed her drink. The years had not been kind to her and the harsh lamplight only served to accentuate her lines and wrinkles.

Mickey took a sip of ale and licked froth from his upper lip.

Lydia had been gone ten years now and her death still rankled. He'd never had another girl like her. He'd lost girls before. Some punters never knew how much was too much, but he'd shrugged it off. What was yet another dead whore? There were plenty more to be had. But Lydia had been different. Lydia had had class. He'd spent weeks trawling the doss houses and taverns around the docks until someone let a name slip. It had been a further three weeks before the man's ship had anchored. On his first night of shore leave, Mickey had been waiting for him. The man never made it back to his ship. His battered, bloated body had been pulled out of the harbour a week later.

Mickey nursed his pint in contemplative silence. 'You don't think . . .?'

'That it was Lydia's kid?' Tina laughed harshly. 'I won't say the thought hadn't crossed my mind but what are the chances?' She swirled the remnant of port in her glass. 'The age would fit, though.' She met Mickey's gaze, then shook her head. 'Nah, impossible. It would be too much of a coincidence, and I don't believe in coincidences.' She nodded at the glass in her stepson's hand. 'Drink that. We must get back. Those new girls need keeping an eye on.' Tina drained her glass and put it on the sticky tabletop. 'You've got to knock them into shape, Mickey,' she said, getting to her feet and taking her coat off the back of her chair. 'They're far too spirited.'

'I'll have a word,' replied Mickey, swallowing the last of his ale. 'Keep an eye out for that girl next time you're at the market,' he said casually, as he put on his coat, 'and let me know if you see her.'

'You really think there's a chance it could be her?' Tina queried, unconvinced.

'Unlikely but it's worth investigating. She'd be, what, early twenties?' He smiled wolfishly, pulling on his soft, goatskin gloves. 'I never got much of a return on my investment thanks to that worthless . . .' He'd never wanted a woman the way he had Lydia. He grinned. If it was the daughter and she looked like her mother . . . The thought of doing to her what he'd done to her mother gave him a thrill like no other.

Turning up his collar against the bitter wind and driving snow, he stepped out into the night, letting the door bang shut behind him. Tina had to put out a hand to avoid being hit in the face.

Three weeks later, he happened to be passing St Mary's Church. There had been a big thaw recently and melting snow streamed down the road. Mickey scowled at his muddied shoes, and at the churning tumult of filthy water, debating whether to risk crossing. A carriage and pair rounded the corner, spewing dirty water into the air. Mickey jumped back in disgust. He swore loudly, shaking his fist after the offending driver. Leaning against the churchyard wall, he delved into his coat pocket for his handkerchief and, muttering curses, proceeded to clean himself up. As he brushed at his coat, his gaze strayed to the notices pinned to the church noticeboard. He sucked in a lungful of air as the name Wheeler jumped out at him. Rebecca Lydia Wheeler. It was too much of a coincidence. He read the notice with interest. The banns were being read for Miss Rebecca Lydia Wheeler, spinster of this parish, and Mr Gordon Graham, widower of this parish, if anyone knows of any impediment . . .

Mickey smiled, his soiled coat forgotten as he ripped the notice from its fixings and stuffed it into his pocket. So, his dear old stepmother hadn't been mistaken after all. Little Becky was in Whitechapel. He scanned the street for a more suitable crossing point. Becky had given him the slip once before, but she wouldn't defy him again. He grinned as he crossed the road, jauntiness in his step.

CHAPTER THIRTY-ONE

1893

'Harriet, be gentle with your sister,' Rebecca said, dumping the boiled potatoes into a metal colander. A cloud of steam billowed into the air. 'She's smaller than you.'

Four-year-old Harriet looked up at her mother. With her curly blonde hair and blue eyes, she was the image of Rebecca, while two-year-old Eliza, with her dark hair and hazel eyes, took after her father.

'I'll take them out the back to wash before supper,' eight-year-old Betty offered, looking up from where she was doing her homework at the kitchen table. She scraped her chair back. 'Come on, you two,' she said, holding out her hands to her two little half-sisters.

'Thank you, Betty,' Rebecca said, brushing a strand of hair from her damp cheek. 'Would you call the boys in, as well, while you're out there, please? And make sure they wash, too.'

'I will.' With her two sisters dancing along beside her, Betty went out into the scullery. Rebecca could hear her calling for her older brothers over the splash of the water pump, and she smiled to herself. Adding a dollop of butter to the potatoes, she beat them with a wooden spoon, marvelling at how quickly the past five years had gone.

It seemed only yesterday that she had stood at the altar in the draughty church, a posy of early spring daffodils trembling in her shaking hands as she'd recited her vows. After the short service, Chrissie, Joe and the boys had joined her, Gordon and her new stepchildren for a meal at the nearby Blind Beggar. The food had been excellent, but Rebecca could only pick at hers, she'd been so anxious about the upcoming wedding night.

She remembered the fear and pain of Kenneth's attack, and by the time bedtime came, she had worked herself up into such a state, she was close to tears. Believing it to be nerves, Gordon had been so understanding that she'd found herself blurting out the truth. He'd been horrified. 'He sounds a nasty piece of work,' he'd said, stroking her back as they sat next to each other at the edge of the bed. 'But the marriage bed doesn't have to be a place of fear.' She'd leaned her head on his shoulder, letting his gentle tone soothe her. 'I'm content to wait until you're ready,' he'd told her, looking into her eyes. His expression had been so kind, so loving, that Rebecca's desire to please him had overcome her aversion to his advances. He'd been gentle and patient, the total opposite to what she had been expecting, and afterwards they'd slept in each other's arms.

She'd fallen pregnant with Harriet almost straight away. It hadn't been an easy pregnancy. She'd suffered debilitating morning sickness and, coupled with the swollen ankles and backache, Gordon and Chrissie had insisted she give up work and rest. It had been while she was resting one afternoon that she'd been alarmed to see the face of Mickey Fox glaring up at her from the newspaper Gordon had left folded on the chair

273

arm. 'Spitalfields Man Jailed for Living Off Immoral Earnings' the headline screamed below Mickey's face. Along with the relief that he would be off the streets for the next four years, she'd also felt a twinge of regret that she'd rushed into marriage with Gordon. She quelled the thought immediately, ashamed of her ingratitude. Gordon was a good man. He loved her and he treated her like his queen. There and then she'd vowed to be the best wife she was capable of being. Gordon deserved nothing less.

Harriet was born early the following January, with an ease and swiftness that surprised everyone. Three months later, Gordon suggested that the time had come to move his family to a more suitable home. He released some of his investments and purchased a little house in Shoreditch.

Chrissie had taken on the general running of the shop, and she and her family had moved into the flat above. Rebecca still did the shop's accounts. Neither Chrissie nor Joe had a head for figures, and she enjoyed it. It made her feel as though she was still involved in the day-to-day running of things. Joe had eventually given up his job as night watchman to work in the shop, alongside his wife, and Alex and Simon, whom Chrissie was training to become master pie makers.

Rebecca stared round her steam-filled kitchen as she cleared away Betty's school books and set about laying the table for supper. It was the largest room in the three-bed terrace house, and where her growing family spent most of their time. It boasted a walk-in larder and a large scullery, with a door leading to a decent-sized yard that housed the privy and water pump, which they shared with their neighbours on either side. Two battered armchairs sat at angles to the fireplace, a black, shiny range took up one of the walls, the large table was pushed against another. The freshly washed slate floor gleamed. A clothes rack hung from the ceiling. They only used the front parlour when company came, though if it was Chrissie, she preferred to sit in the kitchen, and drink her tea at Rebecca's large, scrubbed-pine table while the children played out in the street.

She heard the clatter of feet in the entryway and Thomas and Christopher entered the kitchen, weary from a long shift at the brush factory.

'How was your day?' Rebecca greeted them, as they pulled out chairs and sat down at the table.

'Hard,' Thomas replied morosely. He was thirteen now, tall and gangly, his strawberry-blond hair standing on end.

'Boring,' said Christopher, who had just turned twelve.

'You've only been there a week.' Rebecca laughed, tousling his hair.

'Can't we work in the pie shop instead?' he implored his stepmother.

'You know what your father said,' Rebecca reminded him. 'As soon as Alex and Simon have learned their trade and are ready to move on, you can take their place.'

'Me as well?' Betty asked, returning to the kitchen with her little sisters. Eliza beamed at the sight of her big brothers and, letting go of Betty's hand, bounded over to Thomas and attempted to scramble onto his lap. He reached down and lifted her up. She snuggled against him, beaming at Harriet across the table.

Rebecca placed the bowl of mashed potatoes in the middle of the table alongside a dish of braised beef. She wiped her hands on her apron, only half listening to the children's noisy chatter as she buttered slices of fresh white bread.

'Here's Father,' Thomas said, as they all heard the front door open.

'Daddy!' shouted Eliza, squirming to be let down. Thomas let her slide off his lap, and she went running into the small hallway, followed by Harriet. The girls' excited shouts were abruptly silenced. Rebecca frowned.

'Hello, sweethearts,' she heard Gordon say, as the front door closed with a soft click. 'Don't be shy. This is an acquaintance of mine, Mr Osborne. My dear,' he called out. 'We have company.'

'Lay another place, Thomas,' she instructed, whipping off her apron as she checked her appearance in the mirror. Her cheeks were flushed from cooking, and tendrils of hair clung to her damp cheeks.

Offering up a silent prayer that the meal would stretch to feed the unexpected guest, Rebecca plastered on a welcoming smile. Gordon strode into the kitchen, Harriet and Eliza nestled into the crooks of his arms and peering shyly over his shoulder at the man who followed.

'Mr Osborne, may I introduce my wife. Becky, this is Mr Osborne. He's recently joined the club.'

Rebecca stared at the man in horror, the blood draining from her face as the room began to spin. She gripped the back of the nearest chair as her mind struggled to understand how Mickey Fox could be standing in her kitchen when he was supposed to be in prison. And why had Gordon introduced him as Mr Osborne?

'A pleasure, Mrs Graham,' Mickey said, extending a gloved hand. Rebecca stared at it as if it were a snake about to strike. She was aware that Gordon was regarding her curiously, clearly wondering at her sudden loss of manners. But she couldn't move. Mickey would be in his early forties now, Rebecca

276

surmised. Prison had clearly taken its toll. His skin was pasty, and his hair was streaked with grey, his skin lined. His eyes were the same, she noted, cold and unfeeling, as they silently mocked her.

'Becky?' Gordon prompted, his voice seeming to come from far away.

'Mama?' Harriet said. It was Harriet's anxious tone that brought Rebecca to her senses.

'I'm so sorry, Mr Osborne,' she said, taking his hand as she forced herself to calm her jangling nerves.

Gordon set down Harriet and Eliza and introduced Mickey to the boys and Betty.

'What a charming family you have, Gordon,' Mickey said, his smile sending a shiver of revulsion down Rebecca's spine. Feeling as though she were moving through treacle, she took her own place at the table, carefully avoiding Mickey's blatant scrutiny.

'You have no family yourself, Mr Osborne?' Gordon asked, passing him the bowl of potatoes.

'Alas, I never married,' Mickey said, as he tried to catch Rebecca's eye. She stared at her plate, studiously ignoring him. He gave a short, deprecating chuckle. 'I never found a woman who would put up with me.'

'After my wife passed away, I never thought I'd find love again,' Gordon told him, 'and yet, here I am, a happily married man once again. So, there is hope for you yet, sir.'

'Perhaps, Gordon.' Mickey nodded. 'Perhaps. Excellent mash, Mrs Graham,' he said, reaching for his glass of water.

'It is indeed,' agreed Gordon. He patted Rebecca's hand. 'My wife ran a pie and mash shop in Tannery Lane for several years,' he told Mickey.

Mickey raised an eyebrow. 'Did you indeed?'

'Yes,' Rebecca choked out. The food tasted like sawdust in her mouth. Clearly her husband had not associated Mickey with the drawing in the newspaper, she fumed inwardly. But, then, it had been a long time ago. The thought hit her like a thump to the chest. What a fool she was. Harriet had turned four last January. She had read about Mickey's imprisonment when she was expecting. His time was up. He was a free man. Bile rose her throat. She swallowed it, attempting to distract herself by cutting Eliza's food into manageable pieces and replenishing Harriet's water. The three older children ate in respectful silence as the conversation between their father and his guest drifted between a variety of subjects, none of which was of any interest to anyone else at the table. Rebecca played with her food, waiting for the moment she could excuse herself and escape to the scullery.

After what seemed an interminable time, Gordon and Mickey left the table for the parlour. The boys went out to join their friends in the street.

'Take Harriet and Eliza and go out to play,' Rebecca told Betty as she helped clear the table.

'What about my duties?' Betty responded in surprise.

'I'll do them,' Rebecca said, mustering a smile for her stepdaughter.

Betty grinned. 'Thank you.' She gave Rebecca a hug. 'Come on, you two.' She held out her hands to her younger sisters. Delighted by this unexpected extra playtime, Harriet and Eliza each grabbed Betty's hands, and hurried off to join the other children taking advantage of the long summer evening.

Rebecca pressed her face into her hands. She was shaking. How could Mickey be here, in her home? It didn't make sense.

She felt violated just by being in the same room as him. She swallowed hard as fear clutched at her with long, cold fingers. She took a deep breath. Hopefully Mickey's friendship with Gordon would be short-lived. Had he known who she was when he'd accepted Gordon's invitation to supper? But why had Gordon invited him? They seemed unlikely acquaintances.

She could barely concentrate as she washed the dishes, scraping the leftovers into a bucket for the neighbourhood pig. She dried up and put the dishes away, listening to the children's laughter drifting in from outside. She knew Gordon would have something to say about her letting Betty off her duties: he always said she was too soft with the children, but she'd needed to be by herself. She needed the solitude to remind herself that, thoroughly unpleasant man though he might be, Mickey Fox, or whatever he called himself now, was no longer a threat to her.

She picked up the bucket of scraps and went out into the yard. The back gate opened into a narrow walkway that led to the allotments where Sally, a huge, black and white saddleback pig, lived. She was attempting to sort out her troubled thoughts when she heard footsteps behind her. She half turned, expecting a neighbour on their way to the allotment, so the sight of Mickey Fox striding purposefully after her knocked her for six.

Her breath caught in her throat as she looked round in panic. There wasn't a soul about. And no windows overlooked this section of alleyway. She pressed herself against the wall, holding the bucket in front of her like a weapon.

'Don't come any closer,' she said. 'Unless you want a bucket of slops over your head.'

'Now, now,' Mickey drawled, with a contemptuous smile, coming to a halt at what he perceived to be a safe distance away. 'Is that any way to greet an old friend?'

'You're no friend of mine,' Rebecca hissed. 'Where's Gordon?'

'He's gone across the street to help a neighbour with something. I thought we might take the opportunity to have a little chat. Catch up on old times.'

'Does he know you're a convicted criminal? Is that why you changed your name?'

'Sadly, the name Mickey Fox is somewhat tarnished,' Mickey sneered. 'I go by the name Michael Osborne now. It sounds rather grand, don't you agree?' He moved quickly, catching her off guard. Knocking the bucket from her hands, he gripped her chin in his hand, yanking her face towards him.

'I'll scream,' she hissed. Mickey laughed. 'I wouldn't, if you know what's good for you.' He inclined his head back down the alleyway. 'Those girls of yours are very pretty. I'd hate for one of them to get hurt.'

'Don't you dare touch them!' Rebecca tried to squirm out of his grip. His fingers tightened around her jaw, sending pain shooting up into her head. Her eyes watered.

'Your mother was the best whore I ever had,' he whispered, his mouth close to her ear. 'I shelled out a lot of money to cover your debts, and had she lived, she'd have been worth every penny but, thanks to that low-life sailor, who I took care of, by the way,' he added, sending a shiver of fear down Rebecca's spine, 'I never got much of a return on my investment. Now I've come to collect the debt.'

'I owe you nothing,' Rebecca spat.

Mickey loosened his grip, and gently ran his finger along Rebecca's chin. 'You're so like her, in spirit as well as looks,' he said, his tone softening. 'It took me a while to get Lydia to come round to my way of thinking, but she did in the end. They all do. And you'll be the same.'

'Don't you dare speak about my mother like that,' Rebecca snapped, massaging her bruised throat.

Mickey laughed. His eyes glinted as his hand closed over her wrist. He yanked Rebecca towards him, his lips curling in a parody of a smile. 'You owe me, Becky Wheeler, and I'm here to collect.'

'You'll get nothing from me,' Rebecca replied. She wished she could stop shaking. 'I'll report you to the police for extortion.'

'Oh, I don't think so, Becky,' Mickey said, his voice brimming with menace. 'I'm capable of things you can't even imagine. Remember old Nora? She found out to her cost that I won't be crossed. If you care anything for your man and your kids, you'll do as I say. It's a shame you're no longer a virgin,' he murmured, as Rebecca recoiled in horror. 'I would have enjoyed being your first.'

'I'm not afraid of you,' Rebecca snapped, snatching her arm free. 'I'm a married woman. You have no business speaking to me like this. When my husband hears of it . . .'

'That wet blanket?' Mickey scoffed. He rubbed Rebecca's cheek with his thumb, and she shivered. 'Do I repulse you that much?' He laughed.

'You disgust me.'

'No matter.' Mickey grinned. 'You're mine, Becky Wheeler. Your mother sold you to the devil when she accepted my offer of help. You're what kept me going in that godforsaken prison.' Mickey smiled. 'Meet me down at the Spitalfields Arms on Thursday evening. I'll book a room. And, Becky,' Mickey said, over his shoulder as he turned away, 'don't even think about running, because I'll find you, wherever you go. Please tell your old man thank you for a pleasant evening and I was looking forward to our game of draughts but, alas, business has called me away. Until Thursday, Mrs Graham. Good evening.' He tipped his hat and blew her a kiss. Rebecca watched him go, hardly daring to breathe until he'd turned the corner and disappeared.

Her insides felt like water as she attempted to clear up the vegetable peelings scattered across the ground. She tipped the scraps into the trough, absently scratching the pig between its ears as it snuffled up the food.

She returned to the house, relieved to find the children were all still out playing. Gordon was standing by the open front door, scouring the street. He heard her coming up behind him and turned. 'Mr Osborne seems to have disappeared,' he said, scratching his head in a perplexed fashion. 'I went across the street to help Mr Adams with something, and when I returned, he'd gone. We were about to start a game of draughts,' he said, indicating the game set up on the card table in the parlour, visible through the open doorway.

'Why did you invite him?' Rebecca asked, evenly, leading the way back to the kitchen.

'I'm sorry, my dear. I didn't stop to consider what an imposition it would be for you.' He sat down by the fireplace and began tugging at his tie. 'It was all rather strange really,' he said, unfastening his top button. 'I've seen him at the club a few times but today was the first time he spoke to me. He practically invited himself for supper.' Gordon shook his head. 'I must say, he's all charm and good graces but I found him to be rather an unpleasant fellow. I don't think it's a friendship I wish to pursue.' He reached for Rebecca's hand and kissed it. 'I apologize again for imposing him on you and the children.'

'It's done now,' Rebecca said. She slid her arm around Gordon's neck and kissed the little bald patch amid his greying brown hair. 'Let's say no more about him.' She got up to make tea, a knot of anxiety forming in the pit of her stomach. She had no intention of keeping their rendezvous on Thursday, but she knew that Mickey wouldn't hesitate to follow through on his threat towards her family.

Later that night, unable to sleep, she crept quietly from the bedroom. With Gordon's gentle snores following her, she made her way quietly down to the kitchen where, finally, she let the tears fall.

CHAPTER THIRTY-TWO

'I have a civic meeting tonight, my love,' Gordon said, hooking his braces over one shoulder and then the other. 'It may finish late, so don't wait up.'

Rebecca's heart sank. She hated it when Gordon left the house, especially at night. In the three weeks since Mickey's visit, she had been expecting him to make good on his threat to hurt Gordon or one of the children. She spent her day scanning the street as the children played. She was dreading the thought of Betty going back to school next week.

'Be careful,' Rebecca said now, straightening Gordon's collar. 'It's not safe after dark these days.'

'I will be.' Gordon fastened his cufflinks, and kissed Rebecca goodbye. She followed him to the front door, her anxious gaze immediately falling on Harriet and Eliza, who were sitting on the kerb, playing with their rag dolls. Further down the street a rowdy game of football was in progress. Everything looked perfectly normal. She glanced at the house across the street where Betty had spent her time ever since her friend Minnie Clarke's cat had given birth to nine kittens. She was driving them to distraction pestering her parents every evening to be allowed one of the kittens. Gordon had been firm in his refusal, but Rebecca could tell he was weakening. She'd be very surprised if, by the end of next week, when the kittens were old enough to leave their mother, the Graham household wasn't welcoming a furry addition.

'What are you doing today?' Gordon asked, glancing up at the sky, and wondering if he should take an umbrella.

'I thought I'd pop over to the shop,' she replied hesitantly. 'I haven't been in for a while, and I'd like to see Chrissie and Mary.' In truth she'd been putting it off, not wanting to risk bumping into Mickey.

'Why don't you invite Chrissie and Joe over for dinner on Sunday? It'll be nice to see them again.'

'I will, thank you.'

Deciding against an umbrella, Gordon dropped a kiss on each of his youngest children's heads and set off down the street. Rebecca returned to the kitchen. Her fear at leaving the house was like a physical ache in her chest. She knew Mickey would not forgive her for failing to keep their rendezvous and that it was only a matter of time before he made good on his threat. She'd thought about going to the police but was too frightened.

She kept her eyes peeled during the walk to the pie shop, and a firm grip on Harriet and Eliza. Despite her worry, she enjoyed her time with Chrissie and Mary, who both doted on the little girls.

'Of course, we'd love to come to dinner on Sunday,' Chrissie said, as she and the girls took their leave. 'I'll look forward to it.'

They visited the park. There were only a few days of the summer holiday left and the park was busy. All the while the girls were playing, Rebecca kept up her vigil. No one looked out of place, but she felt only relief when it was time to call the girls to her and get ready to leave.

'Mama, Mama,' Harriet cried, running towards her, arms spinning like a windmill, Eliza following, her little legs struggling to keep up. 'I want to stay longer.'

'I'm sorry, love, it's almost dinner time. Perhaps we'll come again tomorrow, if the weather holds,' she compromised, taking their hands in each of hers. It was pleasantly warm. The bank of dark clouds that had hovered above the rooftops earlier had dissipated, leaving a deep blue sky in their wake. They walked home in the sunshine, Rebecca smiling at the girls' incessant chatter. She spent the afternoon standing in the street, talking with neighbours while they kept an eye on their respective children until it was time to go in and start the supper preparations.

'Is Father home?' Thomas asked sleepily, frowning in the candlelight.

Rebecca shook her head. 'Not yet,' she whispered, swallowing her own sense of dread. She glanced across to where Christopher was snoring softly, one arm flung across the pillow. 'Go back to sleep, Thomas. He'll be home when you wake up,' she said, praying it was true.

Thomas mumbled something incoherent and buried his face in his arm. Rebecca tiptoed onto the landing. She'd already checked on the girls. All three were fast asleep. Careful not to step on the loose floorboard, she crossed the landing to her own bedroom and went to the window, peering down at the empty street. A black and white cat emerged from the shadow of Minnie's house. The mother taking a break from her demanding offspring to do some nocturnal hunting.

Rebecca scanned the street both ways, her senses on

heightened alert for anything amiss. After a while, she drew the curtains and climbed into bed. She blew out the candle. She'd left the lamp burning in the parlour for Gordon. She hoped he wouldn't be too much longer. The bed felt cold and empty without his solid presence. She lay awake, listening to the downstairs clock chiming the hours until eventually she fell asleep somewhere around midnight.

'Mama?'

Rebecca woke with a jerk, her heart racing wildly. 'What is it, Eliza?' she asked the small white figure hovering beside the bed.

'I can't sleep.' Eliza replied, holding out her arms.

Rebecca lifted the covers and Eliza scrambled in beside her. With Eliza cradled in one arm, Rebecca reached out to Gordon's side of the bed. It was cold. As if on cue, the downstairs clock chimed three, deepening her sense of dread. Something had happened to him. With a dreadful sense of foreboding, she eased her arm from under Eliza and slipped out of bed. Barefoot, she padded to the window and peered out. The streetlamps cast pools of yellow light over the cobbles. There wasn't a soul to be seen, not even the cat. Feeling a chill of apprehension, Rebecca pulled on her dressing-gown, and went downstairs. The parlour lamp had died out, but the street-light gave enough brightness for her to see by. Pulling open the curtains, she settled herself in the window seat, where she kept watch until morning.

'Mama! Mama!' She was woken by Eliza's distressed cries.

'Coming, coming.' As quickly as her stiffened limbs would allow, Rebecca hurried up the stairs.

Eliza was standing on the landing, looking close to tears. 'I didn't know where you were,' she whimpered as Rebecca scooped her into her arms, hushing her, as her mind raced wildly. Clinging to the vain hope that Gordon had come home while she'd been asleep in the parlour, she hurried into the bedroom but that hope was soon dashed. She sank onto the bed, at a loss to know what to do.

CHAPTER THIRTY-THREE

'No one of that description has been reported injured, ma'am,' the policeman said, running his finger down the page of a thick ledger. He peered at Rebecca over his steel-rimmed spectacles. 'I shouldn't worry, ma'am. I reckon he's had a skinful and passed out somewhere. He'll be home once he's sobered up.'

'My husband rarely drinks,' Rebecca informed him, as calmly as she could. She wanted to take the sergeant by his collar and shake him. Could he not understand the urgency? 'And he certainly wouldn't stay out all night. I've told you, threats were made against my family by Mr Fox. He calls himself Michael Osborne now. Please, you must investigate.'

'Do you have an address for this Mr Fox, or Osborne?' the policeman asked, kindly.

Rebecca shook her head. 'He's a member of the Hamilton Club, same as my husband. They'll know his address.'

'I'll get someone to go round to the club,' the policeman promised, 'ask a few questions, but, unless you can prove your husband has been a victim of foul play, there's not much else we can do. Have you tried the hospitals?' Rebecca nodded wearily. She and Chrissie had spent the morning touring the hospitals but no one of Gordon's description had been brought in. Joe had visited the civic society offices, only to be told that the meeting had ended at eight o'clock and, as far as anyone knew, Gordon had been heading straight home.

Rebecca left the police station with a sick feeling and the policeman's empty promise that they would do what they could.

The day passed slowly. She'd sent the children out to play and tried to pretend everything was normal, but she couldn't concentrate on even the simplest household tasks. She spent hours standing by the parlour window, watching for anyone coming or going. She went to the doorway, her gaze straying from the children playing to the end of the road, her stomach churning. Thomas caught her eye. He and Christopher had taken the day off work and had spent the morning searching the surrounding streets and alleyways. At thirteen, he was old enough to know something was seriously wrong. Rebecca summoned a smile. Thomas tried to reciprocate but she could tell, even from that distance, that he was close to tears.

Minnie's mother, Martha, came out wielding a broom and waved. 'Afternoon, Mrs Graham. Lovely day again.'

Rebecca nodded and smiled. 'Lovely,' she agreed, her voice barely audible above the noise of the street. Not wishing to engage in conversation, she went back inside, shutting the door behind her. She knew Martha would think her behaviour odd – no one shut their door during the day – but she didn't care. She couldn't face anyone until she knew Gordon was safe. She resumed her position by the window, marvelling at how life was going on as normal beyond the glass. Martha was sweeping her front steps, talking to Mrs Adams, who was jiggling a crying baby on her hip. A group of neighbours stood in a huddle

290

further up the street, chatting amiably while keeping an eye on the children. A horse and cart trundled by, and a dog chased a cat up a drainpipe.

Rebecca sighed, her shoulders slumped. She must think about starting supper. She had no appetite, but the children had to eat. It took all her self-will to muster the energy to go into the kitchen where she stood for several minutes in the larder just staring at the shelves, her mind too numb to think. Her gaze settled on the loaf of bread. She had tomatoes and beans she'd picked in the allotment. They would have a cold supper. She busied herself preparing the simple meal, her gaze straying to the backyard in case Gordon came in through the back gate. The knife fell from her hand with a clatter. She knew Thomas had checked the alleyway but she needed to be sure. Wiping her hands, she wrenched open the back door and crossed the yard, her breath coming in frantic gasps. She fumbled with the latch on the gate, and stepped into the narrow alleyway that ran between the houses. The air smelt of chicken manure and pig, as she hurried in the direction of the allotments. Halfway along the alleyway a narrow pathway led onto the street. If Gordon had come that way . . . Rebecca paused, scanning both directions, her heart sinking in despair. She could hear children at play drifting from the street. A woman was coming from the allotments, her basket laden with leafy summer vegetables. Rebecca greeted her with a tired smile. Her shoulders slumped and she turned back towards the house, grateful when her neighbour took the path towards the street. She had no appetite for idle conversation today.

Back in the kitchen she finished preparing the meal and went to call the children in. As she opened the front door, she was suddenly aware that a silence had settled over the street. At once she was gripped by a deep sense of foreboding. Everyone, even the children, appeared fixated on something at the end of the road. Rebecca followed their gaze, a coldness spreading through her veins at the sight of the two policemen walking purposefully towards her. She clutched at her throat, knowing that her world was about to come crashing down.

'Mrs Graham?' the older of the two policemen enquired gruffly. He was tall, with greying sideburns, and tired, kind eyes, but Rebecca barely registered his features as she nodded mutely. She was vaguely aware that Thomas and Christopher had followed the policemen to the door. Now they came to stand beside her. Instinctively she put her arms around her two stepsons, knowing she could not protect them from the news to come.

'I'm Sergeant Willis and this is Constable Morley. May we come in?' the policeman asked.

Rebecca nodded mutely. Turning, she led the way into the parlour.

'You might like to sit down,' Sergeant Willis suggested. Rebecca shook her head. She could barely swallow.

'Mrs Graham, I'm afraid I have bad news. The body of a man we believe to be your husband has been found . . .'

Although she had known what was coming, the shock of hearing the words brought a cry of disbelief. Rebecca's knees buckled and Constable Morley had to help her to a chair before she fell. Thomas stood beside her, his young face grim as Christopher started to cry. Rebecca reached out to him, pulling him down beside her.

'What happened?' Thomas asked, his face ashen.

The policemen exchanged uncomfortable glances as Sergeant Willis cleared his throat. 'I'm afraid we're treating his death as murder.'

'Murder!' Thomas exclaimed. 'Why would anyone want to murder Father?'

'We're going on the presumption it was a robbery,' Sergeant Willis said, consulting his notebook. 'Though it looks like the culprit was disturbed for Mr Graham's pockets were untouched.'

Rebecca buried her face in her hands and wept. She knew this was not a robbery. It was her fault. She had defied Mickey and now her dear, sweet Gordon had paid the price.

Sergeant Willis shrugged. 'I'm sorry. Your husband's body is at the police station. I'm afraid we'll need someone to identify him formally.' He coughed into his hand.

'I'll do it,' Thomas said immediately.

'No, Thomas,' Rebecca protested. 'I can't let you.'

'Ma'am,' Constable Morley spoke up, shuffling his feet awkwardly, 'I'm afraid Mr Graham suffered significant injuries. It might be too much of an ordeal . . .'

Rebecca shook her head. 'I want to see him,' she said firmly. 'Thomas, would you go and fetch Betty and the little ones. please?' She got to her feet. 'Thank you, Sergeant, Constable. I need to be with my family now.'

'Of course. The post-mortem is scheduled for this afternoon. You may see your husband any time after that.' Rebecca nodded.

She saw the two policemen out, keeping her gaze averted from the curious stares of her neighbours. She knew it wouldn't be long before they started coming over, but she couldn't face anyone now.

She closed the curtains, plunging the parlour into semi-darkness. Thomas returned shortly afterwards with a tearful Betty. Harriet and Eliza were too young to understand the enormity of the situation, but they picked up on the sombre mood.

At the sight of Betty in tears, Eliza began to wail. Rebecca sank onto the sofa, gathering her brood around her, as she tried to come to terms with her own grief. She might not have been in love with Gordon when they married but she had grown to love him over time and his passing would leave a gaping hole in her life. She sniffed.

'Don't cry, Mother,' Thomas said, wiping red-rimmed eyes. 'I'll look after you.'

Rebecca reached over to pat his arm. 'You're a good boy, Thomas.'

The days followed in a blur. Chrissie had turned up that evening and had immediately begun making cups of tea for the seemingly endless stream of callers. Joe had accompanied Rebecca to the police station where she'd almost collapsed at the sight of Gordon's swollen, bloodied face. He'd been kicked and beaten to death, Sergeant Willis had explained grimly. 'Poor Gordon,' Rebecca whispered, wiping her eyes and turning away as the coroner gently pulled the blanket over his face. 'You didn't deserve this.'

Chrissie closed the café for a week as a mark of respect and threw herself into helping plan the funeral. Gordon's sister, Elizabeth, arrived. Her inconsolable grief only served to remind Rebecca of her guilt, which made her own grief so much harder to bear.

The funeral was held in their local church. Following the coffin down the aisle, Rebecca was warmed and touched by the sheer number of mourners squashed into the pews. She barely noticed the cloying scent of the lilies, or the way the slanting ray of sunlight fell across the burnished coffin. She hardly heard the vicar's address, but she forced herself to concentrate on Thomas's eulogy. Squashed between her mother and Christopher, Betty sobbed quietly into her handkerchief. Rebecca had made the last-minute decision to leave the two youngest children with a neighbour but now she found she missed the distraction. The two little girls' natural exuberance had been a much-needed balm to the rest of the family's grief over the past week.

Chrissie nudged her from behind. The vicar had concluded his sermon and the pall bearers were waiting to take Gordon to his final resting place outside. Rebecca nodded quickly, and got to her feet, the rest of the congregation following suit. She walked with her head bowed, her eyes flooded with tears. In her peripheral vision she was vaguely aware of the sea of pale, solemn faces.

Suddenly a dark figure moved into her peripheral vision. Her breath caught in her throat, and her head snapped up. Mickey Fox stood to one side. He smiled, his cold gaze boring into her and sending a shiver down her spine. Rebecca felt as if she was about to be sick. How dare he? How dare he? she screamed inwardly. Where were Sergeant Willis and Constable Morley now?

She burst through the open doorway into the warm late-summer sunshine. Only the faintest hint of a breeze stirred the surrounding trees. Birdsong reverberated through the air as Rebecca picked her way between the rows of weathered stones and wooden crosses. She held tightly to Christopher and Betty's hands. Thomas followed behind, supporting his aunt, who was sobbing noisily into a sodden lace-edged handkerchief. Chrissie and Joe were close behind, their three boys following solemnly.

Afterwards, she stood to one side as the mourners streamed by, offering their condolences. Her face ached from smiling. She just wanted to collapse into bed and bury herself away from the world, but she had the wake to get through yet. Chrissie and Joe had gone on ahead with the children to set out the plates of sandwiches and make the tea. To Rebecca's relief, they'd taken Gordon's sister with them. She was struggling to process her own grief and comfort her devastated children: she didn't have the energy to deal with Elizabeth as well, no matter how fond she was of the woman.

'If there's anything we can do, Mrs Graham . . .' Martha Clarke said, squeezing Rebecca's hand in hers.

'Anything at all,' Martha's husband reiterated, looking uncomfortable in his too-tight suit. He slipped his arm around Martha's waist, nudging her along.

'Mrs Graham, may I offer you my sincere condolences?' Rebecca froze as Mickey Fox stepped in front of her. He held his top hat in his gloved hands, looking every bit the respectable gentleman. 'My stepmother regrets that she couldn't attend but she sends her deepest condolences,' he said, with faux-sincerity.

Rebecca was unable to tear her gaze from his. Her heart was racing. She clenched her fists, willing herself not to break down in front of this hateful man. To her horror, he leaned towards her, his face drawing level with her. With his mouth close to her ear, he said in a low voice, inaudible to all but herself, 'I warned you, Becky. No one defies me. No one.' He drew back, his voice low enough for only Rebecca to hear. 'Unless you want another funeral in your near future . . .' he added, looking pointedly at Betty, who was being comforted by her friend Minnie. 'I'll give you time to mourn. I'm not totally heartless.' He smiled, his expression radiating sympathy. 'A couple of months should do it. Then I'll be round to collect what's mine.'

He took her hand and raised it to his lips. Rebecca shuddered in revulsion, snatching it away in disgust. Mickey grinned. Setting his hat on his head, he turned and walked away. Rebecca stared after him, her heart racing.

By the time she arrived at the house where the wake was being held, Rebecca felt physically and emotionally drained. Chrissie insisted she sit and rest while she and Mary took over the serving of refreshments. Grateful to be relieved of the responsibility, Rebecca sat on the sofa, surrounded by her children.

'Are you all right, Mother?' Thomas asked, leaning his head on her shoulder.

Rebecca mustered a smile. He looked so grown-up suddenly, his face pale and drawn as if the weight of his newly perceived responsibilities was already weighing heavily on his young shoulders.

'I'm as well as can be expected, thank you, Thomas,' replied Rebecca, gently.

Thomas nodded. He'd managed to hold his emotions together throughout the funeral service, but Rebecca could see the tears were just below the surface.

She turned slightly to her right to check on Betty, who was sitting silently with Minnie, her eyes red, her cheeks blotchy and swollen, cradling the kitten Minnie had given her as solace for her grief. Harriet leaned against her mother, sucking her thumb. It was a habit she'd almost grown out of but which had resurrected with the death of her father.

Rebecca leaned back in her seat, letting the snippets of conversations wash over her. Her mind was churning and she couldn't stomach even a cup of tea. She would never be free of Mickey. Her whole family were in serious danger unless she gave in to his demands, and she couldn't do that. Kenneth's cruel rape would be as nothing compared to what Mickey would do to her once he had her in his clutches.

She buried her face in Eliza's curls, inhaling her sweet smell, blinking back tears. How could she keep her children safe? She wondered briefly about confiding in Chrissie and Joe, but she would be putting them at risk then. She bit back the scream of terror and frustration that was building at the back of her throat. She would have to leave. She had no choice. Chrissie and Joe could keep the shop. Chrissie could rent the house for her, while Rebecca and the children found somewhere far away, somewhere they'd be safe. At the thought of having to leave everything dear to her yet again, the tears came. Hot and angry, they coursed down her cheeks, with racking sobs that shook her shoulders and brought Chrissie running from the kitchen to shoo the children away and gather Rebecca into her arms.

'Hush, hush,' she crooned, stroking Rebecca's long hair. 'It will be all right, Becky. It will be all right.'

CHAPTER THIRTY-FOUR

Rebecca woke with a start, instinctively reaching for Gordon. Her hand connected with a small, solid form. Eliza stirred and rolled over. Rebecca drew away her hand and sighed. Rolling onto her back, she lay in the darkness, listening to Eliza's gentle breathing. It was a week since the funeral, and she still wasn't used to being without her husband. She and the children were going through the motions of daily life, but Gordon's absence had left a huge hole in their lives.

She was no closer to finding a solution to her predicament and every day she paced the floor, peering first out of one window and then another, terrified that Mickey would grow impatient and come sooner than the two months' grace he'd offered her. Her fear was more for her children than for herself. Once he tired of her, would he start on Betty? There was no telling to what depth of evil depravity a man like Mickey Fox would sink. The thought of Harriet and Eliza falling into his clutches turned her stomach and she tasted bile at the back of her throat. She knew at first hand how a man could turn something so precious between a loving husband and wife into an act of evil cruelty. She gasped. Thinking of Kenneth turned her thoughts to one of the few people she felt she could trust in this world.

She sat up with a jolt. Why hadn't she thought of him before? Jeremiah would help her surely.

The more she thought about it, the more the idea made sense. Even if they couldn't forgive her for leaving as she had, such was their common decency that if she was in trouble, they would do whatever they could to help her. She wondered if Ben was still at the farm. Was he married? The thought caused a sharp stab of pain. Resolving to push aside all thoughts of Ben, she got up and went downstairs. Fetching pen and paper, she sat at Gordon's writing desk where she dithered and debated over her wording for a long time until she was satisfied. As soon as the boys had left for work and Betty for school, she, Harriet and Eliza walked to the post office.

Two weeks passed with no reply, and Rebecca was starting to lose hope when, one evening in early October, while they were seated at the supper table, there came a knock on the door. Rebecca froze, her first thought being that Mickey had come to make good on his threat.

'Shall I go, Mother?' Christopher asked, seeing that his step-mother appeared incapable of movement.

'No!' Rebecca said, quickly, causing the three older children to exchange puzzled glances. She struggled to compose herself as the knocking came again, more insistent this time. 'It's all right, thank you,' she said, getting up, her hand fluttering to her throat in fear.

Heart pounding painfully, she opened the door, and took a step back, her eyes widening in shock at the sight of Kenneth Seymour standing on the pavement.

'Hello, Becky.'

She tried to slam the door in his face, but he put his foot in the way, his hand on the door. 'Please, Becky,' he said. 'I'm not here to cause you any more grief, I promise.'

Keeping the door firmly between them, Rebecca eyed him warily. 'What do you want?'

'I received your letter. I want to help.'

'Your parents are here?' Rebecca said, in a rush of relief. Jeremiah would know what to do.

'My wife is in the cab.' He indicated the hansom cab waiting by the kerb. 'May we come in?'

Rebecca hesitated. The sight of Kenneth had brought back the memory of her ordeal in all its terrifying detail. As if reading her mind, Kenneth let his hand drop to his side, his shoulders sagging. 'I'm sorry, Becky,' he said softly. 'I wanted to tell you that so many times over the years. I don't know what came over me. I . . .' His words trailed off. He inclined his head towards the carriage from which an attractive woman in a mauve bonnet and matching jacket was alighting. 'May we come in?'

Rebecca sighed and opened the door wider.

'Mrs Graham,' the woman said, smiling as she approached. 'Becky? Don't you remember me?'

Rebecca frowned as recognition dawned. 'Polly? Polly Weeks?'

'Well, Polly Seymour now, and has been for seven years.'

They followed Rebecca into the kitchen where she introduced them to her children. 'Finish your supper and get on with your jobs,' she told them, tousling their heads in turn. 'Betty, would you make a fresh pot of tea, please? We'll be in the parlour.'

'Yes, Mother,' Betty replied solemnly.

In the parlour, Rebecca prodded the embers with a poker, stirring the dormant fire into life. 'Did Uncle Jerry and Aunt Holly not want to come?' she asked, setting down the poker, disappointment settling like a stone in her chest as she took the armchair opposite the sofa, on which Kenneth and Polly sat close together.

The couple exchanged uncomfortable glances.

'I understand that they wouldn't want to see me,' Rebecca said, with a sigh. It hurt, but she understood.

'No, Becky, they . . . It was my fault you left. We both know that.' He cleared his throat and Polly laid a hand on his arm. 'Polly knows,' he said, in response to Rebecca's quizzical gaze.

'I was shocked when he told me,' Polly admitted. 'I almost left him.'

Kenneth hung his head. 'I confessed to my parents on their death bed. I couldn't let them believe ill about you, Becky.'

'What?' Rebecca stared at him. 'Uncle Jerry and Aunt Holly are . . . dead?'

Kenneth nodded, his cheeks crimson with shame. 'Influenza. Several people in the district died. Polly and I came down with it. Polly had it particularly bad. She almost died.'

'I'm much recovered now,' Polly said, as Rebecca's gaze swivelled from Kenneth to his wife.

'I'm pleased to hear it,' she said woodenly, her mind still processing the fact that the two people she'd loved like family were no more. 'Ben?' she whispered.

Kenneth shrugged. 'He came to the funeral. He escaped the sickness altogether as far as I could gather.' It was on the tip of her tongue to ask if he was married but she swallowed the question. What was the point of torturing herself? The relief

302

that came from knowing he was alive and well was tempered by her grief for the Seymours. At least Kenneth had done the decent thing by confessing to them. She'd hated them believing the worst of her.

There was a knock on the parlour door and Betty entered bearing the tea tray. She smiled shyly, her cheeks colouring slightly.

'Thank you, sweetheart,' Rebecca said, rising to take the tray. Betty closed the door behind her and Rebecca busied herself pouring the tea, a heavy silence settling over the room, broken only by the crackling of the flames and the clink of china. Her pulse was racing, and she could hardly bring herself to look at Kenneth. How could Polly bear to be with him? she wondered, handing the other woman her tea.

As if reading her thoughts, Kenneth directed his sorrowful gaze at her and said, 'I'm sorry, Becky.' His eyes were red, as though he were fighting back tears. 'I was so jealous of Ben, you see. I was the son and heir. Elm Tree Farm should have been all mine, by rights, but Mother and Father kept taking in these waifs and strays and . . . they were always talking about treating you all as family. I know my father preferred Ben. I was a disappointment to him.' He got to his feet, pacing the small rug in front of the hearth. 'Oh, he never said it in so many words, but I knew. Ben could do no wrong in my father's eyes, and then you fell for him too. I couldn't cope. I was eaten up with jealousy. I loved Polly, but I couldn't bear the thought of Ben's life going along smoothly. I wanted to hurt him, and you. I didn't expect you to leave like that.'

'How could I have stayed?' whispered Rebecca, ashen-faced.

Kenneth slumped back on the sofa, and bowed his head. Polly looked as though she was about to burst into tears. Her lip quivered. 'I believe that is why we've never been able to have children,' she said. 'We're being punished.'

If she was expecting Rebecca to feel sorry for her, she was disappointed. 'How did Aunt Holly react?' she asked.

Kenneth shrugged. 'They were so ill, delirious even. I wasn't sure how much they understood but one evening, near the end, I was sitting with Mother.' Kenneth's voice broke. 'She was so weak,' he choked. 'She said – she said, "I knew my Becky wouldn't have left for no good reason . . ."' Kenneth burst into tears.

'Oh, my dear.' Polly pulled him into her arms.

Rebecca studied the few stray leaves at the bottom of her teacup, her own emotions running amok. She wished so much she'd had the chance to see Holly one last time, but she was comforted by the knowledge that she had died knowing the reason why Becky had left.

'Can you forgive me?' Kenneth asked, struggling to compose himself. He blew his nose loudly and mopped his wet eyes.

'You ruined my relationship with Ben, with Aunt Holly and Uncle Jerry,' she whispered. 'How can I ever forgive that?'

'Ben never stopped loving you,' Kenneth mumbled miserably, folding his wet handkerchief into a neat square. 'We'd always thought he and Ella might wed . . .' Rebecca gasped as if she'd been punched in the stomach. The flood of relief that followed was overwhelming. '. . . but Ben hasn't married. I believe he still pines for you. Ella married a blacksmith from Bourton a few years back. She's got a couple of kiddies.'

Rebecca set down her cup and saucer, which were clattering in her shaking hand. 'You didn't think to tell Ben the truth when you were cleansing your soul, then?' she remarked drily.

'I'm a coward,' Kenneth said lamely. 'He tried to find you,

when you first left. So did Father. Even after it became clear you were long gone, he refused to give up. Day after day he went out looking for you. I felt bad for him. He was a broken man. He eventually left the farm. I guess it held too many memories for him.'

Rebecca blinked back tears, her heart aching at the thought of Ben searching the length and breadth of the county for her. She rubbed her throbbing temples. 'I'm sorry,' she said, getting abruptly to her feet. 'I need to lie down. It's all been a shock. The last few weeks . . . I can't. . .' She clutched her head, her temples throbbing.

'But what of the problem you wrote about in your letter?' Kenneth began.

A glare from his wife cut him off. 'We'll come back tomorrow,' Polly said. 'We're booked in at the inn down the street, the Black Sheep. Send word if you need us.'

Rebecca saw them out and closed the door, leaning against it in relief.

'Mother?' Thomas stood in the doorway, a worried frown marring his youthful good looks.

'I'm fine,' Rebecca assured him. 'I'm just tired, that's all. I may go and lie down for a bit. Will you be all right with the little ones?'

'Of course.' Thomas nodded emphatically.

'You're a good boy, Thomas,' Rebecca said, going to him and giving him a hug. 'Your father was very proud of you.' Thomas hugged her back fiercely, his back ramrod straight as he fought to contain his emotion.

Tomorrow, Rebecca thought as she made her way wearily up the stairs. She would deal with her problems tomorrow. For now, she needed to sleep, and to come to terms with the additional grief over Aunt Holly and Uncle Jerry, as well as processing her feelings at seeing Kenneth again. She realized, to her surprise, as she crossed the landing, that she felt only pity for him. He was clearly not a happy man, and he no longer held any power over her. She only wished the same could be said of Mickey Fox.

CHAPTER THIRTY-FIVE

'Why don't you just report Fox to the police?' Polly asked, sipping her tea. She set the dainty gold-rimmed cup back on its saucer and regarded Rebecca with a quizzical air.

'I wouldn't be surprised if some members of the local constabulary are customers of his,' Rebecca replied, with an air of frustration, her gaze straying to the street beyond the window. She and Polly were sitting in the snug of the Black Sheep Inn where Polly and Kenneth had spent the night.

'Surely your fears are unfounded,' Kenneth said, returning from the bar with a mug of ale. He took a sip, licking froth from his upper lip as he sat down next to Polly, his back to the window, and stretched out his legs. 'I mean, really, what can he do to you? He can't force you . . .' There was an uncomfortable silence. Rebecca looked at her feet and Polly suddenly seemed to find the light fittings of interest. 'What I mean is, he's surely all bluster and threats.' He regarded Rebecca over the rim of his pewter mug. 'I think you're worrying about nothing.'

Rebecca contemplated the scratched, pockmarked tabletop for a moment. 'You don't understand what he's like, Kenneth,' she said at length. 'We have a history.' She looked away, feeling the heat flare in her cheeks. 'You know my father and brothers drowned when I was ten?' Kenneth nodded, and she continued, 'My mother couldn't afford the rent on our cottage and we were evicted. We had no family, no one who could help us. Mickey Fox pretended to be kind. He promised Mama employment. What we didn't know,' Rebecca said harshly, getting up and crossing to the window, 'was that he ran a brothel. He forced my mother to work for him, to . . . to service men.' Her voice broke. She took a breath to steady herself. 'She was murdered by a customer and Mickey wanted me to replace her.' She heard Polly's sharp intake of breath behind her. 'I was twelve years old. My mother's friend helped me to escape, and he killed her. He killed Gordon and he's threatened me on several occasions. If I don't do as he says, and give myself to him, he will hurt my children.' She turned to face her two companions. Kenneth stared back at her, his expression a mixture of scepticism and disgust. Rebecca shivered. Despite the cosy fire, she felt chilled to the bone.

'For all your airs and graces, your mother was nothing but a common whore?' he said, frowning.

'Kenneth!' Polly gasped, slapping his shoulder with her glove.

'How dare you?' Rebecca glared at him. 'You, of all people? After what you did to me?'

Kenneth looked away, shame-faced. An uncomfortable silence settled on the room, broken at length by Polly.

'I'm sorry,' she said, shooting Kenneth an angry look. 'He didn't mean anything by it, did you, Kenny?'

Kenneth exhaled and shook his head. 'I didn't mean anything by it, Becky. I'm sorry.' Rebecca gave a grudging nod. Her dislike for the man was tempered only by her need of his help, though she was beginning to wonder whether he would be any help at all.

'I'm assuming you have no proof to back up your claims against Fox?' Kenneth asked.

'No,' Rebecca replied shortly.

'Perhaps the police could track down one of the girls who worked for him back in Dartmouth,' suggested Polly.

'I think the best thing to do,' Kenneth said slowly, tracing a droplet of condensation down his mug, 'is to ignore him and get on with your life. He's clearly a bully and he's intimidating you, but if you ignore him, he'll get bored and leave you alone.

'Kenneth!' Rebecca exclaimed in frustration. 'It's been fifteen years since I left the brothel. He's not going to give up now. He won't ever give up until I give in or I'm dead.'

'All right,' Kenneth said, shifting in his seat. 'I'll have a word with him then. Get him to leave you alone.'

'I'm not sure that's a good idea,' Rebecca said in alarm.

'Is that wise?' Polly frowned. 'He sounds a nasty piece of work.'

'Like I said, he's a bully. He just needs someone to stand up to him. Where can I find him?'

'He's a member of the Hamilton Club. That's where Gordon met him. He pretended to be his friend and then killed him.' Rebecca saw Kenneth and Polly exchange a glance. She knew they thought she was being paranoid, with her wild allegations of murder she couldn't back up. 'He goes by the name of Michael Osborne. But I really think it's a bad idea, Kenneth. He's dangerous.'

'Then what did you expect me to do? What were you hoping to achieve by writing to my parents?'

'I don't know,' Rebecca admitted. 'I thought perhaps Uncle Jerry would have an idea, connections maybe . . .'

'Why don't you and the children come back to Shaftesbury?' Polly suggested. 'He'd never find you there. I'm sure the hotels and restaurants would be only too glad to buy your pies once more.'

Rebecca hesitated, before replying. 'It is something I've thought about.' Now that she knew Ben was unmarried, the prospect of moving back was suddenly a lot more appealing.

'Think about it,' Polly said. 'One of the cottages on the farm is empty. You'd be welcome to it.'

'In the meantime, I'll seek out this Mickey Fox and have a word,' Kenneth said, draining his pint. He stood up. 'What time am I most likely to find him at his club?'

'It opens about midday, as far as I know, until about eleven at night. Gordon usually went after supper, around six.'

Kenneth nodded. 'I shall go this evening. Shall I walk you home?' he asked Rebecca.

Rebecca reluctantly accepted his offer. If Mickey was lurking nearby, she didn't want to run into him while out on her own.

As the afternoon waned, Rebecca found she couldn't settle to anything. She sat in the parlour, ostensibly darning a pair of Christopher's socks, her face turned towards the window. The damson-coloured clouds were threaded with gold and crimson, the tiles on the roof opposite glinting in the sun's dying rays. She had felt an overwhelming sense of foreboding all afternoon. The muted voices of the older children drifted from the kitchen where they were clearing up after the evening meal. Harriet and Eliza were at her feet, playing with their paper dolls.

She wondered if Polly was as anxious as she was. Surely she must be, Rebecca mused. Mickey was a dangerous man. If Kenneth came to harm, Rebecca would never forgive herself.

She disliked the man, but she wouldn't wish any harm to befall him.

Giving up all pretence of darning, she laid down her work and sighed, massaging the back of her neck. She could feel a headache coming on, no doubt caused by tension.

She tried to tell herself that the Hamilton Club was a respectable place that boasted parliamentarians among its membership. Surely no harm could come to Kenneth there. *But what about after he left?* murmured a small voice inside her head.

She leaned back in her chair, watching anxiously as the sunlight faded from the rooftops. She glanced at the clock. It was twenty minutes past six. 'Come, girls,' she said, stirring herself. 'Time for bed.' She got to her feet, shushing their grumbles, and ushered them up the stairs. She let out a slow breath. It was going to be a long evening.

The clock chimed ten. Rebecca was sitting in the warm kitchen with her three oldest children. It was way past their bedtime but tomorrow was Saturday: Betty had no school and the boys were both on a late shift, so they could enjoy a lie-in. Rebecca hadn't wanted to be alone, and she knew she wouldn't sleep. Instead, she sat at the kitchen table, nursing a mug of cocoa, while trying to quell the anxiety she felt. She had expected Kenneth to come to the house once he'd seen Mickey but he had clearly decided otherwise. Now she would have to wait until the morning to find out what had happened. She could only hope and pray he was safe.

A loud hammering on the front door made her jump. Thomas, Christopher and Betty all turned to her, their eyes wide in pale faces. It had to be Mickey. Rebecca swallowed painfully, her eyes frantically scouring the kitchen for a suitable weapon. 'Thomas, pass me the coal shovel,' she said, aware that her voice was shaking. Thomas's brow furrowed slightly, but he did as he was told. The loud hammering came again.

'Open up. Police!' came the shout.

'Mama?' Betty said, her eyes filling with tears. The last time the police had come to the house had been to inform them of her father's death. Rebecca patted her shoulder and pushed back her chair. Her pulse was racing as she hurried to open the door, her fingers fumbling with the latch.

Two policemen stood on the doorstep, bathed in the light spilling from the hall. 'Mrs Rebecca Graham?' the older of the two asked. He was a heavy-set man with a ginger mutton-chop moustache and florid complexion. Rebecca's heart sank. Something had happened to Kenneth.

'Who wants to know?' asked Thomas, coming up behind his stepmother. He was followed by Christopher. Betty hovered anxiously in the kitchen doorway.

'It's all right, Thomas,' Rebecca said hoarsely, her heart thumping against her rib cage. 'Yes, I am Mrs Graham. Has something happened to Mr Seymour?' The two policemen exchanged glances.

'Mrs Rebecca Graham,' the older man said. 'I'm arresting you for the wilful murder of Mr Kenneth Seymour.'

'Oh, no,' Rebecca wailed. 'Kenneth's dead? I knew it. I knew he shouldn't have gone, but he wouldn't listen.'

'Mother,' Thomas said, frowning. 'Did you hear what the policeman said?'

'Yes, Kenneth is dead,' she whispered. 'Murdered.'

'You need to come with us, madam,' the policeman said, sternly.

As he took hold of her arm, Rebecca's shocked brain finally

comprehended the man's words. 'You're arresting me?' she whispered, unable to believe what was happening to her. Blood rushed in her ears and the hallway began to spin. She would have fallen if Thomas hadn't managed to catch her.

'This is ridiculous,' Christopher spluttered, turning his anguished gaze on his stepmother. 'My mother has been here all evening. You've got the wrong person.'

'We have a witness,' the younger policeman said, his face devoid of expression. He was thinner, smooth-shaven with thick brows and a nose that looked as though it had been broken. 'You'll need to come with us, madam,' he said, nodding at his superior.

'This way, madam,' the older policeman said, motioning to his right. At the sight of the black cart waiting alongside the kerb, Rebecca's stomach lurched in fright. A dark, hooded figure sat up on the driver's seat, staring ahead. The black horse tossed its head and whinnied softly.

'Mama?' Rebecca looked back over her shoulder, in panic. Betty had come into the hall, her eyes pleading. 'Mama, tell them you didn't do it. Tell them.'

'I won't be long,' Rebecca said, biting back a sob as she reached out to grab Betty's hand. 'I'll be home soon, I promise. Look after Harriet and Eliza until I get back.' She turned to the policemen. 'Where are you taking me?'

'You'll be held at Whitechapel police station overnight,' the younger policeman replied gruffly. 'In the morning you'll be transferred to Fenchurch women's prison. Your children can apply to visit you there.'

The commotion had brought a few of her neighbours to their doors where they watched open-mouthed as the policemen ushered Rebecca towards the prison cart, her face burning with

313

shame. Betty's sobs rang in her ears. The policemen opened the back and she climbed inside, trembling. The door slammed behind her, plunging her into near-total darkness. Her only source of light was the faint glow of a streetlamp through the metal grille set high above her head. She could hear Thomas and Christopher arguing with the policemen. Betty was sobbing louder now, and she was relieved to hear the voice of Minnie's mother, Martha. Martha would take care of the children until she came home. The thought of her two youngest blissfully asleep upstairs was like a knife to her heart and she began to weep.

The air stank of stale urine and vomit. Fear pressed down on Rebecca, turning her insides to liquid. The cart lurched forward, and Rebecca grabbed the side to stop herself falling. It was an uncomfortable journey, and it seemed to Rebecca that an eternity had passed before they came to a halt. The door was flung open.

'This way,' barked the first policeman tersely, holding up a lantern. Almost blinded by the sudden light, Rebecca stumbled and half fell out of the cart. The stench of human filth clogged her nostrils, clinging to her hair and clothing, and she was shoved into the police station, her cheeks burning with shame as the policeman ushered her to a cell. There was a narrow cot, and a bucket half full of the previous occupant's waste.

'You'll be interviewed shortly,' the policeman said. He slammed the cell door, the clang reverberating around Rebecca's fevered brain. She sank onto the bed and buried her face in her hands, sobbing quietly.

Shock had set in and she couldn't stop shaking. Kenneth was dead. Mickey had obviously killed him and somehow framed her for his murder. How? She thought of poor Polly. Would she believe Rebecca was the culprit? She knew Kenneth had raped Rebecca, so would it be too much for her to believe Rebecca had killed him in revenge? These thoughts whirled around her brain, driving her frantic with terror. Beyond the bars, people came and went. Constables brought in more prisoners. Metal doors clanged as the police station filled with the dregs of humanity. The crying, screaming and swearing echoed through the building. Rebecca curled up on the bed. The blanket smelt foul and was likely crawling with lice. She thought about Harriet and Eliza waking up in the morning without their mother and began crying again. What would happen to them if she was convicted? At the thought, her chest constricted painfully, grief searing her heart. How would she survive if she never saw her children again?

CHAPTER THIRTY-SIX

Fenchurch women's prison was a dark, turreted building within sight of the Tower of London. With three other women of varying ages, Rebecca was taken from the cart into which they'd been crammed, and ushered down a draughty, stone-walled corridor to a reception area where she was processed, relieved of her clothes and given a drab, shapeless grey dress, a white cap and a pair of wooden clogs. Rebecca changed quickly, shivering in the chill of the damp room.

'What's that?' the female warder barked, pointing at Rebecca's chest.

Rebecca's fingers instinctively curled around her locket. 'It's mine,' she said defensively.

'It looks expensive,' the woman sneered. 'Give it here.' She held out her hand, palm upwards.

'No, please.' The woman had already taken her wedding ring.

'It's the rules,' the woman snapped. 'Hand it over or I'll rip it from your neck.'

Slowly, Rebecca undid the clasp. For a moment she could only stare at the delicate chain and intricately carved silver oval lying in her shaking palm. The warden snatched it from her, making her flinch.

Along with the other women, Rebecca was taken into the main prison. It was on three levels, reached by metal staircases. It was eerily silent, the only sound the echo of their feet on the metal steps. She had to cling to the railing to stop herself stumbling in the ill-fitting clogs.

'In here.' The warden unlocked a door and shoved Rebecca inside, slamming it behind her. The sound of the key turning in the lock chilled her to the bone. The cell was sparsely furnished with a narrow cot, a three-legged stool and a slop bucket. She was relieved to note that the bucket was empty and had recently been scrubbed. She sank wearily onto the low cot. While the bedding was worn and frayed, it at least smelt clean. A square, barred window high above her head afforded her a glimpse of grey sky.

Her mind was in turmoil as she struggled to comprehend her predicament. She'd expected to be released as soon as she'd been interviewed. She had the children as witness that she had never left the house all evening but the policeman who'd interviewed her late the previous night, a pompous, opinionated man, hadn't seemed interested in the fact that she might be innocent. Her entreaties that they investigate Mickey Fox, or Michael Osborne, had fallen on deaf ears. All the policeman would say was that there was a reliable witness.

She had never been so terrified in her life. She had eaten no breakfast and had managed only a few sips of the weak tea they'd brought her at the police station before she was transferred, but she had no appetite.

Time dragged. Patches of blue appeared on the square of sky, shadows moving across the wooden floor. She counted the marks scratched into the wall. Someone had been there five years, judging by the inscriptions. The thought of spending even another day in such a small, confined space sent shivers down her spine. At one point she thought she heard a baby cry, and tears sprang to her eyes as she thought of her children at home. How were they coping without her? What if she never got out? What would become of her children? Especially the little ones? The thought of her sweet babies being taken to the workhouse filled her with a fresh wave of terror and she went to the door, banging hard on the heavy wood. She shouted for the warden until she was hoarse, but no one came.

It was growing dark before she heard the key turn in the lock. A different woman pushed the door open, her baton at the ready. Rebecca looked up dully.

'It's supper time,' the woman announced, without warmth. 'I'm Miss Johnson. You may address me as "ma'am".' Indicating with her baton that Rebecca was to get up and follow, Miss Johnson turned on her heels. Wearily Rebecca followed her down the long flights of steps, along with the three other women who'd arrived that morning. Miss Johnson led them into a large refectory. Women ranging in age from girls barely in their teens to white-haired old crones sat quietly at long wooden tables. They eyed the newcomers with little interest. At the far end of the hall there was a table at which sat three women and four small children. One woman nursed a baby at her breast. Rebecca could hardly tear her gaze away from the tableau, a surge of hope flaring as she contemplated having Harriet and Eliza with her in the prison, but she quashed the idea almost as soon as it came. She wouldn't want her beautiful, innocent daughters being brought up in such a place. But she did need to find out what was happening to them. She resolved to request an audience with the governor as soon as supper was over.

She took her place near the end of one of the long tables. Several inmates were moving up and down the tables dispensing steaming bowls. A scrawny girl with stained teeth and greasy blonde hair plonked a wooden bowl in front of Rebecca. She sniffed it cautiously. To her surprise it smelt quite appetizing. Bits of meat and vegetables swam in a pale broth. Someone placed a platter of bread in the middle of the table.

'It's not bad grub here,' the girl next to her said, under her breath, helping herself to a thick slice of coarse dark brown bread. 'We had a visit from some do-gooders and since then the food's improved no end. It used to be real slop before that. Not fit for pigs.'

'No talking,' snapped one of the three wardens prowling the dining hall.

'I'm Emily,' the girl whispered, when the warden's back was turned.

'Becky.'

'What are you in for?' asked Emily, casting a surreptitious glance down the hall. The wardens were talking among themselves, their attention away from the rows of women bent over their bowls. Emily was a thin girl, with pale features, and tendrils of wavy blonde hair escaping from beneath her cap. 'I stabbed me old man when he beat me black and blue for the umpteenth time. Didn't kill him, fortunately, or I'd have swung by now.' She grimaced. 'I got ten years.'

'I'm innocent,' Rebecca murmured.

Emily laughed. 'That's what they all say.'

Rebecca looked down at her bowl. 'It's true. I didn't do anything. I need to speak to the governor. I have to make him understand . . .'

'Silence!' bellowed Miss Johnson, striding towards Rebecca.

'Just because you're new here, don't think you can flout the rules. Back to your cell, now. Come on.'

Blushing furiously, Rebecca put down her spoon and meekly followed the warden from the room. She could feel numerous pairs of eyes boring into her back.

'I need to speak to the governor,' she said, plucking up her courage to speak, as they climbed the stairs to her cell. 'There's been a terrible mistake. I shouldn't be here, and I need to find out what's happened with my children. I—'

'Save it for your trial,' Miss Johnson snapped, unlocking the cell door.

'Wait, please . . .' The door slammed in her face. Rebecca stared at it in dismay before sinking wearily onto the bed. Her temples throbbed and panic threatened to overwhelm her. Why would no one listen to her? It might be months before her case came to trial. Even if she was acquitted, her children could be anywhere by then. Hot tears scalded her cheeks. She curled up on her bed, her chest heaving as she sobbed into her thin pillow.

The cell grew darker, the small square of light fading with the encroaching night. From beyond she heard the cacophony of hundreds of footsteps on metal stairs, punctuated by the heavy clang of cell doors being banged shut. Rebecca rolled onto her back. Her throat ached from crying and her eyes felt hot and sticky, her cheeks raw. Occasionally a sudden scream would shatter the deep silence, making her hair stand on end, but apart from that, it was easy for Rebecca to feel she was entirely alone.

She drifted in and out of sleep, her tired brain conjuring up weird and frightening dreams and several times she woke with a start, crying out for her children. She was especially worried for the youngest two. Harriet and Eliza were too young to understand that their mama couldn't come home. They would think she had abandoned them, and that pained her more than anything.

The days passed in agonizing slowness. She was allowed out of her cell only for meals and for half an hour of exercise in the afternoon, which comprised a solitary walk around the yard under the watchful eye of one of the wardens.

After she'd been incarcerated for two weeks, she was surprised when, after breakfast, she was informed that, instead of returning to her cell, she was being set to work. 'Your two weeks of solitary confinement are up,' a hard-faced warden, Miss McRae, told her. 'You're in the laundry. Over there.' She pointed to a group of women assembling at the far end of the hall. Rebecca was pleased to see Emily among them. They usually sat next to each other at mealtimes and the two had become friendly, or as friendly as it was possible to be when talking was forbidden.

Emily gave Rebecca a quick smile, earning herself a glare from the overweight prison guard who was waddling towards them, jangling her large bunch of keys noisily.

'Line up,' she barked, unlocking the gate that barred their way. In single file they walked quickly along a wide, draughty corridor, their clogs echoing loudly on the scuffed stone floor.

Twice Rebecca stumbled. Her clogs were large and uncomfortable and she hadn't yet mastered walking in them properly.

'Watch it, clumsy oaf,' one of the women hissed, as Rebecca tripped again, lurching into the woman in front of her.

'Silence!' the guard barked, bringing up the rear. She squeezed her large girth past the group of women who'd come to a halt outside a wide metal doorway. The smell of soap and mildew hung in the air. Patches of black mould bloomed on the low ceiling. The warden opened the door and the women surged into the room.

Rebecca found herself in a large laundry. There were huge vats, industrial-sized mangles, and wooden washing dollies. Wooden racks for drying the clothes on inclement days hung from the high ceiling. 'Graham, you're on the tubs,' the guard said. 'Get those fires lit,' she barked. 'Come along, get moving. No shirking.'

The women hurried to their jobs. Rebecca looked at Emily uncertainly, and she inclined her head towards one of the large washtubs. It was set upon a small stove, which Rebecca had to light in order to heat the water. It was just like her washtub at home, but on a larger scale. Inhaling deeply, Rebecca rolled up her sleeves.

It was backbreaking work. The air soon grew hot and steamy. Sweat dripped down Rebecca's spine. She wiped her brow on the back of her hand, her hair damp against her skull. The washing dolly was heavy, and her shoulders were soon screaming for relief as she continued to churn the heavily soiled items in the tub, the water turning an unsavoury grey. The humidity was making her feel faint and it was a relief when it was time for a water break. She took her dipper gratefully. The water was tepid and unpleasant to the taste, but she was too thirsty to care. She drained the small metal cup quickly, and handed it back, her thirst far from slaked.

By the time they broke for dinner, her hands were raw and blistered from wielding the heavy wooden washing dolly. She'd splashed herself on several occasions and the scalding water had left an angry red weal on her bare forearm. She could barely drag herself to the refectory. Her feet ached and her back throbbed painfully. After dinner, she had to do it all over again.

That night, she fell asleep as soon as her head hit the pillow.

Each day followed the same gruelling routine. One good thing, she mused ruefully, as she stood with Emily in the dank courtyard for their brief half-hour exercise, she was too exhausted to think about her predicament.

'It's visiting this Sunday,' Emily said, shielding her eyes from the glare of the clear October sky, as she shivered in the chill breeze. 'I'm hoping my ma will come. She doesn't always. No one else bothers.' She turned to Rebecca. 'What about you? D'you think your kiddies will come?'

Rebecca wrapped her arms around her thin frame for warmth. Her skimpy uniform offered no protection against the autumn wind. She'd lost weight since being locked up and her dress hung on her like a sack. When she lay on the thin mattress, she could feel her bones through her skin. Her lips and hair were dry and brittle, her complexion pasty. She shrugged her shoulders, torn between the hope that her children would visit, and not wanting them to see her looking so awful. Tears were her constant companion and they stung her eyes now, blurring her vision. She wiped them roughly away.

'There's a lot that don't get visitors,' Emily said. 'It's a long way for some to come just for half an hour.' She lowered her voice, casting a wary glance in the direction of the two wardens who were standing in a corner of the yard, keeping watch. 'At least if visitors bring us food we can keep it now. The wardens used to take most of it but the do-gooders put a stop to that.'

Rebecca felt a surge of hope. 'Do they come round often, the do-gooders?'

Emily shrugged. 'Once or twice a year, perhaps. They come on Christmas Day and bring presents donated by the churches.'

323

'I wonder if I might be able to speak to one of them about my innocence.'

'You could try. They like to spend time with us. That's how they knew about the wardens helping themselves to our stuff. Poor old Sal earned herself a week in solitary for opening her mouth, but at least we get to keep what our family sends us.'

The whistle blew, signalling the end of the half-hour break. A collective groan filled the yard and the women began to shuffle towards the arched entryway.

'Get a move on,' one of the wardens shouted, waving her baton at the stragglers. Rebecca and Emily joined the crowd of unkempt, unwashed women crowding through the narrow brick archway, where they were herded, like cows, down the long passageway back to the laundry.

CHAPTER THIRTY-SEVEN

Rebecca perched on the edge of the bed, her hands clasped together as if in prayer. Her heart beat erratically and her stomach felt hollow. She held her breath as footsteps approached, then passed her cell door. She exhaled, her shoulders sagging in disappointment. Ever since she'd been returned to her cell after the brief church service in the prison chapel, she'd been wondering if she'd be one of the lucky few to receive a visitor. It was now late afternoon and still she hadn't been called. Despair settled over her like a heavy blanket. She'd been hoping, praying that someone would come. If the children hadn't wanted to, and she wouldn't have blamed them, she would have thought Chrissie would make the effort. Unless. She shook her head. Chrissie would never believe Rebecca capable of murder. If only someone would come, just so she knew the children were all right. The not knowing was eating her up inside. It was a month since her arrest and she'd had no news about them at all.

Her mournful thoughts were interrupted by the sound of approaching footsteps and she held her breath, hope igniting in her breast when they stopped outside her door. At the sound of the key being inserted in the lock, she leaped to her feet, facing the door in hopeful expectation.

'You've got a visitor, Graham,' hissed Miss McRae, sourly, standing aside so Rebecca could step past her. Heart racing with excitement, Rebecca walked ahead of the warden down the three flights of steps, her mind whirling as she wondered who it was. Much as she longed to see her children, anyone from the outside world would do.

'This way.' The warden led her through a series of locked gates and up long corridors, until she finally stopped in front of a wide, metal door, which she unlocked, ushering Rebeca inside.

She blinked, finding herself in a bright, airy room. Dust motes swirled in the pale sunlight streaming through the bank of windows opposite. Prisoners and their visitors sat at long wooden benches, similar to church pews, each facing the front of the room, with the three solemn-faced wardens keeping a stern eye on proceedings. Behind them hung a large board listing the many rules and penalties for minor infractions. Rebecca scanned the seats for someone she recognized.

'Sit.' Obediently, Rebecca slid onto the closest bench. The last thing she wanted to do was annoy the woman and risk being returned to her cell.

Miss McRae exited through a door at the back of the room, leaving Rebecca to sit listening to the snippets of hushed conversation drifting from the various groups. A woman with grey-streaked mousy-brown hair was sobbing loudly, while a middle-aged gentleman, presumably her husband, attempted to comfort her.

The rear door reopened, and Rebecca shot to her feet, unable to hold back her sobs at the sight of Thomas walking towards her. His pale face was pinched with anxiety, his dark eyes clouded with worry. Tears streaming down her face, Rebecca opened her arms wide.

'Mother!' He flung himself into Rebecca's arms. She held him close, savouring the feel of his firm solidness in her arms, the smell of his hair and skin. They were both sobbing.

'It's all right, my boy,' Rebecca mumbled, between sobs, stroking Thomas's hair. 'It's all right . . . Your brother and sisters?' she managed to ask, between sobs.

'They're with Aunty Chrissie,' Thomas said, with a shuddering breath, as he drew back, wiping his eyes roughly on his jacket sleeve. 'They send their love. Mother, I . . .' Thomas half turned and, for the first time, Rebecca became aware of a man standing a few paces away.

'Ben?' she whispered, certain it must be a trick of the mind.

'Hello, Becky.'

Rebecca clutched the back of the wooden bench. He had hardly changed in the seven years since she'd last seen him. She flushed with shame, and bowed her head, knowing how she must look to him, in her drab prison garb, with her prison pallor and sour, unwashed smell.

'Look at me, Becky,' Ben said, his voice so gentle she wanted to cry. Slowly, she raised her gaze to meet his. 'I'm going to help you get out of here.'

'How . . . how did you know?' Rebecca asked, as they settled themselves on the hard bench.

'Polly Seymour came to see me,' he explained. 'She told me Kenneth was dead, and that you'd been arrested for his murder.'

'I'm innocent,' Rebecca whispered.

'I know, and Polly knows it, too. Which is why she asked for my help.' He glanced at Thomas, who was sitting as close to

327

Rebecca as he could get. 'She also told me the reason you left the farm,' he added grimly, his fists clenching involuntarily at his side, swallowing his anger. 'I caught the next train up and I've been here ever since, trying to secure your release.'

Rebecca smiled through her tears. Just knowing there were people who believed in her made her heart feel lighter. She clutched Thomas's hand. 'How are the children?' she asked, her brow furrowing.

Thomas shrugged. 'Eliza used to cry all the time, but she's better now. Harriet wets the bed. Aunty Chrissie said it's because she misses you.' He laid his head against her shoulder, a little boy again. 'We all miss you.'

'I know, darling.' Rebecca stroked his head. 'I miss you all too.' How cruel had life been to these poor children, she thought, meeting Ben's gaze over Thomas's bowed head. They'd barely got used to the loss of their beloved father when their mother had been taken from them as well.

'Polly also told me something about your history with this Mickey Fox,' Ben said, when Thomas had gone to get a drink of water. 'You never told me about that part of your life.'

'I'm sorry,' Rebecca said, seeing the hurt on Ben's face. 'It was a very unhappy time and I just wanted to put it behind me. I never thought I'd see him again and I didn't want to spoil things between us.' She gave a hollow laugh. 'But it was spoiled in the end anyway, by Kenneth.'

'I wish you hadn't run off,' Ben said quietly. 'I love you, Becky, and nothing will ever change that. I wish you'd told me what had happened.'

Rebecca stared at him. The sounds and smells of the prison faded away. Had she heard right? He still loved her? 'I was soiled goods,' she whispered.

'No,' Ben hissed. 'I should have protected you. I should never have let you go back to the farm alone.'

Rebecca reached out and stroked Ben's arm. 'You weren't to know.'

'He asked me to be best man at his wedding. Did you know that?' Ben ran a hand through his hair in agitation. 'If I'd known what he'd done . . .'

'That's why I couldn't tell you,' Rebecca murmured. 'I was so afraid you'd fight him. What if you hurt him, or worse? I couldn't bear the thought of you going to prison. That's why I left. To protect you.'

Over Ben's shoulder she saw Thomas making his way back towards them. He'd clearly been crying.

'Are you all right, love?' Rebecca asked, as he slumped on to the seat beside her.

He nodded. 'Are you going to help my mother?' he asked Ben.

'I shall do my best,' Ben replied gravely. 'I've written to the governor,' he told Rebecca. 'You have an alibi in your children. I'm surprised you're even in here. What are the police saying?'

'I told them that at the police station,' replied Rebecca, with a dismal shake of her head. 'But they wouldn't listen. They just kept saying there's a witness. It must be Mickey. There's no other explanation.'

'I think I need to have a word with this Mr Fox,' Ben said.

'No!' Rebecca cried in alarm, earning herself a sharp glance from the wardens, as several people looked round. 'You mustn't go near him,' she said quietly. 'He's dangerous. He'll kill you like he did Kenneth.'

In hushed tones, and aware that Thomas was listening with

ever-widening eyes, Rebecca told Ben all about Mickey. How he had treated her mother, about him killing Nora for helping Rebecca escape, his stint in prison, how he had changed his name, and how he had murdered her husband, while Ben listened in grim silence.

'Time's up,' the warden shouted. 'Back to your cells.'

'You need to find a woman in Dartmouth called Dora,' Rebecca said frantically grabbing Ben's arm as the warden gripped her elbow, dragging her away.

'Dora? Dora who?' Ben frowned.

'I don't know. She used to work at Angel Terrace. Number fourteen. It's just up from the harbour. Please, Ben, she'll be able to help you. You must persuade her to speak up about Nora. If you can persuade the police that Mickey murdered Nora, they may look at him for Kenneth's murder. Please, Ben, I . . . And look after my children. I'm frightened for them. I—'

'Mama!' Thomas's distraught face was the last thing she saw as she was manhandled through the door. It slammed with a deafening clang.

'Back to your cell, Graham,' the warden growled, shoving her.

Rebecca joined the group of dejected women shuffling to the main prison, heads bowed, shoulders slumped. Some sobbed quietly, while the wardens walked silently alongside, stone-faced, devoid of sympathy and empathy.

The days followed in an exhausting blur of drudgery. The only thing that kept her going was the thought that Ben loved her. She had never imagined in her wildest dreams that he would still feel so about her after all this time. And she knew he would do everything in his power to help her. It was also a huge weight off her mind, knowing that Chrissie was looking after the children. She thanked God daily for her friend. She should have known that Chrissie would never have allowed her children to be taken into the workhouse. That gave her some measure of comfort and went some way to relieving her agony at being shut away from them.

The last Monday of November dawned wet and windy. At the shrill ring of the bell, Rebecca threw back the covers, her teeth chattering in the frigid air. Her muscles ached from the cold. They'd all been given an extra blanket when the temperature plummeted, but it had made little difference. Shivering, she pulled on her shawl and slipped her stocking-clad feet into her clogs, ready for the warden. She was looking forward to the steamy warmth of the laundry.

The huge washtub bubbled and belched clouds of steam into the damp air as Rebecca wielded the heavy washing dolly, her shoulders protesting painfully. Emily came by, wheeling a cart laden with bundles of wrung-out laundry destined for the drying room. Though they couldn't talk, they managed a quick smile before Emily disappeared behind a large washtub.

Rebecca churned the washing – the water had long since turned a dirty grey, soapy scum floating on top. She brushed a loose strand of hair from her sweaty face with her forearm, almost losing her balance on the low stool. She steadied herself, her heart pounding. Only last week a girl had put herself in the infirmary by half falling into a vat of scalding water.

'Graham!' Warden Harper's voice cut through the air like a knife. Rebecca froze, aware that every pair of eyes was turned in her direction. Her pulse raced as she stepped off the stool, her mind racing as she tried to imagine what infraction of the rules she had committed.

'This way, Graham,' Warden Harper barked, wending her way between the washtubs. 'The governor wants a word.' She smiled slyly, relishing Rebecca's obvious distress. 'What you been up to, then?'

'Nothing, I swear,' Rebecca said, hastily untying her apron. Her stomach roiled. She met the worried glances of some of the women, and her mouth dried. The governor only asked to see an inmate if there had been a very serious infraction of the rules. Or if there was bad news to be delivered. 'The children,' she murmured anxiously. 'Oh, please God, not one of the children.

'Is it my children?' she asked, attempting to keep pace with the warden as they traversed the draughty corridors, her anxiety growing with every step. 'Has there been an accident?'

'Silence!' The warden glared, keys jangling in her hand, as she unlocked first one door, then another.

Rebecca had never been in this part of the prison before. The air felt warmer and fresher. Warden Harper unlocked another door, and Rebecca found herself in a carpeted hallway. There was a window to her left, overlooking a wide yard. A painting of a daffodil hung on the wall, a splash of colour in an otherwise drab grey world. The warden knocked on the door and a voice from within bade them enter.

'Inmate Graham, sir,' Warden Harper said in clipped tones, pushing open the door and indicating to Rebecca with a sharp nod that she should enter.

'Mrs Graham.' The governor was a thin, wiry man, his dark hair and neatly trimmed beard streaked with grey. A small brass plaque on the desk read 'T. S. Sweetman, PRISON GOVERNOR'.

'Please, sir,' Rebecca stammered. 'Has something happened? Is it my children?'

'Silence!' the warden barked. 'Speak only when you're spoken to.'

'Thank you, Miss Harper,' the governor said mildly. He peered at Rebecca over his half-moon spectacles. 'I have had no news regarding your children, Mrs Graham.'

Rebecca's initial relief was immediately replaced by the nerve-jangling fear that she must have done something wrong to warrant a visit to the governor's office. Or, she thought, as hope surged, perhaps Ben had been in touch, as he'd promised, and the governor wanted to discuss her innocence.

Putting aside his pen, Governor Sweetman slid his paperwork to one side and leaned down to open a drawer. 'I believe this was in your possession when you first arrived?' he said sternly, holding up Rebecca's silver locket.

'Yes, sir,' replied Rebecca, her hand going instinctively to her throat.

'May I ask how you came by it?' Governor Sweetman asked, his expression serious. 'The truth now, mind.'

'It belonged to my mother, sir.'

'Likely story,' sniggered Warden Harper. Governor Sweetman raised an eyebrow.

'If you look inside, sir,' Rebecca said quickly, 'you will see it contains miniature paintings of my parents.'

'I have seen the portraits,' Governor Sweetman said. 'Exquisite work.' He pressed the small clasp and the locket sprang open. He studied the tiny portraits for a moment. 'Well,' he said, regarding Rebecca over the rim of his spectacles, 'I can see the resemblance.' He sat back in his chair. 'Mrs Graham, it would appear that this is one of those serendipitous moments.'

He steepled his fingers, his expression thoughtful. 'Harper,' he said to the warden, 'would you be so kind as to arrange a pot of tea?'

'Tea, sir?'

'Yes. I'm expecting Mr Durnford in the next ten minutes or so and I'm inviting Mrs Graham to join us.' Seemingly oblivious to the incredulous looks on the faces of both women, he smiled, indicating one of two chairs facing his desk. 'Have a seat, Mrs Graham. It is you Mr Durnford wishes to see.'

'Me, sir?' Rebecca frowned, while Warden Harper's jaw dropped.

'Yes, Mrs Graham. You. Something to do with this locket, I believe. Harper? The tea?'

'Yes, sir.' Shooting Rebecca a curious glance, the warden left the room.

Painfully aware of her unwashed skin and sweat-soaked clothing, Rebecca perched gingerly on the edge of one of the chairs. From her vantage point she could see only the top of the turrets on the prison wall, topped by a rectangle of dishwater-grey sky.

'May I ask what is your connection to Durnford? Is he a previous employer?'

'I don't believe I've ever met the man, sir,' replied Rebecca, puzzled.

'Hmm.' Sweetman's frown deepened. He picked up the locket, letting the chain run through his fingers. 'When he recognized this on my desk yesterday, and demanded to know where I'd got it from, I naturally assumed he was about to say someone had stolen it from him. He became quite agitated. He asked me to find out whom it belonged to. Mr Durnford is one of our most generous benefactors, so naturally, once he'd gone, I had the staff questioned and one of the wardens said you'd been wearing it when you arrived. Mr Durnford said he would return this morning at eleven o'clock.'

At that moment, Warden Harper entered with the tea tray, her expression blank. Governor Sweetman nodded his thanks. 'You may return to your duties,' he said, when she hesitated. Avoiding Rebecca's gaze, she backed out of the room, shutting the door firmly behind her.

Rebecca focused on the tendrils of steam curling from the spout of the teapot, her sweaty palms folded in her lap. Her stomach was a knot of nerves. If Mr Durnford was a benefactor, perhaps Ben had spoken to him about her case. Was that the reason he wished to see her?

Footsteps sounded in the hall outside and she squared her shoulders. The door opened to admit a tall, broad, ruddy-faced, well-dressed man with grey hair. Rebecca got hastily to her feet and frowned. Mr Durnford looked vaguely familiar, but she couldn't place him. The way he was staring at her made her feel she should know him.

'Mr Durnford,' Governor Sweetman said, rounding his desk to shake the man's hand, 'a pleasure, as always. Sir, this is Mrs Graham. She was wearing the locket when she arrived, but she assures me it belongs to her.'

'Thank you, Sweetman,' Mr Durnford said. He turned his attention to Rebecca. 'Good morning, Mrs Graham,' he said, the skin crinkling round his eyes as he smiled. 'James Durnford, a pleasure. If I may, I'd like to ask you about this locket,' he said. He sat down, motioning for Rebecca to do the same. Governor Sweetman handed him the locket and he held it in his open palm, the silver oval glimmering in the pale November light.

'It belonged to my mother, sir,' Rebecca replied. 'It came to me when she passed away . . .'

'Lydia is dead?' James cried, his plump face crumpling in anguish.

'You knew my mother, sir?' Rebecca asked, surprised. Her eyes narrowed, suspiciously. Had Mr Durnford been a visitor at Angel Lane? 'How did you know her?' she asked coolly.

'My dear,' James said, 'I'm Lydia's father. Your grandfather.'

'My grandfather?' repeated Rebecca.

'May we have a moment, Governor?'

'Of course.' Governor Sweetman gave a sharp nod of assent. 'Take all the time you need.'

James waited until the door closed behind the governor, before taking Rebecca's hands in his. 'How long ago did my dear Lydia die?' he asked, his eyes filling with tears.

'Fifteen years ago, sir. The nineteenth of March 1878.'

James moaned as if in pain. 'So long ago. All this time, I never knew my little girl was no longer in this world.' He ran a hand over his face. 'I don't know if your mother ever spoke about me,' he said, his expression heavy with sorrow and regret.

'Yes, sir.' Rebecca nodded.

'I was a stupid, proud, arrogant man. Oh, what a fool I was.' He groaned. 'Lydia was my only child. Her mother, God rest her soul, your grandmother, died when Lydia was a child.' He held up the locket. It spun slowly, catching the light streaming in through the window. 'After my wife's death, I went a little mad. I destroyed every painting of her. I was so afraid of losing Lydia. She was all I had left, but instead of protecting her with love and kindness, I became a tyrant. I allowed her so little freedom that of course she was going to rebel. It was inevitable. A girl as spirited and beautiful as your mother was bound to break free at some point.' His eyes glistened with unshed tears. 'She fell in love with your father. Well, of course I forbade her to have anything to do with him.' He let go of Rebecca to rub a hand over his face. 'So she eloped. I was so angry, I refused to go after them. Let her come crawling back, I thought. She'd soon discover how difficult life can be without the privilege of money and status. But she didn't. She wrote to me, but I never replied. I was a selfish fool and now I'm a lonely old man. It's my own fault.' His expression was bleak. 'You must have been but a child yourself when you lost your mother.'

'I was twelve,' Rebecca told him gently. 'It was only eighteen months after my father and brothers perished.'

'My child,' James cried, 'life has treated you unfairly.'

'She wrote to you,' Rebecca said, remembering. 'We were facing eviction and Mama wrote to ask for your help. You never replied,' she said, her eyes heavy with accusation.

'I was out of the country,' James said. 'The house was let. My post was to be redirected, but I was travelling . . .' He turned his grief-ravaged face to Rebecca. 'How can you ever forgive me?'

'What's done is done,' Rebecca said dully. She tried to smile but she couldn't help wondering how differently her life might have turned out had her grandfather received her mother's letter.

'Sweetman tells me you're being held on a charge of murder,' James said, breaking the uncomfortable silence.

'I'm innocent,' Rebecca protested. 'The person who framed me for murder is the person who, in a roundabout way, is also responsible for my mother's murder.'

'What?' James recoiled in shock. 'Lydia was murdered?'

'I'm sorry, sir, yes.' As quickly and gently as she could, Rebecca told her grandfather everything that had befallen her since she and her mother had left Leonard's Bay all those years before. She faltered a little when she came to the part where Kenneth had attacked her, anxious that Mr Durnford might think she was to blame, that she had led Kenneth on in some way.

'The scoundrel,' her grandfather growled. 'You haven't told the police this, have you?' he asked, his frown giving way to worry. Rebecca shook her head. 'Good. We don't want to give them motive. Please, my dear, continue.'

A heavy silence filled the room when she finished, broken only by the cawing of a rook on the prison wall. Her grandfather's face was ashen. 'This Michael fellow must be brought to justice and your name must be cleared,' he said, a quiver in his voice.

'A friend of mine has written to Governor Sweetman, declaring my innocence. I believe he's trying to find some of the girls who work for Mickey in the hope they can be persuaded to testify.'

'Tell me this person's name and where I can find him.'

'Ben Troke.' Rebecca gave him the details. There was a discreet cough outside the door and they started.

'It may take some time, my dear,' James said, getting to his feet as Sweetman opened the door. 'But we will sort this out.' He paused in the doorway, his hat in his hand. 'I saw you once,' he said. 'At a concert. I thought at first that you were Lydia but then I realized you were too young. If only I'd had the courage to approach you . . .' His voice was laden with regret. 'Well, good day to you, my dear. I shall see you very soon, I promise.'

Rebecca returned to the laundry, her mind whirling, her locket nestled safely under her dress. That was why Mr Durnford had seemed familiar. He had been the man she'd noticed staring at her at the concert with Gordon. She went back to work, ignoring the curious, questioning glances from inmates and staff alike, as she tried to make sense of the past hour.

As soon as the whistle blew, signalling their half-hour break, she was swamped with questions. Even the wardens appeared less frosty, loitering on the periphery of the group, clearly eager to hear what Rebecca had to say.

'Mr Durnford's your grandfather?' one woman shrieked. 'You lucky girl. He's loaded, by all accounts.'

'I'm not sure what it means for me, yet,' Rebecca admitted.

'It means you'll soon be getting out of this godforsaken place,' Emily said, tucking her arm through her friend's. 'I'm so pleased for you, Becky. It's like a fairytale come true.'

'I don't want to get my hopes up,' cautioned Rebecca. 'If Mr Durnford and Ben can come up with some evidence against Mickey Fox, then . . .' She shrugged.

'If anyone can get to the truth, it's Durnford,' another woman said. 'He'll get you out.'

'He will,' Emily agreed confidently. 'It's thanks to him things have got better in here. He'll leave no stone unturned. You mark my words. He'll have you out of here quick as a flash.'

CHAPTER THIRTY-EIGHT

'Syphilis, you say?'

The nun nodded sorrowfully. 'I'm afraid so, sir. Quite mad, she was, by the end.' A cold draught blew down the corridor at the asylum and, despite his thick coat, Ben shivered. Candles flickered in their sconces, casting eerie shadows up the ancient stone wall. 'Was Dora a relative of yours?' the nun asked, as she escorted Ben down a wide corridor to the front door.

'No,' Ben replied. 'A friend of a friend. Thank you for your time, Sister.'

'Go well and go with God,' the nun said.

The heavy, metal-studded door swung shut. Ben set his hat on his head and sighed. The address in Angel Terrace Rebecca had given him was now occupied by several families. After a lot of dead ends, a discreet enquiry had led him to Maddy, a gin-soaked dock dolly who'd told him, for a price, about Dora. He'd arrived at the asylum a day late, the young nun who answered his knock had told him.

He yawned. He'd barely slept in days. The temperature was dropping. The narrow streets were deserted. It was even too cold for the prostitutes. Deciding he might as well call it a night, he turned and headed for the tavern where he'd booked a room.

He ordered a pint of ale and settled himself in front of the roaring fire in the smoke-filled snug. The publican's ancient bulldog snored loudly on the hearthrug. Nursing his pint, Ben stared into the flames. He was still reeling at the revelations of the past few weeks.

When Polly had turned up at Angus's farm, she'd been in a right state, and who could blame her, having just lost her husband in such a brutal fashion? 'They've arrested Becky for it.' Her words were like an arrow to his soul. A person could change in eight years, he knew, but with every ounce of his being he was certain she could never have committed such a crime. 'There's something else,' she'd said, as she was about to leave. 'The reason Becky left was because . . . because . . .' She faltered, her face twisted in pain. 'Kenneth, he raped her. She thought you wouldn't want her any more.'

Ben had stared at her in growing anger, his fists clenched at his sides. By God, if Kenneth had been standing in front of him just then . . . He checked himself. The man was dead. Impotent with fury, he'd taken the axe and burned off his anger by chopping wood.

The following day he'd taken Rebecca's address from Polly and, telling Angus he had personal business to attend to, caught the next train to London.

He had been a jumble of nerves as he'd walked into the prison with Thomas. How would Rebecca react at seeing him again? The expression on her face told him all he needed to know. He could see the love shining in her eyes and, despite her awful predicament, it seemed to Ben that his soul soared in delight. She still loved him. He had been determined to prove

341

her innocence, even if only for the memory of what they once were to each other, but now, knowing she still loved him, he was all the more determined.

He sipped his ale, and rubbed his tired eyes. His trip to Dartmouth had proved a dead end. He sighed, and massaged his aching head, thinking of Rebecca. He had always assumed she would marry, but that didn't stop the shock when Polly had told him about Gordon Graham. Much as he'd wished things had been different, he couldn't blame her. It was one thing to look back in hindsight, but who knew how he would have reacted, had she told him about Kenneth? His anger, even now, was such that he might well have done something he came to regret. He drained his glass, staring morosely into the glowing embers of the fire. The thought of his Becky languishing in prison for the rest of her life sent chills down his spine. He couldn't allow it. There had to be something he could do.

The following morning, having caught the early train to London, he held his scarf over his nose and mouth to ward off the stench of the factories and made his way to the pie shop.

'Ben?' Chrissie eyed him hopefully across the steamy café.

He shook his head. 'Dora's dead,' he said bluntly. 'You mentioned he was running a brothel in Spitalfields?'

'That was years ago,' Chrissie said, leading him out the back where they could talk privately. 'He's working under a new name now,' she explained, pouring Ben a mug of tea. 'He's still running girls, just more discreet.'

'I'll ask about,' Ben said.

'Be careful,' Chrissie warned him. 'And stay away from the Hamilton Club. That was how that Kenneth ended up murdered.'

'I can take care of myself,' Ben said. 'Thanks for the tea.'

Every night during a cold, bleak December, Ben traipsed round the streets of Spitalfields. He spoke to every prostitute he saw, giving them money, but none of them knew anything or, if they did, they weren't talking. Each afternoon, after catching up on a few hours' sleep, he made his way to Rebecca's house in Shoreditch. He was building quite a good rapport with the children, Thomas, in particular, who was grateful for everything Ben was doing to secure his mother's release.

'Any news?' he asked Thomas now, as he removed his boots by the kitchen fire.

Thomas shook his head. 'The police have no leads,' he said grimly. 'I don't think they're trying too hard. As far as they're concerned, Mother did it.'

'When will Mama come home?' Harriet asked, climbing onto Ben's knee.

'Soon, sweetheart,' Ben said, praying he wasn't setting the child up for more heartache. 'Soon, I promise.'

'This came for you today,' Betty said. Wiping her hands on her apron, she took an envelope from the table and handed it to him.

'It's from a Mr Durnford,' Ben said, scanning the letter with a frown. 'He says he's Becky's grandfather.' He looked up, to be met by several puzzled expressions. Ben shrugged. 'Anyway, he wants to meet me, and find out how my enquiries are going into Mickey Fox. Right.' Ben set Harriet on the carpet. 'No time like the present. I shall go to his hotel now.'

James Durnford had taken a room in a modest hotel not far from Petticoat Lane. He greeted Ben like a long-lost friend. 'Welcome, welcome,' he said, ushering Ben to a group of chairs around a roaring fire. 'Please sit. I'll order some tea.'

While they waited for the tea to arrive, Ben filled James in on his recent visit to Dartmouth.

'That's a shame,' James said regretfully. 'She may have been able to corroborate Becky's suspicions that Mickey killed her friend, Nora. And the other girl, Maddy?'

'I couldn't get much sense out of her, sir. The gin . . .'

James nodded. 'I've written to several influential acquaintances. The police investigation relies solely on the false evidence of this Michael Osborne, apparently.'

Ben recoiled in shock. 'But he's the culprit. Mickey Fox, don't you see? He's framing Becky for a murder he committed.'

'You and I know that, but not the police.'

'He's probably paying them off,' Ben said in disgust. 'Thank you,' he said, looking up at the waitress as she set the tea tray on the low table in front of him.

James picked up the teapot and poured the contents into china cups. 'As you were saying,' he said, 'we need someone who can reliably point to Fox as the culprit.' He leaned back in his chair, his expression thoughtful. 'I shall arrange for protection,' he said at length. 'Becky would never forgive me if anything happened to you.' He smiled at Ben's surprise. 'Oh, I may be old but I'm no fool. I could tell by the way she spoke of you that she's in love with you, and that the feeling is mutual.' He cocked a quizzical eyebrow.

'I do love her, sir,' Ben said.

'Then let's have that girl released so you two can get on with your lives.'

A bitter wind whipped along the narrow alleyway as Ben trudged through the piles of filth. Bursts of laughter drifted from a nearby public house, the cobbles gleaming sickly yellow in the light spilling from the windows. A drunk lay slumped against the wall. His jacket was open, and it was clear to Ben that the man had been recently robbed. He glanced behind him nervously. The man following paused and nodded. Ben nodded back. James Durnford had hired a burly ex-seaman to accompany him. If his sheer brawn wasn't enough to deter anyone with evil intent, then the several knives he had concealed about his person would probably do the trick. Reassured, Ben continued on his way. As he left the light of the public house behind, the alley grew darker, the light of the crescent moon barely penetrating the thick smog.

It was a few days before Christmas yet there was little cheer in the mean alleyways of Whitechapel. He'd lost count of the number of child beggars he'd come across during his nightly expeditions, the sight of their bare feet, blue with cold, and pinched, hungry faces had tugged at his heart. He wasn't a wealthy man, but he'd given what he could. He passed two now, a boy and a girl, huddled in a doorway, with only a thin shawl to protect them from the bitter winter cold. He reached into his pocket, ferreting around for his last coin, and handed it to the girl. She looked up at him with eyes too old for her young face. 'Thank you, sir.'

'Oi!' came a voice. 'What are you doing, you filthy pervert? Get away from my kids. They aren't for sale.'

Ben turned as a large, buxom woman came barrelling down the lane towards him. She was clearly on the game, her heavily made-up face garish in the thin moonlight. She pointed a small fish knife at Ben's stomach. At once Jim, his minder, was at his side. The woman's face registered fear. The two children huddled against her skirts, looking up at Ben with a mixture of fear and resignation.

'Leave my kids alone,' the woman said, but her voice had lost some of its edge.

'I don't want to hurt them,' Ben said. 'I'm after information.'

The woman frowned. 'What information? I don't know nothing.'

'Michael Osborne?' Ben said. The woman blanched. 'Look, I can pay you for anything you can tell me,' he said, knowing that James Durnford would pay well.

'How much?' the woman said, her curiosity aroused. Ben mentioned a sum and she balked. He could see her mind working as she imagined what she could do with the money.

'You could get yourself and your children well away from here,' Ben said. 'Start a new life.'

'Where can we talk?' She glanced around nervously.

'My name's Jenny,' she said, once they were seated in a quiet corner of the public house. Jim and the children were sitting near the fire, where the children were gobbling a bowl of stew each as if they hadn't eaten in days, which, Ben surmised, they probably hadn't.

'I've never met Michael Osborne but I know him by reputation. He's a nasty piece of work. Girls working for him have a tendency to go missing,' she said, swallowing a mouthful of ale.

'You don't know where I can find someone who works for him, do you?' Ben asked, handing her a folded banknote.

Jenny's eyes gleamed. 'No one will talk,' she said. 'They're too scared. I'll be leaving here tonight.' She sighed. 'There's a woman, Tina. Tina Fox. Rumour has it she's related to him, but they had a falling out. She frequents the Nautical Arms down near the river. She might talk.'

'Thanks,' Ben said, standing up. 'Get yourself somewhere safe, and good luck.'

'Not the sort of place I'd usually visit,' James Durnford said drily, as he and Ben pushed their way through the doors of the Nautical Arms. The air smelt sour and the sawdust scattered across the flagstone floor was in need of changing. It being a weekday morning, the place was deserted but for a lone woman sitting close to the fireplace, nursing a bottle of gin.

'Mrs Fox?' James said, approaching her from behind.

The woman turned and it was all Ben could do not to gasp at the jagged scar running down one side of her face. 'Who wants to know?'

'I'm James Durnford and this is Ben Troke. We're after information about Mickey Fox.'

Tina snorted. 'I opened my mouth once before, and look where it got me,' she said, taking a swig from her bottle.

'I can pay you handsomely for your trouble,' James said, taking the seat beside her and motioning to Ben to do the same. 'If he's incarcerated, he can do you no harm.'

'He's a nasty piece of work, that stepson of mine,' Tina said, fixing her red-rimmed eyes on Ben. 'He's got blood on his hands, all right.'

'You remember Becky Wheeler?' Ben said.

Tina flinched. 'Becky? Oh, I knew she'd be involved somehow. He's got a real fixation on her, Mickey has. He was obsessed with the mother, and when she was done away with, he transferred his obsession to the kid. That's why he killed Nora, cos she helped the kid get away.'

Ben stiffened. 'Do you know that for sure?' he asked. 'Proof we can take to the police?'

'I was there,' Tina said dully. 'I lured her into his trap. He killed Becky's husband, too, to teach her a lesson. He's got no conscience, that man. I always thought there was something wrong with him.'

'Do you know whether he killed Kenneth Seymour?' Ben asked urgently, leaning forward and resting his elbows on his knees. 'Please, it's important.'

Tina shrugged. 'Mickey turned up here out of the blue a few months back wanting my help. He'd cut himself. Seems his latest victim attempted to fight back. Mickey had a big gash in his side. I patched him up best I could and sent him on his way.' She smiled. 'There is something,' she said, with a triumphant gleam in her eyes. 'He drank quite a bit of brandy while I was stitching him up, for the pain, and he was rambling about teaching Becky a lesson she'd never forget. That if he couldn't have her, no one would.'

'Would you be prepared to tell that to the police?' Ben asked, unable to quell his growing excitement.

'I'll go to prison as his accomplice,' Tina whined fretfully. 'I might even hang.'

'You're going to prison anyway,' James said, sternly. 'But if you tell the police everything you've told us, I can speak on your behalf and get you a lighter sentence.'

Tina stared into her almost empty bottle. 'All right.' She sighed. 'I don't have much choice, do I?'

CHAPTER THIRTY-NINE

Rebecca threaded the heavy sheet through the large industrial mangle. Water gushed into the tub, splashing her skirt and showering the grey slate floor. She guided it through the rollers and into the waiting basket, then heaved it onto the handcart. She leaned on the edge of the mangle, wiping a hand across her damp face, and massaged her aching shoulders, careful to make sure none of the wardens were looking her way. She had noticed that, since Mr Durnford's visit three weeks earlier, their attitude towards her had warmed slightly.

She sighed and gathered up another wet sheet. She'd heard nothing more from Mr Durnford, and she was becoming agitated. Tomorrow was Christmas Eve and she was dreading spending Christmas away from her children. It was also Sunday, so she was hopeful Ben would visit with them. Perhaps he would bring encouraging news. She kept hoping and praying that he or Mr Durnford had discovered Dora's whereabouts. But would she be prepared to go to the police? Rebecca turned the handle, forcing the threadbare sheet between the heavy rollers. Most days she alternated between cautious optimism and black despair.

'Graham! Over here. You're wanted in the governor's office.'

Rebecca inhaled deeply. She met Emily's gaze. Her friend gave her a reassuring smile. Barely daring to hope, lest she be disappointed, she wiped her hands on her apron and hurried to where the warden who had called her, and whose name she didn't know, was standing with Warden Harper. They were eyeing Rebecca with what looked almost like respect.

'Let's go, Graham,' Warden Harper said, with a jerk of her head. Someone cheered, and another whistled as several of the women began clapping. 'Silence!' snapped Warden Harper, glaring over her shoulder. She pushed Rebecca between the shoulder-blades, propelling her through the open doorway and into the cold, dank corridor. Rebecca walked quickly, her breath clouding in front of her, the air bitingly cold after the steamy warmth of the laundry.

She hardly dared breathe as they approached Governor Sweetman's office. Warden Harper rapped loudly, and the door was opened immediately.

'My dear Rebecca.' James beamed.

'Mr Durnford,' Rebecca murmured, her heart ricocheting off her ribcage. Did her grandfather's jovial attitude mean he had some good news?

'Call me Grandfather, please,' he said, ushering her into the office. A fire crackled in the grate and the side table was set for tea.

'Have a seat.' Rebecca glanced at Governor Sweetman, who blushed slightly, half rising in his seat. 'Please,' he said, indicating an empty chair. 'That will be all, Warden,' he said, dismissing Harper with a wave. She left the room, the door closing with a soft click.

'My dear, let me tell you what we have discovered, your

young man and I,' James Durnford said, taking his place at the small round table.

'That young man is smitten by you, my dear. And why not?' His hand closed over Rebecca's. 'You're a beautiful girl, just like your mother.' His voice faltered, a shadow crossing his face. 'I made so many mistakes . . .' He shook his head. 'Anyway, let me tell you where we are with our investigation.' His smile broadened. 'It is my pleasure to tell you that Mickey Fox is now a resident at Her Majesty's pleasure in Brixton.'

'He's been arrested?' Rebecca exclaimed, her shoulders sagging in relief. 'You found Dora, then?'

'Sadly not,' James said, as Governor Sweetman poured the tea, his expression impassive. 'I'm afraid Dora passed away. Syphilis, I believe the nurse at the asylum told Ben.'

'Oh, that is sad,' Rebecca said, thinking of the woman who had been Nora's best friend. She picked up her cup, then put it down again. 'So how . . .?'

'Ben did some snooping around Fox's establishment in Spitalfields.' Rebecca paled, as she imagined the danger in which Ben would have put himself. 'I made sure he had protection at all times, my dear.' James patted her hand. 'It was Mickey's stepmother, Tina. She's a nasty piece herself but she came good in the end. 'She's in prison now, too, but she's given the police a written confession implicating Mickey in a number of murders, including your friend Nora's, your husband's and Kenneth Seymour's.'

'But why?' Rebecca wept. 'Gordon didn't deserve to die. Neither did Kenneth.'

'According to Tina, Mickey was obsessed with you.' James proceeded to tell Rebecca everything he and Ben had learned from Tina.

351

Rebecca placed a hand on her grandfather's shoulder. 'Thank you.'

'It's the least I can do. If it hadn't been for my selfish pride, none of this would ever have happened.' He inhaled deeply. 'So, Mickey Fox will likely hang for his crimes.'

Rebecca could feel no sympathy for the man who had blighted her life for so long, and who would have happily watched her go to the gallows if not for the determination of her grandfather and Ben. Dearest Ben. She couldn't wait to see him again.

'All charges against you have been dropped,' Governor Sweetman said. 'You're free to go.'

'My carriage is outside,' James said. 'Let's get you home.'

'Mama! Mama! Mama's home!' Harriet and Eliza ran down the hallway to fling themselves at their mother. Rebecca sank to her knees, her arms spread wide, and they fell against her, as she gathered them into a hug, simultaneously laughing and crying. They were followed by Betty, who was crying copiously, and the two boys, both of whom looked close to tears.

'Oh, my darling children!' Rebecca cried, reaching out to gather the three older children to her. She buried her face against them, savouring their warm, familiar scents. They were all crying now, even Chrissie and Joe, who were watching from the parlour doorway.

They moved into the parlour, the children all talking at once.

'I'm so glad you're home,' Chrissie said, smiling through her tears.

'So am I,' Rebecca said, as the two women hugged tightly. 'Thank you so much for looking after them. You have no idea how much that comforted me.'

'It was the least I could do,' Chrissie assured her. 'You've got good children there,' she said. 'You can be proud of them.'

'I am,' Rebecca said, smiling indulgently at the children clamouring for her attention.

A sound in the doorway made her jump. She had lived with fear for so long, it would take time for her to learn not to start at every sudden noise.

'Hello,' called a familiar voice. 'It's just us.'

'We're in the parlour, Mr Durnford,' Chrissie called. 'I'll go and make a fresh pot of tea,' she said, bustling off to the kitchen.

'There's someone to see you, Rebecca,' James said, coming into the parlour.

Rebecca's heart sped up when Ben walked in behind her grandfather, looking even more handsome than he had the last time she'd seen him at the prison. 'Ben,' she murmured.

'Hello, Becky,' he said, his eyes crinkling as he crossed the room towards her. Close up, she could see that the past few weeks had taken their toll. There were lines around his eyes, and across his forehead, and a few grey streaks in his hair at the temples. Only too aware of how she must look, Rebecca hung back. She was wearing the dress she'd been arrested in. It was too large for her now, and the smell of prison clung to her. As if reading her mind, Ben took her hand. 'You look beautiful,' he whispered. Breathing a sigh of relief, Rebecca rested her forehead on his shoulder, and cried.

'It's all right,' Ben murmured, as he stroked her back. 'Let it all out. You've been brave for so long.' When her sobs finally receded, she looked round, surprised to find they were alone. 'Chrissie took everyone into the kitchen,' Ben said. 'Becky, we need to talk,' he said, leading her to the sofa by the window.

'So much has happened, Ben,' Rebecca said, with a sigh. 'So

much has changed since I left. Gordon . . . I have to mourn him, Ben. He was my husband, and I did love him. Not the way I love you, but . . .'

'I understand,' Ben said softly, his lips against her hair. 'That's why I'm leaving tomorrow.'

'So soon?' Rebecca said, with a jolt of disappointment.

'I must,' he said, with a wry grin, entwining his fingers with hers. 'I couldn't trust myself to stay away unless there was a good distance between us. Once a decent amount of time has passed, I shall court you properly. We'll get to know one another again.' Rebecca smiled and leaned her head against him. 'I never stopped loving you, Becky,' he said.

'I'm sorry I left,' Rebecca whispered.

'No regrets,' Ben said quietly. 'We can't change the past. What's done is done. All we can do is look to the future. And now I shall leave you. You need this time with your children.' Rebecca walked him to the door.

'Goodbye, Ben.'

'Goodbye, Becky. I'll soon be back, and then I'll never let you go.' With a last chaste kiss to her cheek, he set off down the street.

Rebecca watched him go, her heart lighter than it had been in a long time. Tomorrow was Christmas Day and she would be at home to celebrate with her family and friends. They would raise a toast to dear Gordon, God rest his soul. Ben wouldn't be there but the knowledge that he would wait for her until she felt ready was enough. She watched him now, as he turned at the end of the road to wave. Rebecca waved back until he disappeared round the corner. Then she went inside to join her family, shutting the door firmly behind her.

EPILOGUE

Sixteen months later

Rebecca leaned her hands on the windowsill and gazed out at the garden. Apple blossom, vibrant pink and creamy white, drifted across the lawn. The sound of birdsong wafted through the open window on the warm breeze, along with the more strident sound of church bells.

The church was only across the way, a stone's throw from the cottage in Raspberry Lane that would be her home from today when she became Mrs Benjamin Troke.

She could hear the children, their excited cries echoing from the rafters as they explored their new home. Since arriving from London two days earlier, they had been staying at the Grosvenor Hotel. The manager had remembered Rebecca and had been only too happy to offer her a reduced rate, for herself and for Chrissie and Joe, who had closed the shop for the weekend.

'Some of the customers were none too happy,' Chrissie had told her with a grin, 'but I wasn't missing my best friend's wedding for anything.' She came into the room now. 'Are you nearly ready? Becky! You look beautiful!'

'Thank you.' Rebecca smiled, turning to study her reflection in the mirror. 'I can't believe I'm marrying Ben at last.'

'It was always meant to be,' said Chrissie, standing behind her and smiling at her in the mirror. Rebecca leaned her head against her friend's shoulder.

He'd given her almost a year to mourn Gordon. It had been a difficult time. She'd had to adjust to life without a husband. She returned to work at the pie shop part time, though Gordon had left her and the children well provided for.

The newspapers had been full of Mickey Fox's murder trial. Once it became public knowledge that he was safely behind bars, more women had come forward, providing the police with detailed accounts of blackmail and murder. He was found guilty on eight counts of murder and hanged a few weeks later. Tina had been sentenced to ten years with hard labour. If not for James Durnford's intervention, it was likely she, too, would have hanged.

'I came to tell you we're going over to the church,' Chrissie said now, adjusting her dove-grey hat. 'I'll see you there.'

'You will.' Rebecca smiled. When Chrissie had gone, she walked to the window, watching her friend emerge from the cottage. She was holding Eliza's hand. Thomas and Christopher walked ahead with Chrissie's boys, their amiable chatter drifting through the window. Betty followed, with Harriet, the two girls clutching little posies of spring flowers. Joe brought up the rear, looking dapper in his suit. A movement in the lane caught Rebecca's attention. Polly was standing by the gate, her face half hidden by the brim of her hat. She was wearing a pale green silk dress and holding the hand of a small boy. Kenneth had died not knowing his wife was expecting their longed-for child. Polly hadn't realized until some weeks later. She'd given birth to a boy, Donald.

As Rebecca watched, Eliza let go of Chrissie, ran to where

Donald and his mother were waiting, and clasped the little boy's hand. Polly and Chrissie greeted each other with a smile. Rebecca saw Chrissie nod and take Donald into her arms. Polly glanced up at the bedroom window. Bending down she lifted a box and started up the garden path. Frowning, Rebecca hurried downstairs to meet her.

'Polly, is everything all right?' Her gaze fell on the box in Polly's arms. It was one she recognized. 'Oh,' she said, her hand going to her throat.

'Holly's china tea set.' Polly nodded. 'She wanted you to have it, Becky. She gave it to me when I married Kenny but I know she really wanted it to go to you.' Polly set the box on the small side table.

As she gently unwrapped one of the delicate china cups from its tissue-paper nest, Rebecca was instantly transported back to the parlour at Elm Tree Farm. She could almost hear Holly's voice as she wished her well on her wedding day. 'Thank you,' she whispered, misty-eyed.

At the sound of a discreet cough, both women turned, smiling at the sight of James Durnford standing in the doorway. 'You take my breath away, my dear,' James said, as Rebecca crossed the room to give him a hug.

'I'll see you in the church,' Polly whispered. Giving Rebecca's hand a squeeze, she hurried out of the door.

'You look very handsome yourself,' Rebecca said, kissing James's freshly shaven cheek.

'Your Ben is a very lucky man.' He smiled.

'I'm the lucky one,' Rebecca said. 'I've been given a second chance.'

James pulled out his pocket watch. 'Five to,' he said. 'Are you ready?'

'One minute,' she said, running back up the stairs. In her room, she took out a little jewellery box. Inside lay the brooch Ben had bought her all those years ago at the Shaftesbury market. It was a little tarnished now with age but, to Rebecca, it was one of her greatest treasures. With her mother's locket resting against the satin bodice, and the brooch pinned to her high, lace-edged collar, she made her way slowly down the stairs to her grandfather. 'Now I'm ready.'

The churchyard was quiet, the bells had fallen silent, and the only sound was the birds serenading her as she took her grandfather's arm.

'Shall we?' he asked, his eyes smiling. Rebecca nodded. With the fingers of her free hand lightly clasping the silver locket that hung around her neck, she walked slowly down the aisle to the altar where Ben and her future were waiting.

Lily Fielding lives in Dorset and used to work at her local branch of WHSmith, where she was fondly known as The Book Lady. She also writes as Karen Dickson.

ACKNOWLEDGEMENTS

There is so much hard work that goes into a book between my delivering the manuscript to the publishers and it landing on the bookshop shelf, and so I'd like to thank everyone at Transworld, especially my editors, Lara Stevenson, Alice Roberts and Vivien Thompson, and my copy-editor, Hazel Orme, for their insight and advice. I'm also grateful to proofreaders Hugh Davis and Sarah Hulbert for their expertise in picking up all my many mistakes and inaccuracies.

I'd like to say a big thank you to my husband, John, and the rest of my family for their continued support and encouragement. I also want to thank my agent, Judith Murdoch. I will always be grateful that she saw something in my writing that she felt was worth pursuing. Thank you, Judith, for your unending support, advice and encouragement.

Lastly, thank you to you, the reader. Thank you for picking up this book. I hope you enjoy it.

Turn the page to solve
some puzzles based on
A Locket Full of Hope.

Share a photo of your scores
on Penny Street to connect with
other historical fiction readers.

A Locket Full of Hope wordsearch

```
Z T H M U T A E N M M G W V C V Y W O P
N B G L B U F V B S G M H R W X U Y S B
I F L R E F D I C D A E W X F R A W H M
N B N U S L N C V O G C R Y J S P I O G
C A L Q J D X T D A Z E A C B Q M Q M K
J C N T Y U A I O K N L S D R H D C X F
Z U Q D J Y T O N S C Y C M I A J N M A
C R Y E Y E E N Z D N D F U B R E Z T M
Q G W I F F X I Q L T I C Y B B Z D O I
F K S V B A N F D S C A P W O O T A N L
Y A Y Y T C X T B N X C Q J N U C R A Y
A T X M U Q L A S N L K Q J E R E T M J
Z B X W D E U Z R S Y O F I N N M M S O
P D R V X Q J K H N H P C I H V P O T B
Q W A U O C A A J H R H W K P G O U D D
W R V Z I F K R M O S R C B E H R T D A
F I S H I N G B F P I T T N C T I H R U
D X U V U L E Q U E P J O K H I U E V X
B Y O J O U G N V Z Y O K R X B M V O D
S I M E O N G R E B E C C A M R Z P Z K
```

Rebecca	Hope	Dartmouth
Lydia	Storm	Ribbon
Ivan	Harbour	Emporium
Simeon	Fishing	Family
Locket	Eviction	

A Locket Full of Hope word scramble

Can you unscramble these jumbled words?

1. NLREAUF → _____

2. RHTEEWA → _____

3. THLIGEHOSU → _____

4. HRHCCU → _____

5. AWBROTO → _____

6. DWONIW → _____

7. TREAH → _____

8. KAWLER → _____

9. RHETOM → _____

10. GLRIVLAE → _____

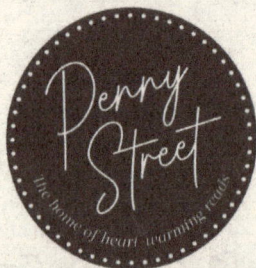